PRAISE FOR
JAMES BECKER'S NOVELS

The Lost Testament

"Extremely satisfying and ridiculously exciting! I was glued to *The Lost Testament*. . . . Let the fast pace, the exciting plot, the likable leads, and the spot-on prose carry you away." —For Winter Nights

Echo of the Reich

"Amazingly good." —Fresh Fiction

"It deserves the widest possible audience."
—Reviewing the Evidence

"Clever and imaginative twists . . . highly recommended."
—Euro Crime

The First Apostle

"Fast-paced action propels the imaginative and controversial plot." —*Publishers Weekly*

"This is an utterly spellbinding book . . . stunning and breathtaking. . . . I was left shattered and stunned."
—Euro Crime

continued . . .

ALSO BY JAMES BECKER

The First Apostle
The Moses Stone
The Messiah Secret
The Nosferatu Scroll
Echo of the Reich
The Lost Testament

THE LOST TREASURE OF THE TEMPLARS

JAMES BECKER

A SIGNET BOOK

SIGNET
Published by the Penguin Group
Penguin Group (USA) LLC, 375 Hudson Street,
New York, New York 10014

USA | Canada | UK | Ireland | Australia | New Zealand | India | South Africa | China
penguin.com
A Penguin Random House Company

First published by Signet, an imprint of New American Library,
a division of Penguin Group (USA) LLC

First Printing, July 2015

 REGISTERED TRADEMARK—MARCA REGISTRADA

ISBN 978-0-451-46646-4

Printed in the United States of America
10   9   8   7   6   5   4   3   2   1

Prologue

"We have no choice. We agree or we die. All of us. It's that simple."

Pierre de Sevry, the marshal of the Knights Templar in the Holy Land, rested his left hand on the pommel of his sheathed battle sword and looked around at the assembled company. His white tunic, bearing the unmistakable symbol of the order, the bloodred *croix pattée*, which had been used in various forms since 1147 to signify membership of this illustrious company of warrior monks, was ripped and torn and heavily stained with blood, some of it his own. His plate armor was dented, holed, and scratched from the almost continuous close combat that had been a daily feature of the siege of Acre since the first Mamluk attack on the city.

The Mamluks—an elite caste of warrior slaves who had fought for the Egyptian rulers for over a century—had assumed power in Egypt a short time earlier, ending the reign of the descendants of the great Muslim leader Saladin. Thirty years earlier they had utterly destroyed a Mongol army at Ain Jalut, south of Nazareth, and had been undefeated ever since. By any standards, they were formidable opponents.

A deep voice cut across the suddenly silent chamber.

"For myself, I would be happy to give my life in this glorious mission."

De Sevry looked at the knight who had spoken, a man he knew had acquitted himself with conspicuous valor over the last few days, and nodded.

"None of us doubt either your courage or your resolve, my brother, and all of us have been prepared to give our lives for the honor of God every day since we arrived in this place. But I have no wish to sacrifice myself or any of this company to no purpose. We are a mere handful of men, less than two hundred strong, and by our latest count the sultan Khalil has mustered an army of over one hundred and fifty *thousand* soldiers, not to mention his siege engines and catapults, and his miners who are probably even now tunneling somewhere in the ground under our feet. Even if each of us in the coming battle managed to slay five hundred of the enemy, there would still be well over fifty thousand of them left. This is a fight that we simply cannot win, no matter what we do or how courageously we conduct ourselves. If we decide to fight, then it is inevitable that we are also deciding to die. And if we die, then the only chance the forces of Christendom have of regaining the Holy City will die with us."

De Sevry paused in his grim recitation and again looked around at the company of his most senior knights, a bare dozen men whom he considered his brothers in Christ as well as his most trusted comrades in arms. All of them looked haggard and wearied by over six weeks of unrelenting and utterly brutal hand-to-hand combat, facing the teeming hordes of Mamluk attackers who had thrown themselves, wave after wave, against them.

From the very beginning, the sultan's siege engines and catapults had been raining missiles down on the city, their target the massive outer wall surrounding Acre. The wall was studded with ten separate and formidable towers, the principal entrance tower possessing walls almost thirty feet thick, a huge structure that had looked utterly impregnable to some of the inhabitants. But that hadn't proved to be the case.

As well as the knights of the Templar order, the beleaguered garrison included Hospitallers and Teutonic Knights, and a joint force of Templars and Hospitallers had barely repelled a determined attack by the Mamluk soldiers on Saint Anthony's Gate on May fifteenth. But already the writing had been on the wall: the siege was only ever going to end one way, and all of them inside the fortress knew it.

Three days later, a sound like distant swelling thunder had echoed off the old stones of the city walls as all the war drums of the Mamluk attackers had been sounded simultaneously, the noise growing rapidly until people within the city were almost deafened. And then with a suddenness that was almost shocking, the drumming stopped and there was the briefest of instants of total silence.

And then the screaming had started, the awe-inspiring sound of tens of thousands of voices bellowing their battle cries to the heavens. Then line upon line, wave upon wave, of Mamluk soldiers had begun running headlong over the rough ground toward the fortifications, converging on the battered structure from all sides simultaneously, their unsheathed swords glinting like a sea of silver in the rays of the morning sun. Above them, the sky had darkened as tens of thousands of arrows had flown overhead, the archers targeting the soldiers waiting on the walls. It had been the beginning of an unrelenting and all-out assault on the city.

And of course it wasn't just the Mamluk soldiers that the defendants faced. The sultan had assembled an array of siege engines, massive catapults, and trebuchets that could hurl rocks ranging from the size of a man's head up to massive boulders three or four feet in diameter that might require a dozen or more men to lift into position on the weapons.

The moment the war drums had fallen silent, the siege engines had fired, the rocks arcing up into the sky before plummeting to earth with devastating force, obliterating anything they hit. For a whole number of reasons, the weapons were inaccurate, but there were so many of them that accuracy was not really an issue. Even the handful of boulders that had smashed into the inner wall of Acre's defenses had been enough to cause significant damage, and most of the rocks that missed this target had slammed into the area beyond the defenses, causing utter carnage among the soldiers and civilians who were unfortunate enough to find themselves in the impact area.

The first breach on one of the towers—the so-called Accursed Tower—had occurred that day, and immediately the attackers had swarmed through the opening driven into the wall, forcing the beleaguered Christian defenders to retreat to the next line of defense, the inner wall, fighting all the way.

And it had been on that very same day that the tragic event occurred, which had unexpectedly thrust Pierre de Sevry into the position of commanding the few remaining Knights Templar.

Guillaume de Beaujeu, the grand master of the order,

had been taking a brief rest from the fighting when he was told that the Mamluk attackers had actually forced their way inside the city. Without pausing to don all his plate armor, Guillaume had immediately rushed out and taken his place at the forefront of the defenders, as was the norm for Templar grand masters, wielding his double-edged battle sword to lethal effect against the swarm of Mamluk besiegers.

In the heat of the battle he had raised his weapon to strike down another attacker when an arrow slammed into his body underneath his upraised arm. His full armor would probably have stopped the missile, but the mail he was wearing was insufficiently strong to deflect it. The arrow had delivered a fatal wound, and he had died within the day.

The next most senior officer was de Sevry, and when Guillaume de Beaujeu had drawn his last breath, the marshal of the Knights Templar reluctantly assumed the mantle of leadership. But it was clear to all the knights that there was very little chance de Sevry would retain the title he had inherited for very long. Or, at least, that had been what everybody believed until a few days later, on May twenty-fifth, when an unarmed emissary sent personally by the sultan al-Ashraf Khalil had arrived at the gates of the Templar castle with an unexpected offer.

Unexpected, because the Mamluk forces had very quickly gained the upper hand after the outer wall had been breached. The less substantial defenses of the inner wall fared little better, the first crack occurring in the area controlled by the Hospitallers, a battle during which their grand master—like Guillaume de Beaujeu, a man who had commanded his troops from the front—was seriously wounded. Mamluk forces had poured into the gap created in that wall, and then the besiegers had managed to open the Saint

Anthony Gate, allowing them unfettered access to the interior of the fortification. At a stroke, hordes of the attackers had swarmed inside, indiscriminately slaughtering soldiers and civilians as they did so.

The battle had raged on the open ground inside the wall, but the outcome was never in any doubt: the city was going to fall. Fighting every step of the way, the defenders were forced back before the waves of determined Mamluks, retreating to the safety of the sea and the handful of boats that still remained, or taking refuge in the Templar castle, the last unbreached redoubt.

The Mamluks had quickly gained the upper hand, and the streets and buildings had echoed with the howls of agony of the wounded and dying. For those who were unable to hide or make their escape, no quarter was given. As soon as the city had been secured and the fighting largely over, the Mamluk soldiers had worked their way steadily down the ranks of prisoners, dragging out all the men and the elderly of both sexes, as well as the infants, and summarily executing them. Young boys and women of childbearing age were spared, only to be clapped in irons to be later sold as slaves, or worse.

But despite the overwhelming superiority of numbers and the resources of the besieging army, one single building, the Templar fort at the southern extremity of the city, still stood, massive and solid, somehow having managed to resist and repel every attack the Mamluks had launched against it.

Most of the Templar knights, the pitiful few still left, could have escaped by sea—the fortress possessed its own guarded access to a small loading dock where a handful of boats were still moored—but that option had never even been considered by de Sevry and his colleagues for one very simple reason: the other people in the fort. Even before the outer wall had been breached, a ragged and desperate clutch of women, many with their infants and older children in tow, had taken refuge in the fortress. The creed of the Templars was simple and inviolate: one of their duties was to protect the innocent, and there was insufficient space in the boats for everyone to escape, and so they had vowed to fight on to the end.

The fortress had held out for five days, the final obstacle standing in the path of the sultan, and still the massive outer walls showed no signs of crumbling under the almost continuous assault by the siege engines. And this failure by his troops to eliminate the last remaining group of enemy soldiers had clearly rankled with the Mamluk leader, for on the sixth day the assaults had suddenly ceased, and a single unarmed figure, carrying a white flag of truce, had walked up to the immense wooden doors that guarded access to the castle.

It was the offer that man had conveyed that the Templar leaders were now discussing. If the sultan was to be believed, and not all of the Templars assumed that suggestion was a given, then in return for handing over the fortress, the Mamluk sultan was prepared to allow all the women and children sheltering inside the fortress to leave the building unharmed. Not only that, but he had also stated that the Templars themselves could walk out, with their weapons and anything else they could carry. It was a remarkably generous offer, and that was why the Templars were immediately so suspicious of it.

They all knew, as, presumably, the sultan also knew, that eventually the fortress would fall. No building or garrison could hold out forever, and especially not against such overwhelming odds. The Mamluk leader was perhaps getting impatient or maybe, as one knight suggested, he wanted to avoid any further deaths among his own men, though the way he had conducted his campaign suggested that this was extremely unlikely to be a consideration on his part.

"I do not trust this infidel," another of the knights stated flatly. "What is to stop him cutting us all down the moment we leave the safety of the castle?"

"Nothing," de Sevry immediately admitted. "They could slaughter us all within seconds. But that might almost be preferable, a quick death in the open, fighting man to man, rather than being crushed beneath the stones of the walls of this castle when the siege engines finally finish their work."

Again he looked around at the other knights. Every one of them met his gaze unflinchingly, their expressions hard and determined.

"If we accept this offer," he continued, "there is at least a chance that we can leave this place with the women and children who have entrusted their lives and their souls to our care and protection. If we reject it, then both we and the innocents will surely die and, as I said before, the one true religion that we serve will lose the last hope of ever regaining the Holy Land."

He paused for a moment. "I know this is a heavy burden to bear, as you will be speaking on behalf of your fellow knights who do not have a voice in this matter, and a difficult decision to make, but the envoy requests and requires an answer, one way or the other. So what do I tell him?"

For a few seconds, none of the armored knights responded. Then one man took a half step forward.

"I am unconcerned for my own life," he growled, "but our master is right. We have accepted into our charge and care the innocents, the women and children who have taken refuge within our fortification. If we do not accept this offer, then they will surely die or end their lives as slaves. If we agree to leave this castle as the Mamluk has requested, then there is at least a chance that we can continue to offer our protection to these people. I vote that we accept."

De Sevry noticed that several of the other knights had nodded agreement at the man's suggestion.

"Very well," he said, his gaze resting briefly on each member of the company in turn. "Am I to assume that that suggestion is acceptable to you all? If not, speak now."

No dissenting voice was heard, and the newly elected grand master himself nodded.

"Very well. Resume your posts, my brothers, and have the sultan's envoy brought before me. I will address him myself."

Within the hour, a group of roughly one hundred Mamluks, a significant force and each armed with both a scimitar and a curved dagger mounted on a belt worn outside his robe, strode boldly toward the closed doors of the Temple castle. But before they reached it, de Sevry, who had been watching their approach from the crenelated wall above the gate, ordered it to be opened, as soon as he was satisfied that only this group of men was close enough to enter the building.

The Mamluks swaggered inside the fortification, looking around them with interest at the battered and bone-weary defenders who had held out against their attacks for so long. Like the Crusader knights, many members of the Templar order spoke at least some Arabic, but when the leader of the Mamluk group made his first demand, none of the knights present would allow it. But during his earlier conversation with the envoy, de Sevry had been told precisely what the enemy soldiers would wish to do, and had reluctantly agreed to it. In a tired and resigned voice he instructed one of his knights to lead them to the highest point of the castle, where the flagpole stood.

It was the work of only a few seconds to haul down the distinctive battle flag of the Knights Templar, the black-and-white *Beauseant*, and replace it with the sultan's own personal standard. As the new flag reached the top of the pole, a light breeze briefly fluttered it, revealing its colors and design to the watching men. The Mamluk group immediately responded to the sight with a ragged cheer, the sound instantly echoed by a thunderous roar of approval from members of the encircling army. Sultan al-Ashraf Khalil now had nominal possession of the castle, and the inhabitants, under the terms of the accommodation de Sevry had agreed to with the envoy, would vacate the building within twenty-four hours.

In the courtyard below, several knights had already begun packing their few possessions, ready to leave, and in other places groups of the women and children who had sought refuge in the building were also beginning to assemble. Through this scene of hurried preparations the Mamluk soldiers strode, confident of their own superiority and invulnerability, there in the very heart of the enemy camp.

De Sevry and a handful of the senior members of the order stood together on one side of the courtyard, watching the activity with jaundiced eyes.

"When we leave this place," the grand master said quietly, "ensure that your sword arms are unencumbered. We may walk out of here freely, but that does not mean that we will easily be able to pass through the enemy lines."

"You do not trust the infidels?"

"I do not," de Sevry replied flatly. "They may still plan

to fall upon us the moment we step beyond the gate. As I said before, we may simply be exchanging a quick and honorable death in battle to a more prolonged process of dying if we allow the siege to continue. But we will know soon enough."

A shrill scream, suddenly silenced, echoed from somewhere within the gray stone walls of the fortress, and instantly each knight reacted. With a metallic slithering sound, battle swords were drawn from their scabbards as they attempted to identify the unseen threat.

"Spread out," the grand master ordered. "Find out what's happening."

The knights dispersed in different directions, each trying to identify the source of the sound. It didn't take long to find it.

One of the senior knights rounded a corner in one of the passageways and was confronted by an appalling scene. Two of the Mamluk soldiers had apparently happened upon a woman and her young son and had set upon them. The woman lay, clearly unconscious, on her back, her face bloodied and bruised, while the Mamluk heaved his body on top of her. The boy was still conscious, but the second Mamluk had effectively silenced him by twisting a length of cloth around his neck. The boy had been bent forward over a barrel, his clothes ripped asunder, to allow the Mamluk to enter him from behind.

The knight didn't hesitate. The scene before him was an affront to every tenet of the order and to simple human decency. His sword was already in his hand, and in two swift strides he reached the infidel who was sodomizing the boy. He seized him by the shoulder, dragged him backward, and swung his sword around in a lethal arc, the broad double-edged blade cutting deeply into the man's body.

The other Mamluk scrambled to his feet and reached for his curved scimitar, but he never had time to draw his weapon. As the first man tumbled backward to the ground, already dead, the knight withdrew his blade and swung it toward the second Mamluk. The end of the sword cut through the enemy soldier's right arm just above the elbow, and the man screamed in agony. An instant later the knight reversed the direction of his blade and swung the tip through the Mamluk's neck, instantly decapitating him. His body collapsed to the ground as his head bounced to one side.

The knight stood for a moment, sword still in his hand and ready for immediate use should any other danger present itself. After a moment, he heard the sound of running footsteps approaching him and turned to face this potential new threat, raising his sword with a two-handed grip.

But the man who appeared was not a Mamluk, but another member of the Templar hierarchy, and immediately the knight lowered his weapon.

The newcomer sheathed his own sword as he stared at the two dead men.

"We should never have trusted these infidels," he said bitterly.

He strode across to where the boy still lay spread-eagled over the barrel, removed the length of cloth from around his neck, and helped him stand up.

The first knight bent down beside his decapitated victim and cleaned the blood from the blade of his sword with the Mamluk's robe. Then he sheathed the weapon and knelt beside the woman who'd been raped. She was still unconscious, but at least she was breathing. The knight rearranged her clothing to cover her thighs and groin, affording her a slim measure of decency, and then stood up.

Moments later, Pierre de Sevry himself appeared on the scene with two other senior knights, his face reflecting the fury he felt at what had taken place.

"I was perhaps too hasty, Master," the first knight said, somewhat hesitantly, "but when I saw what was happening I reacted instinctively."

De Sevry shook his head. "No, my brother. You did what any of us, what any decent man, would and should have done."

He paused for a moment, and then nodded, his decision made. He turned to the knights standing beside him and issued three simple orders.

"Find them," he said. "Find them all, and kill them all. When you've done that, tear down that rag and hoist the *Beauseant* in its place. And then summon Tibauld de Gaudin to my presence."

"I am unhappy about this," de Gaudin said, sitting on the opposite side of the table to the grand master. "I feel that my place is here, with you and the other members of our order, until the end comes."

De Sevry nodded.

"I know that," he replied, "but we have to look at the whole situation. Because of what happened here today, and no matter what transpires tomorrow, this fortress is going to fall. Perhaps not this week, perhaps not even next week, but within a month the siege engines and the miners will have done their work and the walls will give way. I know that you are unconcerned for your own life, but we have charge of these women and children and the only hope they have is you, my brother. I have already ordered my men to load the chests onto the ship. As soon as they have completed that work, I want you to take on board the vessel as many of the women and children as the ship will physically hold, and then sail as quickly as you can to Sidon and to our castle there. That would at least ensure that we salvage something from the disaster of Acre, even if it is only the lives of the innocents."

"Very well," de Gaudin said, "if that is your order, then I will of course obey. When I reach Sidon I will organize a force to sail here as quickly as possible to assist you."

"Do not bother, my friend. I have a feeling that this will all be over long before any reinforcements could possibly arrive."

That evening, while it was still light enough to see, the galley that had been allocated to Tibauld de Gaudin, the treasurer of the *Pauperes commilitones Christi Templique Solomonici* in Outremer, the land beyond the sea, moved slowly and silently away from the dock that was protected by the Templar castle. Positioned in a line above the keel were half a dozen ironbound and locked chests, and sitting or standing on every available few square inches of space on the deck were the women and children fortunate enough to have been selected to accompany him.

The galley headed directly away from the shore, opening out to the west, so as to put some distance between the vessel and the archers of the besieging Mamluk army as quickly as possible. Only when the crew was certain they were out of range did the heavily laden vessel begin a slow and somewhat cumbersome turn to starboard, around to the north, for the fifty-odd-mile journey up the coast to Sidon.

In those days, vessels rarely sailed at night, for a num-

ber of reasons, but on this occasion they had had no option, and they did have one device that helped them in
their mission. Next to the helmsman, illuminated by a
shielded oil lamp, was a small container of water in which
floated a piece of wood carrying a slim length of steel,
one end bearing a daub of red paint. The Templars were
one of the first groups ever to use a basic compass, and
there were still discussions about exactly how and why it
worked, but the pragmatic view was that it did and so
they employed it. For whatever reason, the red end of the
metal always pointed in the same direction, and that was
all the sailors of the order needed to know.

Tibauld de Gaudin stood in the stern of the craft, behind the helmsman, and stared back toward Acre. A few
lights flickered in the Templar castle, the torches placed
in sconces on the battlement walls, and beyond them he
could see the much brighter and more obvious illumination from the blazing fires that delineated the front line
of the besieging army. De Gaudin stared behind the slow-
moving galley until he could no longer see anything save
for a dull yellowish glow in the sky, and then he left his
post to stare with equal intensity into the blackness of the
night ahead of the ship.

He knew with absolute certainty that he would never
see any of his Templar brothers from Acre again.

And in this belief he was perfectly correct.

The morning after de Gaudin had made his somewhat
reluctant escape from the doomed city of Acre, another
envoy arrived at the Templar stronghold bearing a further
message from the sultan, in response to the brief explanation de Sevry had already provided for the continued
presence of the Templars. According to the envoy, the

group of Mamluks who had entered the fortress the previous day had clearly been guilty men who had acted in an unacceptable manner, and the sultan was so embarrassed by their conduct that he wished to apologize in person to the commander of the Templar forces and give his personal guarantee that the terms agreed for the surrender of the fortress would be respected.

In hindsight, the Templars should have known better than to have even listened to the man. But in accordance with the expressed wishes of the sultan, de Sevry and a handful of his senior knights left the fortress and strode toward the center of the encircling army. The moment they were outside bow shot range of the fortress walls, they were surrounded, swiftly disarmed and forced down to their knees, and then one by one beheaded to the accompaniment of the spaced beats from a single Mamluk war drum. The defenders of the castle looked on in horror, but were powerless to do anything to intervene.

One of the great strengths of the Templar order was that if a leader fell in battle or was otherwise unable to continue in his post, the members of the order simply elected a new leader and carried on fighting. As was the custom, a senior knight was duly elected to command the force inside the castle, but it was already obvious that his tenure in the post was likely to be even shorter than that of his predecessor.

Three days after de Gaudin had left, the Mamluk miners set fire to the stacks of timber that they had placed in the tunnels they'd dug under the outer wall of the castle, and within a matter of hours the first crack appeared in the outermost wall of the structure. And as soon as that happened, an attack was launched against the building by over two thousand Mamluk soldiers, the attackers outnumbering the remaining defenders by more than ten to one.

But even as the final battle for the Templar castle began, other sections of the wall that had been seriously undermined by the tunneling operations simply collapsed, crushing most of the attackers as well as virtually all of the defenders. Once the dust had quite literally settled, hundreds of other Mamluk troops swarmed into the ruins, slaughtering every Christian they found.

At Sidon, when news of the fall of Acre reached the Sea Castle, de Gaudin was elected grand master of the order of the Knights Templar in Outremer, though his command now only comprised a bare few dozen knights. About a week after he had safely landed his human cargo at Sidon, he returned to his galley and ordered the crew to sail back out into the eastern Mediterranean to the island of Cyprus, then owned by the Templars, in order to raise reinforcements to protect and defend the last remaining Templar mainland strongholds in the Holy Land.

But in this quest de Gaudin was unsuccessful, and the relieving force he had hoped to create never materialized. After he left, Sidon itself was attacked and quickly fell to the massive army of the marauding Mamluks. The few surviving knights, squires, and sergeants of the order made their way to Tortosa, but that stronghold, like the other remaining mainland Templar castle in the Holy Land, Athlit, was abandoned in August that year, even before the Mamluks had launched an attack on either.

The last redoubt for the Templars proved to be the tiny fortress island of Ruad, located about two miles off the coast of the mainland, where the few surviving members of the order gathered. It held out for some time, but in 1303 it, too, was besieged and then captured by the victorious Mamluks. The defenders who managed to survive the siege were either randomly slaughtered as soon as the walls finally tumbled or marched in chains to Cairo where they were slung into the dungeons and later died through starvation and ill treatment.

De Gaudin blamed himself for the failure to summon reinforcements. He had both called for volunteers to fight against the infidels as a simple Christian duty and tried to hire mercenary soldiers, without success. Clearly even mercenaries were only too aware that attempting to take on the Mamluks was simply opting for an unusual form of suicide, and no amount of money would act as a sufficient inducement.

The reality was that never again would Christian forces occupy the Holy Land. The Crusades were over, and in less than twenty years the *Pauperes commilitones Christi Templique Solomonici*, the Poor Fellow Soldiers of Christ and of the Temple of Solomon, would effectively cease to exist, betrayed by the greed, cupidity, and treachery of the king of France, Philip the Fair.

De Gaudin died a bitter and broken man less than two years after the fall of Acre, and was succeeded as grand master by Jacques de Molay, one of the senior knights who had accompanied him to Sidon and then on to Cyprus, and with whom he spent many hours talking in private.

And during one of those quiet conversations, toward the end of his life, de Gaudin finally and almost reluctantly confided a single piece of information to the man who would succeed him, vital information that de Molay would himself jealously guard during his tenure as grand master of the Knights Templar, and the agonizing end of his own life in the so-called cleansing flames of his execution pyre in Paris.

1

Robin Jessop gazed curiously at the leather cover of the book in front of her. The lettering on the spine was nearly illegible, and the front of the volume, which should arguably have been better protected if it had, as she'd been told, been stored in a proper bookcase over the years, showed considerable signs of wear, although the title was still readable. What it said didn't make any sense, but she could certainly read it.

" *'Ipse Dixit,'* " Jessop murmured to herself. "Who on earth would give a book that title? And why? And no author's name, either."

It was Latin, obviously, the two words translating more or less as "the master has spoken," which Jessop, as a former classics scholar, albeit some time ago, and, lately, a somewhat reluctant antiquarian bookseller and valuer, a young woman operating in a world that was normally occupied by elderly and shortsighted men, had not the slightest difficulty in translating.

It had seemed like an easy, if rather dull and tedious, assignment. A middle-aged man named William Stevens who lived just outside Torbay had received an unexpected bequest from an uncle whom he barely knew existed. It wasn't money, but simply the entire contents of the old man's library, a collection of well over one thousand books that ranged from a couple of hundred paperback novels published over the last few dozen years through early-twentieth-century hardback books to almost one hundred ancient leather-bound tomes. And it was these latter volumes that the beneficiary of the will hoped might be worth a small fortune.

When Stevens had first telephoned Jessop, she explained to him at some length that age in itself was no guarantee, or even a reliable indicator, of a high price. Condition, edition, and rarity, she went on, were the three most vital words. To have real value, the book had to be in as good a condition as possible, and the older the book the less likely it was that the condition would be fine enough to command a high price. And a first edition would invariably be worth more than all the subsequent printings, and by definition there were always a smaller number of first editions printed.

Stevens had seemed unimpressed, and Jessop, who had seen the way the conversation was heading and didn't much like it, because she really didn't want to have to waste her time looking at a collection of worthless old volumes, had marshaled her final arguments. A lot of old books, she had told Stevens, were so common and so undesirable that they might only fetch a few pounds at auction, and probably a lot less if they were sold to a dealer, especially as a job lot. The days of a genuine treasure turning up, like a fragment of a Guten-berg Bible or other fifteenth-century relic of the very earliest days of publishing, were long gone. There was even less chance of anything older being in the collection. Antiques programs on television and the arrival of the Internet had more or less ensured that almost all the genuine finds had been, not to put too fine a point on it, found.

"But you don't know that for certain," Stevens had insisted. "As far as I know, old Isaac inherited this collection from his great-great-grandfather, and from what I've been able to find out it was always kept in the library at the old family home, and had been for centuries."

That had sounded to Jessop like something of an ex-aggeration.

"The paperback novels as well?" she'd inquired mildly.

"No, of course not. I meant the old stuff. It's only seeing the light of day now because they're having to sell the house up in Scotland. Bloody death duties, of course."

"Scotland?" Jessop had asked.

"Yeah. Had to hire a bloody van to get it all down here, and now the boxes are blocking up half of my ga-rage. Anyway, I hear what you say, but I still want you to look at the collection. If it's worth anything, you can buy it off me and sell it through your shop, because I certainly don't want it. I live in a small apartment, and I've got no room for it here. If you tell me that none of the books are of any value, either you can have them for nothing and sell them through the trade or I'll get them picked up from your shop and give them away to some charity shop, I suppose. They seem to take pretty much anything these days. And if you don't want the books I'll pay you a rea-sonable fee for your time," he added, before Jessop could point out that she had no option but to charge for the time it took her to do valuations.

Part of success in life lies in recognizing a fait accompli when you're looking at one. Robin Jessop knew that Stevens simply wasn't going to let it go, not least because she was well aware that there were no other antiquarian bookshops anywhere in the area she could suggest as alternatives, and she had finally and reluctantly agreed to inspect the collection on the terms Stevens had suggested.

Pretty much ever since the seven large heavy-duty cardboard boxes had been delivered to the back door of her shop, she'd been regretting her decision. Even as she'd unpacked the first box, she saw immediately that there was almost nothing in it of any obvious value. But she'd persevered, emptying all the boxes before picking up any of the books to inspect them.

As a first step she'd gathered together all the paperbacks, some of which had been packed into each box, and replaced them in the largest of the cardboard boxes after only the most cursory of inspections. Paperbacks were disposable items, in her view, and almost none of them had any value at all. But she did check the first few pages of each book, just in case. A first edition paperback of Ian Fleming's initial "Bond" book, *Casino Royale*, and signed by the author, for example, would be of very significant value. But she quickly saw that there was nothing of any interest, just a somewhat broad selection of Westerns, thrillers, and a few historical novels, none signed by anybody and all in only average condition.

Shifting those had cleared the decks somewhat, and then Robin had begun working her way through the rest of the collection, but that had proved to be almost equally disappointing. She'd looked at a handful of religious books, a couple of old—but not valuable—Bibles, books of hymns, and others of common prayer, none of them first editions and all rather tatty. There were collections of significant English writers, including most of the usual suspects—Shakespeare, Bunyan, Milton, Keats, Wordsworth, and other Lakeland poets among them—but these books seemed to have been bought for their decorative appearance, for their leather spines to grace a bookshelf, rather than to be read. At least, as far as Jessop could see, none of them had ever actually been opened. All were comparatively recent reprints, just as she'd expected. Some charity shop, she thought, as she packed them away in one of the boxes, would probably be delighted to take them.

Then there was a motley selection of hardback novels, and these she looked at with more care. Until the advent of the Kindle and its hideous electronic kin—devices that Jessop privately regarded as the work of the devil, and which had changed the face of publishing for all time, and much for the worse, in her opinion—most novels had been published first as hardbacks and only later, perhaps as long as a year or even more after hardback publication, being released as paperbacks. Some of these hardback editions had sold in very small numbers, but if for some reason the paperback had then shot into the bestseller lists, many of those first edition hardbacks had acquired significant rarity value, especially if the author had written anything in them. Or, ideally, had written something and then died. So she checked the printing record and the first few pages of each one carefully.

There were a dozen or so first editions of little-known novels by obscure authors, all in reasonable condition, but none of them were signed. These Jessop put aside for checking later and packed the rest of them away. She had spent another couple of hours going through the remainder of the newer books—those less than a hundred years old—and had picked out another handful of books that looked interesting. And then she'd started working her way through the really old stuff, the genuinely ancient volumes.

In the early days of publishing, most of the books produced were religious in nature, all lineal and spiritual descendants of the very first mass-produced book in history, the almost priceless forty-two-line Gutenberg Bible. Nobody knew for certain how many copies of that first book had been printed: two contradictory letters had been written in 1455, one stating that the total was a hundred and fifty-eight, while the other claimed one eighty. Most modern researchers agreed the total was probably over a hundred and sixty, but what was known for certain was that only a mere forty-eight had survived the trials and torments, the fires and floods and general neglect, of the almost six hundred years since they were printed in 1455, and only twenty-one of those were complete works, the others being incomplete in one or another respect.

Robin was well aware of the value of the Gutenberg Bible. The last time a complete copy had been sold, back in 1978, it had fetched 2.2 million dollars, and most informed estimates suggested that the current value of such a volume would lie in the twenty-five-million to thirty-five-million range. Even individual pages, properly authenticated and with a provenance that stood up to scrutiny, could fetch anything between twenty thousand and a hundred thousand each.

Of course, she wasn't expecting to discover such a treasure, and in this she had not been disappointed. There were more Bibles—another seven of them in all—a couple in pretty good condition with heavy and ornate leather covers, the pages intact and virtually unmarked, each of which had most likely come from a parish church somewhere. Those, too, she put aside, because they clearly had a value, if only as decorative objects. She also picked out another ten books on various subjects that seemed interesting enough to merit further study, and consigned the remainder of that pile to the cardboard boxes. And there were a few other books, on very specialized subjects, that she believed one or two of her longtime customers would probably want to buy, though in all honesty she couldn't charge very much money for them, because those particular areas of the market were both extremely limited and not especially popular.

And that just left her with a final couple of piles of about forty old volumes to look at. She'd found the book entitled *Ipse Dixit* about halfway down the final pile, and it had puzzled her immediately. Her business was books, especially old books, and she normally expected to recognize every volume she saw, and to know it well enough to be able to state the date of its first printing to within a decade or two, to provide a précis of its subject matter, and certainly to know the identity of the author, if the book had been written by a single individual.

But the *Ipse Dixit* volume puzzled her, because not only had she never seen one before, but she'd never even heard of it, although she knew the title had been used on a recent memoir written by an American judge. Unless her professional knowledge was woefully lacking, that particular ancient tome had never appeared in any of the catalogues or listings with which she was familiar. That could make it unique, or possibly so, and that fact alone implied that it would have some value.

She placed the book on one side of her desk, deciding to look at it only after she'd examined the remaining volumes. It might take quite some time to locate any information about it. Or, she thought, with a sudden frisson of excitement, to perhaps fail to locate any information about it, to establish that it really was a genuine lost volume of some sort, a book never previously known, seen, or catalogued by anyone.

Just under an hour later, Jessop stood up from her desk, picked up the final three books she'd checked, and carried them over to the last of the cardboard boxes that lined the passageway, a box that was still under half-full because of the collection of books she'd put to one side to value separately.

Looking at all those took almost another two hours, and by the time she'd finished, her back was aching from the constant bending as she'd studied the volumes on her desk. But she was fairly satisfied. She'd identified almost twenty books that would be worth selling through a specialist auction house. She'd jotted down her estimates of the likely values they could achieve, and even after deducting her fee for providing the valuation and examining all the volumes, and the commission charged by the auction house, she hoped William Stevens would be pleased. He should come out of it with at least a few hundred pounds in his hands. She would have to discuss it with him, obviously, and arrange for all the other books to be removed and disposed of, but it was actually a far better result than she had expected.

She placed all those books in a separate box and moved it to one side of her study, leaving all the others out in the passageway, and made herself a cup of instant coffee in her tiny kitchen, a room the builder of the property had obviously decided was too small to serve any other function.

She lived literally above the shop. Downstairs and fronting onto the street was her bookshop, a corner-shop-sized premises comprising a largish single room lined with bookshelves and with stand-alone bookcases forming a kind of small literary maze through which browsers could amble at their leisure, hopefully plucking volumes from the shelves as they did so. At one end, near the counter, she'd positioned a low coffee table and four small armchairs, to encourage potential buyers to sit down, to enjoy a coffee or tea, and flick through the books they'd selected.

She still wasn't sure that was a good idea, combining the functions of a café and a bookshop, but her business adviser had assured her it would help get her shop off the ground. And so far it had helped; the receipts from the drinks sold sometimes exceeded the sales of books.

It also helped that Betty Howarth, who ran the shop most of the time, was an accomplished home cook, with a noticeable skill when it came to baking, and her home-made cakes proved to be something of a draw, even for people who had apparently never read a single book in their lives and had no obvious intention of doing so at any time in the future. Betty, a slightly plump, dark-haired middle-aged lady who lived across the river in Kingswear, shared Robin's love of books, even if she didn't share her knowledge. That didn't matter, because everything on the shelves was priced, and in the event of a query Robin could be downstairs in less than a minute.

Above the commercial premises was a small two-bedroom flat. When the estate agent had sent her the details of the property, the apartment had been described as "charming and compact." Like almost everything said by estate agents, this was not actually a lie but certainly required the truth to be interpreted in a somewhat elastic manner. When Robin had seen the "spacious living room," which supposedly doubled as a dining room, she almost pulled out there and then.

"I doubt," she'd said to the agent, "if you could swing a six-week-old kitten in that room, and if you tried it with a fully grown cat you'd hit all four walls every time. That would certainly piss off the cat, and it doesn't do much for me, either."

"Actually," the agent had replied, "that expression—"

"I know," she'd interrupted. "It refers to a very different kind of cat. You don't need to tell me."

The agent had nodded—Robin suspected that all estate agents went through some kind of training course that taught them that whatever customers said you always had to agree with them—but pointed out certain advantages that she might not have appreciated. The small rooms would make it cheaper to heat in the winter, and she wouldn't have to buy as much furniture with less space to fill. And he had closed his argument by emphasizing the unpalatable facts Robin already knew: that particular shop with the apartment above it was the only property for sale in the town that came anywhere near fitting her requirements and was also within her modest price range, and he did have three other clients who had all expressed a serious interest in the building.

So she hadn't discussed it any further, but simply said she'd take the property, subject to the usual survey and the bank deigning to grant her a mortgage in exchange for a slice of her soul and a large proportion of her disposable income for the next quarter of a century, and had moved in just over six weeks later.

And, in fact, it hadn't worked out too badly. The master bedroom—if the enlarged box room could be dignified with such a grandiose title—just about accommodated her six-foot-wide bed, albeit with only about a foot of space on either side and around five feet at the end of the bed. The so-called guest bedroom she had immediately turned into a study, and apart from that, and the minis-cule living room, she also had a bathroom with a separate lavatory and a kitchen that was about six feet square.

Compact it certainly was.

She carried the mug of coffee into the study, maneu-vering carefully around the cardboard boxes—even the central passage of the flat was quite narrow—and then resumed her seat, slightly altered the angle of the adjust-able light on the desk, and positioned the mysterious book squarely on the leather desk protector in front of her. She took hold of the hand-tooled leather cover and lifted it.

Then she sat back in her seat, an expression of mild shock on her face, because something totally unexpected had just happened. She'd made a discovery that both sur-prised her and also, she suspected, served to explain some-thing that up until then she hadn't understood.

The *Ipse Dixit* book wasn't actually a book at all.

2

Helston, Cornwall

One of the biggest problems with performing genealogical research is that it can be incredibly addictive, as David Mallory had already discovered. In fact, there were three problems with doing it. Apart from the addiction question, it was also comparatively expensive and definitely time-consuming.

His interest in the subject had been triggered by an apparently inconsequential remark his mother had made to him, just a few days before she'd died in the hospital the previous year after a long illness. At the time, he hadn't given much thought to what she'd said—there were far more pressing matters occupying his mind in the days immediately before and following her death—but as the months had passed, his thoughts returned to what she'd told him, and he'd begun to wonder if she was right.

He'd also wondered if it mattered. And, although he was quite sure that it didn't, the switch that engaged his curiosity had been tripped, and there didn't seem to be any easy way of turning it off. So he'd done a little research on the Internet, but he had quickly realized that to fully explore his ancestors he would need a piece of specialized software to enable him to plot his family tree, because his standard word processing program just wasn't capable of doing it and he didn't want to have to write a database to do the job. He would also need a list of Web sites and other resources that he could access to obtain the information he was looking for. Successful genealogical research, he had quickly realized, was more a matter of knowing *where* to look rather than just knowing *what* to look for.

Once he'd bought and loaded the genealogy software, which cost less than he had expected, and had more or less gotten used to its quirks and foibles, Mallory had started rolling back the years, tracking his ancestors through time. And he'd found it simply fascinating, not to mention all-consuming.

Not the names themselves, of course, because that was what they were, just names and dates with links to other names and other dates, but the time he spent wandering off into the endlessly intriguing byways of history, fleshing out the characters behind the names on his charts, the men and women to whom he quite literally owed his very existence.

He'd quickly established that his mother's throwaway remark—she'd told him that he was the eldest son of an eldest son of an eldest son of an eldest son, though she couldn't remember all the names—was absolutely accurate. For whatever reason, he appeared to be the end product of a patriarchal lineage that had invariably involved firstborn male children, or that, at least, was what his researches had shown so far, and he had already managed to dig back as far as the end of the eighteenth century with some of the branches of his family tree.

The problem he was facing, and which he found was taking up more and more of his spare time, was that the further back he tried to go, the more difficult and time-consuming the search became. He'd been able to access the first, the most recent, records without even stepping out of his study, because he'd found them online, but he very quickly ran out of options there, and even the extensive records held by the Mormon Church didn't contain all the information he sought. Instead he was having to physically visit cemeteries and churches, looking for weathered and faded headstones in forgotten weed-choked corners of graveyards, or search handwritten parish records, ancient property deeds, and the like. That sometimes necessitated spending a day off or even a full weekend traveling to another town and often booking a hotel room for one or two nights, and that meant his new and compelling hobby was starting to get expensive as well, with the escalating cost of fuel, meals, and accommodation.

But for the moment, he could afford it. Or, rather, he *would* afford it, which wasn't exactly the same thing, because now the bug had really bitten. And his mother's death had left him a house he didn't like and didn't need and was actively trying to sell, and a bit of money as well, so it wasn't as if he was exactly strapped for cash.

In his own mind, he rationalized his new and almost all-consuming pursuit as a kind of tribute to his mother, a way of celebrating her memory by investigating and describing in detail her family tree, as if establishing her lineage would somehow help to reinforce his memories and recollections of her.

He barely even remembered his father, who'd died in a road accident when he was still a child, and his mother was all the family he'd ever had, or had ever known. His father's untimely demise had robbed his mother, Mary Anne, of any chance of having any other children, and him of the possibility of growing up with any siblings. She had never expressed the slightest interest in finding another man with whom to share her life, and had settled down, grieving but apparently contented, to raise her son alone. It was only when he became a teenager that he finally realized that some of her irregular weekends away with one or other of her female friends, or slightly longer visits to distant and usually unnamed relatives, weekends and periods when the young David would be farmed out to a neighbor or another friend, might admit of an alternative explanation.

Not that he blamed her in the slightest. Ever since he first considered the matter, David Mallory had been convinced that each of us has only one life, and the secret to happiness is to be content with what one has, to play the cards fate has dealt. And fate, in the person of a driver so drunk that when he'd been cut from the wreckage of his car, suffering only from a broken arm, he was hardly able to stand, let alone drive, had at a stroke orphaned David and made a widow of his mother. As far as he was concerned, whatever it took to get through life was fine with him, and his mother, like everybody else, had needs and wants that had to be satisfied.

So in his opinion, establishing a full and complete family tree was one small way in which he could honor the memory of the woman who had brought him into the world and had largely been responsible for shaping him into what he was.

And so, when his workload permitted, he continued pursuing his hobby. At the age of thirty-two, Mallory was already established in his third career. He'd left school at nineteen, not having quite made the grade to get into even a minor redbrick university to read anything he thought would enhance his employment prospects. He couldn't see a bad media studies degree doing much for him, and that was about all that was on offer. Instead he'd joined the police force for a brief and inglorious career.

The reason he'd left had nothing to do with his wishes but everything to do with the jagged scar that ran in a faint zigzag pattern down the left side of his cheek, white against his tanned flesh. He hadn't wanted to leave, but his superiors had made it very clear to him that he and the police force were about to part company, permanently. And, the superintendent had told him on the day when Mallory handed back his warrant card, he was extremely lucky not to be facing prosecution himself over what almost everybody in the Bristol police force had begun calling "the Incident."

He had always had a knack with computers, writing his first program in C while still a teenager, and after he had shed his dark blue uniform for the last time he gravitated toward information technology. He hadn't wanted to get into programming because he'd always found the coding and seemingly endless debugging terminally frustrating, but IT support seemed a more attractive prospect, and he'd started doing that for a local company.

But almost five years of explaining what to do to people apparently too dense to actually follow simple instructions, and fixing problems that a reasonably bright fourteen-year-old could do in his sleep, had soured that for him as well, and he'd left after his mother died, to set up his own business.

He called himself a computer consultant, which meant pretty much whatever he wanted it to mean: everything from tuition on application software, through virus re-

moval and security advice, up to systems analysis and sup-
plying, installing, and commissioning complete systems
for companies installing or upgrading networks.

He was able to pick and choose his jobs, big and small,
and even when he was working that usually just meant he
had to be available on the end of a telephone and have
access to a computer with a broadband link to the Internet and hence to his client, but not necessarily physically
in any office building, which he was finding very convenient as he pursued his new interest.

That afternoon, he'd left the company where he'd just
finished installing a small network to replace their older
system and driven the short distance back to his cottage,
a square and uncompromisingly rugged granite-built
house that had stood in its small patch of land at the edge
of a village near Helston for almost two hundred years,
changed and modified by successive owners but still re-
taining much of its original character.

Mallory had recently begun contacting other people
who were carrying out genealogical and related research,
finding them through Web sites, blogs, and chat rooms,
and offering to supply copies of the information he'd so
far established, in exchange for any help they could provide with the data he was still seeking. So far, this had
proved to be a largely unproductive field of investigation,
with almost nobody who had responded being able to
give him any information that he hadn't already uncov-
ered for himself.

So when he'd made himself a coffee and switched on
his laptop computer to check his e-mails that afternoon,
he frankly wasn't expecting very much from the various
e-mail replies he'd been sent.

But actually the fifth message he opened seemed potentially hopeful, and when he opened the attachments

the sender had provided and looked at the contents, at the scans of the documents his new correspondent had unearthed and the sections of the family trees he had managed to create, Mallory realized that he was looking at what amounted to a part, an important part, of the missing data in his own searches. Because a number of the new genealogical charts he was looking at unquestionably related to at least some of his forebears.

And when he read one of the accompanying notes that supported the family trees, he also realized that his research would now have to start heading in a direction that he had half suspected from one earlier trail he'd followed.

It looked as if he'd been right in his guess, and if so, that meant his family actually had its roots not just in a very different part of Britain, but in an entirely different country.

3

Dartmouth, Devon

"How very curious," Robin Jessop murmured to herself as she looked at the book that wasn't a book.

Even on a close examination, it still looked as if that was what it was. The cover was black leather, fairly plain in design but with an embossed border, and with the words *Ipse Dixit* in capital letters impressed and picked out in gold leaf on both the spine and what looked like the front cover. Both titles were quite worn and the name on the spine, especially, quite difficult to make out. But it wasn't a front cover, because it simply didn't open. The edges of the pages, too, looked more or less as one would expect, but were firmly stuck together. The giveaway was a narrow flattened oval hole that ran through the sealed pages, more or less in the center of them but just below the front cover, obviously intended for some kind of key.

A key that, of course, she didn't have.

But that wouldn't necessarily be an obstacle, she reasoned. It was clearly a book safe, and it looked so much like a genuine book that she was quite certain that would be its principal defense against discovery. It was like the old adage: where do you hide a tree? Answer: in a forest. So where do you hide a book? In a library, obviously. The probability was that dozens or perhaps even hundreds of people might have seen the object on one of the bookshelves in the old house belonging to William Stevens's relative and had never even thought to take it down and examine it. If anyone's gaze had rested on it for more than a few seconds, he would probably just have assumed it was just a dull old book and ignored it.

And if she was right, and that had been the intention of the person who'd constructed it, the locking mechanism would quite probably be something fairly simple, a very basic key of some kind. What she needed to do was to try to find out exactly how the mechanism worked before attempting to open it, not just jam a screwdriver or something into the slot and hope for the best. And to do that she needed two things: a much brighter and more focused light and a magnifying glass.

The lens was no problem because she had two on the desk in front of her. One was quite small but powerful, offering a magnification factor of fifteen or twenty—she couldn't quite remember which—that she used for detailed examinations, while the other was much bigger and low powered, a tool she used when the quality and size of the print inside books required it. She always mentally referred to that as her "Sherlock Holmes glass" because to her eyes it was very much like the magnifying lens the fictional detective was often portrayed as holding.

The light was more difficult, because it needed both to be bright and to have a very narrow beam to allow her to see right down into the interior of the flattened oval keyhole on the side of the object. Her desk light was bright, but far too diffuse to be much help, even when she angled it directly toward the keyhole. As she'd expected, she could see almost nothing inside the opening. For a few moments, she held the object in her hands, considering it. She shook it, but as far as she could tell it was empty. Certainly nothing inside it rattled or moved, and it weighed about what she would have expected, assuming it was basically an iron or steel mechanism inside the leather binding.

She needed a flashlight of some sort, and strangely enough, the best one for the job was probably the cheap and tiny battery-powered LED light attached to her car key ring. The light was sold as an aid to locating a keyhole in the dark, which was never necessary with modern cars because of the remote central locking system they all possessed, but she had found it useful on a number of occasions when trying to insert her Yale key into the back door of the shop. The beam wasn't particularly powerful, but it was bright and well focused, and that was what she needed.

The keys to her Volkswagen Golf were in a shallow ceramic dish on the narrow hall table, which stood at the end of the passageway next to the door to her apartment, behind which a circular flight of metal stairs led down the outside of the building to the single-car parking space and the rear door of the shop. It was the work of just a few seconds for her to step into the passage, collect the keys, and return to her desk.

But when she sat down, she didn't immediately do anything, just sat in thought for perhaps a minute, because before she went any further she definitely needed to contact William Stevens. At that moment, the object still belonged to him, and before she spent any time trying to open it, she needed to either buy it off him or get his permission to go ahead.

She touched the space bar of her laptop computer to wake it up and composed a detailed e-mail to him. In it, she explained that she had assessed the collection of books and the vast majority were of little or no value. However, she added, there were a number of older volumes that clearly were of some importance. She listed the titles and the latest auction values she had been able to find for each of them, included the dates and locations of those auctions so he could check them himself if he so wished, and then added all the values together. It came to just under eight hundred pounds. From this sum, Robin added, the auctioneer's commission and charges would need to be deducted, and her own fee for valuing the collection.

She also described the book safe, for want of a better expression, describing it as accurately as she could and pointing out that it was most likely merely a curiosity and as far as she could tell from examining it, it did not contain anything and was locked. She finished the e-mail with a proposal, pointing out that some of the books were the kind she would be interested in buying as stock items for her shop, and making him a flat offer of seven hundred and fifty pounds for everything.

She marked the message high priority, and then sent it to him. As soon as it had gone, Robin picked up the phone and called Stevens on his mobile number. He answered almost immediately.

"William, it's Robin," she said. "I've gone through all the books you sent me, and done my valuation bit on them. There aren't a lot there of high value, frankly, but there are a few that would be worth selling and that I would be interested in buying myself. What I've done is send you an e-mail listing those books and giving you the latest auction valuations that I've been able to find, and then I've made you a cash offer for the lot, for the entire collection."

Stevens's response was almost exactly what she had expected.

"How much?" he asked.

"Seven hundred and fifty pounds," she replied, "and in my professional opinion I don't think you'll get any more than that if you take them to auction, but of course that's entirely up to you."

"That's more than I expected," Stevens said. "They're yours."

"Thanks. But could you please read my e-mail first, see what I've said to make sure you understand my valuations and why I've made the offer that I have? If you're still happy with the figure, then I need your confirmation in writing—just replying to the e-mail would be fine—and your bank account details so that I can do a transfer. If you want cash, I can do that as well, but obviously I'll need to go to the bank first."

"No, a transfer's fine. I'm just around the corner from my house now, so I'll go and check my messages and get back to you in a few minutes."

"Thanks, William."

Robin didn't have long to wait. Less than five minutes later her laptop emitted a musical double tone to indicate the receipt of an e-mail. She opened the program and read the message with a smile of satisfaction. William Stevens had simply confirmed that he was happy to accept the stated sum for the entire collection of books, including the book safe. He'd added his bank details, and within another few minutes Robin had logged on to her business account and arranged the transfer.

As far as she was concerned, the moment the bank's computer reported that the transfer had been initiated and was in progress and could no longer be stopped or amended, the deal was done. She sent another very short e-mail to Stevens confirming that the money was on its way, then pushed the laptop to one side and turned her attention again to the mysterious leather-bound object sitting on her desk.

She propped it up with a couple of books so that it sat at an angle, the small hole in the pages directly in front of her, and shone the small LED flashlight directly into the opening. She took the small magnifying glass, the more powerful of the two, and used that to try to peer into the locking mechanism. It wasn't easy to do, because even the tiniest movement of the magnifying glass meant that everything would suddenly become blurred and out of focus, because of the power of the lens, and it took several minutes for her to finally be able to gain a clear idea of what she was looking at.

Strangely enough, it didn't look to her as if the opening in the locking system was designed for a key at all, because she could see no sign of a lock. In fact, as far as she could tell, the lid of the book safe was held in place only by a catch, or possibly by a number of catches, and all that she would need to do in order to release it was to slide something like a slim screwdriver through the hole until it made contact with the mechanism, and then give it a firm push. The thing that gave her pause was that although it certainly looked like a catch, held in place by a short spring, there seemed to be other levers as well that didn't seem to be directly connected to it, and she had no idea what possible purpose they could be serving.

She shrugged, laid the book safe flat on the top of her desk, and positioned its spine against the horizontal pen holder that was an integral part of her old desk, to give herself something to push against because she expected that the mechanism would be stiff through lack of use and the dust of the centuries. And she didn't think that was an exaggeration because her best guess was that the object was most probably medieval. The mechanism might even, she acknowledged, be rusted solid, though if it had been kept in a library for most of the time, she hoped that wouldn't be the case.

She turned her attention to her small tool kit that, frankly, didn't contain very much: four screwdrivers, a couple of pairs of pliers, and a utility knife with a retractable blade, plus a handful of the screws, nails, washers, and other assorted bits of hardware that seemed to migrate into every toolbox over the years. Two of the screwdrivers had Phillips head bits, and so were of no use to her, and one of the others was simply far too big, the blade too thick to enter the slot. But the last screwdriver had a narrow but quite long blade—she thought it was the kind used by electricians—and she guessed that would probably be long enough, because as far as she could tell from her examination of the book safe, the catch was only four or five inches inside.

Robin slid the end of the screwdriver through the hole cut in the false pages of the book safe, doing her best to keep it straight so that it would make contact with the catch on the inside. She heard the very faint sound of metal touching metal, and then the screwdriver blade would go no farther.

"Here goes nothing," she muttered, changed her grip so that the heel of her hand was on the end of the screwdriver, and pushed firmly.

The screwdriver slid perhaps another half inch inside the book safe. There was a faint click and then a sudden loud thud.

Robin Jessop was so shocked she released the screwdriver and flung herself backward away from the desk, the back of her wheeled chair slamming into the wall behind her.

"Jesus Christ," she said, getting to her feet, her eyes still fixed on the book safe.

4

Helston, Cornwall

As well as establishing the identity of his forebears and completing the various parts of his family tree, Mallory was also creating a map that showed the location where each person he'd been able to identify had been born, lived, and then died, marking each spot with, respectively, a green, blue, and red label bearing the name of the man or woman and the appropriate date or dates for each of those events or periods. He'd bought a large-scale map of the United Kingdom especially for this purpose and mounted it on one wall of the bedroom he used as an office. What he was finding particularly interesting, and obviously predictable, was that, although for the last few generations his family had lived in and around Cornwall and the western parts of Devon, the earlier he trod back in time, the more dispersed his ancestors seemed to become.

There appeared, in fact, to be a steady movement east-ward the further back he went, toward London and the southeast of England, which really wasn't what he had

expected. He had always understood from what his
mother had told him that his family had lived in the far
southwest of the country for generations, but this was
only partially correct. They *had* lived in that area, but
only since about 1875. He had always mentally assumed
that his roots lay in the mysterious country of King Arthur and the land of Tintagel, the rugged promontory that
jutted out into the Atlantic, the most southwesterly point
of England aimed like the tip of a spear toward the far
distant shores of America, the rocks endlessly defying the
pounding waves.

As a child he had been fascinated not just by tales of
Arthur and his Knights of the Round Table and Avalon,
but also by the stories he had heard of the legendary land
of Lyonesse, which centuries, countless ages, ago had
supposedly sunk forever beneath the waves somewhere
off the Cornish coast, and he'd even briefly wondered if
his ancestors might have been descended from the rem-
nants of the noble families who had apparently perished
in that long-forgotten tragedy.

Later in his childhood, he'd been equally enthralled
by the tales of the wreckers and smugglers who, only two
or three hundred years earlier, had haunted the rocky
coves of the Lizard Peninsula—that name alone evoca-
tive and intriguing—using lights to lure ships onto the
saw-toothed rocks and the unfortunate sailors to their
deaths.

And it wasn't as if the stories were all wild flights of
fantasy. The sheer number of known wrecks around the
coast of Cornwall was a persuasive argument that suggested that at least some of the tales of the wreckers had
to be based in fact. There was one cove on the west side
of the Lizard where gold coins from some wreck had
been found so often that it was known locally as "Dollar

Cove" in preference to its real name. And there were other echoes as well, somewhat less substantial than the discovery of an occasional gold coin, locations where shadowy figures had allegedly been seen in the night, apparently reliving some traumatic event from hundreds of years earlier, and still other places, lonely beaches, where the ghosts of long-dead sailors were said to walk the sands when the cold sea mist rolled in from the Atlantic.

These romantic, if somewhat gory, notions had colored his childhood dreams and his outlook, and he'd been secretly proud of the imagined feats of his ancestors, but now it looked as if at least some of his forebears had far more likely been soft city folk, probably scratching out a living as tradesmen somewhere near London, or possibly farmers, rather than the tough and ruthless land-based Cornish pirates he'd conjured up in his imagination. And that was actually rather disappointing.

But the information he'd just read related to another branch of his family, and their origins seemed to lie a long way from London. The genealogical search results he'd just been sent showed a steady migration toward London from some way north of the Scottish border and, even further back than that in the early fifteenth century, the earliest dates Mallory had yet seen, from northern France.

And not only that, but even his family name had been altered and amended along the way, the double *L* appearing as a permanent feature only in the late eighteenth century. Before that, there were numerous variants, the *O* and *A* changing places to give "Molary" and "Malory," and occasionally one letter vanishing altogether, so there were several "Molorys" and "Malarys" among his forebears.

But it was the French arm of his family that he was

beginning to find the most interesting, and what was driving his interest there was less the location than the spelling of the surname, and the possible implications if his parallel research into another, and totally unconnected, subject produced the results he was hoping to see.

5

Dartmouth, Devon

Before she did anything else, Robin Jessop picked up her car keys and walked out of the apartment and down the spiral staircase to the parking area at the back of the building. Halfway down, she used the remote control to unlock her car, and when she reached ground level, she opened the vehicle's trunk and took out a pair of heavy gloves that she kept there in case of having to change a tire. Then she locked the car again and climbed back up to her apartment, pulling on the gloves as she did so.

In the study, she sat down and slid the chair close to the desk and looked closely once again at the book safe. Gingerly she stretched out her gloved right hand, picked up the screwdriver she had been using, and, at arm's length, carefully eased the tip of the tool under the lid of the object, trying to lift it. But it remained firmly closed, which was actually what she had expected, bearing in mind what had just happened. She would have to probe the lock again and try to free the mechanism a second time.

She mentally reconstructed the sequence of events, re-membering the way the screwdriver had reached a dead end as it touched the latch mechanism, and the faint click she had heard when it freed some part of the catch. That was what she had been expecting.

But what had taken her completely by surprise was the loud thud that had followed as an appallingly effective medieval antitheft device had been activated. In that split second after the catch had been released, powerful springs had obviously been triggered by a mechanism within the book safe and had forced two rows of needle-pointed spikes out of opposite sides of the relic, one set driving through the spine of the "book" and the other set through the false pages on the opposite side.

If she had grasped it by the spine, which she had very nearly done and which would have been the obvious way to hold the object while opening it, when the catch was released, three or four of those spikes would have been driven into, and very possibly even through, her left hand. And if she had used a screwdriver with a shorter blade to free the catch, her right hand could have been punctured as well.

She thanked her lucky stars that she'd used the pen holder instead to brace the object, and doubly so when she bent forward and looked even more closely at the rows of spikes. Despite the fact that the metal had prob-ably been forged well over half a millennium earlier, not only were the points clearly still very sharp, but each also carried a faint discoloration. Robin knew quite a lot about medieval tactics, and guessed that as well as the agonizing pain that the spikes would cause when driven into a per-son's hand, there was a very good chance that they had also originally been painted with some kind of poison or toxin. Whether or not it would still be viable after such a passage of time was another matter altogether, but she definitely had no wish to find out.

Wearing the heavy gloves as protection for her hands, she pressed down hard on the leather cover, holding the object firmly in place against the pen holder, then slid the point of the slim screwdriver back into the slot, taking care to avoid touching the protruding spikes even with her gloved hand. This time, the end of the tool entered slightly farther than it had done previously before striking metal.

Robin took a deep breath—not that doing so helped in any way, of course—and then pushed the screwdriver gently. Nothing happened, so she increased the pressure steadily, concentrating on keeping the tool straight. For a few seconds she thought the blade must be resting on the wrong piece of the internal mechanism, because nothing seemed to be budging. But then there was a very faint click and the screwdriver slid perhaps a quarter of an inch farther inside the book safe.

Nothing else seemed to happen. No other spikes emerged, and the relic appeared unaltered. But when she removed the tool and carefully slid the point under the front "cover" of the old object, she found that it lifted up quite freely.

She used the screwdriver to open the lid of the book safe all the way so that the interior was completely exposed, but she didn't touch any part of it. She guessed that the spikes were the only protection the object had, because it wasn't very big and there was no sign of any other mechanism inside it still waiting to be triggered, but she wasn't prepared to take any chances. Instead, for several minutes, she just sat at the desk and studied the book safe.

Now that the lid was open, it was quite easy to see the

mechanism. Carried on a metal frame that was secured to the bottom of the book safe with a single pillar was the central catch. In fact, there were two separate catches. Releasing the larger of these, the one closer to the opening and which any metal object slid into the hole would touch first, freed two other catches. These held the mechanism controlling the two rows of spikes in place. They looked something like the head of a garden rake, a pair of slim metal base plates on which the sharpened spikes had been positioned. When the catches were released, these two plates had been forced apart by a pair of powerful springs, with the result she had witnessed just a few minutes earlier.

Then there was a second and smaller catch, located perhaps half an inch behind the first one and that controlled the second and fortunately harmless mechanism she'd triggered. Pressure on it did nothing more than release small spring-loaded bolts on the three sides of the "book," at the top, bottom, and side. Once they had been tripped, the cover could be opened.

She studied the interior carefully, but could see no indication of any other devices. As a check, she tapped and prodded all around both the inside and the outside of the book safe using the long screwdriver from her tool kit before she touched any part of it with her gloved hands. Nothing happened. No other mechanisms were triggered, and after a few minutes she was satisfied that the object was safe to handle.

She'd been wrong about one thing in her e-mail to William Stevens. The book safe wasn't empty. Not quite. Underneath the latch mechanism was a length of parchment rolled into the shape of a scroll and lying beside it was a short length of frayed leather, which had presumably originally been tied around it.

She didn't immediately pick it up. Instead she slid the point of the screwdriver into the end of the roll and lifted it an inch or two, just in case it was somehow connected to any other kind of antitheft mechanism built into the book safe. Then she lowered it again and repeated the operation at the other end of the scroll. Finally she took a second screwdriver and used both tools to lift the scroll completely out of the box and deposit it on her desk.

Still wearing the heavy leather gloves she had taken from the trunk of her car, she picked up the book safe, carried it across to the metal filing cabinet that stood against one wall of the room, and placed it carefully on top. Then she took off the gloves, because they were too cumbersome and clumsy to allow her to examine the parchment, and instead opened one of the drawers on her desk, removed a pair of white cotton gloves, and pulled them on. Old books were often delicate and needed special handling, and she almost always wore gloves when she was examining books and manuscripts more than about one hundred years old.

And there was another reason as well. The spikes fitted into the book safe had been a nasty surprise, and it was not beyond the bounds of possibility that the medieval mind that had conjured up that device could also have decided to protect the parchment itself, perhaps by coating it with poison, or mixing a toxin into the ink. The one thing she certainly wasn't going to do was touch any part of it with her bare hands or even with her gloves.

She used the screwdrivers to maneuver the parchment, took a pair of pliers from her toolbox, opened the roll a couple of inches, placed them at the top to hold it in place, and again used the screwdrivers to carefully and gently unroll the remainder of the document, placing a second pair of pliers at the bottom of it. Then Robin put down the tools, picked up her low-power magnifying glass, and bent forward over the parchment scroll.

She read the first few lines carefully. Or, to be absolutely accurate, she looked at the first few lines and tried to make sense of them, without any success. She'd expected whatever was written on the scroll to be in Latin, a language with which she was quite familiar, but although the writing obviously used the Roman alphabet, she didn't recognize any of the words. They certainly weren't Latin, nor did they belong to any other language that she could identify.

Of course, there were any number of ancient languages that the author could have used, including ones like Catalan and Occitan, which were still spoken by communities in Europe—by millions of people, in fact, in the case of Catalan—or a language that had died out since the Middle Ages. But she had seen enough ancient texts to be able to at the very least recognize the probable language employed. She would normally be able to identify the odd word, or even the root of a word, but that wasn't the case with the text in front of her. The more she looked at it, the more convinced she became that it wasn't written in any known language, but was actually enciphered.

If she was right, then this opened up a host of new possibilities and questions, beginning with the obvious one: what kind of cipher had been employed? Cryptology was a subject about which she knew very little, and one obvious problem, even if she had been an expert on the subject, was that ciphers had developed over the centuries, and without knowing exactly when the text on the parchment had been prepared, she had no way of knowing what types of encryption methods would have been employed at that time.

But there was one thing she could try. She removed her cotton gloves, took a sheet of paper from her desk drawer, wrote out the alphabet across the top of it from left to right, and then wrote out the alphabet again directly below it but this time backward, so that the letter *Z* appeared directly under *A*, *Y* under *B*, and so on. That was a decryption code for one of the oldest—and the simplest—ciphers known to exist, the Atbash.

Originally intended for use with the Hebrew language, Atbash was the most basic possible substitution cipher, encryption being carried out by simply replacing the plaintext letter selected from the conventional alphabet with the cipher letter that corresponded to it. So the plaintext English word *FOREST* would appear as *ULIVHG* in Atbash. Although the encrypted text would appear indecipherable, the standard cipher had only one possible key—the reversed alphabet—and was hence extremely weak and easy to crack. Technically, it was a monoalphabetic substitution cipher, and was known to have been used as far back as the time of Julius Caesar, and there were even a couple of examples in the Book of Jeremiah.

Robin wrote down on the paper the first half dozen words of the first line of text written on the scroll, using capital letters. Then, using the alphabet and its mirror image, she replaced the letters in each of those six words with their Atbash equivalents. Then she tossed her pencil down on the desk in frustration. The six words she had copied had appeared to her to be simple gibberish, but the Atbash-deciphered equivalent words that she had just created were equally incomprehensible, words that she was quite certain were not a part of any known language that she had ever encountered. If the text was enciphered, and she was virtually certain that it was, then whatever encryption method had been used was clearly far more complex than conventional Atbash, and that could mean that the document was much more recent than she had first supposed, cryptology getting more and more sophisticated with the passing centuries.

What she needed to do now were two things. First, she should definitely try to find out if the book safe was of any value in itself, though she had her doubts about that. Not everything dating from the medieval period—and that was her best guess as to its likely date—was worth much, and the fact that the object contained the spring-actuated spikes added a further level of complication. What she had was essentially a book-sized antipersonnel device, a sort of clever medieval switchblade, and it was quite possible that selling it could actually be illegal. She might end up having to give it to a museum somewhere, just to get rid of it.

That was the first thing, and she guessed that she could get some results immediately thanks to Google and the Internet. She woke up her laptop again and entered the search term "ipse dixit book safe" and pressed the ENTER key. As usual, the search generated a number of replies—she couldn't ever remember entering any search term that didn't produce at least some results from Google, but none of them on the first two screens she scanned looked hopeful. She tried other variants, adding the words *key*, *medieval*, *text*, *parchment*, *cipher*, and *encrypted* in various combinations as well. But she found nothing, no sites or references that seemed to describe anything like the object she had acquired. She widened the search, just looking for "book safes," but even that didn't produce any useful information.

By the end of her search, she had only really discovered that such objects were unknown in the medieval period, apparently being relatively recent innovations, and she had found no mention at all of any safes that included anything like the antitheft mechanism she had just experienced firsthand. It looked as if what she had was unique, and that could make it an important and potentially expensive object. Or it could simply be an ancient curio, of no value whatsoever, and she had no way of telling which.

That seemed to be a dead end, though obviously she would have to spend longer investigating it, perhaps talking to experts in a museum, or people from an auction house that specialized in early mechanical objects. But that was something for the future. What she needed more urgently was help from someone who knew about ciphers, somebody who could show her how to begin decoding the text on the parchment.

Hopefully her extensive customer database would help her track somebody down. Because she tended to acquire books on a wide variety of subjects, she had a comprehensive mailing list of people who were in the market for specialized volumes. At the last count, that database had contained over three thousand names, and at least two or three of those people, she was quite sure, had put down markers with her for volumes dealing with codes and ciphers, though so far, if her memory served her correctly, she hadn't acquired or purchased any books dealing with this subject.

She closed down her browser window and clicked on her customer database. It included a basic search facility, which she opened. She typed "cipher" in the correct field and pressed the ENTER key. Less than a second later, three results appeared on the screen in front of her.

She looked at the three names but was fairly sure she'd never met any of them in person, though that was unimportant, then accessed each short file in turn. The information she kept on each customer was fairly limited—name, address, telephone number, e-mail address, purchase history, and preferred method of payment, and not all those fields were completed in every case—plus a subject listing, which was where she performed most of her searches when new books arrived in the shop, and a larger section in which she recorded whatever else she knew about her customer. Or rather her customer's wishes with regard to books.

Robin opened the first customer record and flipped straight to this last part. The information she read had most likely been taken verbatim from an e-mail sent to her by the customer, and just stated that the man was looking for any books relating to either the activities of Bletchley Park, the highly secret British code-breaking establishment that operated during the Second World War, some aspects of which were still classified even in the twenty-first century, as well as books written in English about German encryption techniques with particular reference to the Enigma encoding machine. That seemed specific enough. She doubted very much if that man would have the slightest knowledge of or interest in medieval ciphers. She shrugged and opened the second record.

That immediately looked a lot more promising. That customer had told her, again in an e-mail, that he was looking for books dealing with the history of ciphers, and particularly those used in the early days, basically pre-Roman and onward. He was also searching for books on two entirely unrelated subjects and had, Robin noticed, not only bought several books on both topics from her in the past but also had a kind of standing order with her for volumes of one particular kind. Books dealing with that subject were extremely rare, but at the same time of no literary merit whatsoever and little monetary value, and only rarely survived the centuries, but there had been two in the Stevens collection.

Robin copied his e-mail address and then moved on to check the third record that had matched her search criteria. But she immediately rejected that customer as a possible source of help, as his main focus was on the importance of secret communications as they related to government, politics, and international relations in the twentieth century. Things like the Zimmermann Telegram.

She created a new e-mail, pasting in the address she'd just copied, but before she wrote anything except the salutation she stood up and walked over to the box containing the books she was keeping and rooted through it for a couple of minutes before she found what she was looking for. She pulled out two slim volumes and nodded in satisfaction as she read the titles. She hadn't wanted to just ask for the man's help in a cold call, as it were, but these two books exactly matched one of the other two categories in which he had expressed an interest. So she could legitimately contact him to ask if he would be interested in buying them, and then bring up the matter of the enciphered text almost as an aside. That would be far more subtle, she decided.

She quickly composed the e-mail, listing the titles, dates of printing, and condition of the two books now lying on the desk in front of her, and the prices she was asking for each of them. She took a small but sophisticated digital camera out of her desk drawer, placed the first book in a clear area on her cluttered desk, and took a picture of it, then repeated the process with the second volume. She took the data card out of the camera, slid it into the card reader slot on the side of her laptop, and copied the pictures into the e-mail and then added the photographs and details of the books to her database as well.

Then she added the final paragraph to her message, informing the recipient that an ancient manuscript had come into her possession, that the text on it was possibly medieval and appeared to be enciphered, and because of his obvious interest in ancient ciphers, would he have any idea how to decode it? She carefully typed out the first dozen words of the text, then signed the e-mail "Robin Jessop" and pressed the SEND key. Then all she could do was wait for his response, if the man bothered getting back to her at all, of course.

She had two other things she wanted to do before she got back to her regular work. She again put on her cotton gloves, picked up the sheet of parchment and took it across to the small multifunction laser printer that stood on a table beside her desk, and scanned the images of it into her laptop. For good measure she made a couple of copies of the text written on both sides as well, each requiring two sheets of paper because the parchment was both an irregular shape and significantly longer than A4. Then she rolled up the manuscript and slid it back into the book safe, before placing the object inside her safe. She still had no idea if either the object itself or the parchment had any value whatsoever, but she wasn't going to take any chances.

Robin walked downstairs, went in through the back door of the shop, and made sure that Betty was coping, which she was, there having been only five customers through the front door of the shop that day, two of them only buying cakes and coffee. Then she went back up to her study to continue preparing the catalogue that she would send out with her next MailShot to her established customer base, work she had been doing before the cardboard boxes of books had arrived from William Stevens.

Much of her business was done by mail, most of it by people responding to her printed catalogue, sent out once every quarter, or to the electronic listings she posted on her Web site, but her direct approaches to customers when she acquired particular books were also very productive. She believed her buyers felt somehow special when she sent them a personal e-mail with details of new books that matched their search criteria, and in most cases sales quickly resulted from these electronic solicitations.

The books she had acquired from William Stevens would, she was quite sure, be of interest to at least a handful of her regular customers, and as soon as she had taken pictures of the new volumes and prepared accurate descriptions, she would send personal e-mails to all those she thought might be interested in buying them.

With any luck, she might be able to recoup at least half of the money she had spent in buying the collection of books within a couple of weeks, and that would obviously be good news for her cash flow. In the meantime, she put the book safe, its brutal antitheft device, and its curious contents out of her mind.

6

Helston, Cornwall

Because David Mallory was on a number of mailing lists, he picked up between fifty and sixty new e-mail messages every day. The vast majority of these, including the inevitable invitations from people in Nigeria desperate to share a multimillion-dollar fortune they had just stumbled across, and blatantly obvious phishing e-mails urging him to supply his bank account details as quickly as possible to some hopeful cybercriminal who was pretending to work in the security department of a High Street bank he'd never had an account with, he discarded without even opening. Messages sent by members of the various genealogy sites he always looked at, just in case there was anything of interest, and obviously he read anything sent by friends or members of his family, and most of these he replied to.

He'd got into the habit of processing his messages in the evening, when he'd driven home from wherever he had been working—assuming he'd been on-site somewhere that day—or when he logged off from some company intranet if he'd been working on from home. And the other thing he did at about the same time was take a cruise around the genealogy sites and look at some of the latest posts on the various blogs, just in case anybody had come up with some useful information or found any new sources of data.

That evening, when he'd put down his briefcase in the hall, made himself a cup of coffee—he invariably drank instant because he wasn't interested in fannying about with percolators and the like—he walked into the bedroom at the back of his house that he used as a study, put down his laptop, and switched it on. He'd only made the jump from a personal desktop machine to a high-specification laptop when he started his genealogy research, because the advantages of being able to carry not just a few notes but the entire corpus of his work around with him on a single machine were overwhelming. So he'd splashed out and bought the best he could find. The machine had a big screen, two hard drives of one terabyte each, an additional solid-state drive for his operating system and application software, a quad-core processor, and sixteen gigabytes of RAM. It was, in computing terms at that time, about as state-of-the-art as you could get.

He started downloading his e-mails but didn't look at them, and instead went straight to one of the blogs that was on his list of favorites. He scanned quickly through the list of posts, glancing at the subject matter of each one, then clicked on the link to the next blog and repeated the process. Several posts were interesting, but none of them provided any information he didn't already know, just really serving as confirmation of data he'd already established.

His messages had finished downloading a few minutes earlier, so he shifted his attention from his browser to his e-mail client and began weeding out those which were of no interest to him, filing those that he thought he would need to keep and replying to all those that warranted it. About halfway down the list, he came across one that stood out. It wasn't the first time he'd heard from that particular man, and he'd established a cordial business relationship with him, albeit completely one-sided. Mallory was a customer; the man was a supplier.

He read the message with interest, looking at the photographs and the details of the two volumes that the bookseller had supplied. He connected his printer and spat out a copy of the message, then took it over to the bookcase where he kept his research material and scanned the shelves, checking to see if he had already got copies of either volume. He hadn't, he realized, so he would definitely buy the two on offer.

It was only then, as he walked back to his desk, that he looked at the last paragraph of the e-mail message. His steps slowed and he came to a dead stop, his eyes fixed on the sheet of paper he was holding.

"Interesting," he muttered as he sat down again.

One word in the message stood out for him, and that largely determined what he did next. He took a sheet of paper and wrote the letters of the alphabet on it, then wrote the reversed alphabet underneath. Then he glanced back at the information in the e-mail and began writing the sequence of letters printed in it. When he finished, he sat back with a frown, because what he'd expected to achieve simply hadn't happened. He had to be missing something. Either that or his guess was wrong.

Another thought struck him, and he looked back at what he'd done and then jotted down a completely different sequence of letters. That also didn't produce anything that seemed to make sense, so he wrote out a number of other lines of letters, checking his interpretation of each one as he did so. When he read the result of one of them, a smile crossed his face. That actually seemed to work.

He looked back at the e-mail and wrote a short message in reply. Then he smiled again, deleted what he'd written, jotted down a few more letters on the piece of paper, worked out the ciphertext, and sent a five-word reply: "Latin. ZGYZHS OVUG HSRUG VOVEVM." It would be interesting to see what response that produced.

Then he looked again at the e-mail, at the signature block at the bottom. The contact details included both a business and a mobile number, and before he dialed he glanced at his watch. It was almost seven, too late to expect an answer on an office telephone, but not too late to call the mobile.

He decided he would revert to a more old-fashioned form of communication and telephone the man. More personal and much more immediate. So he dialed, and almost immediately a woman answered.

"Can I speak to your husband, please?" Mallory began.

There was a pause that went on a couple of beats too long, and he was just about to speak again when the woman replied.

"I don't seem to have one of them," she said, "so you've probably got the wrong number."

"This is the number that was on an e-mail I was sent today," Mallory insisted. "I'm trying to reach Robin Jessop. He has a couple of books I'd like to buy."

"Ah. Robin is not exclusively a man's name, Mr. Mallory. I'm Robin Jessop, and I was a woman the last time I checked."

This time Mallory paused.

"How'd you know my name?" he asked.

"I'm not psychic and it's not rocket science," Robin replied. "I only sent out one e-mail today, which listed two books for sale so—though we've never spoken before— it more or less had to be you. Normally you just send me an e-mail when I've offered you a book you want, so is there any particular reason why you've called me? After office hours, I mean. I don't think anyone else is going to be queuing to snap up a couple of collections of parish records."

Mallory was slightly nonplussed by the unexpected turn the conversation had taken.

"No, you're probably right there," he said. "I'm doing a lot of genealogical research, and it's amazing what information you can sometimes find in parish records. That's why I've bought every book you've offered me on the subject, and that will include the two you've just told me about, by the way. But no, that wasn't why I was calling you. Have you checked your e-mail this evening?"

There was another short pause before Robin replied, a faint hint of suspicion in her voice, "Not for an hour or so, no. Should I have done, Mr. Mallory?"

"Please, call me David. It's just that I think I've solved your little puzzle, the one you sent me in your e-mail, and I've sent you an e-mail in reply. But I thought I'd call as well, just to tell you I'd cracked it."

"You have? That's brilliant, Mr.—er—David. You solved it?"

"Well, I think I have. You only listed six words, and I have made sense of those."

"It was obviously a cipher of some sort," Robin said. "I got that far myself. What was it?"

"Atbash," Mallory said. "With—"

"No, you're wrong. I tried Atbash and it doesn't work."

"It does," Mallory insisted, "but what I was going to add is that you need to apply a shift. With regular Atbash, you just write the alphabet backward under the normal alphabet, so *A* becomes *Z* and so on. Whoever encoded those six words applied an extra wrinkle that I've never seen on an Atbash cipher before, though I have heard of it being done. They started the reversed alphabet under the letter *P*, so that became *A* in the Atbash cipher, and *O* became *B*, finishing up with *Q* enciphered as *Z*. It's basically a left shift of eleven places."

"You know about ciphers?" Robin asked, sounding clearly interested. "You're not a spy or anything, are you?"

Mallory laughed. "No, much more mundane than that, I'm afraid. I work with computers for a living, but I've always been really interested in encryption systems, and the good old Atbash is pretty much the earliest we know of. I've got a marker out with you for any books you get about ciphers."

"I know," Robin said. "That was why I sent you that message, because you were the only person I've ever had any contact with who seemed interested in the subject. Where are you, apart from standing by the phone, I mean?" she added, after a couple of seconds. "Which part of the country?"

"Way out in the wilds," Mallory replied. "I work in Helston in Cornwall, and I live just outside the town. And you're somewhere in Devon, aren't you?"

"Yes, not quite as far out as you. I'm in Dartmouth, down on the south coast." She paused for a moment, ideas spinning through her brain. "Look," she went on, making a suggestion she hoped she wouldn't regret, "I've got a bit of a mystery on my hands, and I think I'm going to need some help in solving it. And what I particularly think I need is somebody who understands codes and ciphers. I'd be happy to pay you for your time. If you have the time, that is."

"What kind of mystery?" Mallory asked.

"I'd rather show you than tell you. But, briefly, the most bizarre box I have ever seen has come into my possession, and there's a piece of parchment inside it that those six words came from. From the sound of it, you'd be able to decipher it fairly quickly, but it might take me days, if I managed it at all."

It was Thursday evening, and Mallory had nothing scheduled for the next day or the weekend that would follow it. He'd vaguely planned on driving up to Leicestershire to follow up a couple of leads about his ancestry in that area, but that was all. But trying to solve what might be some sort of medieval mystery was a far more enticing prospect, especially if he could charge for his time.

Estimating the age of a woman from her voice alone was almost impossible, and he guessed that Robin Jessop was most probably a lady in late middle age, simply on the basis of her profession: sweet young things tended not to own antiquarian bookshops. He made an instant decision.

"I could be with you by about lunchtime tomorrow, if you wanted," he suggested. "I could take a look at what you've got in the afternoon and hopefully sort out the decoding fairly quickly. Would you be happy to pay for a couple of hours of my time and my expenses? Fuel and so on?"

At the other end of the line, Robin Jessop also made an instant decision. Voices, she knew as well as anybody, could be incredibly deceiving, and she knew nothing whatever about David Mallory apart from the few snippets she had learned during the present telephone call and the fact that he had bought about a dozen books—all of them parish records—from her over the past year or so.

He could be a deranged rapist or murderer, but frankly she didn't think so, and she could quite easily engineer it so that all their meetings, and most especially the first one, would take place in very public areas. She could simply get him to do the decoding, pay him for his time, and never see him again. And she was, quite apart from all that, more than able to take care of herself.

"Thank you, David," she said. "That sounds like a plan."

"Okay, Robin, you've got yourself a deal. Why don't we meet in a coffee shop in Dartmouth that my knackered old GPS will stand a faint chance of tracking down? Maybe you can e-mail me the location and the name?"

"Good idea, and thanks. I'll do that right away."

Robin ended the call with a warm sense of satisfaction. She had been going to suggest meeting in a public place, and was pleased that the idea had come from David Mallory himself. She didn't believe his remark about his GPS having difficulty trying to find her place. If the device could find a café, it could just as easily find her shop or her apartment. In fact, she realized, he already knew her shop address from their previous transactions because it was on all her business correspondence. No, he'd obviously made the suggestion so that she would feel comfortable meeting a stranger, a man, for the first time, and that showed a sense of consideration toward her. She had a feeling that they were going to get on.

She chose a small café that she occasionally visited, looked up the address on the Internet, and wrote a quick e-mail to Mallory, giving him the name and the postcode of the establishment. Then she checked her in-box, spotted the message he had sent to her, and opened it.

For a moment, she stared blankly at the screen, not understanding anything apart from the word *Latin*. Then it dawned on her that he had actually used the Atbash cipher to encrypt the rest of the message, and she reached into the waste bin and pulled out the paper she had used earlier on. After fiddling around for a couple of minutes, she had reversed the coding and was able to read the plaintext that Mallory had sent to her. The message read *Atbash left shift eleven*.

Whatever David Mallory was like as a person, it seemed quite clear to her that he was polite and considerate and had a sense of humor as well as knowing a lot about encryption systems. And in the circumstances, that was really a pretty good start.

7

Via di Sant' Alessio, Aventine Hill, Rome, Italy

The Pontifical University of Saint Anselm was sandwiched between the Magistral Villa and the minor Basilica of Santa Sabina on the Lungotevere Aventino, which ran along the south bank of the Fiume Tevere, a location that offered excellent views across much of Rome and Vatican City from the Aventine Hill.

The Via di Santa Sabina ran behind all three buildings, and directly opposite the university, which was built in the form of a square and enclosed an open courtyard flanked by arches and a covered walkway, the Via di Sant' Alessio extended, arrow straight, for a little under a quarter of a mile down to the southeast. The road was flanked by a number of substantial detached buildings surrounded by gardens and in many cases protected by high walls. Few of these properties displayed any outward indications of what activity or activities were carried out inside, privacy being a jealously guarded benefit in this exclusive and expensive area of the city.

One of these buildings, its external identity being restricted to nothing more than a house number, contained what amounted to the back office facilities of one of the buildings that fronted the Lungotevere Aventino. Different parts of the structure served different purposes for different groups of people within the organization. One of these, one of the smallest, in fact, was essentially a dedicated intelligence unit. It occupied an air-conditioned suite of rooms in the basement, protected by a steel-lined door that was kept locked at all times whether or not anyone was in the suite. The unit had been established almost a century earlier to carry out a very specific type of monitoring activity for a purpose that at first sight appeared to make no sense whatsoever.

In the earliest days of the unit's existence, the small staff had spent their working days reading the occasional novel, but mainly commercially published nonfiction books and especially reports that had been obtained from a number of different sources, some in the public domain but many that had originated within the walls of national intelligence units around the world. Throughout the twentieth century, advances in technology had dramatically increased both the scope and the ability of the unit, beginning with the introduction of telephones and telex machines, and then fax equipment, until finally the staff had started taking advantage of the most flexible, the most comprehensive, and by far the most effective intelligence collecting tool so far developed on the planet: the Internet.

What most users of the Web didn't realize was that every time they went online, they were leaving behind them a trail of electronic footprints that anybody with the appropriate equipment and skills was able to follow. Internet monitoring programs could be set up to record every action that a particular person took, every search term he entered, every Web site and every page on every Web site that he visited, every e-mail he sent and received, and even—if it was considered necessary—every single keystroke that he made.

This kind of comprehensive blanket surveillance was, paradoxically, most often used inside the home, allowing parents to monitor what their children were up to on the Internet in an attempt to keep them safe and out of the hands of the pedophiles who, if the popular press was to be believed, were to be found lurking on every virtual street corner. Husbands and wives also took advantage of this kind of technology when one of them suspected that the other might be playing away from home, and some businesses had been known to covertly monitor the actions of their employees in the same way. This kind of almost total surveillance was specifically and precisely targeted and could reveal a hell of a lot about the chosen subject, but it was usually of little or no relevance to anybody outside the immediate family, group, or company.

Of far more interest to the intelligence unit based in the center of Rome was blanket general surveillance, and in particular surveillance in two apparently dissimilar fields: Internet searches and special interest blogs. One characteristic that almost everybody who used a computer would immediately recognize was that whenever any new piece of information or an unusual word was encountered, almost the first thing most people did was to type the word or phrase into a search engine to find out more about it. Everybody did it because it was quick and easy and in most cases it provided the required information with a fair degree of accuracy.

The analysis of search terms on the Internet was a serious matter because of its importance to companies that primarily traded online, who absolutely needed to know what their potential customers were typing into their search engines so they could tailor their Web sites to respond accordingly. And, just as important, they also needed to know the keywords their competitors were monitoring—the "pay-per-click" system used to drive clients to a particular Web site—on specific search engines. Search engine optimization was a vitally important weapon in the armory of every company trading online.

The remit of the small intelligence unit based in Rome was both broader and in many ways more specific than this. Their task was to identify particular words or phrases that they had been told were significant by their employers, though they hadn't been told why. The main problem they had faced was that nobody knew for certain exactly which words might be significant, because the information on which they were basing their searches was the better part of one millennium old. So the dictionary—for want of a better expression—that they were using contained a huge number of possible search terms, both individual words and combinations of words, and false alarms were very common as a result.

Some of the commercial search engines provided lists of the most popular search terms to anybody who was interested, but these almost invariably just listed the words used by browsers, and that was really only half the story. For the intelligence unit, not only was the search term important, but just as vital was the geographical location and especially the identity of the person who had typed it into his or her computer.

Programmers working for the intelligence unit had developed a number of monitoring tools that would allow the unit to identify search terms of interest that had been entered into the principal search engines, together with the IP—Internet Protocol—address from which the search was generated, and that would allow the location to be established with a fair degree of accuracy.

Multiple copies of the programs ran on different servers, each monitoring a particular search engine, and they had also installed other versions of the programs that used the same look-up word tables in the other main European languages, as well as both Arabic and Hebrew. But the language that the unit had been told was the most important to monitor was, oddly enough, Latin, and all the computers were programmed to monitor a large number of Latin words and phrases as their highest priority.

The blog sites in many ways offered less fertile ground, not least because there were far fewer blogs that needed to be monitored, as there weren't that many that dealt in any way—no matter how obscure—with the subject matter.

So it was perhaps not entirely surprising that when the intelligence unit received the first confirmed hit—confirmed because the two words typed precisely matched one of the Latin phrases in the oldest and most reliable of all the word lists they used—it came from a Web search engine, not a blog.

Once the validity of the match had been confirmed and all the information possible obtained about the person responsible for the Web search, the substance of the hit was reported to the man in charge of the unit.

After that, things happened very quickly.

8

Dartmouth, Devon

Robin Jessop had been sitting at a corner table in the café she'd selected for about fifteen minutes, nursing a rather flat cappuccino and watching the sunlit street outside through the slightly grubby window. She had asked Mallory to get there by one o'clock, and at a couple of minutes past the hour the door of the café swung open and a large, heavily built man with a pronounced beer belly swaggered in and glanced around.

Robin's heart sank. Not only was he twenty years older than she had expected, fat and unattractive, but he was also wearing a wedding ring on the third finger of his left hand. If that was Mallory, the sooner he finished the decrypting and left, the better, she decided. But then the man gave a broad smile and strode past her to another table at the back of the room, where a rather plain and solid woman was sitting, wearing a floral dress that didn't suit her.

She turned around slightly in her seat as he passed her to see where he was going, and when she turned back another man was standing right in the doorway, scanning the patrons, apparently searching for somebody. He was about her age, tall, well built, and with neat blond hair parted on one side, wearing blue jeans and a leather jacket, a computer bag slung over his shoulder. He looked remarkably average apart from the faint white line of a jagged scar running down his left cheek, an obviously old healed injury that immediately drew her eyes toward it. He glanced at her, but then his gaze passed over her.

It was the computer bag that suggested his identity, and Robin half rose in her chair and waved her hand to attract his attention.

"Are you David?" she asked diffidently.

He immediately looked down at her. "Yes. You're Robin?"

She nodded and gave him a quick smile as she gestured toward the seat on the other side of the table.

"Are you okay?" she asked. "You look a little surprised to see me."

Mallory smiled and nodded.

"I'm fine," he said, "but I am surprised. My mental picture of you was as a kind of blue-rinsed academic, all pearls and twinset, and maybe twenty years older."

"Are you disappointed?"

He shook his head. Even with her sitting there and wearing a padded jacket, he could see that she had a proper female figure, the swell of her bosom unmistakable beneath the material. Mallory had never understood the "can't be too rich or too thin" near-anorexic fashion that some women embraced, turning themselves into walking bags of bones.

Her large dark brown, almost black eyes peered at him through the lenses of her spectacles with cool appraisal beneath the dark fringe of her quite short black hair. Her face was slightly rounded, her nose very slightly bent, almost as if at some time it had been broken, unlikely though that scenario had to be, and her full lips were parted to reveal small white teeth. And, although it was an obvious cliché, there was a definite look of determination about her chin. Overall, it was the face of a girl who knew exactly where she was going and precisely how she intended to get there.

But it was her smile that struck him most forcibly. He'd occasionally read in bad novels how the heroine's smile was supposed to brighten up a room, and he'd always dismissed it as simple hyperbole and cheap exaggeration, but in Robin Jessop's case it was absolutely true. It really did, and Mallory found it difficult not to smile back at her. So he didn't resist, and matched her expression with his own.

"You're less geeky than I was expecting," she said, "which is good news. And for a few seconds I thought that you might be the man who's now sitting right behind me."

Mallory glanced over her shoulder as he sat down on the opposite side of the table, then flicked his glance back to her.

"You mean the one with the stomach and the jowls?" he asked.

"Exactly."

"You may be doing him a disservice," Mallory said mildly. "He may well be a teetotal nonsmoker, the perfect family man, completely faithful to his wife, wonderful with children, kind to animals, and all the rest of it."

Robin nodded. "You're right, of course. You should never judge by appearances." She hesitated for a moment, then leaned forward slightly. "I'm sorry, but I just have to ask. Where did that scar come from?"

Mallory didn't respond for a moment, then shook his head.

"You are direct, aren't you?" he replied. "It's from a part of my life I'd rather forget. An incident that ended a career I was enjoying. When—if—we get to know each other better, then I'll tell you."

"I *can* keep a secret," Robin said.

"Luckily, so can I," Mallory replied, then immediately changed the subject. "Look, I'm sorry I'm a few minutes late, but trying to find somewhere to park in this town is well-nigh impossible, and I'm gasping for a coffee and something to eat. Is the food here any good?"

"The coffee is a bit suspect," Robin said, her voice revealing a trace of the irritation she felt over what Mallory had said, or rather failed to say, "but the sandwiches aren't bad."

"Right," Mallory said, grabbing the plastic-coated menu from the holder on the table. "I'm buying. What would you like?"

Five minutes later, they were both tucking in to paninis, and fifteen minutes after that they stepped out of the café, heading toward Robin's shop.

"It had spikes on it?" Mallory asked as she described what had happened when she used a screwdriver to release the catch on the book safe. "I've never heard of anything like that before."

"Nor have I. But quite a number of interesting and unusual devices came out of the medieval period. Some of their chests are absolute works of art with the most massive and complex locking systems built into the lids. One key could control as many as a dozen different bolts spaced around the edge of the chest, a bit like the doors you get on some big safes today. And all the bolts and levers would be curved and carved, sometimes embossed with gold or silver decoration. Really wonderful designs and elegant workmanship. The book safe is frankly quite crude by comparison, but as an antitheft device, it would certainly have been brilliantly effective. If those spikes—and I think it's at least possible that they would originally have been tipped with poison—had slammed through your hand, the last thing you'd be thinking about was what was inside the object. And of course even after you'd prized the spikes out of your flesh, the box was still locked."

Mallory was silent for a few seconds, then glanced sideways at Robin.

"But that means there's a bit of a problem with it, don't you think?" he asked.

"What do you mean?"

"It would work as an antitheft device, obviously, but whoever owned it wouldn't want to trigger the mechanism every time he needed to put anything in the box or take something out. That would just be pointless and dangerous. So there must be some way of freeing the catch to open the lid that won't fire the spikes through your hand."

"Oddly enough," Robin said, "that never occurred to me. But you're quite right. I released the catch just by using the point of a long-bladed electrical screwdriver, but obviously when it was made, there must have been a proper key for it. The hole it goes into is shaped like a wide flattened oval, so presumably that's what a cross section of the key would look like. But just wait until you see this thing. It scared the life out of me when it went off."

"I'm not surprised. You were really lucky in the way you decided to open it."

They turned in to the street where Robin's bookshop was located, but she didn't go in through the front door because she could see a couple of customers in the shop and the last thing she wanted to do was disturb them when they might possibly be in a buying mood. Instead she led Mallory down the adjacent alleyway and around to the rear door of her premises.

"Come upstairs," she said, suddenly aware when she spoke that it was a slight double entendre.

"That's an offer I've not had in a while," Mallory replied, quietly enough not to be heard.

9

Via di Sant' Alessio, Aventine Hill, Rome, Italy

It wasn't the first time Marco Toscanelli had been summoned with such a high degree of urgency to the building on the Aventine Hill, but on this occasion he sensed that things were different. The moment the electric lock on the steel-lined door behind him had clicked shut, effectively turning the entire basement area into a giant Faraday cage, secure from any form of electronic eavesdropping, the feeling of excitement in the air was almost palpable.

"Go straight in," the man who opened the door to him said. "He's expecting you."

Toscanelli strode down the corridor to the door at the end, knocked twice, and then opened it and stepped inside the office.

It was a relatively small room, given the size of the property as a whole, but he knew that most of the space in the basement area was given over to the machines that handled the intercepts and the computers that interpreted the data. The human acolytes who tended the equipment had to make do with whatever space was left over. Despite that, it was comfortable, with a thick carpet on the floor, paintings on the walls, and contemporary Italian furniture. The lack of outside light—this part of the building was entirely underground, but for security reasons no windows would have been provided in any case—was disguised by a false window positioned on the wall behind the desk and covered with curtaining, through which the "sun," a small but powerful light, could be dimly seen.

Silvio Vitale, a slim man with a pencil mustache and dressed in a black suit, the head of the organization, was sitting in the leather swivel chair behind the desk, a number of sheets of paper in front of him. As Toscanelli entered the room he stood up and shook hands in a perfunctory manner and then gestured to the chair that stood to one side of the desk.

Toscanelli took a step over to it and sat down, then pointed at the heavy wooden upright armchair standing in the center of a square of rubber matting that had been placed on top of the office carpet. On one side of the chair was a body bag, unrolled and open, ready to receive a corpse.

"Who?" he asked simply. "And why?"

"Silvrini," Vitale replied. "You do not need to know the reason."

"I think I do," Toscanelli said, chancing his arm. Vitale's short temper and capricious mood swings were legendary. "He was one of my team on the last job, in Venice. As far as I was aware he's a good operative."

"He was, certainly," Vitale agreed, emphasizing the tense of the word, then paused for a moment before nodding. "Very well. With knowledge comes responsibility, so you can perform the duty. He was detected arranging a meeting with a senior member of the Carabinieri here in Rome, apparently intending to provide information about those two eliminations that took place in Ostia last year. The two men that you executed, in fact, so his intended betrayal was very personal to you, Marco."

Toscanelli's male model face—he had elegant, regular features, high cheekbones, a wide mouth, brown eyes, and thick, curly black hair—hardened immediately. "You have proof?"

Vitale nodded and handed him a slim folder.

Toscanelli opened it and scanned the contents, the result of a short surveillance operation that had been performed on Silvrini after suspicions were raised about some of his actions.

"He was stupid," Vitale commented. "He used a disposable mobile phone to make the call, but he used it inside the apartment that we provided for him. He should have known it was bugged."

"Yes, he should," Toscanelli agreed. "He certainly should. Does he know yet?"

"No, but he's waiting outside."

Vitale bent forward across his desk and depressed the button on the intercom system.

"Bring him in now," he ordered.

A few moments later the door opened and a man wearing a light gray suit stepped inside the room. He took one look at the chair, the body bag, and the rubber mat and immediately turned away, trying to leave.

But two other men had entered the room behind him. They, too, were smartly dressed, but they were built like nightclub bouncers, and Silvrini had no chance of getting past them. They grabbed his arms and half dragged, half carried him to the chair and forced him down onto the seat. One man held him in position while the other secured his wrists and ankles to the arms and legs of the chair using plastic cable ties that were easy to use and as near unbreakable as made no difference, pulling them tight with pliers. Then both men stepped back and stood with their backs to the door, waiting impassively.

Silvrini was whimpering in terror, an incoherent muttering that was more babbling than recognizable speech. A dark stain suddenly appeared on the front of his trousers, a clear indication that he had lost control of his bladder and, in Toscanelli's eyes, probably an equally clear confirmation of his guilt.

Vitale waited without speaking, his hostile gaze fixed on the bound man in front of him, until Silvrini finally fell silent.

"You know why you are here, why this is happening to you," Vitale said at last, a statement rather than a question.

Silvrini shook his head violently, and his voice, when he spoke, was pleading, almost whining.

"No, no. I have no idea. You must believe me. This has to be a mistake. Please, Silvio. You know me."

"I do," Vitale agreed, "and it was a mistake."

For the briefest of instants the expression on the bound man's face showed relief, but Vitale's next words clearly dashed any hopes he might still have harbored.

"It was a mistake, and you made it. When you decided to betray the organization that employs you, it was the act of an idiot to make the call to the Carabinieri from the living room of an apartment owned by that organization."

"But I didn't, Silvio. I promise you, I didn't. The brotherhood is my life, you know that. I would never—"

Vitale said nothing, but simply held up his finger for silence. Then he depressed a button on the console in front of him, and suddenly Silvrini's unmistakable voice filled the room, the surveillance tape playing through the hidden speakers of a stereo system. The recording was short but utterly conclusive, the Italian telling the unidentified police officer that he had information about the two unsolved murders, and arranging a meeting in central Rome for the following afternoon—that very day, in fact.

"I wonder how long he'll sit there in that café, waiting for you," Vitale said quietly. "Because you won't be at the rendezvous, obviously. But I expect you already guessed that."

"It's not—" Silvrini began.

"It's not what, exactly? Not an attempt to betray this most holy of orders? Not a direct attack upon the brotherhood?"

Sivrini shook his head again. "Not—"

"Enough," Vitale snapped, and gestured to the two men standing in front of the door. "We'll finish this right now."

Both men strode forward. One held Silvrini's head still while the other wrapped a length of broad adhesive tape over his mouth, silencing the man.

Vitale nodded in satisfaction, then stood up. "Let us pray for absolution for our brother before punishment is administered," he said.

Toscanelli stood up as well, and the four men bowed their heads. Vitale made the sign of the cross and then led them in a short prayer, humbly asking God to accept the soul of their soon-to-be-departed brother, Alberto Silvrini.

The bound man clearly knew what awaited him, and was thrashing from side to side in the chair in a frantic attempt to escape, but the plastic bonds held him firmly in place and the chair was too heavy to be toppled over by his actions: it had been used for similar purposes on numerous occasions in the past, and had been designed to be very stable. All his violent action achieved was to open up cuts on his wrists where the plastic bonds dug into his skin.

As the prayer finished, Vitale made the sign of the cross again and resumed his seat behind the desk. He bent down, opened one of the drawers, and took out a digital video camera and a tripod. He spread the legs of the tripod, attached the camera to the platform at the top, and then adjusted its position until the figure of the helpless man, who was still writhing and struggling to get free, filled the viewfinder. Then he switched on the camera, and waited until he was sure it was recording before he spoke again, the tone of his voice almost regretful, his words measured and carefully considered, after the manner of a judge. Which was, after all, what he was in this case, essentially a triumvirate in the person of a single individual: judge, jury, and executioner.

"Alberto Silvrini. You have been condemned out of your own mouth and by your own words and actions. You have attempted to betray the brotherhood in the most diabolical and underhand way, and for that the sentence is death. But because of the nature of your offense, that mercy will not be granted immediately. You are to suffer before you die, but in accordance with that most ancient of all the tenets that we hold dear, not a drop of your blood will be spilled. Rest assured that you will die whole. Your suffering and death will be recorded for posterity and for our archives, and will serve as a warning to any other members of this brotherhood who might ever contemplate following the unfortunate example you have set."

Hearing his sentence of death pronounced in such a

cold and dispassionate manner had the effect of making Silvrini redouble his efforts to escape, but to no purpose.

Vitale glanced at the two men now standing beside the wooden chair and nodded to them. "You may begin. On my count. One every minute."

What followed was clinical in its brutal efficiency.

The man standing on Silvrini's left reached down, seized the bound man's little finger, and pulled it steadily backward, bracing his thumb just above the knuckle joint as a fulcrum. Silvrini went rigid, his face reddening and flushing as the pain began to bite. There was a sudden dull crack as the bone snapped, and even through the rudimentary gag Silvrini's howl of anguish could be heard. His body slumped against his bonds, his head dropping forward and tears springing from his eyes.

Precisely sixty seconds later, the man standing on Silvrini's right performed exactly the same operation on the bound man's right hand. And so it continued until every one of his fingers was broken and swollen. The thumbs were more difficult because the bones were thicker and stronger, but the two men had come prepared and used pliers to shatter those digits as well.

By the time they'd finished, Silvrini was virtually unconscious from the incredible pain he was suffering, and Vitale ordered Toscanelli to wait until he had recovered slightly before completing the procedure.

"It would be a mercy to kill him now," Vitale said quietly, staring at the bound figure slumped in the chair in front of him, "before he's fully conscious, but we're not really in the mercy business."

A few minutes later Silvrini lifted his head to stare at Vitale. His whole face was red, his cheeks streaked with tears and the agony in his bloodshot eyes clear for all to see.

"Good," Vitale said, "he's awake again. You may begin, Marco."

Toscanelli nodded and stepped forward. He paused for a moment beside the prisoner and stared down at him.

"You've been a real disappointment to me, Alberto," he said. "So this won't be quick, and certainly not as quick as you'd like."

Silvrini looked up and shook his head.

Toscanelli flashed him a brilliant smile and stepped around behind the chair, where he was handed a loop of rope and a short length of wood by one of the men standing there. The chair had a high back, and in the center of the top rail a hole had been bored. Toscanelli fed the loop of rope through the hole and dropped it over Silvrini's head, then slid the length of wood into the smaller loop remaining at the other end.

He gave the rope a sharp tug, pulling Silvrini's head and neck against the chair back, then twisted the wood to start the garrote working. He increased the pressure on the wood, watching critically as the noose started to tighten around the man's neck. Silvrini began to choke, and he released the pressure a couple of turns, allowing the man to breathe again before once more twisting the rope tighter. He did that twice more, taking Silvrini to the point where he couldn't breathe and then easing the pressure, then stepped around to face his victim once more.

He lifted the doomed man's chin and stared into his face, and smiled again as Silvrini forced his eyes open for the last time.

"This is it, Alberto, so take your last breath."

Then he stepped back behind the chair and twisted the rope again, taking his time as he slowly and steadily increased the pressure. Silvrini struggled and choked as the rope began to bite, his body thrashing hopelessly, helplessly, from side to side.

Toscanelli increased the pressure, turning the wood in the loop until it would turn no more, and held it there, watching critically as the man in front of him slowly died. His struggles grew weaker and weaker until finally he stopped moving altogether, but still Toscanelli maintained the pressure, making sure he finished the job completely. He held the wood in place for a two full minutes after Silvrini's last convulsive shudder, just to make absolutely sure.

Only then did he release his grip and step back, away from the chair, before moving forward to stare down for a moment at the dead man's face, the skin an unpleasant mixture of shades of red and black, the eyes open and staring blindly ahead. Then he strode back across the room and again sat down in the chair beside Vitale's desk, to allow room for the two enforcers to complete their work.

"Sometimes," Vitale said, watching as the two men cut through the plastic ties and lifted Silvrini's body off the chair and lowered it none too gently into the body bag, "I think you enjoy that kind of thing just a little too much."

Toscanelli shook his head, reached into the right-hand pocket of his jacket, took out an oblong packet, and opened one end. He extracted an unusually long and thin cigarette with a thin gold band around the filter, put it in his mouth, and lit it.

"Treachery is the only crime you can't forgive," he said, then drew deeply on the cigarette and narrowed his eyes against the smoke. "In fact, in my book, it's more than a crime. I believe it's a mortal sin. If the decision had been mine, I would have broken every bone in his body before finishing him off. What about his family? Had he any close relatives?"

"No wife, of course, just like the rest of us, but he had a sister and a brother as well, at least until about two hours ago. The sister lives in Modena, and he seems to have had no recent contact with her, but his brother was here in Rome. I sent out another team to take care of him as well, just in case he had let anything slip. We can't afford any loose ends, and particularly not at the moment."

"Why now especially?"

"Because we've had a definite hit," Silvio Vitale replied.

10

"So you live above the shop, as they say?" Mallory asked.

"Yes. In fact, I bought this part of the building," Robin replied, leading the way up the metal spiral staircase. "I needed both a shop and somewhere to live, because I really didn't want to have to commute to work, and this seemed to fit the bill. It's pretty cramped, but it works for me."

"It must have been expensive, the commercial premises and accommodation. Selling books must pay well."

Robin glanced back at him over her shoulder.

"Not as well as I'd like," she replied. "But I had a small inheritance from an aunt, and that was enough to cover the deposit and start the business. For the rest of it, just like everyone else these days I've had to sell most of my soul and almost all my income to the bank on the corner of High Street. But I'm building up a customer base, mostly people like you who are interested in specific and unusual subjects, and so far I'm showing a reasonable profit."

She stopped on the metal landing at the top of the

external staircase and took a set of keys out of her hand-bag. She selected a Yale, slid it into the lock, and opened the door.

"The loo's that door there, if you want it," she said, "and my office is the one where the door's open. I'll put the kettle on, but the coffee's only instant," she warned.

"That's fine with me," Mallory said, heading for the lavatory. "Frankly I can't tell the difference."

Five minutes later, they were sitting on opposite sides of the desk, two mugs of coffee steaming but largely forgotten beside them as they stared at the black leather book safe and its two rows of protruding spikes. Both of them were wearing white cotton gloves at Robin's insistence, just in case her suspicion about the spikes originally being poisoned was correct. The pair she'd found for Mallory was the biggest she had, but they were still an extremely tight fit.

He held his hand horizontally over one of the rows of spikes, comparing the thickness of his palm to their length, and whistled softly.

"My hand is a lot bigger than yours," he said, "but I think that if I'd been holding the book safe when it was triggered, those spikes would have gone straight through my palm and come out the other side. They must be nearly two inches long."

"According to my ruler, they measure just over one inch and three quarters."

Mallory nodded, then bent to look even more closely at the two separate mechanisms that were built into the relic: the catches that held the lid closed and the trigger-ing mechanism that was designed to fire the spikes. Then he stared at the slim hole cut into the side of the book safe opposite to the spine, where lengths of paper had been attached to look like the pages of a book.

"That opening," he said after a few moments, "doesn't look to me like it was intended to accept any kind of key that I've ever seen. But that shape is very familiar to me."

"It is? What is it?"

"It looks like the top of a sheath for a sword, or maybe a dagger. It's like a flattened oval, thicker in the middle and then tapering on both sides to where the sharpened edges of the blade would be. And there's something else as well."

He reached over to the pen rest on the edge of Robin's desk and picked up a pencil. He used its sharpened end to point to two small raised areas in the metal on the inside of the book safe, one above and the other below the center of the flattened oval.

"I don't know how much you know about stabbing weapons," he said, "but the blades of most knives and swords intended for stabbing rather than hacking include a grooved channel that's commonly known as the blood gutter, though it should properly be called a fuller, after the blacksmithing tool used to make it. Most people think it's intended to allow a blade to be pulled out of a body more easily, but actually it allows the weight of the blade to be reduced without affecting its strength. I think those two bits of metal were probably intended to fit inside the fullers on a double-edged blade. A particular blade, I mean, so the keyhole, that narrow oval slot, has been designed to prevent the wrong knife blade from being inserted. If that isn't the case, then I've got no idea why they're there."

"You're right," Robin said. "What you say does make sense. And I suppose the mere fact that the 'key,' if you like, was a dagger—a weapon that most men in medieval times wore around their waist every day as a matter of course, just as a part of their normal dress—would have added another layer of protection for the book safe. One dagger, I assume, looks very much like any other dagger, and somebody trying to crack the secret of the book safe wouldn't have any idea there was anything special about one particular weapon. They'd have been able to hide the key in plain sight, if you like."

Mallory was still bending forward over the desk, closely examining the mechanism inside the object.

"I think I see how this works now," he said.

He gestured again with the point of the pencil. "Look here, on both sides of the slot where the blade of the dagger would be inserted. There are two metal bars, one on each side. As the correct blade was slid inside, its edges would have pressed against these two bars, which are hinged. If you move them outward, then the opposite ends would have fitted into these two slots, here"—he pointed at two rectangular cutouts on the pair of metal levers that were attached to the rows of spikes—"and that would have locked the mechanism and prevented it from being triggered. It's really quite sophisticated. Whoever made this had both time and talent, and was also pretty good at metalwork."

Mallory put both hands inside the book safe, rested his thumbs against one of the bars carrying the spikes, and his fingers around the one on the opposite side, and then squeezed them together. The springs were strong, but so were his fingers, and in a few moments his efforts were rewarded by a distinct double click as he reset the booby trap.

"Pardon me for asking," Robin said, "but why have you just done that?"

"For safety," Mallory replied. "If you're right about the age and the history of that thing, the booby trap wasn't triggered for several hundred years, and in all that time the spikes stayed safely inside the book safe. Leaving them sticking out like that is pretty much an invitation for somebody to hurt themselves, so I think it's actually safer if the trap is reset. I don't suppose you'll be sticking a screwdriver in it again."

Robin thought about that for a moment and then nodded.

"You're probably right," she agreed, "and it'll certainly be easier to store it in my safe like that."

Mallory stretched out his hand to the rolled parchment, but Robin stopped him.

"Don't touch it," she snapped, and Mallory drew his hand back as if he'd been burned.

"I can't do much if you won't let me see the manuscript," he said, sounding hurt.

"Sorry. It's just that it's very fragile and you need experience to know how to handle something like that."

"I'm not an idiot. I've been studying old documents in churches and libraries for the last year or so, tracing my family history. I do know something about this."

Robin shook her head.

"Sorry again," she said. "I didn't know that. Most people don't have a clue about the damage you can do to old parchment just by touching it with your bare fingers."

Mallory silently lifted his gloved hands in front of her face, and she nodded.

"I'll need to get some professional advice myself on how best to preserve it," she said.

"So I presume you've copied it?" he asked, sounding only slightly mollified.

"I've copied it and scanned it as well. That was pretty much the first thing I did after I got over the shock of the booby trap triggering."

She lifted the parchment carefully, using a couple of pencils, lowered it into the book safe, and then closed the lid, pressing it down until the catch clicked to lock it. Then she carried it over to the safe from which she had removed it a few minutes earlier, put it inside, and locked the door.

"Do you think it's valuable?" Mallory asked. "That book safe, I mean."

"I really don't know. When I realized what it was, I assumed it was just a curio, and there are people who collect that kind of thing—medieval instruments and weapons and so on—but I really have no idea if this has a significant value or not." She laughed shortly. "The reason I'm keeping it in the safe is so that I don't stab myself with it and nor does anybody else who comes up here, like Betty."

"Betty?"

"The lady who runs the shop for me. I'll introduce you later. I can just see her wandering up here to ask me something and pricking the end of her finger on one of those spikes. But now that we've looked at it more closely, I'm beginning to think that it might well be valuable, simply because I've never seen anything like it before. I've done some searches on the Internet, and although book safes aren't unknown, I can't find any mention of medieval ones, and I couldn't find any that contained any kind of built-in antitheft device. Often in those days, important books included a lock of some sort to prevent them from being opened, but they were still just books, not safes, so I suppose it could even be unique. I'm still convinced it's medieval, and it's in pretty good condition, and rarity, condition, and age are all ticks in the right boxes as far as serious collectors are concerned."

Mallory nodded. "It's an impressive piece of kit and if

you want my opinion—and I suppose that's the reason I'm here right now—without even taking a look at the parchment, I can tell you that whatever it is and says is important. Or at least it was important when it was put inside that relic, which isn't quite the same thing. Nobody would go to this kind of trouble, to have an object like that made, unless the contents were crucial to them in some way. So I guess the next step is to take a look at the text on the parchment and try and find out what it says."

Robin sat down in the swivel chair and pulled open one of the drawers. She took two sheets of paper out of the drawer and slid them across toward Mallory.

"You'll recognize the first few words because those were the ones I sent you," she said.

Mallory nodded, opened his computer case, and took out a sheet of paper on which he'd written the alphabet and the left-shifted Atbash cipher.

"This should be easy enough," he said.

But Robin shook her head decisively. "Not necessarily. After we talked and I read your e-mail, I wrote out the cipher as well, but when I tried it on another section of text, all that happened was I turned gibberish into a different kind of gibberish, but certainly not into Latin or any other language that I recognized."

"Did you, now?" Mallory said, looking down thoughtfully at the photocopy on the paper in front of him. "Well, I think that's good, because I like a challenge. It sounds as if whoever wrote this might have used more than one encryption technique, and that's interesting in itself, because again it suggests that whatever this text says it is—or at least it *was* when it was written—extremely important to somebody."

Mallory looked at the photocopy again, then shook his head.

"It's not that easy to read even in the original," he pointed out. "In some places I can't really see where one word begins or ends."

"A lot of medieval documents were like that," Robin replied. "Paper was a fairly rare and expensive commodity, so the words were crammed together and the whole width of the paper was used. And of course parchment was a lot more expensive than paper."

"Well, we need to get this right, without any mistakes, just in case this reveals the location of the lost treasure of King John or something like that."

"Not very likely," Robin said, with a smile. "So, what do you suggest?"

"I know it will take a lot longer, but I think the first thing we should do is transcribe the whole of the original text onto a computer, letter by letter. That way we'll be able to identify any ambiguous letters and play around with the spacing if we aren't sure where one word ends and the next begins. Then we can print it out because it'll be easier to write the deciphered Latin text underneath, and an English translation under that, in the old-fashioned way, using paper and ink."

"Okay. It'll take a while, but that's not a bad idea. I'm more used to looking at this kind of material than you are, so let me suggest that I read out the letters from the photocopy, while you type them."

Mallory nodded.

"That works for me," he said.

He opened his computer bag again, took out his laptop, and switched it on. He started up his word processing program and created a new file named "parchment.docx," then waited with his hands poised above the keyboard.

Robin removed her spectacles and placed them on her desk, then picked up a pencil.

"You can read without glasses?" Mallory asked.

She nodded. "Yes. They're plain glass, not prescription lenses, more a kind of disguise. I find I get taken a lot more seriously if I wear glasses than if I don't. I know I'm not blond, but I've more or less seen the word *bimbo* forming in the minds of some men—people like my first bank manager here in Dartmouth, for example—when I've been trying to discuss business with them. So now I tend to wear them most of the time when I'm out and about, but actually my vision's pretty near perfect."

Mallory considered her for a moment.

"I get the feeling there's an awful lot about you that I don't know yet," he said.

"You have no idea," Robin replied, "but I would remind you that you're the one who won't talk about that scar on your cheek."

"Touché. Maybe later. Right, let's get started."

Robin began reading out the individual letters that formed the text of the medieval parchment, drawing a neat diagonal line through each one as she did so. Where the letter was in any way ambiguous—sometimes the letter *O*, for example, could look like a *Q*, or *C* resemble a *G*—she drew a circle around the letter and told Mallory to put both the possible letters in brackets for the decryption that would follow.

She also told him to put a space after every letter that appeared to be the last one in a particular word. She was fairly sure she wasn't always getting everything right, because Mallory's earlier comment had been accurate: in a few places the words seemed to run one into the next without any break that she could see, and the quill or whatever had been used to write the text had had a thick point, so the letters themselves were heavy and difficult to interpret. To complicate it still further, in some areas the ink had faded significantly, and the letters were even more difficult to read in consequence.

But they quickly settled into a routine as the parchment began to yield its secrets, or at least the encrypted text, in its entirety.

11

Via di Sant' Alessio, Aventine Hill, Rome, Italy

"It's not the first time this has happened," Toscanelli responded. "Are you quite certain about it?"

Vitale nodded. "We've never before had such a precise result from any of our surveillance mechanisms. This time we are positive that the relic has at last been discovered again after having been lost for so many centuries."

"Please convince me," Toscanelli said.

"The term was entered into a search engine in Britain. In fact, the user carried out quite a number of searches, most of them including the one expression we are almost certain would be used, the Latin *Ipse Dixit*—"

"The master's words," Toscanelli interjected.

"Exactly, but some of the searches, especially the later ones, also included words like *manuscript* and *medieval*, so it seems almost certain that the person who initiated those searches is in possession of the relic. We've printed all the search terms entered from that one location."

Vitale picked up one of the sheets of paper from the desk in front of him and passed it across.

Toscanelli glanced at it with professional interest.

"They got the title right," he said. "As far as we know, the relic bore the name *Ipse Dixit*, and that's not likely to be a mistake. So that looks like a confirmation that they have somehow found it. We need to move fast."

"Faster than you think. We want this sorted within hours, not days. We simply can't afford under any circumstances for the text to be decrypted, not after all the years we've been looking for it."

Toscanelli nodded.

"Where do I need to go?" he asked, "and how big a team am I taking?"

"The target is a man named Robin Jessop and he's in southwest England in a town named Dartmouth. There will be six of you in total, and the other five have already been briefed and are on their way to Ciampino Airport, where there's a private jet waiting for you. You will use your real name, and you alone will be responsible for communicating with this office. All your equipment, including weapons and the documentation you'll need, will be on the aircraft when you get there. As always, none of you are to take any personal identification with you whatsoever. This has to be a completely deniable operation. Under no circumstances are the British authorities to find out what is happening, and the usual rules will apply in the event of any of your team being compromised or apprehended."

Toscanelli nodded. "They are to be silenced, permanently, before they can be interrogated."

"Exactly. Ensure that they all know that before the operation commences. In this case, you should meet no problems. The man is a bookseller in a small coastal town in England. He will not be armed, and may well be elderly—so far, our systems have not been able to determine that. Once you have retrieved the relic, any and all evidence that he may have already deduced about it is to be either recovered and brought back here or destroyed. Fire is probably the preferred method, as it will conceal almost everything."

Vitale handed over a black-colored folder. "All the information we have is in here. The whole sequence of events, the search terms used, and of course all the address details for this man Jessop."

Toscanelli nodded again. The operation sounded simple and straightforward, and he only had one final question to which he thought he probably already knew the answer. But for the benefit of the recorders that he knew would be running in the background in the office, he needed to hear the instruction. "And Jessop himself? What about him?"

"He is to be eliminated. If possible, make it look like an accident. If not, use any method that seems expedient and effective. But it is essential that he is dead before you leave the scene."

12

It took the pair of them well over an hour to transcribe the entire text of the parchment into the computer, a long, boring, and tiresome operation.

When they'd finally finished, Mallory copied the file onto a memory stick and gave it to Robin, who transferred the file onto her own laptop and printed two copies of the transcribed text on her laser. Then she handed back the memory stick, stood up from her chair, and stretched.

"I don't think I can face starting the decryption right now," she said. "I need a caffeine injection as a matter of some urgency, and this time I'm buying."

"Good idea."

Mallory stood up as well, closed the lid on his laptop and unplugged the charger cable, then slid the computer back into his bag.

Robin looked at him quizzically.

"I can't afford to lose this machine," Mallory said simply. "I do a lot of my work for my clients offsite, and so I have a lot of commercially sensitive material on this computer as well as some expensive utility programs, plus all my personal stuff. So where I go, the laptop goes."

"Even fifty yards down the road for a coffee?"

"Even fifty yards down the road for a coffee," Mallory confirmed.

Robin locked the apartment door behind her and at the bottom of the spiral staircase she opened the rear door to the shop and led the way inside.

A pleasant-looking middle-aged woman turned around from her seat behind the counter as they walked in, lowering the novel she had been reading as she did so.

"Betty," Robin said, "this is David Mallory. He's helping me with a little project I'm working on." She turned to Mallory. "Betty runs the place," she went on. "I simply couldn't manage the shop without her. I know that's a cliché, but in this case it also happens to be absolutely true."

The coffee in the café Robin had selected was far better than it had been in the one where they had met. Somewhat revived and fortified, they were back in her office within twenty minutes, and Mallory started work on the decryption almost immediately. And almost immediately he ran into problems.

"You're quite right," he said. "It's only the first nine words that I can decode using the Atbash cipher with the eleven-place shift to the left. It doesn't work for the tenth word, nor the eleventh or twelfth." He thought for a few seconds, then continued. "I suppose realistically there are only two possibilities. Either whoever wrote this switched to a different type of encryption method, or they simply used a different shift but carried on using Atbash."

"If it's medieval, and I still think that's the most likely period, then I have no idea what other possible types of cipher were around, if any. Do you know?"

"Oddly enough, yes. Ciphers of various sorts have

been around for a long time. Researchers have identified three kinds of monoalphabetic ciphers in the Old Testament, and there are even records of an early type of steganography—that's a technique for hiding a message inside another medium—using wax tablets from around the fifth century BC. The idea was to scratch the real message in plaintext on a block of wood used as the backing for a wax tablet, then apply the normal wax surface to hide it and write another, entirely innocent, message on the wax. Melt the wax off the wood, and then the important message could be read."

Mallory laughed shortly.

"That was a fairly efficient method of sending a hidden message, because it could travel as fast as the messenger could run or a horse could gallop, but there was another classic example of steganography that was a lot slower. According to Herodotus, in ancient Greece a vital message about Persian invasion plans was tattooed on the shaved scalp of a slave. Weeks later, when his hair had grown long enough to hide the tattoo, he was sent off to the recipient of the message, his head was shaved again, and the warning was delivered, but that was obviously a really slow option."

"I've actually heard of steganography," Robin said. "That includes things like microdots, doesn't it?"

"Microdots and almost everything else, yes. There was a famous case back in the sixties when an American serviceman who'd been captured by the North Vietnamese blinked his eyelids to spell out the word *torture* in Morse code during a press conference he was forced to attend, which is one of the more unusual examples. These days, because of digital transmission media, you can hide data or images in almost everything from pictures to sound files and documents.

"One very simple and obvious way of doing that would be to include a passage of text in a blank area of a word-processing document, and to make the text the same color as the background. It would be invisible to anyone reading the document, but if the recipient knows where it is he can simply highlight the block, change the text color, and read it. But more usually the text would be shrunk down to the size of a full stop or other punctuation mark and embedded somewhere in a document, or reduced to the size of a single pixel and then hidden in an image file of some type.

"Then there was a thing called a Polybius square, developed by a Greek historian in the second century BC, which was used to convert letters into numbers, most commonly employed in signaling. A variant of that is still in use today. And it was most probably Julius Caesar who used what you might call a shifted Atbash in his military communications, usually without reversing the cipher alphabet, and a monoalphabetic cipher of that kind is still known today as a Caesar alphabet. He also did things like substituting Greek for Latin letters. Coming a bit more up to date, the Vikings used simple encryption methods in some of their rune stones, and in the thirteenth century, Roger Bacon wrote quite a lot about the cryptography methods that were then in common use. Techniques for encrypting messages and information have been around in various forms for a long time. There's even a section in the Kama Sutra about the importance of using and understanding ciphers."

"The Kama Sutra?" Robin asked. "I thought that dealt with slightly more interesting subjects, like sex."

"It does." Mallory grinned. "And those are the only bits that everybody reads, but there's a lot more in that work than just finding the right—or even the wrong—position to adopt when you're in bed with somebody."

He looked back at the printed text in front of him.

"But almost all of these methods were various types of substitution ciphers," he finished, pointing at the paper he had been scribbling on, "and I'm pretty certain that this is just a kind of Atbash, nothing more complicated than that. And using this method of shifting, there are only twenty-six possible alternative keys, or fifty-two if we include the nonreversed cipher alphabets. I'll write out all of them and then we'll pick a word that's fairly short, four or five letters, something like that, and try each of them until we find the one that decodes it."

Writing them all out was laborious, but easy, not least because Robin did half of them.

"I'll start from the beginning," Mallory said, "with a right shift of one place, and see where that gets us."

The short answer was nowhere, because it didn't work. Nor did the right shift of two, but when he tried the next possible key, right-shifted three places, the first four-letter word he had selected deciphered as *deus*.

"That looks like Latin," he said.

"That's because it is," Robin confirmed. "It's the Latin word for God."

Mallory quickly decoded the nine words that followed the first group he had deciphered.

"If the guy who wrote this was following a pattern," he said, "I'll probably need to use a different key for the next word."

But to his surprise, he decrypted the next word, the nineteenth in the manuscript, using the same key, and did the same with the following eight. However, the twenty-eighth word refused to decipher using that key, and Mallory took several minutes, trying each possible Atbash key until it finally yielded to a left shift of seven. That worked for the next eight words, but not for the ninth.

"That's interesting," he said. "There's obviously something important about the number nine, because I've now used three different Atbash ciphers, two of them decoding nine words each and the other one decoding eighteen, which is of course nine multiplied by two. I'll bet this cipher works either for nine words or for a multiple of nine."

It did. The thirty-seventh word didn't decode until Mallory tried a left shift of eight, and then he was able to decipher the next eight words to make a total of nine for that particular key. The next group decoded using Atbash shifted eleven places left, and the following eighteen using a right shift of three.

"He's starting to repeat himself," Mallory said, "and that might make it a bit easier—or at least quicker—to sort out the rest."

The first section of the document was eighty-three words in length, and because Mallory could guess where the cipher changed and what the subsequent one was likely to be, he made short work of decrypting the text into Latin. But when he tried to decode the first word of the second paragraph or section, none of the keys he'd used before decrypted it, and in fact none of the twenty-six possible shifted Atbash keys worked, and nor did the keys using the nonreversed alphabet.

"I didn't expect that," he said. "This section has obviously been written using either a different encryption method or a different type of Atbash cipher. I know I told you that there weren't that many alternative types of code in use in the Middle Ages, but I think we're looking at one."

"But however it was done," Robin said, "it surely can't be that sophisticated?"

"Probably not. Atbash is the simplest possible type of

monoalphabetic substitution cipher, and it wouldn't be that great a leap of logic for somebody who used that code to make the transition from it to another type of substitution cipher, but using a keyword or several keywords, instead of just the alphabet written forward or backward and shifted left or right."

Robin looked slightly blank.

"Let me give you a very simple example."

Mallory jotted down the letters *A* to *F* in a horizontal line on the paper, and then wrote *BRANDY* directly underneath them.

"Right, that's the first part of the alphabet and let's assume that *BRANDY* is the keyword you've chosen. Suppose you wanted to encode the word *DECADE*. You do it exactly the same as you'd do in Atbash: just read off the letters from the code word that correspond to the plaintext letters, so *D* would be enciphered as *N*, *E* as *D*, and so on. So using that code word, *DECADE* would be encrypted as *NDABND*. Two ciphers that are still in use today—the single and double substitution ciphers—use exactly the same technique. In theory, you can't decrypt the text without knowing what the code word was, and certainly not with a double substitution cipher that uses two different code words that both have to be applied. You encrypt the plaintext using the first code word, then encrypt the enciphered text using the second code word, so it's really difficult to crack. But that's a comparatively recent technique, and I don't believe that's been used here."

"You said that in theory you can't crack it, but what about in practice? Is it possible?" Robin asked.

"In practice, the biggest problem in decoding encrypted text is usually time. Today, given enough computing power and sufficient time, almost any code can be cracked. That's what places like GCHQ out at Cheltenham do. That's their job over at Spook Central, the whole reason they're there. They have banks of supercomputers, things like Crays, and they run what are called brute force attacks, trying every possible combination of letters, numbers, punctuation marks, and symbols against messages they believe are important. That technique only works because these computers can try tens or hundreds of millions of combinations every *second*. I don't have access to a supercomputer, obviously, but with simple ciphers there are things you can do quite quickly to try to work out what at least some of the encrypted letters stand for. Have you ever heard about a technique called frequency analysis?"

"Oddly enough, yes, if you're talking about an alphabet. In English, the most commonly used letters of the alphabet are, in order, *E T A O I N*. Don't ask me how or why I remember that, but I just do."

"Exactly," Mallory said, looking at her with new respect. "Most people have never even heard of it. So looking back at my simple example using *BRANDY* as a code word, if you applied frequency analysis to the result, you could reasonably assume that either the encrypted letter *N* or *D* represented the plaintext letter *E*, and of course you'd be quite right: it's *D*. The bigger the sample you have to work with, the more accurate the result is likely to be. Unfortunately I don't know the frequency analysis details for Latin, so that method wouldn't necessarily be much use to us here. And the other problem is that if the person who wrote this text decided to change the key every nine words, we might never be able to decipher it completely because we just wouldn't have enough material to work with."

"So, is there anything we can do?" Robin asked.

"That's really where you come in. I've deciphered the first eighty-odd words of this, so we now have the Latin text. If you can translate that into English so that I can understand it, then we might find a clue."

Ten minutes later, Robin passed Mallory a sheet of paper on which she had written out a translation of the Latin text. He took it eagerly, but the expression on his face changed as he read it. Then he put the paper on the desk and looked across at Robin.

"Unless I'm missing something," he said, "this just looks like a waste of space. It's a long rambling prayer or invocation about the importance of accepting God's will and living a life based on a strict rule."

Robin nodded.

"You haven't missed anything, unless I've missed it, too. That's exactly what it is, and it's typically medieval in its sentiments. I really can't think of any good reason why anyone would want to hide something like that away in the book safe. The important bit has got to be contained in the rest of the text, the part that we can't decipher."

She glanced at her watch. "I don't know about you, but I'm getting hungry and it's nearly seven, so let's make tracks for a restaurant. You might have a sudden brain wave when you're halfway through a chop or something."

Mallory nodded. "A break often helps when you're stuck on something, in my experience, so let's go. You can tell me all about your life and your deprived childhood and your deepest fears and fantasies and dreams," he added with a smile. "Or not. It's entirely up to you."

"I'll keep my fantasies and dreams to myself, thank you very much, and my childhood was depressingly un-deprived."

She watched Mallory shut the lid of his computer and

put the laptop in his bag, along with the photocopies of the parchment and the sheets of paper they'd been working on.

"You really can leave that here, you know," she said. "I'm sure it'll be perfectly safe."

"Sorry. The habit of a lifetime, but I'll worry if I can't see it."

"Is that the only peculiarity about you?" Robin asked as she locked the door to her apartment and they started walking down the stairs. "Or have you got a whole raft of neuroses and psychoses that you're just gasping to tell me about over a bowl of soup? In short: are you normal?"

"I think anyone's definition of the word *normal* depends largely on where and when they're standing, if you see what I mean. What was normal in Rome in the first century AD would have been considered completely abnormal in Victorian England. But as far as I'm aware, by the standards of this century and in this country, I'm pretty normal. I just tend to worry quite a lot about my laptop."

"You could have given me the short answer," Robin complained, leading the way down the alley to the street. "A simple yes would have done."

13

Exeter Airport, Devon

"India Bravo Echo, Exeter Tower, land runway two six and take the taxiway on the left."

"Thank you, Tower. Cleared to land and to turn south off the active. India Echo."

The tower controller lifted his binoculars to his face as the pilot of the Cessna Citation X lifted the aircraft's nose just prior to touchdown on the active runway. The main landing gear straddled the center line, both wheels touching the concrete at the same moment, producing twin puffs of blue smoke and leaving a pair of short black skid marks. Moments later, the nose gear made contact with the runway and the high-performance executive jet began slowing rapidly, angling away from the centerline and toward the entrance to the taxiway, close to the western end of the runway. A few moments later, the pilot called the tower again.

"India Echo is clear of the active."

"Roger."

"Pretty aircraft," the controller's assistant remarked,

watching the sleek white-painted jet move along the taxi-way.

The controller nodded.

"Pretty, really expensive, and very quick," he agreed. "Now that Concorde is no longer with us, what you're looking at is the fastest civil aircraft in the world. For your fifteen million quid or so, you get a jet that'll do better than point nine Mach, with a range of well over three thousand miles. Nice piece of kit. Don't see that many of them here, and especially not with Italian registry."

The assistant was still watching the aircraft.

"Maybe it's the Mafia come to call," he suggested.

"I think it's a bit too high profile for them," the controller replied. "Far more likely to be some fat Italian businessman on the take, traveling with a small flock of his mistresses."

A few minutes later the pilot shut down the Cessna's engines in the private aircraft parking area and the side door opened. Six heavily built men wearing dark suits emerged and walked briskly across to the ECA—Exeter Corporate Aviation—facility. Neither the controller nor the assistant saw them, because by then their attention was directed elsewhere on the airfield, but none of the new arrivals looked like businessmen, fat or otherwise.

About forty minutes after that, the six men drove away from the building in a pair of black Range Rovers, which they had hired while the aircraft was still in the air somewhere over France. They turned right out of the main gate and headed west along the A30 until they reached the Sowton Interchange, and there they turned south to follow the M5 Motorway, the second vehicle holding position about a hundred yards behind the first.

Both drivers set their Range Rover cruise controls to

hold them at exactly seventy-three miles an hour, because they couldn't afford to get stopped by the police for something as mundane as speeding. One reason was that they were in a hurry. The clock was ticking and they didn't want to be delayed.

The second reason was just as practical. After they'd cleared the customs and immigration facilities at the airport, one of the flight deck crew had returned to the Cessna, ostensibly to check on how much fuel they would need to buy for the return journey. When he'd rejoined his passengers outside the ECA building, he handed over half a dozen small but quite heavy black plastic cases that he'd recovered from a hidden compartment in the aircraft's cabin and then concealed in his bulky flight case.

The contents of these were now tucked away in the jacket pockets of the men sitting in the two Range Rovers, but would result in their immediate arrest if any British police officer knew what they were carrying. Of course, the organization that employed them would be able to secure their release without too much difficulty, but the operation would require negotiation with the British authorities—something that their masters in Italy would most especially want to avoid—and take a considerable amount of time.

And time was the one thing they all knew they were short of.

14

The restaurant was small, only accommodating about a dozen tables, and four of those were positioned by the long windows that overlooked the river Dart. They managed to secure the last of these, at the far end of the room, and for a few minutes after the waiter had led them to the table, they both sat in a companionable silence looking out at the water.

Through the open windows, they could hear the melodic tinkling of halyards on metal masts, and on the opposite side of the river Mallory could see a large number of sailing yachts of various sizes moored in lines, with the lights of cottages and streets on the opposite side of the river just beginning to be switched on. It was a scene that was quintessentially English, but with just a hint of a Mediterranean playground about it.

"It is beautiful," Robin said, somewhat wistfully. "I never get tired of sitting and looking out at the river. It's never the same from one day to the next. There's always something going on, something to watch."

"I presume you're a regular here?" Mallory asked.

Robin nodded. "I probably come here at least twice a month, usually as my treat to myself for getting through another week without going bankrupt. Sometimes I bring Betty along as well, just to keep her sweet. It's not desperately expensive, the food is pretty good, and we all have to eat somewhere."

"Look," Mallory began, "I know we agreed you'd cover my expenses and my time, but let me pay for this meal. I've had quite an entertaining day so far, and I'd be quite happy to pick up the bill."

Robin scowled at him. "I noticed you only said that *after* I told you this wasn't an expensive restaurant." Then she smiled, her face lighting up. "No, a deal is a deal. Dinner is on me."

Mallory shrugged, then looked out the window again and pointed across the river, to the opposite bank. "I've never been here before. Is that another bit of Dartmouth over there on the other side?"

Robin shook her head. "No, that's Kingswear. It's actually separate, and there's a ferry you can use to get across there. And you'll notice that most of the yachts are on trots on that side of the river, the east. That's because the main navigable channel of the Dart is closer to the west bank in this area."

" 'Trots'?" Mallory asked.

"Moorings. There's so much nautical stuff about in Dartmouth that even a confirmed landlubber who's never so much as sat in a rowing boat—someone rather like me, in fact—still absorbs some of the local expressions, possibly by some form of osmosis. Don't forget that this town's main claim to fame, apart from Agatha Christie's house, which is some way upriver, is the Royal Navy College, HMS *Britannia*, a kind of concrete battleship. If you came in on the main road, you must have seen it. A massive building on the left-hand side as you start driving down the hill into the town, and pretty impressive, not to mention being stuffed full of extremely fit young men."

"Could that possibly have had anything to do with you setting up shop here in the town?" Mallory asked innocently.

"Oddly enough, no. I prefer my men to be a bit more mature, and to have slightly wider interests than the ability to discuss the tactics employed at the Battle of Matapan or Trafalgar. Most of the young officers in training that I've met here have been fairly single-mindedly set on making it to the admiralty, and the idea of becoming Mrs. Commander Blogs, just a kind of decorative attachment worn on the left sleeve of a naval officer's uniform, has never appealed to me. I want to do more with my life than play second fiddle to any man, or any woman, for that matter."

Mallory looked at her for a long moment.

"You're not—" he began.

"If you were going to say 'gay,' the answer is no. I enjoy the company of women, but only as long as they've got their clothes on."

"And men?"

"That depends on the man, obviously. I notice, by the way," Robin added with a smile, "that we haven't even ordered yet, and already the level of conversation has descended to navel level and below, and that's *navel* with an *e*, nothing to do with the boys up the road wearing dark blue."

"I could say that you started it, banging on about the college," Mallory said. "But you're right. Let's order something, and then try and decide what we should do about that piece of parchment."

A waiter stepped over to the table, pad and pen poised, and a couple of minutes later he scurried off back toward the kitchen.

Over a couple of steaks—served with salad for Robin and french fries for Mallory—and a bottle of half-decent red, they began exploring possible ways that they could decipher the remainder of the encrypted Latin text.

"I wonder if we need to start looking at numerology," Mallory said. "The shift in the Atbash cipher took place every nine words—except for those two runs of eighteen words, but of course eighteen is nine multiplied by two—so I think it's a reasonable assumption that the number nine is important for whoever encrypted this. And of course we also have other numbers, the value of each shift in the cipher. In fact, each shift could generate two numbers, because a left shift of ten, say, is the same as a right shift of sixteen in an alphabet of twenty-six letters. Was the Latin alphabet twenty-six letters, by the way?"

Robin shook her head. "That question isn't easy to answer because it depends upon what period you're talking about. The archaic Latin alphabet, which was in use after the seventh century BC, contained twenty-six letters, but five of those letters came from the ancient Greek alphabet, and the order was slightly different as well. For example, the letter *Z* came between *F* and *H*. Then the classical Latin alphabet appeared in the first century BC, but that only contained twenty-three letters, missing today's *J*, *U*, and *W*, so Julius Caesar's name would actually have been spelt *IVLIVS*."

She paused and took a sip of wine. "But by the Middle Ages, the present Latin alphabet had been pretty much established, including the letter *W*, which of course isn't a double *U* at all but actually a double *V*. That's one reason why I think the parchment dates from that period in history, because you've been using the full twenty-six letters in your decryption, and it's been working. And the other two indicators of date are the interpunct and what was known as *scriptio continua*. Or, to be exact, the absence of both of them."

"I presume you're going to tell me what the hell you're talking about. I spend my life working with computers, and Latin is pretty much all Greek to me, if you see what I mean."

Robin smiled at him.

"That's the point," she said. "We're different but complementary. I know all about the old stuff and you know something about the new stuff."

Mallory raised an eyebrow at that remark and the emphasis she'd used, but Robin bashed on without a pause.

"Right, an interpunct was a punctuation mark used to indicate where one word ended and the next word began. It was usually a dot, but sometimes a small triangular shape, and most often it was vertically centered on the line of text, not at the bottom of the letters, which is where a comma or a full stop is placed today. It's still used in some languages like Catalan to indicate where there are two syllables separated by a dot and where the sense would alter considerably if it was omitted. One common example is *cella*. Without the dot, which is known in Catalan as a *punt volat* or 'flown dot,' the word means an 'eyebrow.' Put the dot between the two letter *L*'s and it means 'cell,' and is pronounced differently.

"Anyway, the interpunct was used in Latin for a while, but was gradually replaced by *scriptio continua*, continuous script, where there were no breaks at all between the words. That sounds as if it was probably a retrograde step, but you have to appreciate that at this time written text was handled in a different way than it is today. Speakers would read the text a number of times in order to memorize it, and so the script, which was usually written on a scroll, was used more like a prompt sheet or an aide-mémoire that the speaker would glance at occasionally just to refresh his memory."

"I didn't see any dots on the parchment," Mallory pointed out, "and most of the words were definitely separated by spaces. Small spaces, I grant you, but they were there."

"Exactly. By about one thousand AD it was the norm for words to be separated by spaces, just as they are today, and certainly this was well established by the medieval period. So, as I said before, that's why I'm fairly certain that the text on the parchment dates from no earlier than the Middle Ages. Anyway, you said something about numbers?"

"Oh yes," Mallory replied, placing his knife and fork on his now-empty plate and leaning back in his seat. "Whoever encrypted that text is clearly leaving us clues of some sort. Otherwise there'd be no point in changing the shifts in the Atbash cipher the way he has. He could simply have encrypted the whole thing using a single setting. So the number nine is important, and possibly the numbers employed in each shift as well. Or, I suppose, perhaps it's not the numbers but the letters. I mean the letter that corresponds to the first letter of the alphabet in the shifted cipher."

Robin finished her main course a few moments later.

"But you do think you can work it out?" she asked.

"I'll do my best. There are lots of options, but there are definitely enough clues, as far as I can tell, so it's really a matter of trying a number of different code words that are based somehow upon either the numbers or the letters, because we've tried all the possible Atbash shifts.

Unless there really was a different kind of encryption method being used, then the obvious solution has to be that the author carried on using the Atbash cipher but with something more subtle than the reversed alphabet or a position shift. That more or less has to mean another code word, and working out what it is could take a while."

He paused for a moment, thinking over what he'd just said, then nodded.

"What?" Robin asked.

"There are really only two possible scenarios here," Mallory replied. "Either the author of the manuscript wanted the text to be readable only to somebody who possessed a special code word, or he didn't. In other words, did the manuscript have to be decoded using an entirely separate secret code word that would only be known to another member of whatever group or society was involved, or was it internally consistent? Is the clue to the second code word somehow incorporated within the text itself?"

"Well, which?"

"I don't know, obviously, but my guess is that it is internally consistent. If a separate code word was needed to decipher the text, why was the first part encrypted just using different shifted Atbash ciphers? Why not encrypt the whole thing using that secret code word? No, I think the clue must be hidden somewhere in the text itself."

They left the restaurant about a quarter of an hour later, both of them having resisted the calorie-laden delights of the dessert menu and settled instead just for coffee. True to her word, Robin paid the bill for both of them without flinching noticeably when she saw the total, and they walked slowly through the darkening streets back toward her apartment.

"It's getting late," Mallory said, glancing at his watch. "I really ought to go and find a hotel somewhere. Deciphering this is going to take longer than I had expected."

"You don't have to worry. I've got a couple of friends who run a little B and B just down the street from the shop. It's cheap and cheerful, very clean, they do a decent breakfast, and they do have at least one vacancy tonight— I called them this morning, just in case you had to stay over. I'll ring them when we get back to the apartment."

Robin led the way down the alley that led to the back of her shop, and then started up the stairs.

She was only on the third step when a black-clad figure materialized from the shadows beside Mallory and grabbed him firmly by the right arm.

"You are Robin Jessop?" he asked in heavily accented English.

15

Dartmouth, Devon

Mallory hesitated for the barest fraction of a second. Who the man was he had not the slightest idea, but the stranger exuded an almost palpable air of menace. And because he had approached Mallory, he was clearly not acquainted with Robin herself and hadn't realized that name could be used by a woman, so what he wasn't going to do was place her in the firing line.

"Yes, I'm Robin Jessop," Mallory said, before Robin could reply. "Who are you, and what do you want?"

The man in black didn't reply, just nodded almost imperceptibly and with a casual grace that belied his size, he reached into his jacket pocket with his other hand and pulled out a small automatic pistol, which he pointed at Mallory.

"You have something we want," he said, and gestured for Mallory to climb up the staircase in front of him.

Mallory was no coward, but he was unarmed and facing not only one man carrying a pistol but two armed men, he realized a moment later, as he took a couple of steps toward the staircase. Another man, with the same heavy build as the first stranger and dressed in a similar kind of dark suit, had just stepped into view, and he, too, was holding a pistol.

And then Mallory discovered that the odds were stacked even higher against them. The second man half turned away and raised his left arm. As he did so, the headlights on a large SUV—it looked to Mallory like a Range Rover or maybe a Toyota Land Cruiser—parked a few dozen yards up the street flashed once briefly in acknowledgment. He and Robin were facing a group of at least three men, and he knew that two of them—and quite probably all three of them—were armed.

Robin looked down at him, a shocked expression on her face, and opened her mouth as if to speak, but Mallory shook his head decisively and she turned away and continued climbing up the staircase to her apartment.

Mallory was thinking furiously, running different scenarios through his mind, but the problem with all of them was the fact that he was only one man, and facing two other men both of whom were bigger than him, plus another one in the SUV. Even if the two he could see hadn't been carrying pistols, he knew perfectly well that if it came to a straight fight he would probably lose.

He glanced back, wondering if by some chance he could swivel on the spiral staircase and kick out to knock out the man behind him, but it was immediately apparent that this wouldn't work because the stranger was keeping well back, and certainly out of kicking distance. He was still aiming the gun directly at Mallory's back, and would be able to fire it at the first sign of any resistance. Something told Mallory these were not the kind of people to make idle threats: the mere fact that they'd both produced firearms suggested they would be quite prepared to use them.

Whatever plan he managed to come up with—assuming he thought of anything, of course—Mallory knew it would have to wait until they were in the apartment, where the small and cramped rooms might just possibly provide him with an opportunity to disarm at least one of the strangers. Beyond that strategy, which was vague in the extreme, he really had no idea what he could do.

"Open the door," the first man demanded when the three of them reached the metal landing outside Robin's apartment. The other man was following them and was already halfway up the spiral staircase.

Robin glanced at Mallory, but both of them knew they had absolutely no option but to obey. She slid the key into the lock, turned it, and pushed the door open.

"Now wait."

The man gestured with his pistol, forcing Robin and Mallory to stand to one side while the second man walked into the apartment, his weapon held out in front of him. It wasn't a big flat, and in less than two minutes the man returned to the door, where he exchanged a couple of sentences in high-speed Italian with his companion.

"You get inside now."

Again Robin and Mallory had no option but to obey, and in a few seconds all four of them were standing around the desk in Robin's tiny office.

"Who are you and what do you want?" Mallory demanded again, and this time the man replied.

"You have relic, codex or perhaps scroll, that is property of my employer," he said, staring at Mallory, his English not fluent but understandable and heavily accented.

Mallory had never been a believer in coincidence, and he was already quite certain that he knew exactly which item in Robin's stock of ancient volumes the man was after. From what he'd seen when they walked through the shop downstairs, everything she had for sale was a book of some sort, not a codex or scroll. The man's next words confirmed it.

"You call it *Ipse Dixit* when you sent question on Internet. That is relic we come to collect."

"How did you find out about it?" Mallory asked, his professional curiosity aroused.

"We have good monitoring of Web. Hand over relic now, and we leave."

"And what about us?"

"All we want is relic. We no interest in you or girlfriend."

The words were reassuring, and the man's tone of voice neutral. But there was a veiled and lethal silent threat behind the dialogue that was quite unmistakable to Mallory, and when he glanced over at Robin, who had so far not said a word since the two men appeared, he was certain that she had picked up on it, too. He met her eyes and saw her give a barely perceptible shake of her head. It looked as if she was reading exactly the same subtext that he was.

"Where is it?"

At that moment, Mallory realized that the only possible weapon they had was the book safe itself, and he thanked whatever god watched over adventurous IT specialists that he'd decided to reset the antitheft device before Robin replaced the relic in her safe.

"It's locked away in the safe in the corner," Mallory replied, pointing at the square dark green metal box. "Mary—she's my secretary—has the key."

He nodded at Robin, though as she was the only woman in the room he didn't think either of the two thugs would be in any doubt exactly who he was referring to.

The man immediately switched his attention to Robin and then pointed toward the safe.

"Open it," he snapped.

Robin still had her apartment keys in her hand, and without responding she walked across to the safe, bent down in front of it, and unlocked the door.

The moment the door swung open, the other man slipped his pistol into his pocket, stepped across to her, pulled her upright, and shoved her roughly back toward the desk. Then he bent down to inspect the contents of the safe.

The biggest thing in it was the *Ipse Dixit* book safe, and he immediately pulled it out and read the faded inscription on the front cover. Then he spoke in rapid Italian to his companion, who gestured for him to place the object on the desk. Mallory picked up a name from the dialogue: it sounded as if the first Italian—he recognized the language they were speaking—apparently the leader, was called Giacomo.

Giacomo—assuming Mallory was right—issued another order in his own language, and the second man took out his gun again and aimed it at Mallory. Satisfied that the situation was under control, Giacomo slid his own weapon into his jacket pocket, then picked up the book safe and examined it carefully.

"What in it?" he demanded. "Scroll? Codex? Parchment?"

Mallory looked at him.

"If that object really had been stolen or taken from your employer," Mallory asked mildly, "surely you would already know what was inside it?"

"Answer question. I no have patience."

"It's an old scroll," Mallory said. "We haven't been able to decipher it, and we put it back inside the box for safekeeping."

The Italian turned the relic over in his hands a couple

more times, then held it close to his ear and shook it. The box safe was of course locked—Robin had done that after Mallory reset the antitheft device—and almost immediately he looked at Mallory and asked the obvious question.

"How you open it?"

Mallory again glanced at Robin before he replied, because he knew this was the only chance they were going to get, the only way they had any possibility of walking out of that room alive.

"There's a small slot on the side of the relic opposite the spine. You have to slide a metal object inside it and then push firmly to unlock it. You need something like this letter opener."

Mallory took a step forward and stretched out his hand toward the pen holder on Robin's desk, but immediately the man raised his arm.

"No touch," he said threateningly.

Mallory stepped back and just waited, because now there was nothing else he could do.

"The mechanism is stiff," he said, "so you need to push quite firmly."

The Italian nodded, then leaned forward and picked up the paper knife, a flat steel blade with a wooden handle. He looked closely at the book safe, slid the point of the paper knife into the slot opposite the spine, took a firm grip on the relic with his left hand, and then pushed the blade firmly home.

16

There was a faint metallic click, followed almost immediately by a heavy thud, and then a brief moment of silence before the Italian started screaming as the medieval booby trap was triggered for the second time in twenty-four hours.

Half a dozen of the metal spikes slammed through the palm of his left hand. And as a brutal bonus, the blade of the letter opener was so short that three of the spikes on the opposite side of the book safe drove deep into his closed right fist. At least for a few moments, the man was completely incapacitated, both hands pinned to the ancient relic.

As Giacomo's scream echoed around the small room, Mallory took two quick strides forward to where the other Italian was standing, his mouth open in shock, his pistol now pointing toward the floor.

But then something totally unexpected occurred: Robin beat him to it.

"Get the other one," she said urgently, and then moved.

She stepped towards the second Italian, pivoted on her left foot, and lashed out with her right. The sole of her shoe—she was wearing a pair of comfortable pumps—connected violently with the Italian's right wrist and there was an audible crack as something broke in his arm. The gun went spinning across the floor to land under the desk. She continued her fluid and well-practiced movement, landing on her right foot and swinging her left leg around in a short and lethally targeted arc, her heel slamming into the left side of the Italian's face. He crumpled to the floor in an untidy and unconscious heap.

The moment Mallory realized that Robin was perfectly capable of handling the second man, he switched direction and dived around the desk. The other Italian—Giacomo—was still screaming, still trying to pull his hands away from the spikes, but the noise stopped moments later when Mallory's right fist, driven by all of the considerable power of his right arm, and given added impetus by the combination of fear and rage that he was experiencing, crashed into his chin.

Once he was certain the man posed no further threat to them—at least until he woke up—Mallory looked over to his right.

"Are you okay?" he asked, though even as he formed the words he realized the question was superfluous.

Robin was not only okay, but had already turned the Italian onto his face and pulled both his arms behind him.

"Perfectly," she snapped. "Now don't just stand there gawping. In the bottom right-hand drawer of the desk you'll find a handful of plastic cable ties held together with an elastic band. Fish them out and let me have them, please. And another thing," she added, "much as I appreciate your chivalrous action in pretending to be me, if we find ourselves in the same kind of situation again, can you please think of a more attractive name for me than Mary?"

"First name that came into my head," Mallory replied, stepping back around the desk and opening the drawer. "It was my mother's name, actually, or the first part of it, anyway. She was called Mary Anne."

"Sorry."

It was, Mallory thought as he rooted around in the drawer, a somewhat surreal conversation, bearing in mind what had just happened in the room over the last few seconds, and he had a number of obvious questions he wanted to ask, but they could all wait. He found the bundle of cable ties and tossed them over to her.

The second Italian was still lying unconscious on the floor, but they had no idea how long that convenient state of affairs would last. Robin stripped a cable tie out of the bundle, looped it around the unconscious man's left wrist, and pulled it tight. Then she dragged his right arm close to his left, threaded the second cable tie under the first, and pulled it tight around his right wrist. For good measure, she took two more of the ties and repeated the process, then lashed his ankles together in a similar fashion, pulling each plastic tie as tight as she could. When the Italian did finally wake up, he would be completely immobilized.

Giacomo was also still unconscious, and the first thing Mallory did was reach into his jacket pocket and take out the automatic pistol that the Italian had threatened the two of them with when they arrived at the apartment. He searched his other pockets as well and pulled out a cheap mobile phone, a spare magazine for the pistol, fully loaded, and a suppressor to screw onto the end of the barrel. That simply reinforced Mallory's belief that he and Robin had not been intended to survive the evening. He placed the weapon and equipment on the desk, removed a slim wallet from the Italian's inside jacket pocket, and then turned his attention to the man's hands.

They were, not to put too fine a point on it, a mess. Six of the needle-sharp spikes had been driven right through the man's left hand, and the wounds were bleeding steadily. In fact, there was rather less blood than Mallory had expected, probably because the spikes themselves were to some extent plugging the wounds. He couldn't tell for sure whether or not any of the spikes had shattered the bones in the man's hand, but he reckoned that was quite probable. He certainly wouldn't be playing the violin any time soon.

There was no such doubt about the injuries on Giacomo's right hand. He had obviously been holding the paper knife firmly in his closed fist in order to push the knife into the lock mechanism, and three of the spikes had been driven deep into his hand, one into the web between his forefinger and thumb, and the other two had slammed through the bones of the knuckles of his first and middle fingers.

"That looks really painful," Robin said, with not an ounce of compassion in her voice, as she leaned over Mallory and looked down at the Italian's hands.

Mallory nodded.

"Your hands and feet are often the most difficult parts of the body to repair, because they're full of small bones. He's going to have serious problems sorting out his hands."

"Shame. You do know they were going to kill us, don't you?"

"That was my guess. Where the hell did you learn to kick like that?"

"I'll tell you another time," Robin replied. "First, I

want that book safe back, so you're going to have to pull his hands off the spikes, and the best time to do that is right now, while he's still unconscious."

Together they turned Giacomo until he was lying on his left side, and then Mallory trod firmly on the Italian's left wrist, seized both ends of the book safe, and pulled, trying to slide the spikes out of the man's hand. The Italian moaned in pain, but didn't come round, and with a sudden jerk the ancient relic came free.

Robin bent down, looped a couple of the cable ties around his wrist, and pulled them tight.

"Two birds with one stone," she murmured. "As well as acting like handcuffs, these will also function as a tourniquet."

When the spikes had pulled free, they had both noticed that the flow of blood from the wounds increased significantly.

Mallory rolled the unconscious Italian onto his right side and tried to repeat the process, but because two of the spikes had been driven deep into the bone of the knuckles, he couldn't simply pull them out.

"I need a lever," he said, "something to use to free the spikes."

The letter opener was still sticking out of the slot in the side of the book safe, and Robin bent down and pulled it out.

"Here," she said. "Try this."

Mallory slid the steel blade into the narrow gap between the edge of the book safe and the bleeding knuckles of Giacomo's right hand and then levered firmly.

This time, the pain must have been far worse, because the Italian moaned and grunted, and then his eyes flicked open. He started to move, trying to roll onto his back, the movement pulling the book safe out of Mallory's grasp.

Robin stretched her right arm around Mallory and, apparently quite gently, pressed the web of her hand against the Italian's throat. Almost immediately he stopped moving and his eyelids flickered again before he slumped back into unconsciousness.

"Before you ask," she said, "that was called a push choke, and he'll be out for at least ten minutes, so you've got plenty of time."

Mallory didn't reply, simply grabbed hold of the book safe again, taking care to avoid the protruding spikes, placed his foot on Giacomo's wrist to keep his arm steady, and redoubled his efforts with the steel blade of the letter opener.

It was messy work, the man's hand sticky with the blood leaking out of the puncture wounds, but after another minute or so of levering and moving and pulling, there was a faint cracking sound and the book safe suddenly came free.

"I'll take that," Robin said, reaching down for the medieval relic and taking it from him, using a tissue to avoid touching the blood that had been splashed liberally over the leather cover. Then she dropped the bundle of ties beside Mallory. "Get another couple of these around his wrists," she said, "and don't forget to do his ankles as well."

He rolled the unconscious Italian onto his side, pulled both his arms behind his back, and quickly lashed them together and then secured his ankles with another four cable ties.

As he did so, Robin placed the book safe on one end of the desk and then bent down to reach under it, stretching out her hand to retrieve the second pistol.

"Hang on a minute," Mallory said. "Don't touch it."

Robin stopped, her outstretched fingers just inches away from the butt of the semiautomatic weapon.

"Why not?" she asked. "We can't just leave it there."

"I'm just thinking ahead. We don't want to leave our fingerprints on that pistol. Use your cotton gloves and then put it on the desk, well away from the other one."

"When you say 'the other one,' you mean the one you took out of his pocket using your bare hands? That one?"

Mallory grinned at her briefly. "That's exactly what I mean, and before I did that I should have waited and thought it through."

Robin stood up, pulled on the white cotton gloves she had been wearing earlier, then bent down again and retrieved the pistol, placing it at the opposite end of the desk to the one Mallory had already recovered. Then, still wearing the gloves, she searched the other man, removing his wallet, mobile phone, and a second suppressor and spare magazine: the two men had been carrying precisely the same hardware. She placed everything at the end of the desk, then slumped down in her chair and stared across at Mallory, who'd just finished immobilizing Giacomo.

"So, who the hell are these two comedians?" she demanded. "And what do we do now?"

17

Dartmouth, Devon

"Those are two good questions," Mallory replied, sitting opposite her and glancing down at the two unconscious men lying on the floor of the small office. Then he looked back at Robin and noticed that, although her voice was steady, her hands were shaking slightly, obviously a physical reaction to what had just taken place.

"And have you got any good answers?" she asked, her glance straying toward Giacomo and the blood still pumping, albeit now more slowly, out of the wounds in his hands.

"Not right now, no," Mallory said.

He paused for a couple of beats.

"Look," he went on, "don't feel bad about letting that man trigger the antitheft device. If we hadn't, and the mechanism hadn't worked, we might both be dead by now."

"I know. It's just that I've never had to react like that before. Up till now, I've only ever used martial arts in training, never for real."

That was shading the truth more than a little, but at that moment Robin didn't feel like explaining herself in any detail. "It's good to know I've got the skills," she added, "but it's still a bit of a shock to see what happens to somebody when I do it in a live situation."

"Karate?"

Robin nodded. "I do Shotokan karate and aikido, mainly, and that was a *mae geri* followed by a *mawashi geri*, to be exact. A front kick and then a roundhouse kick." She shook her head in frustration. "So, what are we going to do now? Call the police? Get that one to a hospital? He's bleeding all over my carpet, quite apart from anything else. It's not a very good carpet, but bloodstains certainly aren't going to improve it."

"I think," Mallory said after a moment, "that the best thing we can do is leave, if we can."

"What do you mean?"

"There's at least one other man waiting outside," Mallory replied. "You were already climbing the staircase when one of these two signaled to somebody in an SUV parked about fifty yards down the road. The man in the driving seat must have a clear view of the back of this place and the staircase as well. What I'm not sure about is what he's likely to do if we leave, what his orders are. These two were carrying pistols, so it's quite possible that he is as well. And I'm not even sure it's just one man. There could be two or three more of them in that vehicle, just waiting for us."

"Oh God. I didn't realize that." She paused for a second or two, then continued. "Look, is there any good reason why we can't just lock the door, call the police, and then wait for them to show up?"

"I think calling the cops is a really good idea," Mallory

replied, "but what I'm not so certain about is whether or not we should still be here when they arrive."

"Why?"

"You might not know how the institutional police mind works, but I do. I've had dealings with them before, close up and personal. If a couple of your local rozzers walked in here now and saw these two men lying on the floor, they would be whisked straight off to a hospital and we would be arrested for possession of firearms and assault. Probably," Mallory went on, pointing at Giacomo, "for causing actual or grievous bodily harm in his case. The fact that he actually triggered the antitheft device on the book safe himself would be deemed to be irrelevant. We both knew what would happen when he stuck the letter opener into the slot, and in the mind of a policeman that would be just the same as if we'd sat on him and then hammered nails into his hands."

"But they were going to kill us," Robin protested.

"That's true, but also irrelevant. The law these days invariably favors the perpetrator, not the victim."

"What about the guns?"

"That was why I stopped you touching the second pistol with your bare hands. If you had handled it, which a fingerprint comparison would show, how could you then prove that one of these two Italians brought it here? Even if you did your best to wipe it clean, there could still be partial prints on it that would incriminate you. And possession of a pistol in this allegedly free country, I should remind you, invariably results in a mandatory prison sentence."

Robin nodded slowly.

"I see what you mean," she said. "So, what do we do?"

Mallory stood up.

"We leave," he replied, "but we have to time this right, and we will definitely be calling the cops."

He stepped out of the office and checked that the door of the apartment, which had been closed when the four of them entered, was locked. It was, the catch on the Yale lock having clicked into place. Then he walked back to the desk, pulled on the second pair of cotton gloves he'd been wearing earlier, picked up the pistol that Robin had removed from underneath the desk, and ejected the magazine. Using his thumb, he stripped all the nine-millimeter cartridges out of it, the gleaming brass ammunition forming a small pile on the desk, and replaced the magazine in the butt of the weapon. Then he pulled back the slide and an additional cartridge, which had been in the chamber of the pistol and ready to fire, spun out of the breech.

"It's not a very big pistol," Robin said, "but that's a lot of bullets."

Mallory glanced at the model number etched into the slide of the weapon.

"I've never seen one of these before," he said, "but I have fired the odd automatic before, thanks to a friend of mine down at the Royal Navy Base at Culdrose. This is a Beretta, an Italian weapon, and according to this the model is a PX4 Storm in nine millimeter. The magazine holds fifteen rounds and there was another one in the chamber, so that's sixteen in total. The fact that the weapon was ready to fire is another reason why I think these two men probably intended to kill both of us, and quite apart from being a really uncomfortable thought, that does raise a bunch of other questions."

Mallory slid the second pistol, the one he had already handled, into his jacket pocket, together with one of the suppressors, the two fully loaded spare magazines, and all but three of the ejected cartridges.

"You're taking that with you?" Robin said, more as a statement than a question.

Mallory nodded.

"There's a lot about this situation that really worries me," he replied, "and I think that having a weapon we can use is a really good idea, just in case anybody decides to start shooting at us."

"So, what about the other pistol?" Robin asked. "What are you going to do with that?"

"I'm going to put it back in his pocket along with the suppressor," Mallory said, pointing at the second unconscious Italian, "and the magazine and these three cartridges in Giacomo's jacket. When the cops arrive, that will more or less guarantee that both these men end up in the slammer. There'll probably be a bit of head scratching over why one man has the weapon and the other one has the magazine and ammunition, but I don't think either of them will be back out on the streets for quite a while."

"But who are they?" Robin asked again, watching closely as Mallory did exactly what he'd described.

"I don't know." Mallory sat down again, reached across the desk, and picked up one of the two wallets they'd taken from the pockets of the unconscious men. "Perhaps there's something in here that might give us a clue," he added.

His touch was clumsy inside the cotton gloves, and he fumbled as he extracted the contents, which proved to be somewhat sparse and largely unhelpful. There were two currency sections at the back of the wallet, one containing exactly one thousand euros, and the other precisely two thousand pounds sterling, both consisting of crisp new high-value notes. There were no credit cards, driving licenses, business cards, passports, or anything that conveyed the slightest indication of the actual identity of the man lying on the floor.

"I'll make you a prediction," Mallory said. "I'll bet that the second wallet contains exactly the same amount of cash, even the same denomination of notes, as this one."

"And that means what, exactly?"

Mallory didn't reply for a moment but stretched out his hand again and opened the second wallet, to reveal the same amount of cash, exactly as he had expected.

"It means," he said then, "that these two men have been given the same weapons, money, and equipment, and no identification documents." He pointed at the two mobile phones sitting on the desk, took a handkerchief out of his pocket, and carefully wiped the one that he had touched with his bare hands. "They've even got identical phones. Whoever they are, it was obviously intended to be a deniable operation, with no link between these men and the organization or government that's employing them."

"Government?" Robin asked, the pitch of her voice rising sharply in alarm. "You think some government sent them?"

"Probably not, but I do know it's standard practice to make sure agents sent on sensitive operations carry nothing to identify them, just in case they get caught. If nothing else, that muddies the waters so that there can never be actual proof that they are employed by any particular country or government. It's called a deniable operation."

Mallory took out his own wallet and slid all the cash into it, then carefully wiped both of the wallets he'd emptied to remove any trace of his fingerprints and tossed them back onto the desk.

"You're stealing that cash?"

"Damn right I am. They won't be needing it where they're going, and we can certainly use it."

Robin nodded.

"Fair point," she said, "as long as you split it fifty-fifty with me. Now, how do we get out of here without whoever it is in the SUV seeing us? Bearing in mind that the only way down to street level is to use the spiral staircase, where we'll be clearly in view."

"Timing is everything," Mallory said, standing up, "and we need to go now, before the bad guy in the Range Rover starts to wonder why his friends are taking so long to retrieve what they came to collect and to dispose of us."

He picked up the book safe, taking care not to touch any of the coagulating blood on the leather cover, cleaned the blade of the letter opener, and then slid the steel point into the slot. He waited for the click that would show the lid was unlatched, opened the book safe to remove the parchment, and then quickly reset the mechanism. He cleaned the cover, shifting as much of the blood as he could, using most of a packet of tissues that Robin produced from her handbag.

"The safest place for the parchment is back in this, I think," he said, "and then you should probably put it in your safe. I don't think we want to be carrying it round with us."

He picked up the parchment and replaced it in the medieval book safe, then pressed the lid closed. Robin carried it over to her safe, placed it inside at the back of one of the shelves, and then locked the door.

Mallory looked at the two Italians again, but both men were still unconscious. He had no idea how long that happy state of affairs was likely to last, but he knew the clock was ticking. He took a last glance around at the office, making sure that neither of them had missed anything, then nodded to Robin.

"Now we can call the cops," he said. "But we don't have to tell them anything. Well, only one thing, just in case the man or men in the SUV are also carrying weapons. I'll handle that. As soon as I've got through, you scream. Then I'll leave the phone off the hook for a few seconds so they'll know exactly where to come. Okay?"

Robin nodded.

"I'll do my best," she said, "but I'm not really much of a screamer."

"Oddly enough, I didn't think you were," Mallory replied.

He lifted the receiver from the phone on the desk and laid it down. Then he dialed triple nine, and as soon as he heard the call connecting he pointed his finger at Robin, who obliged with a piercing screech. Then Mallory took over, muffling and changing his voice by the simple expedient of partially covering his mouth with his left hand.

"Oh my God," he yelled. "He's got a gun! He's holding a pistol!"

He thumped and banged the desk quite violently, and slammed one of the chairs into it. They could both hear the tinny sound of the emergency operator's responses from the earpiece of the telephone handset, but then Mallory ended the call.

"Are you sure that was long enough?" Robin asked. "For them to locate where the call was coming from, I mean?"

"It should be, yes. Establishing the location is the first thing they do, and if they think there's a woman in danger—and that was a pretty convincing scream, thank you—and especially if there's a chance of firearms being involved, they'll be here in minutes."

"So your plan is?"

"We wait until we hear the sounds of the sirens, because they're bound to have their blues and twos working. We'll hear them coming at the same time as the guys in the SUV, and as soon as we do we leg it out of here and down the staircase. Then along the alleyway to the main street, and then we just walk away. The opposition will probably see us, especially if they switch on their headlights, but unless they get out of the car and follow us on foot, we'll be long gone before they can drive around to the main street and intercept us. And they might not be so keen to leave their vehicle if they know a police car is going to be arriving within a matter of seconds."

"And if they do decide to risk it and chase after us down the alleyway?" Robin asked. "What then?"

"We can probably outrun them, but even if we can't I've got a whole pocketful of nine-millimeter reasons why they should keep their distance."

And then there was no more time for talking, because both of them simultaneously heard the distant but quite unmistakable sound of a siren, the atonic wailing noise almost immediately getting louder.

"Quicker than I thought," Mallory said. "That sounds like our cue to get out of here."

He picked up his computer bag, looped the strap over his shoulder, and led the way to the door of the apartment. He listened for a few seconds, concentrating on the noise of the approaching siren, then nodded: it sounded as if the police car was only a matter of a few hundred yards away.

Mallory turned the handle of the Yale lock and pulled the door open wide, the noise of the police siren immediately virtually doubling in intensity.

And for a moment, he just stood there, realizing that there was a third possible course of action that could be taken by the opposition that he had never even considered. In the same instant, he realized another fundamental truth: that in a dangerous situation having a weapon tucked away in a pocket and largely inaccessible was exactly the same as having no weapon at all.

Because standing right in front of him, a pistol held loosely in his right hand, was another black-haired and heavily built man wearing a dark suit.

18

Dartmouth, Devon

It was difficult to know who was the more surprised—
Mallory or the unidentified stranger—but perhaps predictably it was Robin who reacted first and fastest.

As the man outside the door raised his right arm to
aim the pistol, she stepped forward to put herself in front
of Mallory.

A half smile appeared for the briefest of instants on the
man's face as he watched the diminutive dark-haired girl
approach him. Perhaps he was wondering who she was,
but it didn't look as if he perceived her as any kind of
threat.

A split second later, he realized his mistake.

Robin stretched out her left hand, the fingers and
thumb open, settled it apparently quite gently on his right
forearm and slid the web of her hand down to his wrist, as
if she wanted to simply force the aim of his pistol away
from her. But that was only a part of her attack strategy.

Moving with sudden speed, she ducked down under
his arm and swiveled so that her back was toward him.

And then she pulled down with both hands on his right arm, her movements fluid and well practiced. Her back acted as a fulcrum, and the stranger, who weighed at least twice as much as she did, sailed apparently effortlessly over her to land flat on his back, his breath forced explosively out of his lungs. But she didn't let go of his right arm, and as he tumbled onto his back, she braced herself and tugged, instantly dislocating his shoulder.

The man took a sudden intake of breath, and almost immediately released it in a howl of pain.

Robin twisted his wrist sharply, and the pistol fell from his grasp to clatter against the top step of the spiral staircase. She took two steps forward and kicked out, flicking the weapon off the step and sending it tumbling into the darkness below. She knelt beside the man and applied pressure to his neck, rendering him unconscious, and quickly used a couple more cable ties to lash his wrists and ankles together. As a final refinement, she used another cable tie to secure the arm that she hadn't dislocated to the lowest part of the steel rail that ran along the edge of the balcony.

Then she turned back to look at Mallory, as the headlights of an approaching vehicle washed briefly over the scene, the flashing blue lights on its roof bar leaving them in no doubt about its identity.

"Now we really must go," she said, and immediately began descending the staircase, holding on to the metal rail and taking the steps two at a time.

Before he followed her, Mallory bent down, checked the man's pockets, and took out exactly what he had expected to find—a spare magazine for an automatic pistol and a wallet stuffed with crisp new notes—then stepped over the recumbent figure lying on the external landing and quickly descended the staircase.

At the bottom, they turned toward the main street and ran down the alleyway, only stopping when they emerged at the other end, because a couple running would attract too much attention. But they walked as quickly as they could, side by side, heading away from Robin's shop.

On the street behind them, the interior light of a second Range Rover illuminated briefly as the doors opened and two men climbed out. At the same moment, the big engine of the SUV rumbled into life, and the vehicle moved slowly away from the curb and down the street, well ahead of the approaching police car.

One of the two men on foot ran quickly down the alleyway, taking exactly the same route away from the scene as Mallory and Robin were following, but perhaps nearly a hundred yards behind them. At the end of the alleyway, he turned right and continued running, looking ahead through the evening gloom until he was sure that he had identified his quarry. Then he slowed to a brisk walk, fast enough to catch up with them.

His instructions were quite clear: the girl was expendable, but the man Jessop had to be taken alive so that they could recover the relic. But "alive" didn't mean undamaged, and as he ran, closing the distance, he pulled his Beretta pistol from his pocket and screwed on the suppressor. As soon as he got close enough, he'd take down the woman and stop the man, maybe by shooting him in the leg. Then he could grab the relic, if he had it in his pocket, or drag him into the car and make him tell them exactly where it was. Either way, it would be the endgame.

Toscanelli climbed swiftly up the spiral staircase and walked into the apartment. He stared at the scene that confronted him in the office with an expression of disbelief on his face, then walked the couple of steps to the desk, closed the lid on the laptop computer—Robin's machine—sitting there, and unplugged the power adapter, which he slid into his pocket.

Taking the computer was only the first of the actions he knew he had to take, and which had been made clear to him back in Rome. He looked down at both the unconscious men, reached into his other pocket to remove his Beretta pistol, took out the suppressor, which he attached to the end of the barrel, then walked across to the first man, Giacomo.

"You stupid, stupid man," he said in Italian, crouching down to look at the injuries to the man's hands. "What happened in here?" he wondered, because he had no idea what could have caused the damage he was seeing.

He knew Giacomo would need medical attention, and quickly, and leaving him there was a risk Toscanelli knew he simply couldn't take. He stood up, slipped off the safety catch on the Beretta, and fired a single shot through the man's head. The report of the pistol sounded like a dull wet thud.

He walked over to the second man and shook his shoulder, trying to revive him. The man moaned softly, but was clearly still unconscious. Toscanelli listened for a moment. The noise of the siren had died away, and he could see from the flashing lights outside that the police car had come to a stop. That probably meant the occupants were already on their way over to the building, so he had no time to lose, and certainly no time to wait for his companion to recover his senses.

His orders from Vitale were clear and unambiguous: no information about their mission was to be revealed to anyone, so the last thing he was going to do was leave any of these men alive to be questioned by the British police. He pulled the trigger of his Beretta a second time.

Still holding the weapon, he picked up the laptop, stepped outside the apartment to where the third man lay incapacitated and moaning, his wrist lashed to the balcony railing, and fired another single bullet through his head as well.

He took a final glance round, satisfied that he had sanitized the scene as well as he could in the circumstances, then ran swiftly down the spiral staircase to ground level and walked through the alleyway to the main street, where he turned left to rendezvous with the Range Rover, which was already illegally parked perhaps two hundred yards away, engine idling, the driver waiting for him.

"Where are we going?" Robin asked as they strode quickly along the street. As she spoke, she took a step closer to him.

"Away from here," Mallory replied. "Apart from that, I really don't—"

He broke off as the shop window they were just passing suddenly shattered, shards of glass tumbling onto the pavement beside them.

Mallory looked behind them. He'd been checking the street at intervals, but he hadn't spotted anyone following them, a mistake that could have been fatal.

About forty yards back, a dark figure in a black suit was taking aim for a second shot at them with a silenced automatic.

"Run," Mallory shouted.

As Robin dodged behind him and began sprinting along the pavement, Mallory pulled the Beretta pistol from his pocket, aimed the weapon vaguely in the direction of their pursuer, clicked off the safety catch, and pulled the trigger.

The report was deafening in the near silence of the narrow street, and he had no idea where the bullet went: forty yards was a long distance for accurate shooting with a pistol, especially one he'd never used before.

But the shot had precisely the effect he wanted. The man who'd fired at them clearly hadn't expected them to be armed, and had ducked down low the moment Mallory fired.

Mallory aimed toward the pavement in front of the crouching figure, and pulled the trigger a second time. He hoped the bullet would perhaps shatter on contact with the stone, and that maybe one of the fragments would hit the man, slow him down a bit.

That might even have worked, because as he turned away he heard a strangled yelp from behind him.

And then Mallory was running, Robin about ten yards in front of him, both moving as fast as they could. Mallory glanced over his shoulder. Their pursuer was also up and running, so clearly if any part of the bullet he'd fired had hit him, it certainly wasn't slowing him down.

Mallory heard another dull thud from behind, and a bullet slammed into the wall of a property just to his right. But he kept on running, knowing that it would need to be a really lucky shot if either of them was hit while their pursuer kept moving.

He was gaining slightly on Robin, and when he looked back, the gunman had dropped back slightly and was now perhaps fifty yards behind him.

"Next right," Mallory yelled as Robin approached a side street.

She gave no sign of having heard him, but when she

reached the corner she dodged to the right and vanished from sight.

Mallory followed her around the corner of the building, but when he'd covered about thirty yards up the street, he turned and waited for a moment, aiming the Beretta back toward the street they'd just left.

But within a few seconds he saw that the gunman was too experienced to just blindly run around the corner in pursuit of his quarry. Instead he came to a dead stop, his body shielded by the building, and just looked up the side street, his head the only part visible.

But that was enough for Mallory to shoot at, and he pulled the trigger twice, the noise of the shots again echoing from the surrounding buildings. Even as he fired, he saw the man pull his head back, ducking into safety behind the solid brickwork of the building on the corner.

Then Mallory turned and ran on, hoping he'd gained perhaps another ten yards, and that the gunman might wait for just a few more precious seconds before continuing the pursuit.

Robin was almost at the end of the side street, and at that moment she glanced back to see where he was.

"Go left," he called, and watched her angle across the street and over to the opposite pavement.

Mallory stayed on the same side of the street, reached the end, and then turned to face back the way he'd come.

The gunman was still not in sight, but as Mallory looked, he stepped around the corner. Once more Mallory lifted the pistol and fired, and again their pursuer vanished from sight.

Immediately Mallory crossed the street to follow Robin. His hope was that the gunman would remain behind the building until he himself had disappeared, so that he wouldn't know which way they'd run. That, too, might gain them more precious seconds. And he knew his car was now only a few dozen yards away. If they could reach that, they'd be safe.

As he ran after Robin, Mallory switched the pistol to his left hand and fumbled in the pocket of his jacket for his car keys. He pulled them out and pressed a button. Immediately the hazard lights on a black Porsche Cayman parked on the opposite side of the street ahead flashed obediently.

Robin obviously saw the car's lights flashing and immediately raced across the street toward it, running around behind the Porsche and wrenching open the passenger door as soon as she reached the vehicle, Mallory only yards behind her.

As she did up her seat belt, he pulled open the door and dropped into the driver's seat, sliding the key into the ignition and turning it as he pushed his computer bag into the space behind the passenger seat and dropped the pistol onto his lap. The engine started with a roar, and Mallory engaged first gear, hit the lights, turned the steering wheel, and powered the car out of the parking space.

As he did so, Robin reached over and behind him, pulling out his seat belt and clicking the buckle into place as quickly as she could. Like Mallory, she was panting from the unexpected exertion.

Mallory grabbed second gear, powered down his window, and picked up the pistol again. Seconds later, the car reached the end of the side street they'd run along, and they both saw the dark figure just reaching the junction.

The gunman saw the Porsche at the same instant, and immediately raised his pistol, taking aim at the car.

Mallory stuck his right arm out of the window, aimed

the Beretta, and pulled the trigger. He had no real hope of hitting the man, not from a moving car, but he hoped firing at him would spoil his aim.

The gunman fired at the same moment, the sound of Mallory's unsilenced weapon drowning out the dull thud of the suppressed pistol. Mallory clearly saw the man's arm move to absorb the recoil, but the bullet apparently missed, because he felt no impact anywhere on his car.

The gunman ducked and crouched down as Mallory fired at him a second time, and then the Porsche was past him, accelerating hard down the street.

Mallory was switching his attention between the street in front of him and his mirrors, and as he watched he saw the man step out into the street, aiming his pistol. There wasn't room in the fairly narrow street for him to swerve or try to dodge, so he just had to rely on speed. And Porsches were good at speed. That was what they were built for.

He left the gear lever in second, the speedometer needle hovering at around sixty miles an hour, the engine screaming its banshee wail.

Robin flinched slightly as the rear window of a parked car they were driving past exploded with the impact of a bullet, but then they were out of pistol range. But not, Mallory guessed, out of trouble.

"Thank God for that," Robin said.

"We've still got problems," Mallory said, slowing down slightly. "That man wasn't just shooting at us," he added. "I was watching in the mirror. When he fired that last shot, he was also talking into a mobile phone."

"Which means?"

"Which means there must be other people out looking for us. We're not out of the woods yet. Where the hell are we? And how do I get out of this town?"

Robin looked through the windshield.

"I know exactly where we are," she said. "Take the next right. We need to get onto College Way because that's the main road out of the town."

She gave him further directions, which Mallory followed, now making sure he stayed at or below the speed limit. With a loaded pistol in the car, the last thing he wanted to do was get pulled over by a policeman.

"Right," Robin said as they made another turn. "This is Newcomen Road. Keep going straight through the one-way system, and then we'll end up down by the river, on the North Embankment. You have to turn left at the end of that to go past Coronation Park. Then you go left again, and that's College Way, the A379. No problem."

Despite the running gun battle they'd been involved in, the town of Dartmouth seemed quiet and normal, with no signs of any unusual activity, though Mallory assumed that the area around Robin's shop and apartment would be knee-deep in rozzers by then. The traffic was light, and they encountered no holdups.

"That's Coronation Park, right in front," Robin said, "so we're nearly there."

Mallory nodded, swung the Cayman around to the left to follow the street, and then left again to start climbing the hill, the looming bulk of the Royal Naval College clearly visible over on their right.

And then, when they'd almost reached the top of the hill, seemingly out of nowhere, a black Range Rover materialized from a side turning directly in front of them, perhaps sixty yards away, stopping broadside on to block the left side of the street.

Both the windows on the right-hand side of the car

were lowered, and in the light from the Porsche's head-lamps Mallory could see two bulky figures, arms extended, both holding pistols that were pointed straight at them.

It wasn't over yet.

19

The control room operator who had picked up Mallory's triple-nine call had had very little information to go on. But she had heard, and heard very clearly, the shouted statement that some kind of firearm was involved in the incident, as well as the agonized scream of a woman. Those two factors had immediately increased the importance of the call, and her response to it, with the approval of the duty inspector in the control room.

As well as ordering the nearest regular patrol car to head for the address in Dartmouth that the automated location system had provided, she also ordered the crew of an ARV, an Armed Response Vehicle, from the Tactical Aid Group of the Devon and Cornwall Constabulary, to attend.

The ARV was a BMW estate car, painted with the usual distinctive pattern of blue-and-yellow high-visibility squares, but with two small yellow squares on each end of the front bumper just below the headlights to indicate that the occupants were armed, the only external indication of the vehicle's special status.

The car was on the road between Plympton and Ivybridge when the call came through. The driver immediately flicked on the roof bar lights and siren and headed east as fast as the traffic would permit along the A38 dual carriageway, while the codriver talked with the control room operator to try to get as much information as he could about the incident.

"Could be a hoax, from the sound of it," Eddie Fulton said as he concentrated on covering the ground as quickly as he could.

The BMW had just passed the outskirts of South Brent, the speedometer needle holding steady at a hundred and ten miles an hour as the car headed northeast. One problem both the officers were well aware of was that they weren't then actually heading toward Dartmouth, there being no fast roads that offered a direct track to the address they had been given.

"Which route are you going?" the codriver, Dave Chambers, asked.

"Not a lot of choice, really. I'll stay on this as far as the interchange, then go east to Totnes and south and east to Dartmouth from there. You'd better tell the operator we're going to be at least another twenty minutes on the road."

Chambers made the call, adding that unarmed officers should not approach the scene until they arrived, just in case there really was a man there waving a gun, unlikely though he thought that would be in sleepy Dartmouth, and it wasn't the far more probable scenario of a couple of drunken locals having a laugh.

In the end, they made better time than Fulton had expected, and he pulled the BMW to a halt a little under seventeen minutes after Chambers had passed his original estimate. Two other patrol cars were already on the scene at the back of the building from which the call had been made, and an ambulance was parked a few yards away, the crew waiting inside the vehicle in case they were needed. Another patrol car had been parked at the end of the alleyway that terminated on the main road to cover that exit, its flashing blue lights reflecting eerily from the windows of the antiquarian bookshop that the police had already established was owned by a Robin Jessop, the same person who owned the apartment from which the emergency call had been made.

Inevitably the relatively heavy police presence had attracted a crowd of interested observers, most of them eagerly recording the scene with the cameras in their mobile phones. Uniformed officers were doing their best to keep them away from both the front and the back of the building.

Moments after Fulton stopped the BMW, he and Chambers climbed out and opened the trunk to unlock the firearms safe. Two minutes after that, both men were fully equipped, Glock semiautomatic pistols in holsters at their sides, and each carrying a Heckler & Koch MP5 submachine gun, all weapons primed and ready to fire.

The on-scene commander was a uniformed inspector—his name tag read WILSON—and before doing anything else, Fulton and Chambers reported to him.

"Evening, sir. What's the situation?"

"What have you been told?"

"Very little. The control room operator who took the triple-nine call heard a scream, possibly from a woman, and then a man's voice, slightly muffled, shouting that somebody had a gun. That's it."

The inspector nodded.

"There's not a great deal that I can add," he said. "We've secured the perimeter, and since the first car arrived on-site, nobody has entered or left any part of the building."

Wilson paused for a moment and pointed up toward the second floor level. "There's at least one light switched on in the apartment, and the entrance door is standing ajar, but we've seen no sign of any movement. One of the constables thinks he heard a couple of thumping sounds when he arrived and got out of his car, but that's it, and we've no idea what could have caused them. And of course they might have nothing at all to do with this incident."

He turned back and smiled somewhat bleakly at the two armed officers. "Anyway, you're the cavalry, so over to you. The only access we can see to the apartment is up that metal spiral staircase, though there might be some internal stairs as well leading down into the bookshop. Both parts of the property are owned by somebody called Robin Jessop. We've been trying his mobile phone, but it's switched off and we have no idea where he is at the moment. Obviously our major concern is that he's up there in the apartment, perhaps injured or worse, but we've been ordered to wait for you before investigating further. I've got floodlights positioned already, but I assumed you'd rather make a covert approach to start with."

"Yes, thank you, sir," Chambers said. "In this case, I think quiet is much better than noisy. Now, could you please pull your men back to a safe distance, and we'll take a look. If you monitor our transmissions, we'll give you a shout if we need the lights."

Both men checked their weapons and equipment, each running his eyes over his companion's gear as well as a final check on their mutual readiness, and then they began moving forward slowly until they had a better view of the apartment and the external staircase leading up to it.

They stopped about ten meters from the base of the staircase and for a few moments just studied the scene.

"I think I can see a shape up there on the balcony. Could be a person, or maybe just a pile of something, clothing maybe," Chambers whispered. "I don't see anything else."

"Nor do I. Let's go. I'll lead. We're going in now."

"Understood," Wilson's voice came through loud and clear in their earpieces. Both armed officers were equipped with specially designed radios that allowed them to transmit without removing their hands from their weapons.

Fulton stepped forward, his submachine gun aimed and ready, covering an arc in front of him as he approached the base of the staircase.

When he was a few feet away he stopped and looked down for a few moments.

"This is Fulton," he said quietly into his microphone. "There's a pistol lying on the ground here near the base of the staircase. It looks like a Beretta, and the magazine is in place. Suggest you upgrade the status of this incident accordingly."

"Copied," Wilson responded.

"I'm starting to climb the staircase now."

Slowly and really carefully the armed police officer began ascending the metal spiral staircase, his weapon pointing upward to where any threat would materialize. Chambers stood a few feet away from the base of the staircase, also aiming his Heckler & Koch upward but ensuring that his colleague was never in the line of fire, scanning the entire balcony and looking out for any signs of danger.

Moments later, Fulton had climbed high enough so

that he could see along the length of the balcony at the top of the staircase. The vague shape that he and Chambers had spotted from the ground was now only a few feet from him, and it was immediately clear that he was looking at a man.

Fulton paused for a moment, trying to check whether or not he was looking at a dead body or at a person who could offer a threat to him, perhaps lying in wait to attack him as soon as he stepped onto the balcony. But almost immediately he could see that the man was lying in an awkward position, facedown and with his arms pulled behind his back, the wrists together. He could also see that the man was not moving, though in the darkness he had no idea of his condition.

Fulton cautiously climbed up the last few steps and crouched down to examine the figure. What he discovered didn't make sense, but there was enough light for him to clearly see the man.

"This is Fulton," he murmured quietly into his radio. "One male lying on the balcony, his wrists and ankles secured with plastic cable ties, and he's been shot through the head, clearly dead. Proceeding inside the apartment."

"Copied," Inspector Wilson said.

"I'm coming up after you," Chambers murmured. "I'll wait on the balcony until you've cleared the apartment."

The door was not open quite wide enough for Fulton to slide through the gap, so he cautiously eased it open a little farther, then stepped into the tiny hall, checking all around him as he did so. Most of the apartment was in darkness, but the internal door directly in front of him was standing open and clearly that room was the source of the light that had been visible from the ground below.

Taking extreme care to make as little noise as possible,

Fulton eased forward until he could see inside the room, the submachine gun held ready to fire throughout, his right forefinger resting lightly on the trigger. But what he saw inside the room made as little sense to him as the condition of the man lying on the balcony. Two heavily built men, both clearly dead, shot execution-style through the head, and who had clearly been restrained by the almost unbreakable plastic cable ties wrapped around their wrists and ankles, lay on the floor of the room. The amount of blood on the floor and their visible head injuries showed him that checking for a pulse or any other sign of life would be completely futile.

"Two more males inside the office, both dead with shots to their heads. That's the room with the lights burning just down the corridor from the apartment door," he reported in a quiet voice. "Both of them incapacitated, wrists and ankles tied, just like the man outside. No threat. I'm clearing the rest of the apartment."

20

Mallory reacted instantly.

Shooting their way past simply wasn't an option, not against two armed men in a stationary car. Their only option was to outrun them somehow. On the open road, it would have been no contest—the Porsche would simply leave the Range Rover in the dust—but in town, especially a town as constricted as Dartmouth, sheer speed was unimportant. They would have to outthink their pursuers, as well as outdrive them.

As both of the men fired their weapons, one bullet carving chucks out of the tarmac right beside the Porsche, Mallory hit the brakes, swung the steering wheel hard over to the right, and at the same time pulled on the hand brake, hard. The rear of the Cayman swung out to the left, tires howling in protest, and as it did so Mallory stamped on the power again, swinging the car round to head back the way they'd come.

"A J-turn," Robin said, sounding unexpectedly calm. "I am impressed."

"Don't be," Mallory snapped. "Just tell me how the hell we get out of this town."

In his rearview mirror he could see the SUV swinging around to follow him down the hill. They had a lead of over a hundred yards at that moment, but Mallory was certain that would quickly evaporate once they found themselves back in Dartmouth's narrow streets. And then a couple of well-placed bullets to shoot out the Porsche's tires, and it would all be over.

"Keep going straight," Robin ordered. She pointed at the dashboard clock and asked, "Is that accurate?"

Mallory looked where she was indicating and nodded. "Yes, pretty much. Why?"

"Just a thought. Keep going."

The Porsche swept down the hill, its speed well over the limit because now Mallory's priorities had changed. The street forked at the bottom into the one-way system that ran around Coronation Park, and Mallory suddenly saw a possible escape route. He slowed up slightly to steer round the bend and glanced across at Robin. "We can do a U-turn round this park thing, then go straight back up the hill and out of town. They won't catch us on the open road."

"You can't guarantee that, not on the kind of roads we have around here. We need a lot more space between us and them."

"Have you got a better idea?" Mallory asked, his voice clouded with irritation.

"As a matter of fact, I have," she replied, glancing to her left as Mallory made the turn by the Floating Bridge Pub and swung the car south onto the road running between Coronation Park and the river Dart.

"Now what?"

"Timing is everything," Robin said enigmatically. "Go round the park again, quick as you can."

Mallory saw two cars in front as he straightened up, a couple of slow-moving sedans, and weaved and accelerated hard to get past them before they reached the sharp bend ahead. Both drivers hooted in irritation, probably because they simply hadn't seen him coming, but then Mallory was past, steering the car to the right, rear tires smoking and leaving black streaks of rubber on the street, and heading back toward College Way. As he made the turn, he saw the Range Rover almost two hundred yards behind them, heading down the stretch of road that ran beside the river.

"Now what?" he asked again.

"Go round again, but slow down when you get near that pub."

"What are you trying to do? Get behind them?"

"Not exactly. I'm trying to get us out of here," Robin said.

Mallory powered the Porsche around the corner at the junction with College Way, tires squealing and the lateral g-force pushing Robin against the passenger door. He headed back toward the river, retracing the route he'd followed less than a minute earlier.

"Now," Robin said, sitting forward in her seat and staring straight ahead. "Slow down. More. Slower. Now. Go straight on, there," she finished, pointing slightly to her left.

Mallory braked harder, turning the car off the main street and down a short section of street that led directly to the river.

And then he saw exactly what she had planned.

Right in front of the car, a man was just closing the barrier at the stern of a ferry that was clearly preparing to leave on the short crossing over to the other side of the river Dart.

Robin leaned over in front of Mallory and gave an imperious toot on the Porsche's horn. The man glanced toward them, opened the barrier again, and waved them onto the vessel, closing the gate behind them. Seconds later, the ferry began to move, easing slowly away from the bank.

"Clever," Mallory acknowledged, switching off the Cayman's engine. "That's why you wanted to know if the clock was accurate."

Robin nodded. "Yes. I use the ferry quite a lot, so I know the timetable. I looked at the ferry when we passed the pub the first time—the fact that it's called the Floating Bridge is a bit of a clue—and I could see they were just getting the last couple of cars on board. If we'd joined the queue then, the bad guys would have been right behind us, and that would probably have been it, but by going round the park one more time, it worked out just right."

As if motivated by a single thought, they turned simultaneously and stared through the rear window of the car. The black Range Rover had just pulled to a stop on the short stretch of road leading to the ferry dock, and as they watched, two dark-haired men wearing black suits got out and stared impassively at the stern of the departing vessel. Then they climbed back into the SUV and the driver reversed it away from the dock.

"They'll probably go round by road and try to intercept us on the other side," Mallory said.

Robin nodded. "Yes, well, that's the point, you see. They'd stand more chance of catching us if they simply stayed in Dartmouth and caught the next ferry over, because going by road is a hell of a long way round. Their fastest route would be to go all the way west to Halwell, then north to Totnes and east toward Paignton, because all the minor roads are really narrow. That route's like three sides of a square. If we were heading to Paignton, we'd only be doing one side of the same square, driving seven or eight miles instead of over twenty. More important, by the time these men reached Paignton, we could be halfway to Exeter, and then they'd never catch us."

"Okay. So, two obvious questions. First of all, where are we going? Second, who the hell are these people? And what the hell have you dragged me into?"

"That's three questions, actually," Robin said sweetly, "but oddly enough the answer to each of them is exactly the same: I don't have the slightest idea."

Marco Toscanelli was extremely unhappy, and whenever he was unhappy everybody around him knew all about it.

In one fell swoop he had lost half of his team, which was pretty much a disaster. Granted they'd been executed by his own hand, though he still couldn't see what else he could have done, because if any of his men had been interrogated by the British police, Toscanelli knew he himself would probably have been the next occupant of the scarred wooden chair in Vitale's office.

That was bad enough, but if he'd recovered the relic, that would have been written off as collateral damage. Unfortunately he still had not the slightest idea where the lost parchment was, but he thought it was a reasonable assumption that the man Jessop probably had it with him. But what was really puzzling him was what had happened in that small apartment. How had an unarmed bookseller and his girlfriend managed to overpower and knock out three of his men, all of whom were carrying pistols, and all of whom were trained and experienced assassins?

That was a question he obviously couldn't answer, or at least not now. And it was a distraction from the business at hand, which was finding Jessop and his girlfriend again and beating the information about the parchment out of them. That was something Toscanelli was really looking forward to doing.

In the meantime, although he knew exactly where his quarry was—in fact, if they were on the dock he would still be able to see them on the river—there was no way he could get to them. Or not right then, anyway.

"Head back into the town," Toscanelli ordered, taking out his mobile and dialing a number. "We'll pick up Mario and then decide what to do next."

The man beside him nodded and steered the Range Rover along the road that ran beside the river.

Toscanelli finished the call, telling Mario where they would meet him, then opened a road atlas to work out their options. When he saw the circuitous route they would have to take to drive to the other side of the river Dart, he cursed fluently in Italian because the situation was far worse than he had expected.

There was no possible way they could get to the other bank of the river in time to intercept their quarry. No matter how fast they drove, the Porsche would be long gone. In fact, their best option, Toscanelli realized, was to wait in Dartmouth and take the next ferry across to the Kingswear side of the river. He didn't know how long the actual crossing would take, but he guessed about five minutes. Add another five minutes at either side of the river to unload the vehicles and pedestrians, and then repeat the process, and that would put them a minimum of twenty minutes behind their targets, a lifetime in terms of an active pursuit, but still a better and faster option than going by road.

"Back to the ferry dock," Toscanelli ordered as soon as Mario climbed into the backseat.

The driver looked at him quizzically.

"The road isn't going to work," Toscanelli told him through gritted teeth. "The ferry is the fastest way over there."

In fact, the crossing took rather longer than he had expected, and by the time the Range Rover rumbled off the floating bridge ferry on the opposite bank of the Dart, by Toscanelli's estimate they were at least half an hour behind the Porsche, and in reality had not the slightest chance of even following it, far less catching it, not with the network of roads on that side of the river, any one of which their quarry could have taken.

They would need some help, and quickly.

As the SUV headed in the general direction of Paignton, working on the assumption that Jessop would want to get out of the area as quickly as possible, Toscanelli took a smartphone from his jacket pocket, opened up the contacts section, and scanned down the list until he found a name and dialed a British mobile number.

"Keep following the main road," he ordered the driver.

When the call was answered, he switched languages, but the first words he said were in Latin, not English.

"Laudare, Benedicere, Praedicare," he said clearly, paused for a moment, repeated the phrase, and then continued in fluent English: "In the name of the Spaniard from Guzman, my name is Toscanelli, and I need your help."

"My brother in Christ," the man at the other end replied, a few moments later. "I am a tertiary of the *Ordo Praedicatorum*. Tell me how I may assist you."

21

Dartmouth, Devon

Clearing the building didn't take long. Less than a minute later, Fulton reported that nobody else was in there and stepped back into the office while he waited for his colleagues to appear. Outside on the balcony, Chambers was also waiting.

Fifteen minutes later, with the crime scene secured, Fulton and Chambers, their weapons made safe, were standing in one corner of the office, talking to the inspector.

"This really doesn't make any sense," Wilson said.

He pointed at the bulky man lying on the floor of the small office. Two paramedics from the ambulance were looking at the unexplained injuries to both his hands with puzzled expressions on their faces.

"That man was carrying an unloaded Beretta pistol and a suppressor in his jacket pocket, but without a magazine or any cartridges. The other one had no pistol, but he did have a magazine that fitted that Beretta and three loose rounds of nine-millimeter ammunition. But the other pistol you found at the bottom of the staircase was fully loaded. The man outside had a mobile phone in his pocket, one that's identical to these two other mobiles we found sitting here on the desk, and all of them have the name of an Italian service provider on them, so they're probably either pay-as-you-go or prepaid phones. What the criminal fraternity here call 'burners.' Those facts are bizarre enough, but the bigger question is even more puzzling."

Fulton nodded. "Who incapacitated three heavily built armed men—according to the medics, the man outside the apartment has a dislocated shoulder—and then used cable ties to immobilize them? And then shot them in the head with a gun that we can't find? And what the hell did they do to that man's hands? It looks like they drove nails through the palm of his left hand and then more into the knuckles of his right. It must have hurt like crazy, and there's no way any man would have sat still while they did it. And why was it done? To make him talk or what?"

"I have no idea," Wilson agreed, "but there obviously has to have been more than one other person involved. The other thing is what these men look like. All three of them have black hair and swarthy complexions. To me they don't look English, and the suits they're wearing are definitely Italian—I've looked at the labels. So if these three guys are Italian, like their phones and their pistols and what they're wearing, that obviously adds an international component, and that makes me wonder if what we're seeing is gang related, perhaps a punishment for something that one man did. Either that or maybe there's some kind of terrorist connection that we can't see at the moment. And I've also done a bit more checking on the owner of this apartment, and it turns out that 'Robin Jessop' is a woman, not a man. This doesn't look to me like a woman's work."

"And none of them are carrying any identification," Chambers added, and pointed at the desk. "There are two identical wallets right there, next to the two identical mobile phones, both of them empty, and the man outside had no wallet in his jacket, but he was carrying the mobile phone, a suppressor that fits the pistol we found at the bottom of the staircase, and a set of car keys. It looks to me as if these three men had been sent out on a deniable operation, and each of them had been given exactly the same equipment, because otherwise surely at least one of them would be carrying *something* that would identify them, even if it was only a driving license or a credit card."

"That makes sense," Wilson agreed. "But whatever happened and whoever these three are—or were—the first thing we need to do is track down this Robin Jessop as a matter of urgency. Have you done anything with the car keys yet?"

Fulton shook his head.

"Not yet," he replied, holding up an evidence bag containing a key with a plastic fob attached. "It looks to me like a hire car, and probably a Range Rover. If it's okay with you, sir, I'll go down and see if it's parked anywhere nearby. Perhaps there's something in it that will help identify these three."

"Good idea," Wilson replied. "Go and do it now."

Fulton walked down the spiral staircase and crossed first to the BMW Armed Response Vehicle, opened the tailgate, and locked his Heckler & Koch MP5 away securely. Then he depressed the remote locking button on the car key and looked around expectantly. A short distance up the street, the hazard warning lights on a dark-colored Range Rover began to flash.

"Bingo."

Fulton nodded in satisfaction and walked over to it, pulling on a pair of blue latex gloves as he did so, to avoid contaminating any possible fingerprint evidence that might be found in the vehicle. He stopped beside it and for a minute or so simply peered in, the interior illuminated by the courtesy light, but saw nothing suspicious.

Then he pulled open the driver's door and checked all the various storage compartments. Tucked away in the back he found three identical small black plastic boxes with hinged lids that he immediately recognized as pistol cases. All of them were empty, which was not entirely unexpected. They'd only found two weapons at the scene, and as far as they could tell, none of them had been fired, so it was a reasonable assumption that all three men had been killed with the missing third pistol, which had then been removed from the scene by somebody else, presumably the person who had killed the three victims.

The glove box on the dashboard was the last place he looked, and what he found inside it both clarified and at the same time deepened the mystery of the identity of the three men.

Fulton left the plastic boxes inside the vehicle, but opened another evidence bag and placed the contents of the glove box inside it before returning to the apartment and showing Wilson what he had found.

The inspector also pulled on a pair of latex gloves before he examined the three diplomatic passports and an international driving license that matched one of the names.

"Well, that buggers things up nicely," he said, flicking through the first document. "All three of them had diplomatic immunity, which means that they could have walked pretty much as soon as we got them back to the station, despite the firearms we found on them. But of course they can't, because they're dead. And that of course raises the other obvious question: just what the hell are three armed Italian diplomats doing being tied up and then shot dead inside a deserted flat owned by a female bookseller, for God's sake, in Dartmouth?"

"If it was easy, it wouldn't be fun," Fulton remarked, just loud enough for Chambers to hear, then raised his voice slightly. "Well, sir, we'd best sort out our reports and then get back on the road, so if there's nothing else we'll get out of your way."

Wilson nodded distractedly. "Yes, and thanks for getting here so quickly."

Then he turned his attention back to the scene in the apartment, wondering just what on earth he'd stumbled into.

22

Devon

Mallory knew beyond the slightest shadow of any doubt that they were safe, at least for the moment, though in dealing with the gang of thugs they'd encountered, the word *safe* was only a relative term. And even though he was certain that they couldn't possibly be following them, that didn't stop him glancing in his rearview mirrors every few seconds as he pushed the Porsche hard, covering the ground as quickly as he could to put some distance between them and the inevitable pursuit.

Robin, sitting next to him, was confused. And worried, constantly twisting around in her seat to look behind the car.

"You told me yourself," Mallory said as she spun round yet again. "They're stuck on the wrong side of the river."

"I know, I know, but I'm still worried. And so are you, judging by the number of times you've checked the mirrors."

Mallory nodded.

"You're absolutely right. Look," he went on, "we need to talk about this, obviously, and I have a question for you."

"Just the one?"

"Well, no, several, actually. That move you made against the man on the balcony. That wasn't karate, so I suppose it was an aikido move? It's not a martial art I know much about," he added.

Robin nodded. "Exactly. Aikido is really a defensive technique, and that was one of the most basic throws, designed to be used against an attacker with a knife or a gun, or even a punch, and if you follow it through completely you incapacitate him as well, just by not letting go of his wrist. But could I just ask you something? What's your plan now? In fact, let me ask you an even more basic question than that: do you even have a plan?"

"I'd only really thought as far as getting out of Dartmouth, to be ruthlessly honest," Mallory replied, "and now we've managed that. I think what we need to do now is get ourselves somewhere safe and then decide exactly what we're going to have to do about what's happened."

"So no plan, then?"

"Not really, no. I'd just like to try and work out exactly what we're up against, and especially why somebody should be so concerned about a thousand-year old bit of parchment that they were prepared to send three armed men out to get it back, and most likely to kill us—or rather you—in the process. Because one thing we do know is that it was the parchment they'd come for. What that man said made that absolutely clear, and that raises a whole lot more questions, like how they found out about it."

"So, where are we going now?" Robin asked.

"Northish," Mallory replied. "I'm kind of heading for Exeter. That's the nearest big city where we can lose ourselves and lie low for a while. Obviously we can't go back to your apartment, because it'll be heaving with cops and forensic guys for hours, maybe days, while they try and work out just what the hell happened up there. And they'll certainly be looking for you to supply some of the answers because it's your property. Is your mobile phone switched on?"

Robin shook her head. "No. I turned it off before we went into the restaurant."

"Good. You should pull out the battery, because you can be traced through the phone as long as it's powered on, and sometimes even if it's turned off."

Robin looked at him, then opened her handbag, took out her smartphone, slid off the back, and removed the battery, replacing the three components separately in her bag when she'd finished.

"Well, what about your place, down in Helston?" she asked. "I'm not trying to force myself on you," she added, "but we do need somewhere to sleep tonight."

Mallory shook his head.

"I'm not even sure if that would be safe," he replied. "Whoever those three people—and we know there are at least three of them because we saw two of them in that Range Rover, plus the man who was shooting at us—are working for, they have impressive resources. If they were able to pick up your search string on the Internet, I think it's reasonably certain that they can also hack into your e-mail. And if they can do that, then it won't take them very long to work out that I might be involved with you. And if they can do that, then my house will be the next place they'll look. No, I think our best bet is to pick a random destination because if we don't know where we're going, obviously nobody can predict where we'll turn up."

"And then what?" Robin asked.

"We'll find a hotel," he replied.

"I'd already guessed that. What I meant was, once we've thought this through and tried to work out just what the hell's going on, what do we do then?"

"Right now I have no idea. I'm just hoping that somehow we can discover what the rest of the encrypted text on the parchment says, because once we know that we'll have a much better idea about why it's so important. And that might tell us why these people are so desperate to get their hands on it. Before we can do anything else, we need information, much more information."

Robin didn't respond for a minute or so; then she shook her head. "You said we need more information, but have you any idea at all who you think we're dealing with here?"

Mallory shrugged. "I don't know, but there are some pointers, I suppose. Those men are Italian, that much I think is obvious, or at least two of the three men who went to your apartment were—the two who spoke, I mean. And they clearly belong to some kind of large organization."

"How do you know that?" Robin asked. "And what organization could it be?"

"Again, I don't know," Mallory admitted, "but the one I think was named Giacomo talked about the relic having been taken from them years ago, something like that, and to me that obviously suggests a group of people, not an individual. If it was just him looking for it, he would have said 'taken from me,' because his English was good enough for that. And I got the feeling that whoever he works for has been looking for that piece of parchment perhaps for decades, not just a year or two, which again most probably means a long-lived group or organization."

Robin nodded. "That makes sense and it would tie up with what little I know about the history of the object. I always try and find out what I can about the provenance of any book that I buy, just in case there's some interesting or unique feature in its past that would help increase its value or make it easier to sell."

"So a Bible definitely owned by Oliver Cromwell, for example, would be a lot more valuable than another anonymous Bible from the same period. That kind of thing?"

"If you can find me an undisputed Cromwell Bible, I'll pay you handsomely," Robin replied. "Yes, exactly that kind of thing. Anyway, according to the man I bought the book safe from, it was part of a large collection that had been sitting on a shelf in the library of a private house somewhere up in the wilds of Scotland for centuries. Even allowing for a bit of artistic license on the part of the man who sold the collection to me, I think it's quite possible that nobody had actually seen that book safe—or at least realized what it was—for well over a century. And you're right, obviously. That does mean these two must be working for some group or other. But you've still no idea who, or what kind of group?"

"Not a clue, but whoever it is definitely has considerable resources. They were obviously monitoring Internet search engines, or at least the one that you used when you entered the *Ipse Dixit* question, and traced you from that."

"They can do that?" Robin asked, sounding surprised.

Mallory glanced across at her and nodded.

"You'd better believe it," he said. "You'd be amazed at the degree of monitoring that goes on these days. Ever heard of Echelon? Or Carnivore? Or PROMIS or PRISM?"

"PRISM, yes. That was in the news not that long ago,

I think. Isn't it a kind of surveillance operation mounted by the American government that gives them access to stuff on Facebook and Google?"

"Exactly." Mallory paused for a second or two and glanced over at Robin. "Are you sure you want to talk about all this now?" he asked.

"No," Robin replied. "I'm sure it's fascinating stuff, but right now I'm not in the mood for a lecture. I'm more interested in trying to work out who these people are and what they want."

"We know what they want," Mallory said. "They're desperate to recover that parchment and, incidentally, to kill us presumably because we know about it. In fact," he added, "that's not strictly true. It's not the parchment they want, but the encrypted text."

"That seems obvious now that you say it," Robin replied. "The parchment is essentially worthless: it's just a bit of ancient animal skin from a calf or a goat. It has to be whatever information is contained in the encrypted text, so that's what we have to decipher."

They fell silent for a few moments as they came up behind another car traveling much more slowly. Mallory waited until the road ahead was clear and he could see that it was more or less straight, and accelerated past the other vehicle.

"I still find it difficult to believe they could have tracked me just because I entered a search term on the Internet."

"Trust me," Mallory said, "they can. As long as they have the resources, the technology isn't that difficult to implement. They would just have to put a piece of monitoring software in place and provide it with a lookup table containing the words and phrases they're interested in, rather like eBay does."

"You can do that on eBay? I didn't know."

"Yes, really easily. You just enter details of whatever it is you're searching for and save the search. Every time an item matching that description is offered for sale, eBay will send you an e-mail telling you about it and providing a link to the product. It's quite old technology now, but still very effective."

"So that's what you think they did?" Robin finished for him. "Set up some kind of monitoring software on that search engine?"

"Almost certainly. And probably on a lot more than just that one. Whoever these people are, they're organized and powerful."

23

Devon

"We've lost them," the driver—he was using the work name Dante—muttered as the Range Rover plowed on through the night, its powerful headlamps illuminating the entirely empty road in front of them. They were just passing to the west of Paignton, traveling close to the maximum speed limit.

"We lost them back in Dartmouth," Toscanelli snapped. "I don't expect to see them again tonight. But don't worry about it."

"What? I don't understand."

"There's a lot you don't understand, Dante. Just keep driving. Keep heading toward Exeter. That's got the best motorway access, and we'll need to move quickly once I get the call."

"What call? You spoke in English to the man you rang, so we don't know what you said. What can he do to help us?"

"Don't ask questions. Just drive. I'll tell you what you need to know, when you need to know it."

*   *   *

As they entered the outskirts of Exeter, Mallory crossed the river Exe and then took turnings entirely at random, just heading in the general direction of the city center, but with no specific aim in view. All he was looking for was a hotel with off-street parking, ideally underground or otherwise secluded and secure, because he absolutely needed to get the Porsche off the road. It was too easily recognizable a vehicle to risk leaving it on the street. He wouldn't put it past the thugs in the Range Rover to spend all night driving around the streets of Paignton, Exeter, and all the other large conurbations in the area looking for the Cayman.

And if he did park it in the open somewhere, he had no doubt that the inexorable workings of Sod's Law would ensure that it would be spotted by the bad guys or, almost as bad, it would be either stolen or vandalized.

About ten minutes later Mallory pulled the Cayman to a stop by the side of the road and pointed across to the other side.

"That looks as if it would do," he said.

It wasn't a chain hotel or, if it was, it was such an obscure chain that Mallory had never even heard of it, but what had attracted his interest was the large closed garage door to the right of the main entrance, and the sign above it that proclaimed SECURE PRIVATE PARKING.

"Works for me," Robin said. "Do you want me to go in and book a couple of rooms?"

"I'd better do it," he replied. "Nobody's looking for me, but I bet by this time the plods are looking for you. Stay in the car, and we should be able to get up to the rooms from the garage so you won't have to pass the reception desk."

He looked at the expression on her face. "Don't worry

about it. They'll want to question you about what happened in Dartmouth, obviously, but I think it's better if we can try to sort out this mess without the cops getting involved at all, at least at the moment. The keys are in the ignition, just in case," he added, then stepped out of the car and crossed the road to the hotel.

About five minutes later he walked back across to her and sat down in the driver's seat again. "No problem. We've got adjoining rooms on the third floor, and you're my sister if anybody asks."

The garage door opened automatically on the approach of a vehicle, but a ticket was required to leave the underground car park, which suited Mallory. He parked the Porsche in a space over to one side of the garage, and then they went up together in the lift. The rooms each had a double bed and an en suite bathroom, but for a few minutes Mallory stayed in Robin's room while they discussed what they had to do.

"I've never been on the run before," she said, "and I'm not absolutely sure I like it. There is a kind of buzz about it, though."

Mallory just looked at her. "You're actually enjoying this? Getting shot at and chased by a bunch of Italian thugs intent on murdering you?"

"Kind of, yes," Robin replied. "In the excitement stakes it certainly beats trying to make a living flogging a bunch of old books. Now, tomorrow," she went on briskly, "we'll have to go shopping, because the only clothes I've got are what I'm standing up in. I can wash my underwear tonight and it'll be dry by the morning, but I'll definitely need to buy a few bits and pieces."

"That shouldn't be a problem," Mallory said, standing up. "Exeter's a busy place, and I'm sure we can blend right in. Right, I'm going next door. Try and get a good sleep, because we have no idea what tomorrow is likely to bring, but I very much doubt if it'll be good news."

"I'm going to have a bath," Robin said, walking over to slip the security catch on the door behind Mallory, "because I feel grubby after everything that's happened this evening. We'll talk at breakfast, or do you want to get food sent up from room service?"

"I'll think about it. Sleep well, and don't open the door to anybody but me."

In the side compartment of his computer bag, he had a change of underwear, a small washing kit including a razor, a spare summer shirt, and one of the T-shirts he normally used instead of pajamas. He had been half expecting to spend the night somewhere in Dartmouth, and had brought the bare minimum of stuff with him. So it looked as if both of them would need to hit the shops the following day, which, he realized with a jolt of surprise, was only Saturday. So much seemed to have happened in the last twenty-four hours that it felt as if several days had passed since he left home.

He'd already noted that free Wi-Fi was available in the room, and he was still wide-awake, so he took out his computer and plugged the power cord into the wall socket behind the desk on one side of the bedroom. Then he connected his laptop and switched it on, before rummaging in his bag for a gadget that he guessed might greatly increase their degree of invisibility.

Every time a computer connected to the Internet, a thing called an IP—Internet Protocol—address was created. For a fixed network, this might be a permanent address, but any PC logging on through a wireless network in particular would be allocated a temporary IP address. Just like a regular street address, the IP address contained location information for the computer, and it was possible to fix its geographical position precisely, if certain monitoring and tracking tools were available.

With their having just managed to slip away from Dartmouth, absolutely the last thing Mallory wanted was to connect his laptop to the Internet and check his e-mail. Bearing in mind the electronic competence already shown by the Italians, that would be rather like springing up and shouting "I'm over here!" which would be a terminally stupid idea.

But there was something Mallory could do about that. He fished a small white object out of his bag and slid it into one of the USB ports on his laptop. Immediately a green light illuminated on the dongle to show that it was connecting and had been recognized by the operating system. He opened Windows Explorer, navigated to the appropriate USB port, and clicked the icon for the hardware application.

A few seconds later, a somewhat unusual Internet window opened, which confirmed that he was connected and a part of a VPN, a Virtual Private Network, and one of the top-line options enabled him to choose the country where he wanted to appear to be. It wasn't a device Mallory used often: he most frequently employed it when he was on holiday abroad to allow him to watch stuff on BBC iPlayer and other systems, a facility denied to him if the server he was connected to realized he was located in France or Spain or elsewhere. It was an undeniably useful piece of kit.

He decided he would be in America for the duration of this particular Internet session, and selected the appropriate option. As usual, his e-mail contained half a dozen offers of enormous sums of money if only he'd send some "attorney at law" or similar all his contact details, and a few genuine messages from friends and colleagues at the company, none of them important or requiring an immediate reply.

His e-mail dealt with, Mallory checked on the Web to see if any news about the situation in Dartmouth had so far been released, but he could find nothing. It was early days, and he made a mental note to check again the following morning. Apart from anything else, he hoped that when the news of what had happened in Robin's apartment did break, even if it was only reported in a local Dartmouth newspaper, he might learn something useful about the three Italians they'd left immobilized there.

Then he sat back in the chair, wondering what to do next. The encrypted script on the parchment still needed to be deciphered, but he decided he would rather wait for Robin before he started looking at that again. Two heads were often much better than one in trying to work out that kind of puzzle, and she knew Latin and he didn't.

But there was something that rather bothered him about the text on the parchment, and he took out the photocopies Robin had made to look at them again. As well as the encrypted text, there was a symbol on the first page that he hadn't recognized when he first looked at it. It was on the top right-hand corner of the first page, a shape that meant absolutely nothing to him, but which looked important. He didn't really think it was a doodle, because paper and parchment were expensive commodities in medieval times, and people who could write then didn't have the time to indulge in such frivolous pursuits. Everything they put down in ink was important. Unfortunately, although the symbol was clear enough, Mallory had not the slightest idea what it was or why it had been included on the parchment. It looked almost like a kind of stick figure, though it quite obviously wasn't:

He spent a few minutes looking around the Internet in the hope of deciphering it, but without success. For the moment, it remained just another question without an answer.

He would shower in the morning, he decided, and got undressed. Before he climbed into bed, he walked over to the window and peered out into the darkened street below. As he did so, he saw a dark-colored, possibly black, Range Rover drive slowly past the hotel, heading toward the center of the city.

It had to be a coincidence, because he was certain they hadn't been followed, and that make and model of SUV was common enough on the roads in Devon, but it still sent a shiver of foreboding through him. He pulled the curtains firmly closed, walked back across the room, and climbed into bed.

But sleep eluded him for quite some time.

24

Devon

It had been, by any standards, a frustrating night.

Toscanelli was certain that the call he'd made would produce results, but he was also well aware that it would take time for the necessary procedures to be put in place and for the results to be collated and analyzed. And then there would inevitably be a further delay before the man he had contacted would be able to provide him with the information they needed.

Although Toscanelli was certain it would be a waste of time and effort, they'd driven all the way up to the outskirts of Exeter, fairly quickly, then reversed direction and driven back the way they had come, but on the slower coast road, through Dawlish and Teignmouth. The chances of spotting the Porsche were slim in the extreme, and all three of the men in the car knew it, but they did it anyway.

They'd looked in the car park of every hotel they'd seen, without result. And, realistically, they all knew that they couldn't even be sure that they were looking anywhere near the right place, because if Jessop and his girl-friend hadn't stopped somewhere but had driven on into the night on the motorway system, they could by then be halfway to London or Birmingham. Great Britain was not a big country, but it was heavily populated and had an extensive road network and literally tens of millions of cars. Finding any one vehicle—even one as distinctive as that black Porsche Cayman—would be virtually impossible, at least without help. He had a gut feeling that their quarry was still somewhere nearby, but continuing their random search would achieve nothing.

They were driving around the northern outskirts of Paignton when he finally decided to call a halt to their efforts.

"That's it," he said, glancing at his watch. "This is not getting us anywhere. Head back toward Exeter on the main road, and we'll find somewhere to stop there."

"A hotel?" Dante asked hopefully, but Toscanelli shook his head.

"It's gone midnight," he said. "This is a covert operation and three Italian men checking into a hotel at this time of the morning would be bound to attract attention we don't want. No, we'll find a quiet spot somewhere and sleep in the car. And, in any case, there's something else I need to do."

As the Range Rover headed north, back toward Exeter, he opened the laptop computer he had taken from the office in the apartment in Dartmouth and waited for the desktop to appear. It didn't, but instead a password prompt was generated, which caused him to grunt in irritation.

But not only had he been well briefed before he left the building on the Aventine Hill in Rome, but he had also been provided with a number of specialist pieces of equipment in a small custom-built leather case. He shut the lid of the computer again and turned to glance at Mario, the man in the backseat.

"Open up that case," he ordered. "You'll find a couple of discs in there. Give me the one with the word *Boot* printed on it."

Mario did as he was instructed, passing the CD in its case to Toscanelli, who took out the disc, inserted it in the DVD drive of the laptop, and then opened the lid once again. As soon as the screen came alive, he looked at the default message displayed and then pressed the F2 key repeatedly to enter the boot options menu. When he was able to access it, he changed the boot sequence, altering the first boot device from the computer's hard disk to the DVD drive. He saved the change and exited the menu, and then watched the screen as the custom hacking software loaded a cut-down version of the operating system that would allow him to bypass the normal start-up sequence and the password request, and then access all the files and folders that were stored on the hard disk.

As the Range Rover continued north, Toscanelli scanned the directory structure, looking at the names of the folders. It didn't take long to find exactly what he was looking for: Robin Jessop had helpfully labeled one of them "Ipse Dixit," and when he checked the contents he found five files there, one entitled "Original text" and four scanned images. When he checked the dates, he discovered that both the files and the folder had been created within the last two days, which confirmed what he had been hoping. Toscanelli used a universal file viewer program to examine both the scanned images and the text file, and nodded in satisfaction when he did so. There was a lot of data in the text file, none of which he could read, but that didn't matter.

His expertise did not extend to translating Latin—which was what his masters had told him was almost certainly the language used to create the document—but obviously there would be no problem in doing so for some of the experts in the organization back in Rome. What he had to do, very obviously, was get the contents of the "Ipse Dixit" folder sent over to Italy as quickly as he could.

He looked up from the computer screen to the built-in GPS to check exactly where the car was, then expanded the map slightly to see the route ahead.

"We're just coming up to a town called Newton Abbot," he said. "Head toward the center, and then take it slow."

Then Toscanelli took out his mobile phone. Unlike all the other men in the group, he had been provided with a state-of-the-art smartphone equipped with a huge array of apps. He navigated through one of the screens until he found what he was looking for: a detection program that would identify wireless networks. He could have used the wireless facility built in to the laptop, but the phone was less obtrusive—just in case they were seen by a policeman who wondered what they were doing—and the app would probably be a bit faster to react.

"What are you doing?" Mario asked from the backseat.

"It's what the Americans call 'wardriving,'" Toscanelli replied. "I'm looking for an unsecured wireless network that I can tap in to, because I need to send the information on this laptop to Rome."

The equipment he'd been supplied with hadn't included a mobile broadband dongle, probably because his masters hadn't seen the need for one.

"Couldn't it wait until tomorrow, when we could find a cybercafe somewhere?" Dante asked.

"No. It looks to me as if this man Robin Jessop helpfully transcribed all the encrypted text from the original parchment onto this computer. If I'm right, the sooner the people in Rome get it the better, so that they can start decoding it. And if that is what he did, we probably won't have to bother recovering the relic, though that would be a bonus. We'll probably be retasked."

"To do what?" Dante asked.

"Most likely just to kill Jessop and the woman. They know too much about this to be allowed to live. And we owe them for Giacomo and the other two."

Within ten minutes the app Toscanelli was using had identified three unsecured networks. One was no good because it would be impossible to park the car anywhere within range, and he couldn't really stand in the street holding the computer while he sent the data. But the two other wireless networks—both were from closed cafés—had parking spaces conveniently located on the street outside.

Dante stopped the car outside the one that had the strongest signal and Toscanelli picked up the laptop again.

"Keep the engine running and leave the parking lights on," he instructed, "and switch on the interior light as well." He took the map book that he'd been looking at earlier and handed it to Dante. "Hold this up in front of you," he said, "in case some passing busybody or a police officer happens to spot us. You're just a lost motorist studying a map. This shouldn't take long."

He opened the wireless network connection utility, selected the network that had the most powerful signal strength, which was obviously the closest one to the car, and clicked the option to connect to it. But when he tried to do so, a dialogue box popped up asking for the password, and he muttered under his breath in irritation. Sometimes networks that were apparently unsecured asked for a password before access was granted, and obviously that was the case in this instance. Trying to crack it was something he really didn't have the time or the inclination—not to mention the skill—to attempt.

"Mario," he instructed the man in the backseat. "Get out and look in through the windows of that café. There might be a notice on the wall or somewhere that gives the password. If there isn't, we'll have to try the other place."

The bulky Italian opened the rear door of the Range Rover and crossed to the closed and locked door of the café. There was a single low-wattage light burning at the back of the café, positioned almost directly above the till, obviously intended as a rudimentary security feature, but the rest of the area was in semidarkness. Mario peered in through the glass door, shading his eyes so that he could see better, then stepped back and returned to the car.

"There are a couple of signs on the walls," he said. "Something in big letters, but I can't quite make out what it says. I need a flashlight."

"You'll find one in that leather case," Toscanelli said. "Just get a move on, before somebody comes along the road."

Mario walked back to the closed café and shone the thin but powerful beam of the flashlight into the gloom of the building. After a few seconds, he switched direction and aimed the light at the opposite wall. Then he walked back to the Range Rover and resumed his seat.

"It is a password," he announced. "They've got the same notice on both walls. In fact, we could probably have guessed it, because it really isn't all that secure. It's 'DEVON001,' all the letters in uppercase."

"Very amateurish," Toscanelli commented, quickly typed

the password into the appropriate field on the screen in front of him, and then clicked CONNECT.

Within a few seconds he was able to open a Web browser, and he swiftly opened an Italian Web site, one that had deliberately never been listed on any of the major search engines, and which had a lengthy and obscure name that nobody was ever likely to type into a browser by accident. It was also protected by a military-grade log-in system. Once he had signed in, he opened a sophisticated FTP—File Transfer Protocol—utility, navigated to the documents section of the hard disk, selected the "Ipse Dixit" folder, and uploaded the entire contents to the Web site. Then he returned to the home page of the site and set an alarm specifying the folder name for the uploaded files.

Then he shut the lid on the computer and passed it over his shoulder back to Mario, took out his phone again, and dialed a number in Italy that was monitored twenty-four hours a day. When it was answered, he passed a brief message to the man in Rome, explaining to him what had happened, beginning with the unavoidable deaths of half the team members in Dartmouth, but finishing with the news—which he hoped would serve to counterbalance the disastrous beginning of the operation—that he had recovered a computer and uploaded what he believed to be the full text of the long-lost parchment to the Web site. Then he ended the call.

The man he had called was, Toscanelli knew, merely a low-level operative, and it would not be until the following morning—or rather a few hours later that same morning, he realized, glancing at his watch—that anyone in authority in the order would be able to check the contents of the folder. And that same person would be able to issue whatever new or revised orders seemed appropriate in the light of what had happened so far.

As Toscanelli replaced the phone in his pocket, Dante glanced at him.

"So now what do we do?" he asked.

"We find somewhere to spend the rest of the night. No hotel, no guesthouse. We're going to sleep in the car because we really don't have any other options. Turn round and head back along the main road, and then drive north toward Exeter. Then we'll find somewhere quiet out in the country somewhere."

Dante nodded, switched on the headlamps, made a U-turn, and drove away from the café, then swung north back toward Exeter, through the area that they had been searching earlier that evening. They kept their eyes open just in case the Porsche suddenly appeared, though that would have been an extraordinarily unlikely occurrence.

About ten minutes after leaving Newton Abbot, Dante picked a side road that looked quiet and little used, and pulled the car off the road into a small copse that offered some kind of cover from prying eyes. The three men made sure that their weapons were well out of sight, just in case anybody——most especially a policeman—spotted the vehicle and looked through the windows, checked that all the doors were locked, opened a couple of windows a bare inch or two to let in some fresh air, and then settled down to try to get some sleep during what remained of the night.

25

Devon

They woke up with daylight, because they hadn't realized the car was parked facing toward the east and as soon as dawn broke the vehicle was filled with the brilliance of the morning sun, a light simply too bright to sleep through. The leather seats of the Range Rover were comfortable enough to sit in, but had never been designed as beds, and although Dante and Toscanelli had reclined the backs as far as they would go, while Mario stretched out across the backseat as best he could, they all awoke with stiff and aching limbs and very short tempers.

They barely even discussed what they should do that morning, because all three of them first needed something to eat and some hot and strong coffee to drink. Dante started the engine, powered the Range Rover out of the copse, its four-wheel-drive system making short work of the muddy track, rejoined the main road, and headed north into the center of Exeter itself to find a café.

That didn't prove difficult, though getting coffee as strong as the three men liked it was more of a trial, the

English drink tasting weak and insubstantial compared to what they were used to. But it was hot and it was wet, and that was better than nothing. They ordered a second pot while they demolished the basket of bread rolls and croissants that had come with the first cafetière, and then Toscanelli produced the road atlas that he had brought from the car and opened it on the table in front of his companions.

"So I suppose now we start searching again?" Dante asked.

"No," Toscanelli replied quietly, both men speaking Italian, "we don't. We wait for the call I'm expecting."

He used the end of his knife to point at Exeter on the map, then indicated the motorway network that extended around the city. "We're here because we have no idea where Jessop and the woman went. This is a good location because there are fast roads leading in all directions out of the city, so as soon as we have a sighting we can get to the spot as quickly as possible."

"Sighting?" Dante asked.

"The man I called last night is a senior British police officer, as well as being a lay member of the brotherhood. The police here have a clever camera system called ANPR that reads the registration plates of motor vehicles, as well as more surveillance cameras than any other country in the world. I have asked him to initiate a search for the Porsche. With the registration number, it can be tracked almost everywhere it goes, because it is almost impossible for any car to drive through a British city without passing at least one camera."

"So, why hasn't he called already?"

"Because it takes time to collate the information, and although I stressed the urgency of our quest—without telling him what we are doing here, obviously—he can only feed the tracking request into the system as a low-priority task. Otherwise questions would be asked. But I am sure that he will be in contact this morning, at the latest. Then we can track these people down and eliminate them."

"It's a shame we don't still have the other vehicle and the other team," Mario said. "Six pairs of eyes would be better than three."

"I had no choice," Toscanelli replied, in response to the man's implied criticism. "I had no idea what had happened to the others until I stepped into that apartment. In fact, I still don't know what happened, but Giacomo and Gaetano were both unconscious and immobilized with cable ties around their wrists and ankles. Giacomo was also bleeding badly from a number of puncture wounds on both his hands, and I have not the slightest idea how those injuries were sustained. But I could hear the police car approaching, and I knew that I didn't have time to try to revive either of them, though I did try to bring Gaetano round. I certainly didn't have time to cut them free and get them both down the staircase before the British police arrived."

He shrugged and shook his head, almost sadly. When he spoke again, his voice was lower, more confidential, and although they were speaking Italian in an English country town, he was still careful to ensure that none of the other patrons in the café could overhear what he was saying.

"You both know the orders that we were given, and how important it is that no word of what we are doing leaks out. Because I couldn't get the men off the premises, I only had one option to make sure that they would be unable to talk. To anyone. The only consolation, I suppose, is that they were both unconscious already, and so they would have felt nothing when the bullets hit them."

"And what about Valerio?" Dante asked.

"I had the same problem. He was unconscious and it looked as if his shoulder had been dislocated. Just like the other two, somebody had immobilized him with more plastic cable ties. By that time, the police car had actually braked to a stop, and I was expecting the officers in it to approach the apartment within a matter of seconds. Once again, I didn't have enough time to get Valerio down the outside staircase, and so I had no other option. I had to shoot him as well."

Dante shook his head and stared across the table at Toscanelli.

"What?"

"I know the importance of what we're doing," Dante said, "and that the operation must be kept completely secret, but I still think you could have got them out. If you'd taken the suppressor off the pistol and fired a couple of shots in the air, that would have stopped the police coming any closer. Then you'd have had time to revive Giacomo and the other two and get them down the stairs and out of the building. I think you acted too quickly, and without thinking it through."

For a few seconds, Toscanelli didn't respond, just held Dante's gaze until the other man looked away.

"That's why I'm in charge of this operation and you're not," he said eventually, his voice thick with controlled fury. "I did act quickly, but I did think it through first. If I had fired a couple of shots, as you suggested, then I quite agree that the police would have stayed well back. Unfortunately they would also have surrounded the building within minutes. Don't forget that there's a British Royal Navy training establishment just up the road, where weapons are certain to be held, as well as people trained to use them. So we would have had to contend with not only armed police, but also members of the British Royal Navy as well. By the time I could have revived those three, we would have had to try to fight our way out of a cordon of well-armed men around the building, and you know as well as I do what the result of that would have been."

He switched his glance from Dante to Mario and back again.

"So if, Dante, I'd followed the strategy you've just suggested, the most likely outcome is that as well as our three companions being either dead or in police custody, I would have been shot down in the street. Then neither you nor Mario would have the slightest idea where to find Jessop and his secretary or his girlfriend or whatever she is, and you'd have had no option but to return to Rome, and you know what would be likely to happen to you there. Failure is not an option within the order, or in our quest for *veritas.*"

Both men facing him were silent as they contemplated the implied threat in what he had said.

"The only good thing," Toscanelli went on after a few moments, "is that we can at least be sure that this mission has not been compromised in any way. Nobody in this country, apart from the three of us, has any idea why we're here or what we're trying to achieve. I regret those three deaths, obviously, but if I had left any of those men alive, by now I'm quite sure that the British police would already be looking for us, because one of those men would certainly have let something slip under interrogation.

"We also have a minor problem to take care of. The British police now have three dead bodies in Dartmouth, but what they also have is the other Range Rover. I didn't have time to search any of the men for the key of the vehicle, so it was probably in one of Valerio's pockets."

Dante shook his head.

"I don't see that that's a problem," he said. "We made absolutely sure that both vehicles were clean before we left the airport, and the only things in them are our pistol cases, and they don't matter."

Toscanelli stared at him for a moment.

"You're not thinking," he said, a sharp edge to his voice. "Both those vehicles were hired from the same place at the same time using the same credit card, which is in my pocket right now. Even an averagely stupid British police officer is going to eventually make the connection and realize that the people who were driving the second Range Rover could possibly be involved with the three dead bodies they are already investigating. As you know, that vehicle is in one of the parking spots in a side street down the road right now, and that's exactly where it's going to stay."

He glanced around the café again, then continued. "Sooner or later, some patrolling police officer will spot the car, but because we're not far away from the Exeter Central Railway Station, leaving it here will confuse the issue to some extent because they won't know for certain if we climbed onto a train and left the area, or if we did something else. On the way here I checked on the Internet"—he took out his smartphone and put it on the table in front of him for emphasis—"and there's a car hire business located a short distance down this road. So when we drive away from here, we'll be in a different vehicle, one that I'll be hiring with a different credit card in a different name, and that should give us a bit of breathing space."

Before either of the other men could comment or disagree with him, Toscanelli's phone rang, a shrill and strident sound that he silenced almost immediately, lifting the mobile to his ear.

The conversation that followed was almost entirely one-sided, Toscanelli listening to what appeared to be a series of instructions from the caller, and responding only when necessary, usually replying with a monosyllable—*sì* or *no*—occasionally elaborated with another word or two.

When he finished the call, Toscanelli glanced at his two companions.

"That was Rome," he said softly. "The orders stay the same, but the emphasis has changed. The recovery of the relic is now of secondary importance because I was right about the contents of that document on the computer. Our experts are already working on decrypting and translating it. If possible, we still need to find it, and either recover it or make sure it's completely destroyed."

"So what's our first priority now?" Mario asked.

"Simple. We are to find Robin Jessop and the girl and kill them. If possible, we are to make it look like an accident, but however we do it, they are to die before we return to Italy. That is now our top priority."

Five minutes later, the phone rang again, and this time the conversation was longer, and conducted in English, Toscanelli making brief notes in a small book as he talked with the caller. When he finished, he glanced at the other two men.

"We've had a bit of luck," he said. "That was our lay brother in the police force. The analysis of the camera footage shows that the Porsche drove into Exeter last evening, but none of the cameras detected it leaving the city. That means they're still here, and I have a note of the route the car followed. I still don't know exactly where they are, but at least we now know where to start look-ing."

Just under thirty minutes later, the three men piled into a hired Ford sedan, Toscanelli giving directions to Dante based upon what the traffic cameras had recorded. His plan was simple: they would drive to the location of the last camera that the Porsche had driven past and start their search from that point.

And when they found the two people, they'd kill them, and Toscanelli was already thinking of inventive and painful ways they could do that. He wasn't going to bother even attempting to make it look accidental. After what had happened, Jessop and the woman were going to suffer. He would make sure of that.

26

"All that did happen, didn't it?" Robin asked, pouring out coffee into two cups from the pot that had been delivered to her bedroom a couple of minutes earlier. "I mean it wasn't all some complicated and utterly realistic nightmare that I'm just waking up from?"

Mallory had decided room service might be a safer option than going down to the hotel dining room for breakfast. Keeping as far out of sight as possible just seemed to be prudent, in the circumstances. And he had another idea he wanted to suggest as well.

"Unfortunately that was all very real, and we have a lot of questions that still need answering, so we need to get started sooner rather than later," Mallory said.

"Well, I definitely need to go shopping, and I have to call Betty. She'll be worried, obviously."

"I still think you should keep your mobile switched off and the battery out of it," Mallory said. "Otherwise the police will certainly be able to find out more or less where you are, and we definitely need to stay off the radar for a while until we find out what's going on with this parchment and these Italian thugs. Don't forget that we were involved in a gun battle in the streets of Dartmouth last night, and the cops take a very dim view of anything involving firearms, so I'm absolutely certain finding you will be a very high priority."

"But supposing I just made one call? I really need to tell her that I'm okay and tell her to keep the shop open and everything running. Apart from anything else, there are a couple of orders that need to be sent out quite urgently."

"Even one call is one too many," Mallory emphasized. "Mobile phones work by staying in contact with the masts that are dotted around the country. That's obvious, if you think about it. The system has to know where you are so that an incoming call can be routed to you, and the same applies to calls you make: the phone has to be linked in to the system. The downside is that if the police or security services want to find you, the masts can be used to triangulate your location. In the country it's not very accurate, but in a town or city your phone can be located to within just a few meters. So if you do turn on your mobile and make a call, I'd be prepared to lay money that within about ten minutes there'll be a police car on the scene and a bunch of cops looking for you."

"So we need to use a public phone somewhere? Because I really must talk to Betty today."

Mallory nodded. "That's the best option, just in case the police have also placed a tracer on the landline that goes into your shop, which they probably have. Obviously they'll know within minutes where you're making the call from, but if we pick the right spot we can be long gone before they can get somebody to the phone box. The other thing we should do is pick up a couple of pay-as-you-go mobiles, just in case we get separated and need to contact each other. But obviously we won't use them to ring any number that would be known to the police, like your shop, for example."

Robin took a sip of coffee and a bite of toast.

"I know I've asked you this before," she said, "but do you actually have a plan? And if you have, what is it?"

Mallory shook his head.

"I haven't, to be completely honest," he admitted, "because at the moment we don't really know what's going on, and it's difficult to decide on any course of action when you have no information about what the opposition are doing. So the only plan I have, the only way forward that I can think of—apart from keeping you out of the hands of British police, of course—is to decipher what the parchment says."

"And then?"

"That depends on what's in the text, obviously. What I'm hoping is that when we do manage to read the message or whatever it is, then it will become very clear why it's still so important, even today. And I have got some ideas that I'd like to investigate, starting with trying to work out the meaning of that strange symbol on the parchment."

"Why do you think that's important?"

"Frankly," Mallory replied, "I have no idea whether it's important or not, but I do think that it's peculiar, and I simply don't believe that it's a doodle or something like that. The shape is too precise and accurate. Whoever drew that on the parchment put it there for a reason, and I'm hoping that if we can find out what it means, that will give us a clue that will help us to decipher the rest of the text."

He leaned slightly sideways and opened the flap of his

computer bag, which of course he had carried into Robin's room when she opened the door to him that morning, and took out one of the photocopies of the parchment. He laid the page flat on the table between them, and they both stared down at the mysterious symbol for a few seconds.

"About the only thing I've ever seen that looks like that is one of the old Viking runes," Robin said. "They were almost all, as far as I know, based on a central vertical line, and then other marks were added to one side or the other of that line, and frequently on both sides, to indicate different letters or sounds. This isn't a subject I know too much about," she went on, "but I do know that the earliest runes have been dated to around one fifty AD, and that, of course, is almost certainly more than one millennium earlier than the date of the parchment."

Mallory looked interested.

"Were runes still being used in the Middle Ages?" he asked.

Robin nodded. "Yes. There was an established medieval runic alphabet used in Scandinavia, where each symbol represented one phoneme—one sound, if you like—for each letter used in the Old Norse language. And in fact, a different collection of runes—they were known as Dalecarlian runes—were still in use in some isolated parts of Sweden until the nineteenth century, though by the end of this period the runic alphabet being used also included a number of Latin letters, like *B*, *D*, and *M*. There was also some doubt as to whether this alphabet had actually evolved since medieval times, or if the Swedish residents who were found to be using it had learned about it from books and began using it very much later."

"So you think it could be a runic letter, then?"

Robin looked doubtful. "As I said, I do know a bit about it, but this really isn't my field. The fact that the symbol does have a central vertical line suggests that perhaps it could be runic, though I have to say I've never seen any rune with quite as complex a shape as that. The two lines at the bottom of the symbol are the sort of marks you do find on runes, but the kind of sideways capital letter *L* at the top just doesn't look right."

"But it might be a good place to start?" Mallory suggested.

"As good as anywhere else, I suppose, yes. But what you need to remember is that each rune normally only represented a particular sound, so even if that symbol does turn out to be a rune, all it's likely to mean is the sound of one letter of one of the Scandinavian alphabets. Some runes did also represent a word or an idea, but again this was only a single concept, so I don't know how much information you'll be able to get from that symbol, assuming that it is a rune."

"I see what you mean," Mallory said, his enthusiasm waning slightly. "But if you haven't got any better ideas, it's still something that I think is worth checking out."

He glanced around the bedroom.

"Look," he said, "this isn't a bad hotel, and I still don't think that anybody could possibly have followed us here, so why don't we stay here for one more night and then go somewhere else tomorrow?"

"That's fine with me, but I still need to make that phone call, and both of us need to find a clothes shop somewhere, if only to buy some more underwear."

Mallory nodded.

"Absolutely," he said. "Why don't we go now, then come back and start working on the parchment?"

On their way out of the building, Mallory confirmed with the receptionist that they would be staying for one more night, and then they walked the quarter mile or so to a shopping complex and went inside. They hit the shops, paying cash for everything they bought. When they'd both replenished their wardrobes, and also bought a couple of soft bags to put the clothes in, and two cheap pay-as-you-go mobile phones from two different and busy shops, they had a snack lunch in one of the cafés.

"There's another thing I think you should do," Mallory said as they finished their meal.

"And that is?"

"Buy a wig, or maybe even a couple of wigs. The first thing most people—including policemen—look at on a woman is her hair, so if you pick up a long blond wig and change your makeup slightly, you'll completely alter your appearance."

Robin nodded. "Okay, if you really think it's a good idea."

They found a shop selling wigs and hairpieces, and Robin bought a light blond wig and another that was midbrown, one long, the other medium length. At another shop that sold a wide range of cosmetics, she picked up some lipsticks and a set of plain contact lenses that would change her eye color to light blue.

"Now we're set," Mallory said as they walked out of the shop together.

The last thing they were going to do in Exeter, Mallory had decided, was make the phone call to Robin's bookshop in Dartmouth. And she was going to do that well away from the hotel where they were staying.

Rather than risk getting the Porsche out of the garage,

they took a bus across to the other side of the city center, but only after Robin had vanished into a ladies' loo and emerged fifteen minutes later looking so different that Mallory barely recognized her, the blond wig and blue contacts completely altering her appearance.

They rode the bus almost to the end of the line, then got off and walked about a hundred yards to a small shopping arcade that linked two streets, and outside which were a couple of public phones.

"Be as quick as you can," Mallory warned, "because I'm pretty sure there'll be a tracer running on your business telephone line. Identifying the originating phone will take about two minutes, and my guess is that it'll then take the police between five and ten minutes to get a patrol car or motorcycle to this spot. So to be on the safe side, just in case a police car happens to be driving down this street when they complete the trace, please make sure you end the call no more than four minutes after you dial the number, and then come straight into this arcade so we can walk through it to the other street. Okay?"

"You're the boss," Robin said.

"If only that were true," Mallory murmured as he watched her walk the short distance across the pavement toward the nearest booth.

Just over three and a half minutes after she had picked up the phone, Robin walked swiftly across to the entrance to the arcade, her face white and strained. But there was no time for Mallory to ask her anything, because at that moment they both heard the sound of an approaching siren, and just moments later a marked police car squealed to a stop near the two phone booths. They didn't stop to watch what happened, just continued walking through the arcade to the other side.

That street was crowded with people, which would help keep them out of sight. But more important, there were a couple of taxis parked by the curb on the opposite side. Mallory didn't hesitate and crossed the road, Robin right beside him, and climbed into the back of the first one.

"City center, please," he instructed the driver, then glanced at Robin. "Are you okay?" he asked.

She shook her head. "Not really, no. I'll tell you later."

They got out of the taxi some distance from the hotel, deliberately, because Mallory didn't want to leave any obvious trail that could be followed, then walked the rest of the way.

Robin didn't speak again until they were back in her room. Then she sat down heavily on the bed, her head cradled in her hands.

"Tell me," Mallory said softly.

"They're dead," she said, her voice cracking with emotion.

"What?"

"Those three men. The Italians. Betty told me they're dead. Somebody shot each of them in the head."

For a few moments Mallory didn't reply, his mind racing. For the first time he realized he genuinely had no idea what was going on.

"What the hell have we got involved in, David?"

Mallory shook his head, trying to organize his thoughts.

"I have no idea," he said, his words echoing his confusion, "but now we're going to have to be really careful, because we'll be at the top of the 'most wanted' list for the police, as well as having whoever shot those Italians after us as well."

"But we didn't do anything!"

"That probably won't make much difference. Those

three men were killed in your apartment—I presume
that's what happened—and that will obviously make you
a prime suspect, just because of that fact. The old murder
triangle is means, motive, and opportunity, and while you
don't have any obvious motive, the mere fact that it's
your apartment is more than enough to put your name
right up at the top of the list as far as opportunity is concerned, and in ink rather than pencil. We don't have an
alibi, except for each other, and that wouldn't wash because the cops would just assume we were just trying to
protect each other."

"But who killed those men?"

Mallory shook his head again. "I don't know, but
there was such a short window of opportunity that it really must have been another one of the same group, another Italian, I mean. We didn't leave your apartment
until we heard the police car approaching, and actually
saw its lights, so realistically the police would have arrived
on the scene within minutes. So the only person who
could have climbed the stairs to the apartment and then
shot those three men had to be the fourth man in the
SUV. Nothing else makes sense."

"But why would he kill his friends?"

"We don't actually know that those men even knew
each other," Mallory pointed out. "In fact, the more I
think about it, the more it looks to me like a contract, a
job that needed doing in a hurry and for which a group
of mercenaries were hired. That would explain the identical contents of their wallets and the fact they were all
carrying exactly the same types of weapons. As for the
why, the only reason that makes sense to me at the moment is that somebody decided it was vital that none of
them could be allowed to talk to the police or the authorities here. When whoever it was went up into the apart-

ment, he was probably hoping to get the other men out of the building before the police arrived, but when he found that two of them were unconscious and all of them tied up so that they couldn't move, he probably realized that that option wasn't going to work, and so he just walked around pulling the trigger."

"Oh God," Robin said, tears welling up in her eyes. "That means I killed them."

Mallory looked at her.

"Don't be so stupid," he said, trying to snap her out of the mood. "The man who killed those three Italians certainly wasn't you. It was the man who climbed the stairs after we'd gone and fired his pistol three times. That wasn't your fault, so don't you even start to feel guilty about what happened. If you hadn't done what you did back there, the chances are that both of us would now be dead. I don't wish anyone any harm, but if it's a choice between three Italian thugs lying on slabs in a mortuary and the two of us in the same state, then my vote goes to the Italians, thank you."

The briefest of smiles illuminated Robin's face as she glanced across at Mallory.

"You have a way of cutting to the chase and immediately making me feel better," she said, "and because of that I'll even forgive you for calling me stupid. I'm sorry, but I think I'm still kind of in shock because of what Betty told me. She said the police want to speak to me as soon as possible to eliminate me from their inquiries."

Mallory gave a hollow laugh. "That's just police-speak for sticking you in a cell until they can assemble or create enough evidence to charge you with something. Don't you believe it for a second. Our best bet at the moment is to stay well below the radar until we find out exactly what's going on. And the answers must lie within the text on that parchment. We absolutely have to decipher the Latin and then translate what it says."

Robin was silent for a few moments, and when she spoke again her voice sounded distant and somehow detached.

"I don't think I've ever broken the law in my life," she said, "until last evening, anyway, and even then I was only acting in self-defense. But I really don't like the feeling of being a fugitive through no fault of my own. Are you sure we can't just contact the police and make a clean breast of everything? I mean, what's the worst that could happen?"

"That's entirely up to you, but I think it would be a very bad idea, even leaving aside the fact that those three men are now dead. If they hadn't been killed, you'd probably still be in trouble, because it would be difficult to convince the guardians of law and order in this country that you didn't know that the book safe had that vicious antitheft device built into it. After all, they could establish that you'd already sent an e-mail to me containing some of the words from the manuscript—that's how we met, after all—and they could argue that because you didn't try to stop that Italian from trying to open it, that was pretty much the same as assaulting him yourself.

"You couldn't even prove that those men were threatening you. Yes, they had guns in their pockets, but at the end of the encounter you walked away without a scratch on you, and you left one man with really badly mangled hands, another knocked unconscious with a possible concussion and probably a broken wrist—when you kicked his arm I definitely heard something crack—and the third one with a dislocated shoulder. However you weigh that lot up, the obvious conclusion is that you—or both of us—were the perpetrator of the attack and they were the victims.

"And now that we know somebody else walked into the apartment just a few minutes after we had left and killed the three of them, I don't have the slightest doubt about what would happen if either of us went to the police. We would be immediately arrested and we'd spend the next few months in separate prisons somewhere, waiting for the case to come to trial."

Robin nodded. "But we didn't fire a gun. Neither of us. Couldn't we prove it?"

"Proving a negative is extremely difficult. If we'd been arrested at the scene, just after the killings had taken place, then we might have a chance of doing that. There are tests that you can run to show whether or not a person has fired a pistol, and of course you would have tested negative for that, though I would be positive because of what happened afterwards. And neither of us would have had the murder weapon in our possession. In those circumstances, then we possibly could have walked away. But once we'd left the scene of the crime, our chances of doing that would have fallen away to zero. The police could argue that we'd worn gloves, or washed our hands a sufficient number of times to remove all traces of cordite, and lobbed the gun into the sea or a rubbish bin or some ditch miles away from Dartmouth. Something like that. And we'd be in trouble. Probably a lot more trouble than we're in now, difficult though that may be to believe."

Robin nodded.

"Yes," she said slowly. "When you put it like that I know we're doing the right thing. We really do have to solve the puzzle of the parchment and what's going on with these Italians before we even think about talking to the police."

"Apart from wondering if her employer was a triple murderer," Mallory asked, "how was Betty?"

This time there was a real smile.

"Whatever the police may have told her, I really don't think she'd believe that of me. I mean, I sell books for a living! I don't go round killing people, obviously. But I think confused is the word that covers it best. The place was swarming with cops when she arrived to open the shop this morning, and she said she had to produce her driving license and show them her photograph before they'd believe *she* wasn't Robin Jessop. A tense few minutes, apparently. Anyway, there's no damage to the shop, and the crime scene is in the apartment, which of course is entirely separate, although it's obviously a part of the same building. Despite the murders she's told me she'll be happy to keep working there until I get back. Quite a tough lady, our Betty."

"One question," Mallory said. "Can you remember the first thing she said to you when you made the call?"

"Er, yes, I think so. She just asked where I was. Why?"

"If that's what she asked, then I think that more or less proves the police were monitoring the call and telling her what to say, because if she'd found out this morning that three men had been found dead in your apartment, and then you called her, that would have been the first thing she'd want to tell you. The fact that she didn't means she was being closely supervised, and the police were probably hoping that you'd just blurt out your location as soon as she asked the question. You didn't, I hope?"

Robin shook her head. "No. I'm not an idiot. I obviously didn't tell her where I was or why I wasn't at the shop. In fact, I didn't answer her question at all. I just told her about the couple of orders that needed sending out, and tried to keep the conversation as businesslike as possible. And then she told me that three men had been found dead in the apartment. That was a hell of a shock, and I denied all knowledge of what had happened. That wasn't difficult, because it was news to me, and I hope that was obvious from my voice. I was totally stunned because what she said was so completely unexpected."

"You did the right thing," Mallory said. "By being matter-of-fact and just telling her what you needed her to do today in the shop, you will at the very least have raised doubts in the minds of whichever police officers were listening to the call, and that can only be a good thing. But I presume she asked you again where you were, because that's what the police will want to find out."

"She did, yes, but again I didn't tell her. All I said was that I'd had to go away unexpectedly, which has the advantage of being the absolute truth. Then she said that the police wanted to see me as soon as possible. At the end of the call she also told me that they'd already questioned her about my movements and the usual sort of stuff about friends and family members that I might be staying with. This morning the police took Betty up to the apartment to ask her if anything had been taken, and she said everything seemed to be in place, as far as she could tell, except for my laptop. If you remember, that was still on the desk when we left the office, but she was quite certain that it wasn't there when she went up to check out the apartment."

"Obviously whoever killed the three Italians took that as well, and that could be a bit of a problem for us."

"Why?" Robin asked.

"Because the scanned images of the parchment are on

that laptop, as well as the transcription of the encrypted text. If you remember, I copied that from my computer onto a memory stick, and then you saved the file onto your laptop. That means that whoever took your machine—and he's obviously one of the bad guys—will know pretty much the same as we do about the parchment."

"They won't get into it," Robin said. "That laptop's protected by a password."

Mallory laughed shortly.

"If only that were true," he said. "Cracking a Windows password is really pretty basic stuff, and you can download a whole bunch of programs from the Internet that'll do the job in a few seconds, or minutes at the most. And even if they can't do that, there are tools you can use to boot the machine from the optical drive and simply bypass it. Trust me, if they know what they're doing, they'll be able to get inside it." He paused for a couple of seconds. "Did she—Betty, I mean—say anything else?"

"Well, she could hardly avoid mentioning the fact that there was a lot of blood on the floor of the office, though I don't know if the police really wanted her to say that. I think I replied, but I was still in shock and I can't remember what I said. Then she told me again that the police wanted to talk to me, and said I had to get back to Dartmouth as quickly as possible. I told her I couldn't and that I wouldn't be back for at least a week, and then I had a slight brain wave, and I said I couldn't talk anymore because the taxi had just arrived to take me to the airport. I also told her I'd dropped my mobile and broken it. Lies compounded on more lies, but I hoped that would create a bit of confusion."

Mallory nodded approval.

"That was good thinking," he said. "I don't suppose for a moment that the police will believe you, but by now they'll know where you made the call from, and they'll certainly have to run checks on all the passenger lists for flights departing from Exeter Airport, just in case you actually have flown off somewhere. And that will give them something to keep them uselessly occupied while we're working on the parchment and trying to decide what to do next."

27

Exeter, Devon

Dante had driven the Ford hire car down virtually every road in Exeter, using the location of the last camera that had detected the Porsche Cayman as the starting point for the search, and they had seen not the slightest sign of the vehicle. There had been one false alarm when Mario spotted a black Porsche in a side street, but when they'd driven along the street to investigate, the car had proved to be a 911, not a Cayman, and the registration number was completely different.

They'd grabbed a late lunch, just soft drinks and sandwiches bought from a garage when they filled the tank on the Ford, and eaten their inadequate meal parked by the side of the road, all three men keeping a sharp lookout just in case the Porsche suddenly appeared.

"He must have parked the car off the road," Mario suggested, stating what was now obvious to all of them.

"We know that," Toscanelli snapped, not in the best of tempers.

"Well, shouldn't we be taking a look in the car parks?"

"We will," Toscanelli promised, "but that's really the last resort. The trouble is that if Jessop did leave the car in a parking lot, we have no guarantee at all that he would be coming back to it, so even if we found it, we might be no further forward. I was hoping we could find the car outside a hotel, something like that, somewhere we could be sure that the vehicle would help us find the two of them."

Toscanelli's phone rang again at that moment, and he answered it immediately.

"*Sì?*"

Then he switched to English, and when he finished the call he was once again energized.

"Get moving," he said to Dante, looking at the map of Exeter. "Keep straight along this road for about a hundred meters, then turn right. As quick as you can."

"What's happened?" Mario asked.

"That was our lay brother again," Toscanelli replied. "Two things. First, Robin Jessop is now officially a person of interest, not quite a suspect but the next best thing, in the multiple murders that took place in Dartmouth last night. That isn't going to help us, obviously, because it means that the British police will now be looking for him. But the good thing is that because his status has changed, we should learn, through our brother, about every sighting and trace of the man."

"So where are we going?"

"Just to the north of the city center here," Toscanelli said. "Less than fifteen minutes ago Jessop made a telephone call to his shop in Dartmouth from right here in Exeter. I've got the location of the public telephone he used, so that gives us another confirmed position to resume our search."

He paused and glanced at his two colleagues.

"They're still here and we're closing in on them," he said, a wolfish smile on his face.

28

"Is that it?" Silvio Vitale asked eagerly. "Is it what we've been looking for?"

The elderly man standing in front of his desk was dressed in a black suit, exactly like Vitale himself and every other person in that part of the building. It was more than a convention: it was essentially both a uniform and a silent statement reflecting not only their history but also their core beliefs. In the centuries that had passed since the order had been formed, the color of their garb had never altered, although the type of garments they wore had of necessity changed over the years.

"We were obviously hampered by not knowing what the document looked like. If you recall, from the very start of our search, there has been doubt about both the fate of the parchment and the contents of the text. Our brothers who were responsible for the investigation in the first instance were only able to establish that the leader of the heretics had been aware of the moves being made against him and had made his own plans accordingly. But at no point were we ever certain precisely what he had done, only that it was very obvious when our searches were carried out that the objects we sought had been removed and presumably concealed elsewhere. The only other thing we believed to have been established was that a document, an original piece of parchment, had been created, and was generally known within the Order as the *Ipse Dixit* manuscript."

Livio Fabrini paused in his explanation for a moment and looked down at the sheets of paper in his hand.

"I'm quite sure that you have looked at these just as carefully as I have, Brother Vitale, and you will have seen that the title *Ipse Dixit* does not occur anywhere on either the transcription of the encrypted text or the scanned images of the original parchment. However, the folder on the computer from which this data was obtained did bear that name, and that suggests to me that the parchment had been secreted or concealed within an object of some description as a means of concealment. Logically speaking, if the parchment hadn't been protected in this way, it is extremely unlikely that it would have survived to the present day, and I think we can assume that the book or whatever was chosen as a hiding place probably did bear the name *Ipse Dixit* because otherwise it is difficult to see any reason why this person in England should have used that expression."

Vitale contained his impatience with some difficulty. Fabrini was one of the oldest members of the order still working, and his knowledge of its history, and in particular the details of the quest that had consumed so much of its combined energy for most of the previous millennium, was unrivaled. But his speech tended to be pedantic rather than rapid, and he had always been incapable of providing the short version of any piece of information. There were times when Vitale longed for a simple yes or no, but he knew that with Fabrini that was unlikely ever to happen.

"So?" Vitale asked, because the old professor appeared to have come to a stop without actually answering the question he had been asked, although he had provided answers to a number of questions which he had *not* been asked. "Do you think it is the lost parchment?"

Fabrini hesitated for a moment, then nodded almost reluctantly.

"Yes," he said slowly. "Yes, I believe that it is, though to be absolutely certain I would need to examine the original and conduct a number of tests."

Vitale exhaled. At last it seemed as if the end of their quest might be in sight. But there were still several obvious matters that needed to be addressed, the first of which was exactly what the text on the parchment said.

"The Latin is encrypted," he said. "How long before it is deciphered?"

"Two of my assistants are working on it as we speak. The first part is very clearly enciphered using a slightly unusual variant of the Atbash cipher, but the second section has so far failed to yield to this technique. But I'm quite sure that it won't take too long to crack the code. At the moment we are still applying different keywords to the Latin alphabet and using shifted and reversed Atbash, but if this fails to generate the outcome we need, we have sufficient computing power here to attempt a brute-force assault on the cipher."

"Do you think that will be necessary?" Vitale asked. "As I understand it, a brute-force attack could take weeks or months."

"It could," Fabrini agreed, "depending on the complexity of the cipher, and that's why for the moment we are trying the present approach, using different keywords related to the creator of the manuscript and the order he represented. I personally believe that will be the fastest method of obtaining the solution. We are," he reminded Vitale, "dealing with a cunning and heretical mind, but more important a cunning and heretical *medieval* mind, and that means there will be a limit to the degree of complexity he could possibly have employed in the encryption of the document."

Vitale nodded. "You've shown me the translation of the first part, which doesn't seem to be particularly helpful apart from establishing the probable identity of the author, and you will of course let me have the rest as soon as you have succeeded in deciphering it. But have you any idea what this is? And if it's important?"

Vitale pointed at one of the sheets of paper on the desk in front of him, and rested his finger on a symbol at the top of the scanned image of the parchment.

Fabrini leaned forward across the desk, his thin frame, scraggy neck, and long bladelike nose momentarily giving him the appearance of a predatory bird, and looked at the object Vitale was indicating.

"It looks like a rune," Vitale said, "but it obviously isn't."

"You're quite right," Fabrini agreed. "We've looked at that as well, just in case it was in some way important, and it isn't. It provides a hint, if you like, to assist somebody trying to decipher the document, but that's all."

And before Vitale could end the interview or even change the subject, Fabrini switched back into lecture mode and began a long and complex explanation of the origin, use, and derivation of the symbol.

29

"Now that the police obviously know we were here in Exeter this afternoon," Robin said, "don't you think we should leave and go somewhere else?"

"We will be moving," Mallory replied, "but not right now. I'm quite sure that there'll be a large police presence in the city by now, and that will probably be the case for about the next twenty-four hours, but unless there are any other signs that we're still here somewhere, it'll gradually be relaxed. Manpower, cost, other priorities, all the usual reasons. It'll be far safer for us if we just slip away quietly sometime tomorrow afternoon or evening."

"Tricky in that Porsche to do anything quietly, I would have thought."

"You're absolutely right. But just because we arrived here in the Porsche doesn't mean we have to leave in it. In fact, I hadn't planned to. I'm going to slip out later today and hire a dull and boring box on wheels from a local car hire firm, and then stick the Cayman in an anonymous multistory car park for a week or so. Don't forget that the bad guys, these Italian thugs, have never seen either of us close up, so what they have to be following is the car. Remove the car, and we should remove that specific threat. And with that wig on, you don't look anything like Robin Jessop, so even if the police go public and display copies of your photograph on TV and in the newspapers, nobody's likely to recognize you. I barely did when you walked out of that loo."

Robin looked crestfallen.

"Do you really think they'll do that?" she asked.

Mallory nodded. "Almost certainly. They now have three dead men, all murdered execution-style if what Betty told you is correct, and the only common factor in their murders is that the deaths occurred in your apartment. The corporate police mind is a simple structure, fully able to put two and two together and make six or any other number it wants. The men died in your property, so clearly you must be involved. In fact, you'll be their number-one suspect, and if they can't find anyone else, they'll happily try and pin the murders on you."

Robin's eyes misted and she shook her head.

Mallory mistook her emotion, and rested his hand reassuringly on her shoulder. "I'm sorry to put it like that and upset you, but you have to be aware of the reality of the situation we're in."

She shook her head again.

"I'm not upset," she snapped. "Well, I am, I suppose, but more than anything else I'm angry. Two days ago I had a quiet and more or less satisfying life, buying and selling books—which I love—and slowly building up my own business. Now, in just a matter of hours, I'm on the run with a man I barely know, trying to get away from both the British police because they're trying to arrest me for mass murder, and a gang of Italian killers who just want to see me dead. And none of it's my fault."

"You're not dead yet," Mallory said. "We'll work our way through this somehow."

Robin stood up and walked across to the window, pulled back the curtains, and stared out. Then she turned round and looked at Mallory.

"You're the only bit of luck I've had so far," she said, almost bitterly. "If you hadn't driven down to Dartmouth and been right beside me when those Italians turned up, I'd probably have been killed last night."

She strode across to the small desk, pulled out the chair and turned it, and sat down to face Mallory.

"And that wasn't just a throwaway line," she said, a determined expression on her face. "I really don't know anything about you. I mean, I'm sure you're on the side of the angels, because any one of those bullets could have killed you just as easily as it would have killed me, but apart from your name and the fact that you know about computers and encryption techniques, and seem to be very well informed about the world of intelligence and the way the British police force operates, you're still a bit of an enigma."

There was an implied challenge in her gaze, and Mallory nodded.

"Okay," he replied. "What do you want to know?"

"Let's start with the scar," Robin said.

"That's why I know about the police," he replied, "because I was a police officer for a while. I enjoyed the job, but I was asked, or rather forced, to leave."

"What happened?"

"As a young beat constable I was stationed in Bristol, and one night I was sent to investigate a domestic disturbance reported by a neighbor at an address on the fringes of a known red-light district. I was the first on the scene. The door was standing ajar, and I could hear a woman screaming inside the house, so I ran inside. There was a grubby bedroom on the ground floor at the back of the house, and in there I found two people. One was a heavily built middle-aged white man wearing shorts and a T-shirt. He was raining punches at a half-naked young black woman he'd driven into one corner of the room.

"At the time, I fondly believed the police were supposed to protect the innocent, a naive view, of course, and not politically correct today, so I ran over to the man and pulled him away from the girl, who I guessed was a hooker. That was a mistake. As he turned round to face me, the man grabbed a beer glass from a table, smashed the end against the wall, and rammed the broken glass into my cheek. That knocked me backward."

"Dear God," Robin whispered.

"Hence the scar," Mallory said, "but that wasn't the end of it. Then this thug swung the glass again, but this time he was aiming at the woman's face. She ducked and he missed, but then he drew back his arm again for a second go, this time aiming at her stomach. I forgot about my handcuffs, pulled out my baton, and smashed it down on his forearm. I could hear the crack as the bones broke even over the woman's screams. That made him drop the glass, obviously, but he swung his left fist at me. So I used the baton again, and broke his other arm. And I really felt pretty good about that, so I gave him a couple more on his ribs and then dropped him with a crack to the side of his head."

Mallory shrugged.

"Blood was streaming down my face, covering the

front of my uniform, and my whole cheek was numb. I had no idea how badly I'd been hurt, but I'd done my job, as I saw it, stopped a serious assault, possibly even a murder. I thought I might even get a commendation out of it. Anyway, five minutes later the room was full of cops, and I was whisked off to a hospital to get sewn up."

He smiled somewhat bleakly.

"I didn't get a commendation. In fact, I was arrested in my hospital bed for assault and causing actual bodily harm. When the man who'd attacked the girl came down after his drink or drugs or whatever he'd been on, he found a lawyer and decided to press charges against me for police brutality, for an unprovoked assault, claiming that I had burst into the property and attacked both him and his girlfriend—who of course supported his story—and he'd been forced to use the glass on me to stop the attack. And the senior officers at the station, my bosses, claimed they believed the man's story. But the problem was the call I'd received from the dispatcher, telling me to go to that address, which was the only reason I'd been in the property, and they knew it. They tried to make that go away, but they couldn't because it was logged and on the record. So in the end the assault charges were dropped, on the condition I resigned from the force and agreed not to talk to the media about the incident."

"Thank you," Robin said. "Now I see why you have such a low opinion of the boys in blue and also why you know so much about the way they work."

"It was quite a long time ago now," he said, "but the scar is a daily reminder. Now, that's enough about me. We need to work on this blasted parchment. The only way we're going to make any sense of what's happened is if we crack the code and read the full text of the manuscript, so let's make a start right now. Unless you've any other questions for me?"

"I've got lots," Robin said, "but they can all wait. Let's get on with it."

30

Exeter, Devon

Dante had stopped the Ford Focus right at the end of the shopping arcade where the public telephones were located less than five minutes after Toscanelli received the call, and had waited by the curb while the other two men climbed out of the vehicle to begin their search. Then he'd found a parking place, locked the car, and rejoined them.

They were hampered by not knowing precisely what their quarry looked like. The only one of the three who'd actually seen them was Mario, and the circumstances in which his sighting had occurred had been far from ideal. The girl, he'd told them, was pretty and dark-haired, which was hardly helpful, while the man Jessop was tall, solidly built with fair hair, and seemed to have a kind of faint mark, like a jagged line, on his cheek.

As far as Toscanelli was concerned, the girl was almost irrelevant. Their main target was Jessop himself, and they needed him alive because they still had to recover the parchment. If he had the ancient document with him, they could kill him immediately, but if he had secreted it elsewhere, then Jessop would have to be persuaded to hand it over. Toscanelli was actually hoping that the bookseller would need to be persuaded, because he was looking forward to doing that himself.

The three men fanned out, scanning the people in the arcade and then in the adjoining streets, but saw nobody who matched even the vague and uncertain descriptions they were working with. Ten minutes later, they reassembled at the opposite end of the arcade.

"This was just a diversion," Toscanelli said quietly in Italian, after a minute or so. "Did you notice anything about this place?"

"Something unusual, you mean?" Mario asked.

"No, not unusual at all. Just some things that should tell you why we're looking in the wrong place."

He glanced at his two companions, but neither of them spoke.

"Right," Toscanelli continued, "Jessop has already proved he's not stupid, as well as being a dangerous man. He would know that if he made a call to his shop it would be traced, so the one thing he wouldn't do was make the call from close to where he's staying. I don't know if he picked this part of the city deliberately, or if he was just lucky, but four things struck me about this area. First, it's a shopping district, which means there are no hotels anywhere near here. Second, the arcade links two streets, which greatly increases the area anyone would have to search. Third and fourth, there's a bus route running along one street and there's a taxi rank on this street. I think Jessop probably came here on a bus, because he wouldn't be in any hurry, made the call, and then took a cab back to wherever he was staying, to get clear of the area as quickly as he could."

"So you mean we're wasting our time looking?" Dante asked.

"Here, yes, but at least we know that Jessop is still here in Exeter. And if my guess is right and he did travel here by bus, that will give us a route to search along. We'll pick up some bus timetables and backtrack each route. Somewhere along one of them there'll be a hotel with a parking lot that's invisible from the road."

"There might be several hotels like that," Mario said.

Toscanelli nodded. "Yes, and if there are, we'll check them all. Jessop is still here, and we're going to find him."

31

Mallory plugged in his computer and switched it on. He used the dongle to establish a presence on the Virtual Private Network, and this time chose France as his apparent location.

"That should keep the bad guys busy," he said. "The first place they'll have to start looking for us is somewhere down to the south of Toulouse."

He explained to Robin how the device worked, and emphasized that it meant they were completely safe from any normal level of electronic interception. Then he started investigating all things runic, which turned out to be a far bigger subject than either he or Robin had expected.

The earliest runes had been used in the second century AD, and were almost certainly derived from the ancient Old Italic alphabets that were used on the Italian peninsula and that were employed to provide written versions of a number of different languages. These alphabets themselves had in turn originated from the Euboean alphabet, which had been used in Greek colonies in the southern parts of Italy. These archaic alphabets were first written from right to left, because that was the natural way that a right-handed mason carving an inscription would work, but when the use of ink became common, the direction shifted to left to right, again because most people were right-handed, and writing in that direction did not smudge the ink.

By the time the first runic alphabets emerged, left to right was the accepted direction for most writing, though some of the very earliest examples ran in the opposite direction, possibly owing to the influence of other alphabets that were written that way, such as the Northern Etruscan. The first runic alphabet was commonly known as Elder Futhark, the latter name representing the phonemes of the names of the first six runes, and as soon as Mallory looked at it he knew that the symbol he was investigating bore no resemblance whatsoever to most of the letters.

"These runes are all quite simple shapes," he said to Robin, who was sitting beside and slightly behind him. He pointed at the images on the screen. "None of these are anything like as complex as this symbol."

"More to the point," Robin replied, "not one of those runes contains any additional strokes like those on the symbol. I mean, none of them have a horizontal line at either the top or bottom of the vertical stroke, and the only one with a prominent diagonal line is the *L* rune, normally spoken as *laguz*, and which means water or a lake. The diagonal is on the correct side, but it's at the top, not the bottom, of the vertical line. What I was wondering was whether we were looking at a kind of complex or combined rune, where several letters were displayed together, on the same vertical line, but that isn't the case with this version of the alphabet."

"Yes," Mallory said, "but this Elder Futhark was only

in use until about the eighth century, according to this article, so let's take a look at the alphabets that followed it. The next in terms of timescale was the Anglo-Saxon Futhorc."

He clicked on a link and brought up a diagram showing all the letters of the revised runic alphabet.

"This looks pretty much the same to me," Robin said, "though there are a few more letters employed. The Elder Futhark had twenty-four runes, but the Anglo-Saxon version expanded over the years until it contained thirty-three different runes. But none of the new ones had the characteristics we're looking for. Try the Younger Futhark."

Mallory obediently selected another link, and they both stared intently at the screen, studying the new information.

"Several of these are more complex shapes," Mallory said, "especially the medieval versions of the runes—you can see that they've added dots to some of the letters—but I still don't see any shapes that resemble this symbol. I think we're probably on the wrong track."

"That's what I thought right from the start," Robin said, "but it was a useful exercise to do, if only because we've now eliminated the various runic alphabets as a possible source for the symbol. The question now is where we look next."

Mallory shook his head. "I'll just do a few general searches on the Web and see if I can find any references to runelike symbology. That might work, if anything like this has appeared before."

A little over an hour later, Mallory sat back and stretched his arms out above his head, looking across at Robin, who was lying sprawled across the bed.

"Nothing?" she asked.

"Nothing," Mallory confirmed. "Either that symbol is

so unusual that nobody has ever seen it before, or perhaps we were wrong and it really is just a kind of doodle, a drawing that we can't decipher simply because it doesn't actually have any meaning. But to me it still looks too deliberate, too positive in the way it's been created, for that to make sense."

He glanced at his watch. "Look, let's order a pot of tea or coffee or something, and see if we can think of somewhere else we can search. Not everything's on the Internet, you know: it just seems as if it is. Maybe we should be looking in libraries, places like that."

Robin smiled at him, picked up the phone, and placed the order with room service.

"You must be getting desperate if you're thinking about actually reading a book," she said. "I'd more or less got the impression that you lived your life online."

"I have been known to read the odd book," Mallory replied, slightly defensively, "but you're right. I do sometimes feel a bit like that guy in *The Matrix*, living inside a computer program and not having much contact with reality."

When the coffee arrived, he turned his attention back to his Web browser. "I think I covered pretty much all the possible search options relating to runic inscriptions and symbols of that type. Any ideas where we could start looking next?"

Robin thought for a few moments, then nodded.

"Maybe you could try a bit of lateral thinking," she suggested. "Instead of trying to find some way of deciphering that symbol, how about approaching the problem from the other end, as it were?"

"And by that you mean?"

"Try searching for subjects that are a bit less specific. Use terms like 'medieval cryptology' or 'early cipher systems,' that kind of thing, and see if that produces any useful information. I just think that because we don't actually know what encryption system—that's assuming that there *was* an encryption system, of course—was used to create the object, trying to decode it is probably going to be impossible. But if you just look at old cipher systems in general, that might give you a clue as to where you should be looking."

Mallory shrugged.

"You might be right," he said, "and it's certainly worth a try."

To his surprise, although the majority of the sites he looked at dealt with what might be termed conventional cryptography—principally various kinds of letter substitution codes and innovative types of steganography—he actually found the result he was looking for almost immediately.

"I've got it," he said, sounding astonished.

"You have?" Robin was almost equally surprised.

"It's an obscure medieval number code that was apparently developed by Cistercian monks in the late thirteenth century. It used a single vertical stem, just like a rune, and nine different types of line or shape that could be attached to that stem. Depending on which side of the vertical they were positioned, they had different meanings, and any combination of these shapes could be used to represent numbers from one up to nine thousand nine hundred and ninety-nine. It's a simple and really clever system, and according to this Web site, it was used by the monks for a couple of hundred years after it was developed, as an alternative to both the old Roman numerals and the new Hindu-Arabic numbers, which were just starting to be introduced."

Robin shook his head. "I've never heard of it. In fact, I've never heard of anything like that."

"I'm not surprised. Again, if the information on this Web site is to be believed, and I've got no reason to doubt it, the system started as a development of a kind of ancient Greek shorthand that only really became generally known about in the nineteenth century when a carving on a stone was discovered at the Acropolis, a carving that described that shorthand. But the number notation system remained obscure right up to the twentieth century, and it was only investigated then because of a fourteenth-century astrolabe that was auctioned at Christie's in London in 1991. The astrolabe was marked with symbols derived from this numbering system, and that prompted research into their origin and meaning."

"So the symbol is a number? I'm not sure that helps us very much, but now you've got the table of meanings in front of you, you can decode it."

Mallory nodded and pointed at the symbol. "I already have," he said. "The horizontal line at the base of the vertical means one thousand; the diagonal pointing up and to the right decodes as three hundred, while the kind of reversed capital letter *L* on its side at the top of the upright means seven. So the entire number represented by the symbol is 1307, and I really don't see how that helps us very much. My best guess is that it refers to the year the document was prepared. And I suppose it could also mean that the person or people who authored it were quite possibly Cistercian monks. Other than that, I don't think we're that much further forward."

Robin nodded, appearing deep in thought. "I'm not sure you're right about it referring to the year the document was written, because my impression was that the date was much later than that, maybe even a century or two later. But that is certainly one possible interpretation."

Mallory pushed the computer to one side on the table and took another drink of coffee. "Any other ideas, or have we just wasted about half a day working out that the symbol is just an unusual way of writing a date?"

"I don't know. I mean, the number pretty much has to be referring to a year—you've proved that—but I still don't think it means the year the text was prepared. If the author wanted the date to be included, or if the date itself was important to the message in some way, then I would have expected him to have made a reference to it in the text itself. A kind of 'In the year of our Lord' statement, that sort of thing. So in my opinion, for what it's worth, it looks to me as if that encrypted date is another clue of some sort, and perhaps what we should be looking for is something that happened in 1307, an event that might have meant something to the authors of the text. But I've got no idea what that might be, so maybe what we'll need to do is carry out a kind of quick survey of all significant events that took place that year, and try and relate one of them to the encrypted text."

Mallory shook his head, light dawning.

"We might not have to do that," he said.

He reached into his computer case to extract the decryptions they had already done of the first part of the encrypted message. He scanned quickly over the printed plaintext that between them they had decoded and then translated from the Latin, until he found the passage that he had remembered. Mallory turned the paper around on the table so that Robin could see the text, and then pointed at a particular section of it.

"We talked about this before," he said, "but the significance of it escaped me at the time."

"It's still escaping me," Robin said. "This passage is just a kind of general statement about the importance of worshipping God and leading a life according to strict rules. I don't see how any of this helps, so what are you talking about?"

Mallory jabbed his finger at the text again.

"Just read that passage aloud, could you?" he asked. "Only that one short section."

"It says 'only through the observance of strict rules can the penitent sinner expect to enter the kingdom of heaven.' It sounds to me like a typical medieval admonition trying to persuade people to follow a particular path."

Mallory shook his head. "Agatha Christie once wrote a novel where the crux of the plot hinged upon a character not repeating word for word what a dying man had said to her, but upon her interpretation of what he had said. I heard what you said when you read out that passage, but what you read was not exactly what we had translated and what's written on this piece of paper. Look at it again."

Robin glanced down at the sheet and shook her head.

"You're wrong," she said. "I did read out what it says."

"No. You said 'of strict rules,'" Mallory insisted, "but the translation actually reads 'of strict rule.' Singular, not plural."

"Rule, rules. What's the difference? And you might have written it down wrong."

"I don't think I did, so why don't you take a look at the sheet with the decrypted Latin text on it and just check it?"

Robin pulled the paper toward her and looked at it. Then she nodded.

"You're right," she agreed. "The Latin noun is singular, not plural, but I still don't see what difference that makes."

"I think I do. If you remember, the number nine seemed significant when I was decoding the text, because almost every ninth word marked a shift in the Atbash cipher. So we have the year 1307, the number nine, and a reference to a 'strict rule.' Does any of that ring a bell with you?"

"Not really, no."

"Well, I've got a pretty loud ringing in my ears at the moment, and I'm surprised it didn't occur to me earlier. A really significant event happened in October 1307, an event that still has some repercussions even today. That's the date encoded in that numerical notation that was almost certainly developed by the Cistercians, and that religious order is important. Plus, there was one medieval society for which the number nine was important in at least two different ways. And, finally, that same society was famed for its adherence to a particularly strict code of conduct, a 'strict rule,' if you like."

Mallory paused and glanced across the table at Robin, who still looked baffled.

"Put all that lot together," he continued, "and you have three indirect references to perhaps the most mysterious, notorious, and powerful of all the medieval organizations. I think this text has got something to do with the Knights Templar."

32

Exeter, Devon

Half of the secret of success in life lies in looking the part, and this is especially true when it's a case of gaining unauthorized access. Toscanelli knew that wearing the right clothes and carrying the correct accessories enormously reduced the chances of anyone stopping him and asking any questions.

Not that he was trying to get anywhere to which access was restricted. He was simply checking hotels, but as far as possible he wanted to be effectively invisible while he did so. Wearing his dark suit and carrying his briefcase, he looked exactly like every other businessman walking the streets of Exeter, and he simply strode into each hotel they'd identified as if he had reserved a room there, hurrying past the reception desk with a quick glance at his watch and then making his way to the parking area using the lifts or the stairs. And nobody at all had taken the slightest notice of him, as far as he could tell.

Exeter was big, but it wasn't a huge city, and they'd only identified about a dozen hotels that had off-street parking that couldn't be seen from the road. And, in the event, they hadn't had to check every one of them.

When Toscanelli had stepped out of the lift on the first level of the underground parking lot at the eighth hotel, almost the first vehicle he'd seen was the black Porsche Cayman, parked in a bay near the sidewall. He'd walked over to it and checked the registration number, just to confirm it, but he'd known it was the right car the moment he saw it.

There was a grim smile on his face when he emerged from the front door of the hotel and walked a few yards down the street to where Dante and Mario were waiting in the Ford Focus.

"Drive away," he instructed, leaning in through the open window, "but circle round and find a parking space somewhere on the opposite side of the street. Pick a spot where you can see both the garage door and the main entrance of that hotel. I'll wait here until you've done that."

"The car's there, then?" Mario asked.

"Yes, it's in the garage," Toscanelli confirmed. "Now get going."

Less than five minutes later, he resumed his place in the front passenger seat of the Ford, and all three men settled down to watch the hotel where they now knew that their quarry had gone to ground.

33

"Of course, 1307," Robin said. "Friday the thirteenth of October, to be exact, when all the Templar commanderies and preceptories throughout France were raided and their assets seized on the orders of King Philip the Fourth of France, Philip the Fair—who was anything but fair in his dealings with the order."

"Unlucky for some," Mallory said, with a smile.

"If you were a Templar in 1307, definitely. Now, I see the importance of 1307, and I did know that the Templars operated by a very strict rule for all their members, but what was so important about the number nine?"

"A couple of things, really. Do you know much about the Templars?"

"Not a lot, if I'm honest, and probably most of what I know is wrong, because of the way old stories and legends get distorted."

"True enough. Well, I've read quite a lot about them, because they've always fascinated me for one very unusual reason, which I'll tell you about some other time, because it's not relevant right now. Most people know about the way the order was destroyed after 1307, but not many have much idea how it started, and even now there's quite a lot we don't know about that period. But we do know that in about 1119 a French noble named Hugues de Payens, who lived in the Champagne region of the country, decided to create a small military group—I suppose today we'd probably call it a task force—and persuaded eight of his noble relatives to join him in the venture.

"They based the rule and conduct of the order on the Cistercians, and that's why that symbol containing the number 1307 is important, because it reminds us of the year the Templar order effectively ceased to exist. But it also provides an incontrovertible link between the Cistercians—nobody outside that order of monks would probably have known how to use that kind of numerical notation—and the Templars. This was just after the First Crusade, and the idea behind the group was simple enough. What they wanted to do was provide a form of protection for pilgrims from Europe who were on their way to worship at the various holy sites in and around Jerusalem."

"So that's why the number nine is important?" Robin said. "Because there were nine of them?"

"That's one reason, yes. One obvious question that nobody's ever been able to answer is how anybody could reasonably expect a force of only nine knights to protect the hundreds, probably thousands or even tens of thousands of pilgrims who were traveling to the Holy Land. Even if they concentrated their efforts on the area immediately around Jerusalem, there were still too many roads and far too many people to make the idea viable. But obviously Hugues de Payens and his companions were very persuasive, because when they arrived in the city in

1120 they approached King Baldwin the Second and explained their mission, and he allocated them one of the two buildings standing on the Temple Mount to use as their headquarters.

"The area was under Christian control at that time, of course, but the two buildings were Muslim in origin. The Dome of the Rock, which is located more or less at the center of the Mount, was believed to have been built on the site of the Jewish Temple, and was commonly referred to as the Holy of Holies. That was turned into a Christian church known as the *Templum Domini*, or the Temple of the Lord.

"The other building that, like the Dome of the Rock, is still standing, was the Al-Aqsa Mosque, and it was that structure which Baldwin allocated to the new military group, and which then gave them their name. Traditionally, the mosque was understood to have been erected on the site of Solomon's Temple, and it was then known as the Temple of Solomon, the *Templum Solomonis*. Because they were using that building as their headquarters, the fledgling order adopted the name *Pauperes Commilitones Christi Templique Solomonici*, which translated as the Poor Fellow Soldiers of Christ and of the Temple of Solomon. That was a bit of a mouthful, and fairly soon, because they were all of noble birth and based in the temple, they simply became known as the Knights Templar."

"So did they manage to protect the pilgrims in the Holy Land?"

Mallory shook his head. "The short and snappy answer is no, and again the number nine is significant. There were nine knights in this original group, all of whom were related by marriage or by blood ties, and the identities of most of them are known. However, two of the men were known only by their names—Rossal and Gondamer—and the final member of the order is completely unknown to history. There's been speculation about him for centuries, but no believable candidate has ever been suggested. And there's no evidence that any member of this original group of knights did anything to protect pilgrims on the roads around Jerusalem or anywhere else.

"Instead, for nine years—that number again—they stayed on the Temple Mount and inside the building, and the best evidence we have suggests that they spent almost this entire period digging down below the Al-Aqsa Mosque and deep into the caves and tunnels that are known to lie beneath the Temple Mount. It's popularly been supposed that they were looking for something, and it's difficult to think of another cogent reason why they should have done all this excavating. Speculation about the object of their quest has ranged from the Ark of the Covenant all the way to the decapitated head of Jesus Christ. The bottom line is that nobody actually knows what they were looking for, but there is some circumstantial evidence that they did finally find it, because in 1129 they suddenly stopped digging and turned their attention to other matters.

"At the Council of Troyes in that year they were recognized and then sanctioned by the Church, and the order then embarked on a major campaign, but not to fight infidels, which is what they soon became known for, but to raise money. They asked for donations, which could be cash, obviously, but they were also happy to accept land and property, and a major thrust of their effort was directed at the noble families of Western Europe. They were very keen to recruit other nobles to join the order, all of whom brought donations with them, normally handing over their entire property when they swore their oaths of allegiance and were accepted as members of the Knights Templar. The thrust of the recruitment drive was that donations would be used to help the order in its fight against the infidels in the Holy Land, the various Crusades, and it was certainly implied that each donor would also earn himself or herself a favored place in the kingdom of heaven.

"There was quite a lot of resistance at the time to the idea of an order of warrior monks, the obvious argument being that a man of God should not take up arms and engage in battle with anyone. But this belief was quickly turned around by a treatise written by the very influential Bernard of Clairvaux, in which he stated categorically that the religious order could, and in fact should, fight a just war to defend both the Church and the innocent from attack. He also established the belief that a Knight Templar who fell in battle against the infidels would go immediately to heaven, any and all sins being forgiven. At a time when heaven and hell were believed to be absolutely real, and when people were genuinely worried about the fate of their immortal souls, this was a remarkably persuasive argument, and dozens of important nobles flocked to join the order.

"Then the Vatican joined the campaign, and in 1139 Pope Innocent the Second issued a papal bull known as *Omne Datum Optimum*, which basically exempted the Templars from paying any taxes or duties, allowed them the unquestioned right to cross any border, and stated that the order was subject to no authority apart from that of the pope himself. It was, if you like, the ultimate 'get out of jail free' card, because it allowed the Templars to do whatever they liked, and within a very short time the order had expanded enormously, with chapters being created across most of mainland Europe, as well as in England and Scotland."

"But they were a fighting force?" Robin asked. "I thought they were involved in most of the Crusades."

"You're quite right. The Knights Templar became the most feared shock troops of the time, something like the Special Air Service is today. They were well equipped and well trained, but above all they were incredibly highly motivated, largely because of this belief that if they died in battle they were assured of a place in heaven. And their orders in combat reinforced this. They were forbidden from retreating in any conflict unless they were outnumbered at least three to one, and only then if they were ordered to do so by the commanding officer, or if the Templar flag, the *Beauseant*, fell. As a result, in combat they were utterly fearless. It was popularly believed that when battle was imminent the only question the Templars ever asked was where the enemy was, never how strong the enemy forces were, because they simply didn't care. They believed that dying in battle was the ideal way for their lives to end."

"Pretty much the same attitude as radical Islam today," Robin commented.

"There's not much that's new in this world, but I suppose it's interesting how that belief has now come full circle, from being a tenet of radical Christianity to now being held with equal fervor by radical Islam. There's probably a message or a moral in there somewhere. Anyway, all that stuff about the origins of the Knights Templar might be useful background, but it's not actually getting us anywhere. What we need to do is try to decipher the rest of the text on the parchment, and now I think we've got a good shot at doing that."

34

Devon

The police investigation into the triple homicide in Dartmouth hadn't actually stalled, but it seemed clear to everybody involved that it was going nowhere, and not particularly quickly. About the only thing they knew for certain was the identity of the victims and where they had come from.

The names of the three dead men had been established as soon as the bodies were transferred to the mortuary in Exeter, simply by a comparison of the faces of the corpses with the small pictures in the diplomatic passports that had been recovered from the hired Range Rover. By checking the number plate of the car, the police had also established where and when the vehicle had been collected. The SUV had been impounded to allow forensic checks to be carried out on it, although as the murders had been committed elsewhere, nobody was quite certain what results this was expected to yield. It was already clear to everybody involved that the three dead men had traveled from Exeter Airport to Dartmouth in the vehicle, and that had been their only contact with the car.

Almost as an afterthought, one of the staff at the airport had mentioned that two almost identical SUVs had been hired at the same time, and by the same person using a single credit card, and the police seized upon this as another possibly fertile avenue of investigation.

Suddenly, as well as three dead men, they also had another vehicle to trace and three further Italians who were presumably still alive and somewhere in Devon, and who were also clearly a part of the same group as the men who had been killed. A watch order had been issued for the second vehicle, images from speed and traffic cameras being closely scrutinized, and a search mounted for these men, whose names had been extracted from the arrivals details at Exeter Airport. But so far no trace of them had been found. They appeared to have vanished just as suddenly and effectively as Robin Jessop, who was still at the very top of the list of the people whom the police wished to question.

Aircraft of any sort, but especially passenger jets and expensive private aircraft, earn no money while they are parked on a hardstanding somewhere, and the Cessna Citation had been refueled within an hour of landing and then taken off about an hour after that. According to the aircraft's flight plan, it had returned to the Rome airport from which it had departed, and inquiries made by the Devon police through the British embassy in the Italian capital had provided almost no useful information.

The aircraft, the embassy stated, had been hired by a businessman in Rome to convey six of his employees to Exeter, and that was about the total extent of the data that had been forthcoming. Apparently the same or another aircraft would be chartered at a later date to collect the men, although it was also possible that they might be flying back to Italy on a normal commercial flight once

their stay in Britain had been concluded. The businessman had not yet made up his mind, according to the
embassy staff officer who had talked to him. The Italian
had been conspicuously reluctant to convey any information whatsoever about his business interests or the reason
for sending six people to England, or what they were
supposed to be doing there. In fact, he had basically provided almost no information at all to the embassy apart
from his name.

The passports were another problem. The businessman had also failed to explain why the six passengers on
the Cessna Citation were all carrying diplomatic passports. He had refused to make any comment at all about
the origin of those passports, which was a matter of considerable interest because they had not been issued by the
Italian authorities. In fact, when the British police examined the passports, they assumed at first that they were
forgeries because they had never heard of the organization that had allegedly produced them.

Generally speaking, diplomatic passports are issued by
governments to senior diplomats, hence the name, but
the three documents that had been recovered in Dartmouth had not been issued by the government of any
nation, but by the Sovereign Military Order of Malta.

A check with the Foreign and Commonwealth Office
in London had confirmed that both the order and the
documents were entirely legitimate, but that hadn't
helped much. The SMOM, as it was usually referred to,
was an ancient Roman Catholic religious order, originally
based on the island that gave it its name, but at present
with its headquarters in Rome. All communications between the British embassy in the capital and SMOM officials, based in the Magistral Palace on the fashionable Via
Condotti near the Spanish Steps in central Rome, on the

subject of the passports and the men who had been carrying them had been ignored.

So the police had three dead Italian diplomats, killed execution-style for an unknown reason, a missing antiquarian bookseller, and no obvious link between them apart from the flat above the shop in Dartmouth, the site of the killings. In short, it was something of a stalemate. Until officers from the Devon and Cornwall Constabulary could lay their hands on either Robin Jessop or the missing three Italians, nobody really believed that the investigation was going to do anything other than stagnate.

35

"But before we get stuck into trying to decipher that," Mallory said, "I think I just need to go and sort out the cars, find a local hire company, and tuck the Porsche away somewhere nearby. There are plenty of car parks around here."

"I'll come with you," Robin said.

"You don't need to."

"Look, I feel safe when I'm around you, and I know it makes no logical sense, but I'm not going to sit here waiting for a knock on the door that might be these Italians, who've somehow managed to track us down. No, if you go, I'm going with you."

"Okay. Whatever you want."

Robin again pulled on the long blond wig and adjusted her makeup, then announced that she was ready. This time, Mallory made no move to pick up his computer, and she looked at him quizzically.

"You sure about that?" she asked.

"No, but just in case we run into any trouble I want

both hands free," he said, tucking the Beretta into the rear waistband of his trousers. It would be uncomfortable driving like that, but he would feel a whole lot happier having the pistol about his person, just in case.

Ten minutes later Mallory inserted the authorized parking ticket in the machine in the parking lot and waited until the electric motor had lifted the metal door clear of the concrete ramp. Then he gave the Cayman a little throttle and drove the Porsche up the slope and out onto the street.

"I'm sure we're safe enough," Mallory said, "but just keep your eyes open for any black Range Rovers, just in case."

He swung the car around to the left to head toward the car park he'd selected, watching the traffic around him closely, but saw nothing to raise his suspicions. In fact, it wasn't until he pulled the Cayman to a stop on the fourth level of the multistory car park that he really registered the presence of the small Ford sedan that had driven into the car park behind him.

And by then it was too late.

36

Exeter, Devon

The Ford had pulled to a stop directly behind the Porsche, blocking it in completely, and before Mallory or Robin could move, a black-suited man was standing on either side of the Cayman, each aiming an automatic pistol directly at them.

"Oh God," Robin muttered.

"Unless you want this girl's brains splattered all over you," the man standing beside Mallory's door said in completely fluent and almost unaccented English, pulling it open, "you'll do exactly what I tell you."

Mallory glanced to his left. Robin was just getting out of the car, the man beside her pressing the end of his pistol firmly into her neck. Her face gazed at Mallory in mute appeal, but there was nothing he could do to help her. At least, not at that moment.

"As my colleagues must have told you back in Dartmouth, you have something that we want, Jessop, but we'll get to that. First of all, the Ford isn't a very big car for all five of us, so you'll be lending me your Porsche."

Mallory hesitated, though it was clear to him that he really had very little option. And the Italian's next words reinforced that belief.

"Don't even think about it, Jessop. This woman's life means nothing to me. I'd rather avoid bloodshed here, but if you don't do what I tell you, we'll shoot her. Then we'll shoot you, eventually, once you've given us what we want. Now turn off the engine."

Mallory nodded. He reached forward and slowly turned the ignition key.

Never taking his eyes off Mallory, the Italian spoke in his native language to the man standing on the other side of the car, who quickly hustled Robin over to the Ford and made her sit in the backseat. As soon as she'd sat down, he slid in beside her.

"Let me tell you what's going to happen now," the Italian said, switching back to English. "You are going to get out of that car and stand facing it, legs and arms apart and leaning on the roof. Do it."

Mallory climbed out of the driving seat and did precisely as he was told.

The third man emerged from the front of the Ford and quickly and efficiently searched him, almost immediately finding the pistol Mallory had tucked into his waistband. The man handed the weapon to the one who appeared to be in charge, who looked at it briefly, then slipped it into his own pocket.

"One of our pistols, I believe," he said.

The third man finished the search and stepped back. "Good. Now you will sit in the front passenger seat of our car and do absolutely nothing until it reaches its destination. If my colleague in the backseat thinks for even an instant that you might try some kind of violence, I have told him that he is to immediately shoot the woman and then shoot you. I'd rather he didn't have to do either, because of the mess that would make inside the car, but be in no doubt that he is quite prepared to carry out my orders if you make it necessary. It is, after all, only a hire car. Do you understand?"

Mallory nodded again.

"I hope you do, because frankly as far as I can see we don't need either you or the woman. I'm quite certain that the relic and whatever information you two amateurs have managed to extract from it are either in your pockets or possibly locked away in your car, but even if you've hidden it somewhere else I'm sure I can persuade one of you to tell me where."

He gestured toward the Ford Focus. "Now get into the passenger seat, and do up the seat belt. Then lace your fingers together and put your hands on top of your head, where my colleague in the backseat can see them clearly."

With the Italian's pistol pointing straight at him as a silent persuader, Mallory complied, as there was absolutely nothing else he could do. He was also acutely aware of the essential truth of what the anonymous Italian had just said: there was no argument that he could marshal that would be likely to persuade the man that their lives were worth sparing. They had no fallback plan or backup system that would be convincing enough to bother the man with the gun.

Who he was, Mallory still had no idea, but he exuded an air of utterly ruthless efficiency. He would not have been surprised if the Italian had been the man who pulled the trigger of his pistol to silence the three men who had appeared at Robin's apartment. And those three people had presumably been his colleagues. If he had been prepared to summarily execute three people he had been working with, Mallory had no doubt that he would kill him or Robin without a second thought. In fact, he was sure that the only reason he and Robin were still alive was that it was more convenient for the Italians to drive away from the center of Exeter with them still in one piece, which meant that as soon as they reached whatever destination they had in mind, their life expectancy would probably be measured in minutes or even seconds.

The other side of the coin, and what gave Mallory the tiniest sliver of hope, were Robin's impressive martial arts skills. And, Mallory thought, as he laced his fingers on top of his head as he had been told, another useful factor was that the strength of the opposition had just been reduced by a third. Instead of facing three men they were, at least for the moment, only facing two, although that would obviously change as soon as the third man arrived at their destination in the Porsche. It all really depended on what happened next, but at least for the moment the odds had been shortened.

The man behind the steering wheel glanced across at Mallory, checking that his seat belt was secured and that his hands were on his head as he'd been told, then nodded to the man outside the car, reversed the Ford, and drove it toward the exit ramp from the car park.

Mallory moved his head slightly so that he could see the door mirror. In its reflection he caught a glimpse of the Italian placing a slim leather case on the passenger seat of the Cayman, then opening the trunk and looking inside, presumably checking to see if that was where they'd hidden the ancient parchment. Then he was lost to sight as the Ford headed down the ramp.

37

It wasn't a particularly long drive.

The driver swung the Ford out of the parking garage and immediately began heading northwest. Within a few minutes he turned onto the A377, which led up to Crediton, but Mallory doubted if he intended to drive that far.

He was right. They drove past a village called Smallbrook, and about half a mile later the driver slowed down, alternating his glance between the road in front and the built-in GPS. And as he hadn't programmed the unit, presumably their destination had already been entered, even before the car had driven into the parking garage.

At Dunscombe, the Italian turned off the main road onto a minor road that opened up to the southwest, signposted to Hookway.

When Mallory saw the direction the vehicle was going, he guessed that they would end up on some quiet road or possibly on the outskirts of a wood somewhere, a place where the Italians could conclude the business with them well away from the prying eyes of any witnesses.

There was a small wood over to the right-hand side of the road, and Mallory wondered if that was where the car was heading, but the driver continued along the minor road without slowing down. But then he did reduce speed. It was quite obvious that the driver had simply been given the location, and had never been to that particular spot before, because he was following the instructions from the GPS with considerable care. At a crossroads he paused briefly and then took the road on the left and continued for another half a mile or so. As they reached another wooded area on the left, he dropped the speed of the car down to a crawl and began searching for somewhere to pull off the road and get the vehicle out of sight.

There were several pull-offs where the car could have left the road, but the condition of the ground meant that getting back onto the tarmac again could have been quite difficult. After about fifty yards, as the vehicle approached the farther end of the wood, a rutted track appeared, leading to a small clearing. Immediately the driver turned the steering wheel to the right and the car bounced and lurched as it left the metaled road surface. He swung the car round the clearing in a circle so that its front pointed back the way they'd come, toward the road. Then he turned off the engine and for a few seconds nobody in the car moved.

Then the driver unclipped his seat belt, reached into his jacket pocket, and took out an automatic pistol—yet another example of the Beretta Storm model—and pointed it at Mallory.

"Girl stays in car," he said, in broken and heavily accented English. "You get out, then stand still."

The last thing Mallory wanted to do at that stage was give either of the men an excuse to pull the triggers of their weapons, so he moved with exaggerated care, unlacing his fingers and reaching slowly down to his right-hand side to unclip the seat belt. Then, still moving slowly and carefully, he opened the door beside him and stepped out of the car. He took a couple of paces away from the vehicle, then stopped and turned back to face it, holding his hands up in a gesture of surrender. The driver was still watching him closely, the muzzle of the pistol aimed at him.

He heard the driver issue an instruction in Italian to the man in the backseat, and then he, too, climbed out of the car and stood on the opposite side of it, the Beretta still covering Mallory.

After another moment the left-hand rear door of the car swung open and Robin emerged, the blond wig tangled and a fierce determination shining in her eyes.

But for the moment, there was nothing either of them could do. The Italian standing on the far side of the Ford gestured with his pistol for Robin to move closer to Mallory, obviously so that he could cover both of them with his weapon at the same time. As she did so, the other Italian moved a couple of paces to the side, to stand beside his companion.

Whether by accident or design, the two armed men had made it impossible for either Mallory or Robin to react. The biggest problem with martial arts was that any practitioner needed to be standing extremely close to his or her target before any of the techniques could be used, and right now they were both too far away.

In short, until one or both of the Italians came a lot closer to them, there was nothing Mallory or Robin could do to try to resolve the situation. If the two men were going to wait where they were until the third member of their lethal group arrived, then Mallory didn't see how they were going to be able to walk away.

The attention of the two men seem to be focused more on Robin than on Mallory, and they were talking together in low voices while they looked over the top of the car at her. Mallory spoke virtually no Italian, just a handful of words and phrases that were useful in a café or restaurant and that he'd picked up on a couple of holidays he'd taken in Rome and Florence a few years earlier, but it looked to him as if they were contemplating spending a bit of recreational time with her, presumably before they shot or strangled her. That, Mallory thought, would be quite interesting to watch, because he frankly doubted whether either man would survive the encounter without getting something broken, but his guess gave him the first glimmerings of an idea.

If they were planning on raping or assaulting Robin, they would presumably shoot or incapacitate him first, to ensure that he wouldn't be able to interfere. Logically, if that was the case, then the closer he was standing to her the better, because they wouldn't want to kill her by mistake when they fired at him.

He glanced at Robin, who was standing only four or five feet away. She met his glance levelly, and he felt that she almost knew what he was thinking. And then they both moved at virtually the same moment, Mallory stepping toward Robin as she clutched him, wrapping her arms around his body and positioning herself in front of him, so that her back was toward the car and partially shielding him from the view of the opposition.

Immediately the Italians angrily shouted out orders, and then they both moved quickly around the car, apparently intending to physically separate them.

And that was the opportunity that Mallory had been waiting for.

"We'll only get one chance," he whispered to her.

"I'll take one if you handle the other," she murmured, then stretched up and kissed him on the cheek.

At that moment, the Italian who had been sitting in the backseat with Robin reached them first and roughly grabbed his shoulder, pulling Mallory away from her.

As Robin stepped to the side, her muscles already reacting to the threat posed by the other heavily built Italian who was then just a few feet away from her, Mallory turned around, his fist traveling in a short and brutal arc toward the Italian's solar plexus.

But the bigger man was no stranger to street fighting, and moved sideways a few inches so Mallory's blow missed. The Italian swung his own fist, aiming for his ribs. But Mallory danced back, dodging to one side, and the man's fist barely grazed his abdomen. He'd done this kind of thing before as well.

He swung his left fist forward, and the blow slammed into the right side of the Italian's chest. To Mallory, it felt something like hitting a plank of wood, and had no obvious effect on the other man.

He followed it up with a straight jab with his right, connecting with the man's stomach. But it hadn't enough power to even slow him down.

Mallory rocked backward as the Italian drove two powerful blows onto his chest, the breath driven from his body, and he stumbled backward, losing his footing on the uneven ground.

Through a haze of pain, he saw the Italian smile at him, the smirk of a man anticipating a future pleasure. At the same moment, Mallory realized he was reaching for his pistol, pulling the weapon out of his jacket pocket.

He thrust himself forward, slamming into the Italian's body, his left hand grabbing for the man's right hand to prevent him pulling the weapon clear, forcing the man back and toppling him to the ground.

They landed heavily, Mallory on top, and as they fell he brought his right arm up so that he drove his elbow— hard—into the Italian's chest. He felt something snap as they hit the ground, and the sudden grunt of pain from the man probably meant he'd cracked a rib.

But the Italian wasn't finished, not by a long way. He levered Mallory off him and, scrambling to his feet, drew the pistol.

There was only one thing Mallory could do. As the Italian lifted the pistol, the muzzle moving to point at him, he slammed into the man again, grabbing his wrist and forcing the weapon away from him.

It was a test of strength, and Mallory knew immediately that he was going to lose. The Italian was just too big and too strong, and he could feel and see the man's right arm moving, inexorably turning the pistol back toward him. The moment it pointed at him, he knew the Italian would pull the trigger. And that he would die.

There was just one chance, and Mallory took it. He took half a step to his left, then kicked out hard with his left leg, crashing the sole of his shoe into the side of the Italian's right knee. It was a painful and incapacitating strike, and Mallory knew it.

The Italian screamed in pain as his right leg gave way, and the two men fell sideways together, both slamming hard onto the ground. At the instant they did, the pistol fired, and both men lay still.

38

Devon

The sound of the shot seemed to echo through the wood, and Robin was suddenly aware of the sound of a multitude of flapping wings as rooks and pigeons took flight away from the trees around them.

"David," she yelled, turning to look at him.

She'd already dealt with the other Italian. He was lying flat on his back, moaning in pain, his left arm cradling his right, which was clearly broken. But before she went to Mallory, she kicked his Beretta to one side, out of his reach, then seized the man around the throat and used a push choke to knock him out.

Then she jumped up and ran the few feet that separated her from Mallory and the other Italian.

She grabbed him by the shoulder, but even as she did so, Mallory moved, rolling sideways off the man he'd been fighting.

Robin looked at the mass of blood covering his chest and gasped in shock.

But Mallory shook his head as he scrambled back to his feet.

"Not mine," he said, gasping for breath. "I managed to turn the pistol toward him. Then he pulled the trigger."

They looked down at the heavily built Italian, but it was quickly obvious to both of them that there was nothing they could do for him—even if they'd wanted to. His eyes and mouth were open, and he was clearly not breathing.

"It looks like the bullet went in just below his sternum," Mallory said, getting his breath back. "But the pistol must have been angled upward, and I think it went straight through his heart."

He glanced at Robin, who looked a little more disheveled, and her eyes were fixed on the corpse of the man Mallory had shot. Or who had technically died by his own hand, not that that suggestion would be likely to cut much ice with the local police force.

"I think that probably counts as burning our bridges," she said.

"I could definitely argue self-defense," Mallory replied, trying to keep his voice level and matter-of-fact while he mentally tried to come to terms with the realization that at best he'd effectively just committed manslaughter. The fact that he'd saved his own life and probably Robin's as well seemed almost irrelevant as he looked down at the body lying in front of him.

"So that's what you're going to say when you end up in the dock at the Old Bailey, is it?" Robin's tone and the expression on her face were entirely serious.

"Let's hope it doesn't come to that," Mallory replied. "Now we need to get the hell away from here before that other Italian turns up. He seems to me to be by far the most dangerous of all these people we've met so far, and I've got no intention of ending up in a shooting match here in this wood with him."

He gestured toward the car.

"Check that the keys are in it," he said, "and then get in the passenger seat."

"Forget it. I'll drive."

Robin turned back to the injured and unconscious Italian and removed the wallet from his jacket pocket—she guessed they would need more funds, especially cash—then jogged over to the parked car, pulled open the driver's door, and dropped into the seat. She started the engine and drove the vehicle a few yards closer to Mallory.

He reached inside the man's jacket and removed the wallet and spare pistol magazine from his pockets. Then he grabbed the dead Italian by the left arm and tugged the body onto its side. The back of the man's jacket was stained a deep red, and Mallory saw at once that the bullet that had killed him had passed completely through his body. But what he couldn't see was any tear or rip in the fabric of the garment, and when he ran the tips of his fingers over the wound, he felt a small hard nodule.

"What are you doing?" Robin asked again through the open window of the car.

"Just a second. I need the pistol—and the bullet."

Mallory pulled the body the rest of the way, over onto its face, the expression "deadweight" never having seemed more appropriate. Then he slid his hand up the dead man's back, under his jacket, his fingers searching for the bullet that he now knew was there.

In a few moments he found and recovered it, the small conical shape slightly deformed after performing its deadly task. He glanced at it, then took a handkerchief from his pocket, wiped the blood off the bullet and as much as he could off his hands, then wrapped the tiny copper missile in the cloth and put it in his jacket pocket. He picked up the pistol he and the dead Italian had been struggling with and dropped it into his pocket. He daren't leave it there because he had no doubt that his fingerprints would be all over it. His eyes caught the glint of brass and he picked up the ejected cartridge case, the last possible piece of forensic evidence.

Then Mallory clearly heard the distant sound of an approaching car, the engine's exhaust a loud rumbling note that he recognized immediately, and he sprinted the few feet to the waiting Ford. He virtually threw himself into the passenger seat and slammed the door shut.

"Go," he said, his tone urgent.

Robin needed no other instruction. The car was already in first gear and as Mallory fumbled for his seat belt she dropped the clutch and floored the accelerator pedal. The Ford surged forward, bouncing across the rough ground as the tires scrabbled for grip. The front of the car lifted as the wheels hit the road and bounced up, then slammed down again. Immediately Robin swung the steering wheel hard to the right and simultaneously pulled on the handbrake for perhaps half a second.

The rear tires squealed as the back of the car slid sideways across the road surface, and then the car powered forward again, Robin fighting to hold it in a straight line under full-power acceleration. As Mallory clicked the seat belt's buckle into place, he glanced sideways at her profile. She looked cool and determined, and completely under control behind the wheel, snatching second gear as the needle of the rev counter just touched the redline. That raised another obvious question that he needed to ask her, when—*if*—they finally managed to find themselves somewhere safe.

Mallory twisted around in his seat and looked back down the narrow road, seeing the slightly wobbly but near-parallel black streaks where Robin had used every last bit of the power the comparatively small Ford engine had been able to produce to get them moving away from the wood.

As he looked, he saw the unmistakable shape of the nose of his own Porsche Cayman just coming into view down the lane about a hundred yards behind them.

39

When Toscanelli steered the Porsche into the clearing where he'd told Mario and Dante to wait for him, it had taken him a moment to realize what he was looking at.

He had no idea where the Ford Focus was, and for an instant he wondered if he had somehow managed to overtake it on the road as he made his way out of Exeter. But that didn't make sense: he had to have been at least five or ten minutes behind his colleagues.

He'd taken a couple of minutes checking the Porsche to see if by any chance the relic was in the vehicle, then spent a little more time programming the GPS on the Cayman with the destination he had earlier selected. They would be meeting at a place he'd picked at random, what had looked on the map like a quiet wooded area where they could conclude their business with Jessop away from prying eyes. Only then had he driven the Porsche out of the car park, and he'd managed to catch most of the traffic lights in Exeter at red.

Then he saw the two dark shapes lying on the ground

at the side of the clearing and immediately stopped the car.

He reached Mario first, but a single glance was enough to tell him that the man was dead. Toscanelli sprinted the few feet to where Dante lay, moaning in pain, his right arm clearly broken.

"That bitch," the injured man muttered. "She—"

"Keep it for later," Toscanelli snapped, grabbed Dante by the left arm, and with some difficulty hauled him to his feet. He half pulled him across to the Porsche, opened the passenger door, and told him to sit down in the seat. Then he walked back to Mario, checked for the man's wallet—which had obviously been taken by Jessop, who was proving both far more resourceful and much more dangerous than Toscanelli had ever anticipated—and removed the pistol suppressor and mobile phone. There was no sign of either his Beretta or the spare magazine for the weapon.

With the dead body sanitized, or as best he could manage, Toscanelli ran over to where Dante had been lying and picked up that pistol as well, before checking the area to make sure there was nothing he'd missed on the ground. Then he sprinted back to the Cayman and put it in gear.

He suddenly recalled seeing the rear of a car disappearing around a corner as he'd approached the clearing. He hadn't taken much notice of it at the time, because he'd been searching for the rendezvous, but it *could* have been the back of the Ford. He might have missed them by a matter of less than a minute.

But he knew how fast that Porsche could travel. Catching them shouldn't be a problem, he thought confidently as he steered the car back onto the road and set off in pursuit.

"What happened?" he demanded, as he gave the Cayman its head and accelerated hard down the narrow road.

"They did what they were told, no trouble on the way," Dante said, his face gray with pain. "Then when we got to the clearing we told them to get out of the car and stand to one side, to wait for you. They did, but then Jessop and the girl grabbed each other and hugged. You'd told us to keep them apart, and so Mario and I ran over to them to pull them apart. And that's when it happened."

"What?" Toscanelli could actually see the Ford now, perhaps five hundred meters in front. He guessed that he would be right behind it in only another three or four minutes.

"Mario pulled Jessop away from the girl and they started fighting each other. I had my hands full with the girl, so I don't know exactly what happened, but there was a shot and then that bitch knocked me out."

Toscanelli nodded to himself. "I can't believe Jessop's just a bookseller," he said. "He's acting more like a professional, but a professional what I have no idea. I think we've been given the wrong information about him. He's definitely a lot more dangerous than I had ever expected him to be."

Toscanelli glanced at Dante again. "And what happened to you? Did you fall or something when the shooting started?"

Dante shook his head. "There wasn't really any shooting, just that one shot that killed Mario. No, it was that bitch of a girl. I grabbed her to pull her away from Jessop, and I really don't know what happened. She kind of spun round and I think she kicked me, but whatever she did she broke my arm, then kicked my legs out from under me. Jesus, it hurt. I've never seen anybody move that fast.

And then she did something to my throat and everything went black. When I came round again the two of them were just driving away."

That wasn't at all what Toscanelli had expected. He already knew that Jessop was dangerous, but from the sound of it the girl—whoever she was—was every bit as lethal. He'd assumed she was just a secretary, or maybe Jessop's girlfriend, but she was clearly much, much more than that. Suddenly the scene inside the apartment back in Dartmouth began to make much more sense. If the woman was some kind of martial arts expert, it had probably been her who had incapacitated the two armed men he'd sent into the building, as well as attacking the third member of the group just outside the entrance door. He still had no idea what could have happened to Giacomo, what had caused those terrible injuries to his hands, and he guessed he would probably never find out.

Things were going from bad to worse. Mario was dead, Dante useless until his arm could be fixed, and all the evidence they'd so far accumulated had vanished, because it was in the trunk of the Ford. The laptop wasn't too important, because he'd already transmitted the files on the computer to Rome, but they still hadn't recovered the relic, which he guessed might well be in Jessop's pocket.

Toscanelli slammed his fist onto the steering wheel in frustration.

But he could still retrieve the situation. All he had to do was catch up with the Ford. Dante could shoot left-handed, and now there was no time or need for finesse. As soon as they were within range, Dante could pepper the Ford with bullets, and it really didn't matter what he hit—the people inside it, the tires, or the engine—anything to stop it. Then they'd pick over the wreckage, take anything that would be useful to the experts back in Rome, and set fire to the car after making sure that Toscanelli's pistol, the one he'd used to kill the three men in Dartmouth, was placed somewhere near Jessop's body.

That would close one open question, because then the police would be able to prove that the three men had been killed by a pistol in Robin Jessop's possession. Of course, that wouldn't provide an answer to the other obvious question that would be asked after the event—who had fired a dozen or so rounds into the Ford?—but that really wasn't his problem.

Toscanelli smiled for an instant. Perhaps if Dante was fairly careful with his shot placement, one or perhaps even both of the people in that car might still be alive when he lit the fire, and for a brief few seconds he relished the pleasurable anticipation of listening to their screams as the flames from the burning petrol licked across their bodies and began to roast their living flesh.

40

Devon

"You drive like a man," Mallory said as Robin powered the Ford around another corner, the tires just kissing the grass verge that formed the apex. "And I mean that as a compliment," he added.

Robin didn't even glance at him, her entire attention focused absolutely on the road ahead, reading the bends and setting up the car for each curve.

"The product of a misspent youth," she replied.

"What were you? A getaway driver for a gang of bank robbers?"

A smile appeared fleetingly on her face. "Nothing so exciting, I'm afraid. I passed my test at seventeen, and then my father insisted that I learn how to drive properly, as he put it. He enrolled me in a race driver school and made sure I got a competition license. I've still got it, actually, though I haven't raced for a few months now."

Mallory nodded. "Every hour that I spend with you produces yet another surprise, something completely unexpected. I suppose you can also fly a plane?"

"Yes. I went solo after nine hours," Robin replied, "but my PPL—Private Pilot's License—has lapsed because I didn't bother doing the right number of hours each year. My father really wanted a boy—a boy he intended to call Robin, in fact, hence the male spelling—but when I appeared and no other children seemed to be forthcoming, he decided to make the best of a bad job. Learning to fly, the car racing, and the martial arts were all his idea. I'm also quite good on a motorcycle, and I can shoot as well, but I'm better with a shotgun than a pistol."

"He sounds like an interesting man."

"He was," she said simply.

Mallory didn't miss the past tense.

"What happened?" he asked. "If you don't mind talking about it."

"I don't, but not right now, because I can see your Porsche in the rearview mirror. He's maybe a quarter of a mile behind us, but he's gaining fast. I don't think there's much chance of this Ford Focus actually outrunning him, no matter what I do."

"Frankly," Mallory replied, twisting around in his seat to stare out of the rear window of the Ford, "it would be a bit embarrassing if you did. I'd never be able to take my car seriously again."

She was right. Unless there was another black Porsche Cayman driving down that lane, which seemed unlikely at best, the Italian wasn't that far behind them. Mallory had the Beretta pistol in his pocket, but he doubted they would survive a firefight with a man as ruthless and determined as the Italian appeared to be. Their best, and perhaps their only, chance of survival lay in getting away from him.

As he turned to face forward, Robin hit the brakes hard and simultaneously sounded the horn. On the left-hand side of the road a metal gate stood open, and just emerging from it was a large, worn tractor, the dull red paint competing for dominance with large patches of rust. Hitched to the back of the tractor was a wide trailer, hay bales stacked on it.

"That could be our salvation," Robin murmured.

At the sound of the Ford's horn, the tractor driver had stopped abruptly, the front end of the vehicle extending about a third of the way across the lane and leaving a comparatively narrow gap between it and the hedgerow opposite.

It was narrow, Mallory guessed too narrow, to allow them to drive through, but once she was certain that the tractor wasn't going to move again, Robin pressed down on the accelerator and the car surged forward.

"Are you sure—" Mallory began, and then shut up, because the answer to his unspoken question was obvious. If she didn't think there was enough room to get the car through the gap, Robin wouldn't be aiming for it.

She didn't slacken speed, but actually continued accelerating. The wheels on the right-hand side of the car bounced over the uneven ground that formed the verge on that side of the road, the door mirror rattling against the errant branches that stuck out of the hedgerow while others scraped along the side of the car.

Robin had got it wrong, Mallory suddenly thought. The gap was too narrow for the car. He was sure of it.

Involuntarily he pulled his seat belt tight and braced his legs against the end of the foot well in front of him.

The rusty red shape of the tractor loomed ever closer, seeming to rush at them, and at that moment Mallory closed his eyes.

Then he opened his eyes again, ashamed of his brief instant of panic. Now he could see that Robin actually was going to miss the front of the tractor by at least an inch, and that was all that mattered. Scraped paintwork was one thing, but ramming into the front of a piece of heavy agricultural machinery would end the pursuit instantaneously.

The somewhat battered front of the tractor flashed by the side window of the Ford at what seemed to Mallory to be an utterly insane speed. And then they were past it. Robin gave the steering wheel of the car the briefest of flicks, and the Ford bounced off the verge and back onto the metaled road surface, still accelerating.

41

Devon

Mallory looked behind. The man driving the tractor was staring at their speeding vehicle and shaking his fist at them.

"I think you just upset Farmer Giles," he said.

Robin snorted.

"Do I look like I care about that?" she demanded. "All I'm interested in is whether or not he's going to pull out and block the lane."

"He is," Mallory replied, still looking through the rear window of the car. "He's just turned left out of the field and he's following us. That trailer is pretty nearly the width of the lane."

"Good. That'll hold up the Italian for at least a few minutes while he tries to find his way past. So what we need to do is get back onto a main road and lose ourselves in the traffic. And then we should probably ditch the car as well."

"Maybe," Mallory said, "but we'll still need wheels."

*　　*　　*

Less than thirty seconds later, Toscanelli swung the Porsche round the bend in the road, cursed fluently in Italian, and immediately hit the brakes. The Cayman's nose flattened as the massive disk brakes hauled down the vehicle's speed, and it fishtailed along the metaled surface of the lane.

The lane was completely blocked by a wide trailer piled high with bales of hay and moving with agonizing slowness, being pulled, Toscanelli supposed, by a tractor.

He weaved the car from side to side, sounding the horn in one long continuous blare, and trying to look ahead to see where it might be possible to get past the mobile road block. But there were no pull-offs or gates that he could see anywhere in front and suddenly, as if in an angry response to the sound of his horn, the wide load began moving even more slowly.

There was only one thing he could do. Toscanelli pulled the car close up behind the end of the trailer, opened his door, and climbed out. He ran along the side of the trailer until he could see the old red-painted tractor that was providing the motive power, a grumpy-looking middle-aged man sitting in the metal seat.

Toscanelli shouted up at him and waved his arms, and eventually the driver favored him with a brief glance. At that moment, Toscanelli reached into his jacket pocket and pulled out his pistol. He aimed it well in front of the tractor and fired two rounds, making sure that they hit the trunk of a substantial tree to dispel any belief that he might be firing blanks.

The effect on the driver was immediate. He adjusted the controls, a gout of black smoke erupted from the vertical exhaust pipe, and both tractor and trailer lurched forward, the speed steadily and visibly increasing.

Satisfied that he had got his message across, Toscanelli

ran back to the Porsche and sat in the driver's seat, following the wide load along the lane, sounding his horn again and again as a reminder to the tractor driver. Within perhaps two minutes the load moved over to one side of the lane as the driver spotted an area where he could get at least partially off the road, and Toscanelli powered past in the Porsche.

Now as long as the lane was long enough, he could catch up with the Ford and write a satisfactory ending to his mission.

42

Devon

Mallory was checking the GPS, looking for options as the Ford sped along the narrow road.

"We're coming up to a fork in the road in a couple of hundred yards," he said. "Go left there. And if you could avoid leaving a skid mark on the road surface, that would be good."

"But isn't the main road, the A30, right in front of us?"

"It is," Mallory agreed, "but unless this GPS has got it all wrong, there aren't any junctions we can easily use. I think our best bet is to stay on these roads and head right back into Exeter and try to lose them in the traffic there."

Robin powered the Ford left at the fork in the road Mallory had told her to expect. Within a hundred yards or so, there was an almost-right-angle bend in the narrow road, around the end of a wood, which had the bonus of making them invisible to the driver of the pursuing car, which Mallory guessed would be getting closer with every second, though he still couldn't see it behind them.

"A bit of breathing space," he murmured, again studying the GPS.

After a moment he glanced up at the road.

"There's another fork coming up," he said, "and go left again. The fastest way to get to Exeter is then to keep straight on, but if we do that I reckon the bad guys will catch us before we get there, so I think we need to get them ahead of us."

"Now where do I go?" Robin asked as she took the left fork.

"There's a turning on the right. Take that. The road goes through a small wood, and it looks like there's a hamlet, or a few houses at least, just beyond it. In fact," he added, "from there we can take an entirely different road into Exeter."

"Sounds good to me."

Robin saw the junction ahead, hit the brakes hard, but not powerfully enough to leave skid marks, pulled the gear lever from fourth down to second, and turned the car right, accelerating as soon as the Ford was around the corner.

The road was narrow and twisting, like all the others they'd been driving along since the Italian swung off the main A377 what felt like a lifetime ago, and Robin concentrated on covering the distance on the somewhat loose and broken surface as quickly as she could.

Toscanelli had become uncomfortably aware that he wasn't catching the small Ford as quickly as he had expected, and he reluctantly added another tick in the mental list he was compiling about Robin Jessop: clearly the man was an accomplished and very fast driver, another possible indication that he was a professional of some sort. But the Porsche was so much more powerful than the Ford that even if Jessop was a trained racing driver, Toscanelli should still be able to catch him.

Seconds later, Toscanelli reached the first fork in the road and the massive brakes on the Cayman hauled the speed down dramatically. His eyes searched the road surface in front of him, scanning for tire marks or anything else that would tell him which way his quarry had turned. But he saw nothing, flipped a mental coin, and angled the Cayman over to the right, simply because that stretch of road looked straighter, and hence faster.

But moments after he'd started accelerating along it, Dante turned slightly in his seat.

"I think I just saw the car," he said, nodding over to his left. "Way over there, by those trees."

"Are you sure?"

"No, but it was the same color as the car we rented, and we haven't seen any other vehicles on this road, apart from that tractor and trailer."

Toscanelli glanced where Dante was indicating, but saw nothing.

"Right," he said. "Use the GPS. Work out which road that car had to be on and tell me how we can catch them."

Dante leaned over in the passenger seat, clumsily fiddling with the GPS in the center of the dashboard using his left hand, his broken right arm resting on his lap.

"They must be heading toward a village called Whitestone," he said. "Keep going along this road until you get to a crossroads at Heath Cross, then turn left. That road will take us straight to Whitestone."

Less than a minute later, Toscanelli hit the brakes again as the Porsche reached the crossroads, swung the steering wheel around to the left, and powered east along the narrow road toward Whitestone.

"Where can they go from there?" he demanded. "What are their options?"

Dante studied the map displayed on the screen of the GPS for a moment. "Coming from the north, there's a T-junction. If they turn right, they'll be heading straight toward us, so my guess is they'll go left, toward Exeter." Dante was silent for a few moments, looking at the options. "That road will take them back to the city, through places called Nadderwater and Redhills, but it would have been a lot quicker for them if they'd not gone through Whitestone. The road they turned off would have taken them straight there."

He altered the scale on the GPS and then glanced at Toscanelli.

"This is only a guess," he began, somewhat hesitantly, but Toscanelli interrupted him.

"Guesses are better than nothing at the moment. Tell me what you're thinking."

"If they turn left at Whitestone and then almost immediately go right, that road will take them down to the C50. That's not a main road, but it's a better road, and there will be traffic on it. Maybe that's his plan, to lose himself in traffic, because if he stays on these empty roads, we'll catch him."

That made sense to Toscanelli.

"So where do I go?" he demanded.

"When you get to Whitestone, go past the junction on the left and take the next turning on the right. That should put us right behind them."

The end of the narrow lane was looming up in front of them, traffic on the C50 crisscrossing the junction in both directions. The road was nothing like as busy as the main A30 trunk road that they could see right in front of them, but there were still plenty of vehicles driving in both directions.

"Which way?" Robin asked, braking the Ford to a stop at the Give Way sign and looking in both directions.

"Left," Mallory replied without hesitation. "We haven't got time to wait for a break in the traffic so we could turn right. And we need to go left anyway, to get back to the city."

"You got it," Robin said.

There wasn't really a break in the traffic crossing the end of the lane from right to left, either, but that clearly didn't matter. Robin waited no more than three seconds, until the next car had driven past them, then lifted her foot off the clutch and sent the Ford, tires screaming, out onto the road a matter of a few tens of feet in front of the next vehicle, an old Peugeot.

The driver hit the horn and the brakes simultaneously, causing the vehicle behind him to brake and swerve as well, but Robin's takeoff had been so blisteringly fast that there was no danger of a collision. The driver's reaction was more a condemnation of her impatience and bad driving manners—as the man had obviously interpreted it—than anything else.

Robin and Mallory, of course, didn't care. They were now, they hoped, out of immediate danger. What they still had to do was make sure that the Italian couldn't catch them, and that was going to involve more brain work than fast driving. Robin was still driving quickly but had been forced to slow down, to move at the same speed as the other traffic on the road and overtake any slower vehicles in front of them when conditions permitted.

Less than three minutes after Robin had driven out onto the main road, Toscanelli repeated her actions, braking the Porsche to a stop at the same junction. For a moment he didn't move, just looked in both directions, trying to second-guess which way his quarry must have turned. Then he spotted the black marks left by a pair of tortured tires on the road surface, and guessed which vehicle had most likely caused them.

With a similarly cavalier disregard for the vehicles driving along the road he was joining, he swung the wheel left and drove out into the traffic stream, eliciting a cacophony of horn blasts from behind as he did so.

Now it all depended on the superior speed and performance of the Porsche.

43

Devon

"He's still behind us," Robin said, a few minutes later, glancing in her rearview mirrors as she overtook a slower car. "Maybe eight hundred yards back, but he's there and he's catching up."

"Shit," Mallory muttered, and looked back at the screen of the GPS, figuring the angles and the options. "There's nowhere we can go until we get to the end of this road, because there aren't any turnings. There's a T-junction at the end, and we need to go left there, to get back to Exeter. Once we're on that road, we've got options."

"So we need to get to that junction as quickly as possible."

The road bent around to their right, and a medium-sized white van was heading in the opposite direction. The moment it had passed, Robin switched on the headlights, punched the accelerator, and drove the Ford out onto the wrong side of the road, screaming past the traffic in front of them.

Mallory clutched at the grab handle as the driver of a small Renault signaled right, the man apparently not having checked his mirrors. Robin gave a prolonged blast on her horn, and the car immediately moved back to the left, weaving slightly. Then oncoming traffic forced her back into the left lane, diving in between two cars and eliciting angry blasts from both drivers.

"He's still catching us," she said, again checking her mirrors. "How far to the junction?"

"About a hundred yards, that's all."

"What then?"

"I'm working on it," Mallory said. "I'll let you know."

"That works for me. I'll drive. You navigate. I'm heavily into role reversal," she added.

Mallory looked at her and smiled briefly.

"And that's something else we need to talk about," he said.

A few seconds later, Robin braked and swung the car left, again causing oncoming vehicles to brake and swerve. And sound their horns, inevitably.

This road was much busier than the one they'd just left, with quite heavy traffic moving in both directions, but still Robin was able to spot gaps and make use of them, accelerating hard to get past vehicles in front.

But Mallory knew that if they stayed on it, the Porsche would catch them. Their only chance was to get off it and lose themselves in the tangle of side streets on the outskirts of Exeter. He checked the GPS again, then the road ahead, and made a decision.

"Take the next left," he instructed, "and then left again."

"You've got it."

Robin hit the brakes as they reached the junction, swung the car left, and moments later left again. Then she looked ahead as the car dived down a narrow street, houses on both sides.

"This is a cul-de-sac," she snapped. "I hope you know what you're doing."

"So do I," Mallory replied. "I just wanted to get out of sight."

"Well, we've done that. Let's hope that Italian bastard didn't see us," she added, swinging the Ford round to face the way they'd come.

Less than a quarter of a mile behind the Ford, Toscanelli eased the Cayman out toward the middle of the road, checking for a gap in the oncoming traffic. There was an articulated truck directly in front of him that was partially blocking his view ahead. He knew he needed to get past it if he was to stand the slightest chance of catching up with the fugitives.

Three cars were heading in the opposite direction, and another truck was following them, but there was a gap— a small gap but one Tosacanelli felt he could use because of the power of the Porsche's engine—between the third car and the truck.

He dropped back twenty or thirty yards behind the vehicle he was following, to give himself room to maneuver and accelerate, and dropped the car down into second gear. The first two cars swept past, heading in the opposite direction, and then the third. The moment that vehicle drove past the Porsche, Toscanelli signaled and swung out, flooring the accelerator pedal.

The approaching truck was closer than he had expected, and the driver sounded his horn, a single loud angry blare, and flashed his lights as the Cayman accelerated toward him. There was room, just, and the moment the Porsche passed the cab of the truck he was overtaking, Toscanelli swung the wheel to the left and pulled in.

But during the maneuver the Italian had lost sight of the road ahead, and in particular could no longer see the Ford Focus that he believed Jessop was driving. He had spotted the vehicle a couple of minutes earlier, but had obviously been too far behind it to confirm its identity. Now, as he scanned the line of traffic ahead of him, he realized that the vehicle he had been following was nowhere in sight.

For about a minute he continued driving along the road, hoping to catch sight of his quarry. He wondered if the Ford had somehow managed a number of rapid overtaking maneuvers while he was stuck behind the truck and had then got far enough ahead to turn off onto a minor road. If it had done that, he had no idea which turning Jessop had taken.

"I don't see them," Dante said.

"Nor do I. Check the GPS. See where they could have turned off."

As Dante leaned forward to look at the screen, Toscanelli muttered a curse and pulled the car onto the side of the road. There was no point in driving on until he could see if he *had* missed a turning and, if there had been, where it went. The drivers of several of the cars he'd overtaken sounded their horns angrily as they drove past the Porsche, but he ignored the noise, bending forward to look at the display on the GPS.

"There are three turnings they could have taken," Dante said, his voice racked with pain. "You can't go back, so the best option is to carry on and take the next left turn, then backtrack and hope we pick them up."

Toscanelli glanced at the traffic passing him in both directions, and knew Dante was right: there was no way he could do a U-turn and backtrack to take one of the junctions he'd missed. That meant he would have to guess which option Jessop would have taken, and aim to intercept him some distance from the junction. If it had been him, running for his life from an armed man, Toscanelli knew he would have headed for the nearest town. There was always safety in numbers, and the best place to hide a car was in traffic.

He nodded, decision made, signaled, and pulled out, again using the Porsche's impressive acceleration to get in front of a car approaching him from behind. He would have to go the long way round, but there really was no alternative.

"That's long enough," Mallory said, glancing again at his watch. "He must have driven past by now. Go to the end of the road and turn left."

Robin approached the end of the cul-de-sac cautiously, in case Mallory had miscalculated and their pursuer had somehow second-guessed them, but there was no sign of the black car. Satisfied, she swung the car out onto the road and accelerated quickly through the gears.

"Take the third on the right," Mallory instructed, "and then go right at the fork. This area is a mass of streets, and quite a lot of them are not through roads. This route'll take us well away from the road we just left, and that should put some distance between us and the bad guy."

The Ford shot down the residential streets at a few miles an hour above the limit, Robin watching out for pedestrians and, worse, children. Cars were parked haphazardly on both sides, and occasionally she had to weave from side to side to get through the gaps.

At a T-junction, Mallory told her to go left, then right

a couple of hundred yards later, at a crossroads. The road they turned into was wider, and much busier, and led to Exeter town center. Robin settled down to just merge in with the traffic flow. The Ford Focus was a popular car, and even if the Italian did somehow get close enough to see the car, he might well not realize it was the one he was chasing unless he was close enough to see the driver and passenger.

In fact, Toscanelli was no longer chasing after them. He'd guessed where they were heading, and instead of trying to catch them, he was attempting to intercept them. Almost as soon as he'd driven off the C50, he realized that trying to track them down in that morass of residential streets was doomed to failure unless he was lucky enough to catch sight of them. So he'd turned round almost immediately and headed back toward the city center.

When he reached the main bridges over the river, he swung left, turning northwest up Okehampton Street, down which he guessed the Ford would probably be heading.

And as he drove under the railway bridge, Toscanelli found himself staring at the Ford heading directly toward him, the woman in the driving seat.

44

Exeter, Devon

"Jesus Christ," Mallory muttered. "Go, Robin, go."

She didn't need telling twice, just dropped down a gear, waited until a bus passed them going the other way, then pulled out, surging past about half a dozen cars in front of them.

"Get over the river," Mallory said, "and go straight on, down Frog Street."

"Frog Street? Who the hell came up with that name?" Robin asked, whipping past another slow-moving car.

"No idea."

Mallory swiveled round in his seat and looked behind, but for the moment the Porsche wasn't in sight, the driver presumably still trying to turn to follow them.

There was barely a gap when they reached the bridge, but Robin powered the car forward anyway, and a man in a white van had to brake hard to let her join the traffic flow in front of him.

"A taste of his own medicine," she murmured as he

blasted his horn and gesticulated at her. "I get fed up with White Van Man always driving like a complete idiot."

The Ford sped over the bridge and Robin angled right to go the way Mallory had wanted.

"Where now?" she asked.

"There's an interchange coming up called Friars' Green. Go kind of straight on and then take the first turning on the left."

"You've got a plan, then?"

"Of a sort, yes. As soon as you've made that turn, take the first on the right and then go right again."

When they reached Friars' Green, the Porsche was just coming into view, but some distance behind.

"He can't travel much quicker than us on these roads," Robin pointed out, turning the Ford left into Southern-hay.

Thirty seconds later, she made the second turn Mallory had told her to take, and as she did so he pointed in front of the car.

"There," he said. "Drive in there."

"A car park?"

"Exactly. That Italian's following the car, so it's time we dumped it."

Robin drove into the parking lot and stopped the car at the end of a row, where it would hopefully be invisible from the road. Immediately they both got out and Mallory opened the trunk to retrieve Robin's laptop, left there by the Italians. Then they walked briskly away, heading between the Cathedral Court buildings and back toward the Friars' Green interchange. They stopped when they reached the road and looked along Southern-hay to the northeast.

In the distance they saw a black car disappearing around

a gentle bend in the road. It could have been the Cayman, but neither of them could be sure.

"And now?"

"We walk over there," Mallory said, pointing to the other side of the road. "We go into that hotel, have a drink or two, then go to the reception desk and ask them to call us a cab."

"And the blood on your shirt?" Robin pointed out.

"A bad nosebleed," Mallory replied, glancing down. "I'll need to buy a new shirt, obviously."

"We've lost them," Dante said as Toscanelli steered the Porsche along Southernhay East. "They must have turned off somewhere, because if they were still ahead of us we'd be able to see them by now."

"You're right," Toscanelli agreed, "but we're not finished yet. My bet is that they'll be going back to that hotel they were staying at, so we can pick them up there."

He stopped the Cayman by the curb, reprogrammed the GPS, and moments later set off again.

Half an hour later Mallory paid off the taxi outside a car rental company, and they walked into the office. Twenty minutes later he started the engine of a Citroën DS3—he'd picked it mainly because the windows were tinted, especially the rear side windows—and drove away, back toward their hotel. He stopped the car about a quarter of a mile from the building, and for a couple of minutes he and Robin scanned the street ahead of them. They couldn't see the Porsche, but that didn't mean it wasn't there somewhere, tucked into a side street or parked beyond the hotel.

"So do we go in, or forget it?" Robin asked.

"We go in," Mallory said. "I want my computer, and

I don't think there's that much risk, if we do this the right way."

Five minutes later, Robin—now without both the blond wig the blue contact lenses, because she'd been wearing both when the Italian had seen her face-to-face—steered the DS3 across the street and stopped in front of the hotel garage door, which opened slowly in front of her.

Mallory was behind her, virtually invisible thanks to the heavily tinted rear windows of the car, the Beretta pistol clutched in his right hand, just in case.

"I don't see the car," Robin said, barely moving her lips, as the door finally opened all the way.

"Let's hope they've given up," Mallory said.

But when he looked out of the window of Robin's room, the Cayman was clearly visible, parked in a side street on the opposite side of the main street, two shadowy figures barely visible inside it. There was nothing they could do about that, so they quickly packed their few belongings and prepared to leave. But before they did so, Mallory reached into his jacket pocket and took out the cheap disposable mobile phone he'd bought what seemed like several days ago, and dialed the nonemergency number for the police.

"What are you doing?" Robin asked.

But before he could explain, the operator answered and he quickly explained to her that he'd just been robbed at gunpoint in the center of Exeter, and that the thief had got away with the keys to his Porsche Cayman. He added that minutes later he had actually seen it being driven away, through the town. He had no option but to give his correct name and address, and the vehicle details, as well as an accurate description of the man he claimed had robbed him, but apologized that he was having to leave the country immediately to attend a business conference in America, and would be out of contact for at least a week.

"Was that a good idea? Giving all your personal information to the cops?"

"I really don't know," Mallory replied, "but I like that car and I want it back, and now that Italian will have something else to worry about with all the local police keeping their eyes open for both him and the car. With a bit of luck, they'll find it when the Italian finally decides to dump it, and hopefully the police will impound it and keep it safe. And at least they'll now be alerted to the fact that the driver of the vehicle is armed, so they'll know what to expect if they try and stop it on the road."

Robin nodded. "That makes sense, I suppose, but my guess is that the Italian will abandon the car pretty soon, because it's just too distinctive."

Then they picked up their bags, and while Robin took the lift down to the garage level, Mallory paid the bill in cash and picked up another ticket for the garage door.

Two minutes after that, Robin drove the Citroën out of the underground garage and didn't so much as glance at the Porsche in the side street opposite the hotel. When she looked in the mirror a minute later, there was no sign of the car following her, so she presumed that her disguise—or to be more accurate, her complete lack of a disguise—had worked, and the Italians simply hadn't recognized her.

On the eastern outskirts of the city, before they joined the M5 Motorway, Robin stopped the car. Mallory climbed out of the backseat and sat in the front passenger seat alongside her.

"So we're pretty much clear of Exeter," she said. "What next? Where do we go now?"

"One question," Mallory said, not replying to her directly. "Have you got your passport with you?"

"Yes." She nodded. "I always keep it in my handbag. Why?"

"I think it's time we took a holiday together. How does France sound?"

Robin glanced at him.

"French, mainly," she said. "But why France, and won't getting out of England be a problem, with the cops all looking for me?"

"It doesn't have to be France, but that's probably the easiest. I've gone over there by car on the Eurotunnel train a few times, and what always struck me was how lax the border checks were. Quite often there's nobody at all in the British passport control booth, and usually the French just wave you through. It's different coming back, but we'll have to cross that bridge when we come to it. And I know the police are looking for you, but they'll be searching for a woman with short dark hair, probably traveling alone."

"And why France?" she asked again. "You didn't seem to answer that."

"Safety in distance," Mallory replied. "Those Italians tracked us down—or rather tracked you down—to Dartmouth, just because of the search terms you used on the Web. We've been off the grid ever since, but at this moment that last Italian knows we're somewhere in Devon, and if he calls for reinforcements, that's where they'll start looking for us. Plus, the local police still want to shove you into an interview room and try to persuade you to admit to something that you didn't do. So the short version is that Britain, and especially Devon, is probably going to be too dangerous for you quite soon. France just seems like a good bet."

Robin thought for a moment. "Okay, you might be right. We could well be safer in France than this side of the Channel, but I don't fancy just chancing our arm at Dover or Folkestone and hoping nobody spots us, or rather me."

"You've got a better idea?"

"Definitely," Robin said. "I'll tell you later. But where are we going right now?"

Mallory fiddled with the GPS for a few moments, then sat back.

"We'll aim for Taunton," he said. "I've just chosen that place at random, so nobody will ever be able to find us there. I hope."

45

Exeter, Devon

Toscanelli and Dante sat in the Porsche in the side street opposite the hotel for almost two hours without seeing any sign of the Ford Focus. Other cars arrived and departed, and people walked in and out through the main doors, but none of them looked even remotely like their quarry. Toscanelli finally admitted to himself that he had no idea where Jessop and the woman were, or how he could possibly pick up their trail again. They might have driven away from the city, or gone to ground in some other hotel. Or done almost anything else, in fact. But the reality was that he had no clue about their location, and spending any longer in that town was, as far as he could see, just a complete waste of time.

He had taken a short telephone call from the senior police officer who'd told him that the Porsche had been reported stolen, and that meant he would have to lose the car fairly quickly.

The other thing he had to lose was Dante. The man was now barely conscious because of the pain from his broken and grossly swollen arm, and would clearly be of absolutely no use to Toscanelli for the foreseeable future. But he certainly wasn't going to take the time to drive him to a hospital. As far as Toscanelli was concerned, Dante and Mario had screwed up big-time in letting Jessop and the woman get away. Mario had paid the ultimate price for his incompetence, and Toscanelli saw no particular reason why he should do Dante any favors. After all, as a result of what the two men had failed to do, he had now lost track of Jessop. He also lost the laptop computer that he had taken from the apartment, and probably the relic itself as well, because he was pretty sure that Jessop or the woman would have been carrying it. So he wasn't feeling particularly well disposed toward his injured colleague.

He drove away from the hotel toward the city center, then turned the Porsche down a side street and pulled up to the curb.

"Empty your pockets," he ordered.

"What?" Dante stared at him.

"Empty your pockets," Toscanelli repeated. "Take out everything you have."

Using his good hand and moving with difficulty, Dante produced his mobile phone, the spare pistol magazine, and the screw-on suppressor for the Beretta.

"That's the lot," he said.

"Now get out. Walk back to the main street, pick a place where there are a fair number of people around, and collapse. That'll be the fastest way of getting you to a hospital. But let me remind you of one thing," Toscanelli added, an arctic chill creeping into his voice. "The British police might interview you. I don't know. If they do, you will say nothing about what we have been doing over here. You simply tell them you are an Italian businessman who has been mugged and has had everything stolen, and your arm was broken by your attacker. Once you have been treated, contact the Order and we will make arrangements to get you back to Rome. But tell anybody anything at all about this operation, and I will make it my personal business to find you and silence your tongue for good. Are you completely clear on that?"

Dante nodded, his left hand already reaching for the door handle. "I know the rules. I guarantee my silence."

The moment the injured Italian closed the door, Toscanelli engaged the clutch and drove away, watching Dante walking slowly back along the pavement in his rearview mirror before taking another turning and increasing speed.

Ten minutes later, he abandoned the Porsche in another side street and walked away from the vehicle. He walked on until he found a café, because after the events of today so far, he felt he needed both a drink—strong coffee, nothing alcoholic—and something to eat. The establishment he chose was quiet and situated on a corner not far from the main shopping area. Toscanelli ordered a coffee and a tortellini carbonara.

Once his food and drink had arrived, he checked that nobody else was within earshot, then took out his mobile phone and called the number in Rome. As he had expected, he was answered by the duty agent, but what he hadn't anticipated was that his call was transferred almost immediately to Silvio Vitale.

"Do you have the relic?" Vitale asked immediately in Italian.

"No," Toscanelli replied in the same language. He knew there was no point in sugarcoating the truth, and he quickly sketched out everything that had happened since the last time he and Vitale talked.

"So this team of six men has now been reduced to just you, Toscanelli?" Vitale asked, the scorn evident in his voice. "Four of the other men are dead and the fifth is probably on his way to a hospital to have the bones of his arm screwed back together again. And all this damage and mayhem has been inflicted on you by an English bookseller and his girlfriend. If I said I wasn't very impressed, would you understand exactly what I meant?"

Toscanelli suppressed a slight shiver as he heard the Italian almost whisper the last sentence. Silvio Vitale's rages were legendary, and retribution and punishment swift and without mercy, as he knew only too well. On the other hand, Toscanelli himself had achieved something of a reputation within the order, and he was certainly too important to be metaphorically cast aside, even by Vitale. And there was something that he wanted to flag up immediately.

"I'm not so convinced that this man Jessop is simply a bookseller," he replied. "I've met him, and there was an air of competence about him that for me was completely unexpected. He may be just a bookseller now, but I believe there is probably something else in his background that we know nothing about. And if we had known more about him, then my approach might well have been very different."

There was a brief silence between the two men as Vitale digested the clearly implied criticism of the intelligence the order had managed to obtain about the target. But before Vitale could reply, Toscanelli spoke again.

"But according to Dante, Jessop may not be the more dangerous of the two people. He said that when they confronted them in the clearing, it was Jessop's girlfriend who attacked him. Dante said he and Mario went to pull the couple apart, but when he grabbed the girl she simply spun out of his grip and kicked him once in the arm. That was enough to break both the bones in his lower arm, and she followed it up by kicking his legs out from under him. She's clearly an expert in some kind of martial art, and is quite prepared to use her skills."

"I'm not in the least bit surprised that she used whatever abilities she had to protect herself. Any woman finding herself in that position would have done the same. Now, unless we get extremely lucky, I very much doubt if we'll ever see those two again. There's no point in you remaining in England now. Do your best not to come to the attention of the British authorities, and get yourself on a flight out of London and back to Rome as soon as you can. Since we last spoke, we have made some progress with the decryption and translation, and we expect that you will be retasked very soon." Vitale paused for a moment, apparently gathering his thoughts. "The clues seem to be leading us in an unexpected direction."

"Where?" Toscanelli asked.

"The eastern Mediterranean," Vitale replied. "I'll brief you more fully when you get back."

46

Robin pulled off the M5 Motorway at the Taunton turning, and they drove around the built-up area for a few minutes before selecting a small three-star hotel virtually at random. The only thing Mallory was really concerned about was getting the car out of sight of the road, just in case the Italians had somehow discovered he'd hired it, and that particular establishment had parking behind the building, which made it completely invisible to anybody driving past.

They took two double rooms, paying with cash—they obviously had substantial funds, unwillingly provided by members of the Italian group that had appeared so determined to end their lives—and had an early dinner in the dining room before retiring to Robin's room. There was still a lot of information on the parchment that they didn't understand, and the bulk of it still needed to be decrypted and translated.

Mallory connected his computer to the power supply and opened the lid of his laptop to wake it up again. But before he did anything else, he took out the photocopies of the parchment and looked carefully at them. Quite apart from the symbol derived from the Cistercian monks' number notation system, which they had now managed to decipher, there was something about the encrypted text itself that had been niggling away at his subconscious. Not the text itself, with which they were both now quite familiar, at least in its enciphered format, but something else.

Then he spotted it. For no very obvious reason, some of the letters on the same side of the parchment as the Cistercian symbol had dots underneath them. Not big marks, but large and firm enough to suggest that they were deliberate, and not just the result of a lack of care in the writing.

"Look," Mallory said, gesturing to what he'd found. "These letters have dots below them, maybe to emphasize the words, or perhaps just to draw attention to the letters themselves."

"I hadn't seen that," Robin said. "How many dots have you found?"

"About half a dozen so far. If I call out the words to you, can you write them down?"

That didn't take long, but didn't produce any useful results, so then Mallory just called out the individual letters that had dots underneath them. But, again, that looked like a blind alley. The letters were *P, S, C, S, C, I, T, E, S, I.*

"Means nothing to me," Robin said. "Usually when you get a group of letters like that, they refer to an expression that would have been in common use at the time the document was prepared. Something like *FID DEF* or just *F D*, which you still find on all British coins. That stands for *Fidei Defensor* or 'Defender of the Faith,' and it's actually a part of the title of the reigning monarch. Mind you, there are also a few that have never been cracked."

Mallory was still looking at the photocopy of the parchment, and at the letters. Then he held it a little farther away, and after a few more seconds he nodded.

"I think I might have worked it out," he said, "and actually it's really simple, not much of a code at all. It looks to me like a combination of the letters themselves and where they're positioned on the sheet of parchment, which letters they've chosen, I mean. So it's not actually a string of ten letters, but five separate groups of two letters arranged in a very specific shape, like this."

He took a clean sheet of paper and quickly jotted down the letters in the format he had just suggested, one group on the first line, three on the second, and the last one on the third line, so forming a rough diamond shape:

$$PS$$
$$CS \quad CI \quad TE$$
$$SI$$

"I'm none the wiser," Robin said. "You're obviously seeing something I'm not."

"I've put the letters together in pairs, but their positions are pretty accurate. The shape of the letters forms a cross, that's the first thing, a cross with equal-length arms, which is very much like the *croix pattée* used by the Knights Templar. And I think the letters are nothing more than the first and last letters of each word in the official name of the order: *Pauperes commilitones Christi Templique Solomonici*, so that gives us *PS CS CI TE SI*. It's just another hint to get us thinking the right way, to confirm that the parchment contains information about the Templars. And I'll bet that when we finally crack the code that will let us decipher the rest of the text, the code word will be something specific to the order."

Mallory paused for a moment, then pulled out another of the pieces of paper they'd been working on earlier and scanned what they'd written on it. "I thought so. This is yet another pointer toward the Templars. You remember that the first section of the document used the Atbash cipher with different shifts. If you take the first letter generated by each new shift, you get *P C C T S* in sequence, the five initial letters of the full name of the Templar order. Whoever wrote this was making sure there were plenty of clues incorporated in the first part of the text to help steer anyone trying to decode it in the right direction. So now all we have to do is work out what word or words they used as the cipher text in the Atbash cipher so that we can decode the rest of the encrypted text."

"Are you sure that's the answer?"

"No," Mallory replied, "but at the moment that's the only thing that makes sense to me. Why would the author of this text leave so many clues pointing to the Knights Templar unless the key to the cipher text was something to do with the order? We already know that the bulk of the message can't be decoded using the normal Atbash cipher, because we've tried every possible variant, so the word or words used have to be something other than just the alphabet, written in either direction."

"So what words do you think we should try?" Robin asked.

"Well, the most obvious ones to start with are the names of things and people that were definitively associated with the Knights Templar. Things like the *Beauseant*—that's the name of the Templar battle flag—and the important individuals associated with it, people like Hugues de Payens and Jacques de Molay, the two men who were respectively the originator of the order and its last grand master, and Bernard of Clairvaux, whose treatise about fighting a just war was so important to the growth of the order. That document was called *De Laude Novae Militiae.*"

"That translates as 'In praise of the new knighthood,' " Robin interrupted.

"Exactly, and that's another possible set of words we could try. Doing a bit of lateral thinking, we could also try things like the names of the reigning pope when the order was established—he was Innocent the Second—perhaps along with the Latin *Omne Datum Optimum,* the name of the papal bull he issued that exempted the Templars from paying taxes and essentially allowed the order to grow as quickly as it did. We can implement all those suggestions by themselves or in combination with each other, but probably the first, the simplest, and certainly the most obvious group of words we should try is the Latin name of the order itself: *Pauperes commilitones Christi Templique Solomonici.*"

Robin nodded.

"That makes sense," she said. "Let's give it a try."

47

Devon

Inspector Paul Wilson walked from the metaled surface of the lane into the small clearing a few miles to the west of Exeter. He stopped just outside the blue-and-white police tape that had already been positioned around the unmoving figure on the ground. He scratched his head, not easy to do when wearing both latex gloves and a Tyvek oversuit that included a hood, and turned to look at the man beside him.

"Tell me what happened," he said.

"This lane's popular with dog walkers, sir," the uniformed sergeant replied, and pointed to one side of the open area where an elderly man wearing a pair of brown corduroy trousers and a Barbour jacket was sitting in the rear seat of a police patrol car, the door open. On the ground beside him, and securely linked to the man's left hand by a long leather lead, sat a male black Labrador, waiting with the gentle and unmoving patience that only dogs ever seem able to display.

"That's Jeremy Young. He'd let his dog—its name is

Sebastian, and I've no idea why—off the lead at the far end of this copse, and it ran ahead of him and into this clearing. According to Mr. Young, Sebastian just stopped dead and started barking. Wouldn't stop, and so he came in after him and found the body. He had his mobile with him, so he dialed triple nine and then just waited for us to arrive."

Wilson glanced across at the man, who was leaning back in the seat and chatting to a uniformed constable.

"He seems quite relaxed, bearing in mind he's just stumbled over a corpse."

"He's retired now, but he was a doctor, sir, so this obviously isn't the first dead body he's ever seen. Probably buried a few of his patients over the years."

Wilson nodded. "Right, make sure we get all his contact details and a full statement, and then he and Sebastian can carry on with their walk."

Wilson ducked under the tape and took a few steps forward to where another man, also wearing a full body suit, was kneeling beside the body, an open black case beside him. The man glanced back over his shoulder as the inspector approached.

"Good evening, Paul," he said. "Quite clear-cut, at least as far as the cause of death is concerned. He was shot at virtually point-blank range with a pistol. Even with the naked eye I can see some evidence of powder burns on his chest, and at that range the bullet went right through him."

"I don't know why," Wilson said, "but I have a feeling there's a 'but' heading my way."

Reginald Barnes—he'd known Wilson for a couple of years—nodded and grinned.

"Just a tiny peculiarity I need to explain to you," he replied. "When somebody is shot in the chest, death is almost instantaneous, for obvious reasons, and in almost every case the body will fall backwards. But in this case I think the victim was killed while he was lying on the ground, first because of the contained area of bleeding, and also because of the bullet."

"The bullet?"

"In a moment. When I arrived, the body was lying on its front. Once I'd confirmed death, I took a good look around the corpse, and there are definite signs of blood-stains on the ground right beside it."

Barnes pointed to a discolored reddish patch a short distance away from the body.

"I rolled him the other way," Barnes pointed out, "when I put him on his back to continue my examination. So the obvious conclusion is—"

"That the murderer probably moved him after the killing took place," Wilson interrupted. "Or at least rolled him over onto his chest. But why would he have done that?"

"You're the detective, not me, but I can make an educated guess. I said the bullet passed right through his body, and you can clearly see an exit wound in the middle of his back. But I haven't found any rips or tears in the fabric of his jacket, and my guess is that the killer saw that as well when he turned him over. The bullet probably only just made it through the chest of the corpse—he was a very heavily built man with good musculature, and that would have slowed the passage of the projectile—but because he was lying on the ground it ended up trapped between the exit wound and his clothing. It's not there now, so my guess it's either in the killer's pocket or maybe at the bottom of a river somewhere."

"If you're right, that's totally buggered up any chance we have of solving this," Wilson said sourly.

"There's something else as well," Barnes said. "You know I did the posts on the three corpses found in Dartmouth? It may just be nothing more than a coincidence, but I did happen to notice that this man is wearing an Italian-made suit, just like those three were, and there's nothing at all in his pockets apart from a packet of tissues. No wallet, no passport, nothing at all. He's also physically similar to those three, the same kind of tanned complexion and black hair. Obviously none of that's conclusive, but I was wondering if perhaps this man was a part of the same group. You did tell me, if you remember, that the first three were part of a group of six Italians who flew into Exeter in a private jet the other day."

Wilson shook his head.

"Bugger me," he muttered. "If you're right, that means four of them are now dead. That's not going to do much for British-Italian relations, is it? And why the hell are they flying over to Devon to be killed? Why couldn't they shoot each other back in Tuscany or wherever they've come from?"

"As I said, Paul, you're the detective."

"Thanks, Reg. It looks like this is going to be another very long day."

48

Over two hours after they'd started trying to decipher the encrypted text, and having tried a number of different code words and combinations, Mallory took yet another sheet of paper and wrote out the alphabet in a horizontal line across the top, placing each letter in a box with another box directly underneath each one. Then he checked the spelling and copied the first twenty-six letters of the expression *Pauperes commilitones Christi Templique Solomonici* directly below it, finishing with the letter *t* in *Christi*.

A	B	C	D	E	F	G	H	I	J	K	L	M	N	O	P	Q	R	S	T	U	V	W	X	Y	Z
P	A	U	P	E	R	E	S	C	O	M	M	I	L	I	T	O	N	E	S	C	H	R	I	S	T

"I don't think that's going to work," Robin said. "You've got the letters *e*, *i*, and *s* occurring three times in the code word, as well as several other duplicates. That's bound to cause confusion, isn't it?"

Mallory nodded. "Yes, but it shouldn't make much difference because the worst-case scenario is that we'll have to try two or three different letters when we're decoding a particular word. Just as an example, in English the word *sword* would come out as *erinp*, which is fine. But I agree there are a lot of duplicates if these are the right code words. For example, the letter *E* in the encrypted text can stand for *E* in the plaintext, which is unusual in itself, or *G* or *S*. But I would have thought that when you're looking at a decrypted word, it would be fairly obvious which of the three possible options will be the correct letter. Of course, if we don't get anywhere we'll have to think again and try some more different code words. In fact, there's an argument that having multiple possible solutions for an encrypted letter adds a further layer of security to the cipher text, because somebody decoding it might find that a particular word comes out as gibberish, and decide that he's got the wrong code words. Anyway, let's see what we've got here."

They worked as a team, Robin reading out the Latin words of the encrypted message letter by letter and pausing when it looked as if she had reached the end of a sentence. Mallory copied down each letter, then used the table he'd prepared to try to decode the original for Robin to translate. It didn't prove to be as difficult as they had expected, and within half an hour they'd managed to decipher the next section of the encrypted text. As Mallory had predicted, although some letters in the cipher text did have two or even three possible solutions, in almost every case it was very quickly obvious which was the right letter to use. Where there was any ambiguity, he simply placed all the possible letters in a vertical line in the correct place in the word.

Then Robin translated the Latin into English, and read out what it said.

The first section of the encrypted text trod ground

that was already quite familiar to Mallory. It was essentially a summary that explained what had happened to the members of the order in the winter of 1307, beginning with the incredible duplicity of Philip the Fair of France, who had actually invited Jacques de Molay to be a pallbearer at the funeral of his sister on the twelfth of October, the day before the mass arrests of the Knights Templar took place.

The orders for the arrests had been sent out weeks or months earlier, and the author of the text was incredulous that the king of France could be so calculatingly evil as to extend the hand of friendship to Jacques de Molay—in those days to be a pallbearer was not only a great honor, but also a duty that would normally only be performed by a family member or by an extremely close friend of that family—when he absolutely knew that within less than twenty-four hours that same man would be incarcerated in his own dungeon and facing an agonizing and painful death.

It was absolutely clear, the writer went on, that King Philip was motivated by nothing more than greed, and had conceived of the plan to destroy the Knights Templar order simply as a way of resolving his own crippling financial problems. And that, the author added, was the firm opinion of most of Philip's court, as well as almost everybody associated with the Templars.

"That's interesting," Mallory said, after Robin had read out the last part of that particular passage. "There's been something of a debate over the last hundred years or so about what was driving Philip to take the action he did. Opinion is pretty much split between two conflicting suggestions. Some people believe that because Philip himself was extremely religious, and he had heard from witnesses who had attended Templar ceremonies that they practiced heresy as a matter of course, he decided with the typical arrogance of people committed to a particular religious outlook that he was right and they, obviously, were wrong. And when anyone subscribes to that view, it's only a fairly small step to take to have the people you believe to be heretics put to death for the good of their immortal souls.

"In medieval times, that was a valid argument, but what it really doesn't explain is why the arrests of the members of the Knights Templar order were so impressively coordinated and conducted in a single swoop. If Philip really believed the Templars were worshipping false gods and as a good Christian he wanted to help them, then surely he should have begun arresting them immediately, again for the good of their souls, and he certainly shouldn't have allowed the leader of such a bunch of heretics—Jacques de Molay, the chief heretic, if you like—to even attend his sister's funeral, far less be a pallbearer at it."

Robin nodded. "You're right. That argument really doesn't make sense. But if he was actually after the Templar treasury, trying to keep Jacques de Molay in particular in the dark about his plans would have been a good move tactically. He would have kept the element of surprise and allowed his men to seize the wealth of the order, which would probably have been more than enough to bail him out of a financial mess he had got himself into. And I suppose that's more or less the opposing argument that's been suggested?"

"Absolutely right, and these days I don't think that most people who've done any research on the subject have much doubt that his motive was purely financial. And I do find it interesting that this piece of text, which from what we've already translated looks as if it's more or less contemporary with the end of the Templars, supports that view."

Then they started decoding the next section, and that produced more of a surprise. Robin was still reading out the encoded words, letter by letter, which Mallory was then transcribing onto paper before referring to the At-bash cipher text to pick out the appropriate plaintext letters. That produced the Latin plaintext, very little of which he could understand, and he then passed the paper to Robin to translate the Latin into English.

"I hadn't expected this," Robin said, when she'd finished that section. "Just listen to what it says."

In a very matter-of-fact way, the next section of the text revealed that the sudden and unexpected attack on the Templar strongholds throughout France had certainly been sudden, but it had definitely not been unexpected. The order, the writer claimed, had agents everywhere, including somebody inside the court of Philip the Fair, and the Templar hierarchy had actually known about the impending arrests and seizures almost as soon as the king had formulated his plans.

"That does make sense," Mallory said. "The Templars essentially formed an independent state with its headquarters in France, and like every state it would have needed to know what was going on in the neighboring countries. For the Templars, because they were mainly based in France, they were quite literally surrounded by potential enemies, so good and accurate information would have been even more important to them. Intelligence has always been the lifeblood of diplomacy: before any government is able to react to a particular situation, it needs to know as much as possible about the intentions of the other party. It would have been really surprising if the Templars hadn't had spies, or at the very least a number of powerful and influential sympathizers, in the French court."

"So that does rather make you wonder why the Templars didn't do more to resist when French troops came knocking on the doors of their commanderies."

Mallory shook his head. "I don't know that there was a lot they could have done. Although the Templar order was an extremely powerful military force, it was also quite well dispersed, with troops in Britain, Spain, Portugal, Italy, Germany, and Cyprus. But even if Jacques de Molay had recalled all of his knights, it's still unlikely that they could have resisted the French army for very long. Don't forget that they were essentially guests in France, surrounded by enemy territory, and there was no way that any of the Templar fortifications could have resisted a siege, because the French would just have starved them out. In the circumstances, unless Jacques de Molay could somehow have ordered all the Templars to leave the country—and that's something that certainly couldn't have been achieved without King Philip noticing and doing his best to stop the exodus—they would just have had to stay and face the music."

"But according to this, de Molay did actually do something to at least minimize the damage the mass seizures and arrests would cause to the order."

She read out the next section of the translated text, which described how secret orders had been sent out by the grand master to his most senior knights during the late summer and early autumn of 1307. Those orders, according to the document they were studying, had given the most explicit instructions for the removal of the vast bulk of the coins, precious metals, and jewels that were held by the Knights Templar as security for their international banking activities.

The same instructions also specified what action should be taken to ensure the safety of the Templar archives, the vast collection of deeds and titles to properties located throughout Europe, which were ultimately far more valuable than the more conventional forms of treasure that the order held. Finally the document added, many of the more senior Knights Templar had been ordered to remove themselves from the various fortifications in France and do their best to avoid all contact with French troops. They were to leave the commanderies and preceptories as anonymously as possible, and certainly not while wearing any of the regalia by which the Templars were so easily recognized, but were also to ensure that they retained possession of their arms and armor and were to hold themselves in readiness for any summons that might be issued by the grand master. None of these instructions were to be questioned by the recipients, but were simply to be acknowledged verbally to the courier who had delivered them.

"It sounds like de Molay did as much as he could in the circumstances," Mallory said. "There have been suspicions for a long time that the Templars did know about the impending raids at least a few weeks before they took place, but this is the first piece of contemporary documentary evidence I've heard of that actually confirms it. Whatever else we find when we've finished all the decoding, this piece of parchment is going to be a valuable addition to the information we have about the demise of the Templar order."

"The other thing I've noticed about the way this text is written is that it's describing events that took place sometime in the past," Robin said. "I don't believe that this parchment was prepared as early as 1307, but probably several months or maybe even years afterward. Obviously I can't be sure about that, because the text itself is undated, but I get the feeling that the author was providing this as background information before going on to talk about something else. And I'm not even sure that it was written by a member of the Knights Templar."

"You could be right about that. Not all of the most senior members of the order were literate—they were fighting men, not scribes—and in all probability what we're looking at could well have been penned by a monk, possibly even by a member of the Cistercian order, acting on the verbal instructions of one of the senior Templars who had managed to escape. But I do think from what we've seen already that this information did come from the higher levels of the organization, from somebody who knew exactly what had gone on in the lead-up to October 1307."

The next section provided an immediate confirmation of Robin's deduction, because it described in harrowing detail what happened seven years later. Jacques de Molay and Geoffroi de Charney, the Templar preceptor of Normandy, had both confessed to whatever the Dominican monks who acted as the pope's inquisitors had wanted them to say, and had been forced to do so by the most appalling and inhuman tortures. They had then been ordered to publicly renounce their heresy in Paris. In return for this very public and humiliating admission of guilt, Philip the Fair had agreed that they would spend the rest of their lives in prison, as a kind of "mercy" that would, in reality, be simply a lingering and singularly unpleasant death.

But on the day both de Molay and de Charney refused to obey their captors. On a scaffold that had been erected in front of Notre Dame, they instead proclaimed to the assembled multitude that both they personally and the order of the Knights Templar wholly and collectively were entirely innocent of any and all of the charges that had been leveled against them and to which they had confessed simply to relieve their agony in the torture chambers of the French king.

"They obviously both knew what was going to happen to them," Robin said, after she'd read out the last translated sentence of the decrypted text. The calm and almost matter-of-fact way in which the events of 1314 had been described had sobered them both.

"Renouncing a confession meant that the two men were considered, in the eyes of both the Church and the law, to be relapsed heretics," Mallory said quietly, "and they were immediately handed over by their Dominican jailers to the secular authorities for punishment. According to what I've read elsewhere, when the news was delivered to Philip the Fair he was incandescent with rage, and ordered the matter to be resolved without delay. For any relapsed heretic, there was only one suitable punishment, and no further trials or hearings were required.

"On the evening of that same day they were taken out to a small island in the river Seine, where a pile of wood had been hastily prepared and laid around a substantial wooden post. The two men were chained to this post and the fire lit beneath them. As a final sick refinement, the executioners had been ordered to use the driest wood they could find."

Mallory paused for a moment and glanced across at Robin. She nodded for him to continue.

"In those days, death by burning included a number of refinements, some designed to be merciful and others the complete opposite. The bodies of some victims were burned, certainly, but they were actually dead before the fire was even started, because they were strangled, garroted, or stabbed by the executioner after a payment was made to him by either the victim or the condemned person's family or friends.

"You have to remember that in most cases the executioner was not paid by the state or by whoever had authorized the death of the man or woman. Instead the victim was expected to pay the executioner's charges. I know that sounds a bit sick, and in fact it is, but at least if the victim did hand over a bag of money, he or she could reasonably expect that death would be quick, even if it wasn't painless. No payment, or not enough money offered, could mean that the executioner would take three or four blows to behead his victim, instead of one clean stroke with his ax or sword."

Robin shuddered.

"I am thankful that I'm living in the present century," she said. "This is fascinating, even if it is morbidly appalling. So some people were killed beforehand, that's what you're saying?"

"Yes. In other cases, a friend of the victim would stand somewhere near the fire and attempt to shoot him with a bow and arrow as soon as the fire had been started. That was dangerous for the person attempting it, because it was illegal: the victim was expected to suffer. There were also cases where a bag of gunpowder was hung around the neck of the condemned person, the idea being that it would explode when the flames reached it, but apparently this was only rarely successful. By the time the flames reached the powder, the victim would already be in agony, and there was a good chance that the gunpowder would simply flare up, possibly killing him quicker but making him suffer even more in the process. Tying the victim to the stake with ropes was also a kind of mercy, because when they burned through, he would probably collapse into the flames and die a little bit quicker."

"You said for these two men that they were held in place with chains."

"Yes. That would ensure that they would remain upright until the flames had consumed them, keeping them alive and in agony for the longest possible time. The use of dry wood was also calculated to prolong their suffering. If wet wood was used, it would produce clouds of smoke that would choke the victims possibly even before their flesh began to burn. But choosing dry wood ensured that they would literally be roasted alive, and that they would remain burning in the flames for perhaps as long as an hour.

"There was a case I read about in England during the Marian Persecutions—when Protestants were persecuted for their religious beliefs—where the condemned man suffered in the flames for some three-quarters of an hour, the gunpowder trick having failed to work, and for much of that time he was pleading with the onlookers to fan the flames of the fire so that his suffering would end all the quicker."

When Mallory finished speaking, Robin was silent for a few moments, her eyes misty with unshed tears.

"You know," she said finally, "I really believe that more atrocities have been perpetrated in the name of some organized religion than by every atheist and nonbeliever who has ever lived. I think you could argue that every religion is inherently evil, simply because of the way that committed believers absolutely know that they and they alone are right and therefore everybody else is wrong. It's even happening today with militant Islam condemning everything that Christianity stands for, while equally militant Christians do precisely the same thing, condemning all Muslims."

Mallory nodded.

"I have to confess," he said, "that I can't think of any recent atrocity perpetrated in the name of militant atheism. But you're right. I can name dozens of horrendous acts of violence carried out by one group of believers against another group of people just because they didn't happen to share those same beliefs. And that's all they are: beliefs, not facts. It's never about facts where religion is concerned. Anyway," he added, "that was pretty much the end of the Knights Templar, at least as far as we know. Unless this parchment is going to tell us that somehow the order managed to survive, of course."

"We'll find out in a few minutes, I hope," Robin said. "Wasn't there some kind of curse made by Jacques de Molay on the day he died? Something about King Philip and the pope dying as well?"

Mallory shook his head. "There was a legend to that effect, yes, and it's certainly true that Pope Clement died in April of the following year, 1315, after a long illness, and Philip the Fair died in November after falling from a horse, and those two unrelated events were probably the origin of the story. It looks as if the myth of the curse began in 1330 with an Italian writer named Feretto de Ferretis, but he stated that the curse was issued by an unidentified Knight Templar, not by de Molay. But in the mid–sixteenth century the French historian Paul Émile claimed that the words had been spoken by the last grand master himself."

Robin was looking at Mallory with a puzzled expression on her face.

"What?" he asked.

"I asked you before," she said, "but you never gave

me an answer. How come you're so knowledgeable about the Knights Templar? Most people probably know a bit about the order, but every time we talk about it you come up with chapter and verse. That's more than just a casual interest."

Mallory nodded and smiled at her, looking almost embarrassed.

"Two reasons," he said. "In my spare time I'm writing—or I'm trying to write—a book about them, so I've got reams of information about the Templars on my computer that I'm trying to knock into some sort of order. And I've got a pretty good memory for facts."

"That's one reason," Robin said. "What's the other?"

Mallory looked uncomfortable.

"I'm going to keep that to myself for the moment," he said. "It's personal, and it's something I'm still working on. Once I've resolved it, I promise I'll tell you."

Robin nodded. "Okay. I'll hold you to that."

"Anyway," Mallory went on, "the other thing that does support what's claimed in this parchment, about the order having been forewarned about the French plan, is that when Philip the Fair's troops and officials gained access to the Paris preceptory of the Knights Templar to seize the treasure, they found that the cupboard was very largely bare. The same story was repeated at most of the other Templar establishments throughout France. The treasure Philip was hoping to grab simply wasn't there, and the obvious implication is that the order knew about the impending raids and had already moved it to a place of safety.

"That's one thing, and there's also a problem with the numbers. In 1307, the Templars probably numbered well over fifteen thousand—some estimates have put the figure as high as fifty thousand—but only a few hundred

Templars were actually arrested. The reality is that most of the order and the vast majority of its treasure and assets simply weren't there when the seizures took place. I've always believed they had foreknowledge of what was going to happen, and it's great that the text on this parchment confirms that. Of course, what we still don't know is where the knights went, or what happened to their treasure."

"Well, maybe that is the actual purpose of this piece of text, to explain that," Robin suggested. "After all, what we've seen so far in this translation has been interesting but certainly not earth-shattering, and certainly not important enough information to have required the protection offered by that book safe. Perhaps this really is a written treasure map, and at the end of it we'll find out exactly where to look."

She said it with a smile, but there was just enough of a serious tone in her voice for Mallory to realize that she wasn't joking. Or not entirely, anyway.

"Then we'd better get on with it and decode the rest," he replied, "but I really don't think we can do any more tonight. It's nearly midnight, my brain hurts, and I can feel my eyes closing. And we need to decide about France. Are we going to cross the Channel and, if so, how?"

"Yes, I think we should visit the land of the cheese-eating surrender monkeys. And tomorrow morning I'll tell you how we're going to get there."

49

Southern England

They were up and having breakfast in the hotel's dining room just after eight thirty the next morning, and were ready to leave by nine.

"You still think France is the best option?" Robin asked as they placed their bags in the trunk of the car a few minutes later. "I mean, if we just want to go to ground somewhere, what's wrong with Wales, or Scotland, or even London? Sometimes the best place to hide is in a crowd."

"Nothing," Mallory admitted, "and we could still do that. But we now know for certain that that parchment is something to do with the Knights Templar, and that order began its life in France and was ultimately destroyed in France. We still have no idea what other secrets the text will reveal, but it wouldn't surprise me if it involved some part of that country, and if we have to go further afield than that, it's a whole lot easier to travel in Europe because of Schengen. There simply are no border controls anymore."

Robin nodded.

"Right. In that case I need to make a phone call," she said, and pulled out the cheap mobile she'd bought in the phone shop in Exeter. She checked a page in a small diary with a silver cover, tapped out the number on the keypad, and pressed the button to make the call.

She exchanged greetings with the man she'd called—Mallory gathered his name was Justin—and the conversation that followed seemed both inconsequential and pointless.

When she ended the call, she smiled at Mallory.

"Who was that?" he asked.

"That was the man who's going to help us get to France."

"Your boyfriend?" Mallory felt a pang of jealousy as he asked the question.

"No. He'd like to be, but he's a bit too much of a hooray Henry for my liking. Too much breeding, too much money, and too many teeth, but not enough brains or guts. He's got a Porsche as well, as a matter of fact. Two of them, at the last count, plus an Aston and a selection of other high-priced automobiles. He owns most of the bits of Cornwall that Prince Charles doesn't."

Mallory felt unaccountably irritated that she'd called him, which didn't make sense because he had no relationship with Robin Jessop other than having been unavoidably thrown together with her because of the book safe and the ancient manuscript.

"So, what's he going to do?" he asked, somewhat sulkily.

"Not a lot, to be ruthlessly honest, but he will be lending us one of his assets."

"What?"

"I'll do better than tell you: I'll show you. Let's get on the road."

Knowing how competent Robin was behind the wheel, Mallory would have been quite happy sitting in the passenger seat, but she simply shook her head when he offered her the keys.

"You drive," she said. "I get bored if I have to stick to the speed limit."

"Yes. I've noticed that," he said. "Where to?"

Robin leaned forward and spent a minute or so programming the Citroën's GPS.

"There you are," she said, leaning back. "Now just do exactly what the nice lady in that box of electronic tricks tells you to do."

"I don't know if 'nice lady' is an accurate description," Mallory replied. "All the women who live in GPSs sound horribly like one of my old schoolteachers, except that they don't rap me over the knuckles with a ruler every time I take a wrong turn. They just tell me they're recalculating the route, with a kind of weary resignation in their voices."

The programmed route took them out of Taunton, and over the M5 Motorway, which surprised Mallory.

"I think we're heading more or less south," he said. "Is that right?"

"Yes." Robin nodded. "We're going to a place called Dunkeswell."

"Never heard of it."

Within quite a short time the roads grew narrower and the going slower, and occasionally Mallory had to stop the car and pull to the side to allow a larger vehicle to pass in the opposite direction.

"It is a bit inaccessible," Robin admitted as they waited for a cement truck to edge past. "There is another, very easy way to get there, but I'm afraid we can't use it."

Mallory suspected she was deliberately teasing him,

playing on the fact that he genuinely had no idea where they were going or what she'd got planned, but he responded anyway. "I'm sure you're dying to tell me, so I'll ask the question. Why can't we go that way?"

She smiled mischievously.

"Because we haven't got the right equipment," she said.

About ten minutes after that, Mallory suddenly realized what she was hinting at as he saw a light aircraft turning to the left a mile or so in front of the car.

"Ah, now I get it," he said. "Dunkeswell is an airfield, isn't it? And the easiest way to get there is to fly?"

"Exactly."

"And is this Justin guy going to meet us there?"

"Not exactly," Robin replied, and refused to elaborate.

Mallory followed the signs to the large free car park located near the entrance to the airfield, found a vacant space, and slotted the DS3 into it.

"Now what?" he asked.

"Now we take to the air."

They grabbed their bags from the trunk, and Robin led the way over to the aircraft park, where a number of small, mainly single-engine, aircraft were clustered on the hard standing. She stopped at the edge of the parking area and lowered her weekend bag to the ground.

"Just hang on here," she said, and vanished in the direction of what looked like an office. A few minutes later she walked back, a key in her hand, picked up her bag, and led the way over to a high-winged single-engine monoplane wearing blue-and-white livery, which also had a small armorial symbol painted on the door.

"That's Justin's coat of arms," she said, noticing Mallory glancing at it. "He's got some kind of title, but I can't remember what it is."

"So this is his aircraft?" Mallory asked as Robin un-locked the cabin door and lifted her bag up to lodge it inside.

"Yes."

"So who's going to fly it?"

"Me," Robin said simply.

"But I thought you told me you didn't have a license?"

"No. I told you my PPL had lapsed because I hadn't flown enough hours recently. It's only a bit of paper," she went on, "and by the time I land this thing I'll probably have done enough hours to renew it for this year."

"Does Justin know your license has expired?" Mallory persisted. "Are you qualified to fly it?"

"No, of course he doesn't know, but he probably wouldn't care if he did. Look, flying's like driving or rid-ing a bike. Just because my license is out of date doesn't mean I've lost the skills. And you'd be amazed at what I've got licenses for. Now shut up, get the rest of the bags stowed in the cabin behind the front seats, and then strap yourself in."

"Which one?"

"Unless you're planning on driving it yourself, the right-hand seat."

"What are you going to do?"

"The external preflight checks, of course. Tires, con-trol surfaces, checking for leaks, all that kind of thing."

By the time Mallory had tucked everything away and done up his straps, Robin was already climbing inside the aircraft. She sat down in the left-hand seat and put the key in what looked remarkably like an ignition switch.

Mallory watched in silence as she then continued what was obviously a very familiar sequence of internal pre-flight checks, moving the rudder pedals and the control column—he had read just enough about flying to know that it wasn't called a joystick—for full and free movement and checking all the gauges and instruments before she started the engine.

The propeller spun somewhat jerkily for a couple of revolutions before the engine caught, sending a sudden puff of blue smoke into the air, then settling down to a steady roar. She again checked that all instrument indications were normal, then pulled on a headset and gestured for Mallory to do the same.

As soon as he did so, the noise from the engine was enormously reduced, and he could also hear Robin talking on the radio, the selector display of which showed a frequency of 123.475.

"Dunkeswell, this is Golf Sierra Tango in the park requesting taxi instructions for a cross-country navex."

"Good morning, Sierra Tango. Taxi for runway two two on QFE 1008. Call at the holding point for two two left."

"Two two left on QFE 1008. Thank you, Dunkeswell."

"To save you asking a whole lot of irritating questions," Robin said, altering the setting on the altimeter subscale before releasing the parking brake and goosing the throttle to start the aircraft moving, "a navex is a navigational exercise, a normal training evolution, which usually means flying a triangular pattern around three airfields. Two two zero degrees is the magnetic heading of the runway, and you have to fly a left-hand circuit from it. The QFE is the local pressure setting that means the altimeter will read zero feet on the ground here, which helps when you're landing but isn't so important when you're taking off, obviously. And we've got clearance to taxi to the runway, but not to enter it."

Mallory looked at her.

"And Golf Sierra Tango?" he asked.

"The aircraft's registration number, which is also its call sign. Nothing clever there. I didn't memorize it or anything. It's printed right here." She pointed at the control panel in front of her, on which the full registration number was displayed.

"Too much information," he said. "This is all new to me, and I'm not taking it all in. What type of aircraft is this, by the way? I mean, is it reliable and all that?"

Robin nodded but didn't take her eyes off the view through the windshield as she taxied toward the runway.

"It's a Cessna 172 Skyhawk," she replied, "and it's the most successful aircraft ever in terms of the total number built. Cessna has knocked out over sixty thousand of these babies, and it's been around since the mid–nineteen fifties, though this one's only eight or nine years old. So, yes, it is reliable, very."

A few minutes later she braked the Cessna to a stop on the taxiway a few yards short of the entrance to the runway and carried out further checks there.

"Pretakeoff checks," she said to Mallory, then depressed the transmit button again. "Dunkeswell, Golf Sierra Tango, holding short of two two left."

"Sierra Tango. Take off. Wind light and variable, regional pressure setting 1014."

"Roger, Dunkeswell. Sierra Tango."

Robin opened the throttle again, and the Cessna eased forward. She turned it left onto the center of the runway, and opened the throttle all the way. The tarmac rushed past with increasing speed, the aircraft bouncing slightly over uneven sections of the runway, and then the plane gave a small lurch and was airborne.

Robin continued climbing straight ahead to eight hundred feet, the circuit height, then turned left to head away from the airfield.

"Dunkeswell, Golf Sierra Tango is continuing VFR en route. Good day, sir."

"Clear to continue VFR. Squawk 4321."

"Four-three-two-one, Sierra Tango."

Robin did something to a box just to the left of her.

"That's a setting on the secondary surveillance radar transponder," she said. "It just means that any radar unit that detects us will read a 4321 squawk and know that we're a real aircraft, not an angel or anything, and that we're not in receipt of a radar service from anyone."

"I'm not even going to ask what an angel is," Mallory said, "but what's VFR?"

"Visual flight rules. It means we do our own navigation, take our own separation from other aircraft, basically just do our own thing. And an angel is a slang term for anomalous propagation, usually an atmospheric effect that can produce returns on a radar screen that look just like aircraft but aren't."

Mallory nodded slowly as the Cessna continued climbing and opened out to the east. It was a clear and bright day, the few clouds high and well dispersed, and visibility was excellent. He'd never been in a light aircraft before, and the appeal of it was immediately obvious, the experience exhilarating.

"Well, it's good of this Justin guy to let you borrow his aircraft," he said.

Robin was silent for just a second or two too long.

"What?" Mallory asked.

"He didn't actually say I could borrow it, not in so many words. I rang him up to see where he was and what he was doing over the next week or two. When I found out he was going to be stuck in Cornwall for a while doing bits of estate business, I knew he wouldn't miss his Cessna."

"You mean you nicked it?" Mallory asked. "We're flying around in a stolen aircraft?"

"I think calling it 'stolen' is a bit strong. He'll be getting it back, after all. It's more kind of temporarily TWOC'd."

"Twocked?"

"Taken without owner's consent, that sort of thing. A common expression in the police force, I understand."

Mallory stared at her for a moment, then looked out through the windshield again, a slow smile spreading across his face. "In view of everything else that's happened over the last couple of days, I suppose flying about the countryside in a hot aircraft is the least of our worries. So, what the hell? Fly me to France, Robin."

50

Southern England and France

They landed at Biggin Hill in Kent, the old Second World War fighter base, affectionately known as "Biggin on the Bump," to refuel.

Once they'd touched down, Robin steered the Cessna over to what looked a bit like a regular petrol station, albeit with very wide spaces in front of the two pumps, and switched off the aircraft's engine.

"Use my card," Mallory said, "just in case there's a watch order out on yours."

Twenty minutes later, having also used Mallory's Visa card to pay the landing fees, Robin taxied the Cessna back toward the active runway, and minutes after that they were airborne again.

"What about French customs and immigration?" Mallory asked as they climbed through five thousand feet and Robin turned the plane onto a southeasterly heading. "Won't we have to clear them in France?"

"That really depends on how good a lunch the men in peaked caps have had, in my experience. I filed a flight plan when we paid the landing fees at Biggin Hill, stating that we were flying to Le Touquet, which is the closest French airport to Kent. I've flown in there a few times, and usually there's been nobody about apart from a man demanding a fistful of folding money for landing fees. I know Justin quite often nips over there for lunch as well, which means this aircraft is something of a regular visitor, so hopefully we won't attract too much attention."

"So we are going to Le Touquet?"

"Oh yes. Not complying with a filed flight plan is a very good way of attracting official attention really quickly. And we have to land somewhere, obviously. I guess we can just hire a car there and then disappear into the French countryside while we work out what to do next."

Two hours later, with the Cessna fully fueled, chocked, and locked in the aircraft park at Le Touquet, they were sitting in a hired Renault Mégane and had just turned south onto the nontoll coastal autoroute at Abbeville. Robin had the map book open on her lap and was looking at the area down to the southeast of Rouen.

"We can start looking for a hotel somewhere quiet once we get past Rouen. According to the map, it's about a hundred kilometers—roughly sixty miles—away, so it's only about an hour's drive. We'll come off the autoroute once we leave Rouen, and there's bound to be a halfway decent hotel somewhere between Louviers and Évreux."

"Sounds good. We just have to remember that this is France, and the French have pretty rigid ideas about timing. A lot of hotels won't accept new arrivals after about eight in the evening, and that's also usually the last possible time you can sit down to dinner, so ideally we need to find a place by seven."

"You're kidding."

"I'm not. I've been caught out before, driving through France. Some hotels actually lock their doors in the evening to dissuade unexpected paying guests, though I think they've lightened up a bit since the economic crisis started. But there are always places we can stay at any hour. There's a chain called Formula One, for example, and you can get in to those at any hour of the day or night using a credit card, but by all accounts they're pretty basic but very cheap. None of the comforts of home, I mean, but at least you get a bedroom, and they're usually clean. My favorites are the Logis de France. They're usually small places, family-run, and often quite quirky. But in my experience you get a decent meal, and the owners are very friendly, at least by French standards."

Robin was silent for a few moments, and when she spoke again her voice was tinged with concern.

"I've been thinking," she said, "and I hate to remind you about this, but back in the wood you killed that Italian, or at least helped him shoot himself. I know he absolutely deserved it because of what we're pretty sure the two of them planned to do to us, and I don't really have any problems with that. But even if it wasn't your finger on the trigger, if you hadn't been there, he would still be alive. Are you sure the police can't pin that on you?"

Mallory shook his head.

"That's why I took the extra few seconds to recover the bullet and the cartridge case," he replied. "If I'd left them there and they'd found me with the pistol in my possession, I'd be in real trouble because they could fairly easily have matched the bullet to the weapon, and that would be extremely difficult evidence to refute. But as it is, all they have is the corpse of a man who's been killed by a shot from a pistol, and about the best they'll be able to do is have a guess at the approximate caliber of the weapon that discharged the bullet, and estimate how close the weapon was to the man when it was fired. Even if I was arrested and they found the pistol in my bag, I would obviously be in trouble for the illegal possession of a firearm, and that would be bad enough, but there's no way they could pin a murder on me."

"But supposing they find the bullet or the case?"

"They won't," Mallory said firmly.

"How can you be certain of that?"

"Because I dropped them out of the side window of the Cessna when we were halfway across the English Channel, and the handkerchief I'd wrapped them up in followed a minute or so later, knotted around about a pound's worth of my loose change."

"I wondered what you were up to when you opened the window," Robin said. "Anyway, thanks for explaining."

Traffic was fairly light, and so it was quite a bit less than one hour later when they drove through the tunnel and joined the traffic jostling for position on the network of roads to the northeast of Rouen city center.

Robin was still navigating, and doing a pretty good job of it.

"If you see a sign for Pont de l'Arche, follow that road," she instructed. "It looks as if that will take us out to the east and avoid the worst of the traffic."

Mallory saw the sign at the last moment, and dived over to the right, earning himself a couple of horn blasts from angry French drivers, then drove under a bridge and followed the road around to the left. Once across the next junction, the road followed the course of the wide river on which a couple of large motorized barges were heading steadily south.

About twenty minutes later, and well clear of Rouen, he turned onto another nontoll autoroute, following the signs for Chartres and Orléans, but, conscious that it was already nearly seven in the evening, they turned off shortly afterward and headed for Amfreville-sur-Iton to find a hotel.

"Watch out for a small greenish sign saying 'Logis,'" Mallory said.

They didn't see a suitable hotel in Amfreville, but about a dozen miles farther on they saw exactly what Mallory had been hoping to find: a large square hotel on the right-hand side of the road, the green Logis sign swinging in the wind and with most of the lights burning. Luckily there was a choice of rooms, and after a quick freshen-up they went down to the dining room and enjoyed a simple but satisfying meal.

"I think this is ideal," Mallory said as they waited for the coffee to arrive after the dishes containing the last scrapings of their desserts had been removed. "I've checked with the owner and both rooms are available all week, so I've booked for tonight and tomorrow. It's got Wi-Fi, not free but we can afford to pay for it, obviously, and I've bought a coupon that will cover us for a couple of days. With a bit of luck, that'll give us the time—and the peace and quiet—we need to decipher the rest of the text."

"And then what?" Robin asked.

"I've no idea. It all depends on what we find out when we can finally read what's written on the parchment. If it's just a lot of rambling religious nonsense, we'll have to go back to Devon and face the music, I suppose, but I think it'll be a lot more than that. Otherwise why would these Italians be so desperate to get their hands on it, and quite prepared to kill both of us in order to do so?"

"Do you want to start work on it tonight?"

"I think we should," he replied. "We're probably safe here, lost in a randomly chosen bit of the French countryside, but I have no idea how long that state of affairs will last. Sooner or later the British authorities will extend their search for you outside the borders of the United Kingdom, and eventually those Italians might pick up our trail as well. We've got a bit of breathing space at the moment, so I think we should crack on and solve as much as we can of this riddle as soon as possible."

51

France

The following morning they walked down to the dining room and ate their way through a typical Continental breakfast consisting of bread, croissants, and pastries, washed down with glasses of fresh orange juice and coffee served in huge cups, each probably holding about half a pint.

Sated, at least until lunchtime, they walked back up the stairs to Robin's room. Mallory booted his laptop and within a few minutes they were once again using the Atbash cipher text to convert the next part of the writing into Latin plaintext. As he started working on it, Robin pointed out something else that had only just occurred to her.

"At last I think I know why that book safe had such a strange title," she remarked. "*Ipse Dixit* translates as something like 'the master has spoken,' and I think that should be 'Master' with a capital *M*, because quite a lot of what we've read so far has been referring to Jacques de Molay, the last grand master, directly or indirectly."

"That makes sense," Mallory said, carefully transposing letters from one line to another as he did so. "It does rather read a bit like de Molay's memoirs, explaining what happened in the last days of the Templar order. I'm just hoping that whatever comes next in this translation will provide a bit more information, because although there've been a few revelations, most of what we've read so far was already known or at the very least suspected by many historians."

The last two sentences on the first side of the sheet of parchment were perhaps the most enigmatic of all, and when she read them out Mallory could easily detect the uncertainty in Robin's voice.

"I hope that you can make a bit more sense of this than I can at the moment. This is the best translation I can come up with from the Latin: 'Three trials will reveal the heritage and the rebirth, but beware the hounds. Rely two times on him who came before and carried the burden and the rank.' It's almost as if this was written by a different person to the rest of the text, somebody who was trying to be deliberately obtuse."

"It looks to me like the same hand wrote this part of the text as the rest of it, but I quite agree with you. The section we've already decoded and translated was quite easy to understand and factual in nature. This isn't. It looks to me like a deliberate clue, or rather a number of deliberate clues, and my guess is that we'll have to solve them before we find out exactly what the text is referring to. Anyway, let's leave those two sentences to one side for the moment and carry on with the other side of the parchment. There may be something in the next piece of writing that will help clarify exactly what these sentences mean."

But as it turned out, they couldn't do that, because when Mallory applied the Atbash cipher text to the first line written on the reverse of the parchment, even he could see that the result was pure gibberish. He passed the text over to Robin, but really just so that she could confirm his diagnosis.

"This isn't Latin," she confirmed, "and that almost certainly means that the decryption is wrong."

"I agree. The author has obviously used a different cipher text to encrypt this piece of the writing. I'm afraid we'll have to start all over again, trying different words associated with the Knights Templar until we finally work out what he's saying."

Two hours later, Mallory stood up from the desk where he'd been working and stretched, trying to work the kinks out of his back.

"We need to take a break," he said. "I've tried every word I can think of that might be associated with the Templars, and none of them have worked on the next piece of text. The trouble is, even if I've somehow managed to pick the right two or three words, if I haven't got them in the correct order, the decryption still won't work. This could take us a hell of a long time to decode."

"Right," Robin agreed, glancing at her watch. "Let's go and grab a bite to eat in the dining room—they'll be serving lunch by now, I expect—and then take another look at it when we come back."

They tossed the problem back and forth between them during the meal, but didn't seem to be getting anywhere with it. Then Robin suddenly fell silent and fixed her eyes on Mallory, the beginning of a smile playing around her lips.

"We're going about this the wrong way," she said. "We were so focused on using words associated with the Templars that we haven't tried the clue that's already contained within the parchment itself, in the text on the first side."

"What clue?" Mallory looked puzzled for a moment, but before Robin could reply he smacked his forehead in frustration as he realized what she was driving at. "You're right. All that stuff about trials and heritage and dogs, or hounds, or whatever it was. Those two sentences were so obscure and obtuse that the clue to the cipher text more or less has to be in them somewhere."

Neither of them bothered with a dessert, and they were back in Robin's bedroom, sitting at the desk in front of Mallory's laptop computer, a few minutes later.

"Right," Robin said. "You know far more about the Templars than I ever will, so where do we go from here? It looks to me as if there are four possibly important words in the first sentence—*trials*, *heritage*, *rebirth*, and *hounds*—but I frankly have no idea what any of those mean, apart from the literal translation, obviously."

"The bad news," Mallory replied, "is that I don't know, either, which obviously isn't exactly what you wanted to hear. I don't know what is meant by *trials*, but I suppose if we apply a bit of logic to the problem, we could reasonably assume that *heritage* probably just means the legacy of the Templars, if you like, and *rebirth* might be a suggestion that although the order was purged in 1307 and ended in 1314, it somehow endured and rose again."

"I didn't realize it took five years for the Templar order to be dissolved," Robin said. "I thought all that happened in 1307."

"No, it was quite a long process. It was officially disbanded by Pope Clement the Fifth in 1312, and the last grand master was executed in 1314. You have to remember that the Templars weren't subject to secular authority: they answered only to the pope. When King Philip began his program of seizures and arrests, the Templars appealed directly to the Vatican for help, on the reasonable grounds that they owed neither allegiance nor obedience to the king of France, or indeed to any monarch. The problem they had was that Pope Clement the Fifth not only was a very weak pontiff, but was also intimidated by Philip, who bullied him into supporting his actions.

"Even then, the pope refused at first to believe the accusations made against the Templars, and in fact in recent years a document known as the Chinon Parchment was discovered tucked away in the Vatican's Secret Archives. That document proved conclusively that in 1308 the pope actually absolved the leaders of the Knights Templar of the charges made against them, and in the same year Clement sent another document to King Philip of France telling him that all members of the order who had confessed to heresy had been absolved and welcomed back into the bosom of the Church. Philip, of course, ignored this information and simply increased the pace of his persecutions.

"But eventually the king's bullying tactics worked, and in 1312 the pope promulgated the papal bull *Vox in Excelsis*, which formally dissolved the order. What's quite interesting is that Clement actually expressed his own unhappiness at the action he was taking in that bull, and admitted that there was insufficient evidence to condemn the order, and that he was taking that step only for the common good, because of the events that had occurred in France. Anyway, because of the differences of opinion between Philip and Clement, for several years the status of the order remained in something of a limbo, hence the delay in its formal dissolution."

Robin nodded. "None of that really helps us understand what's meant by *rebirth*, though, unless I'm missing something. What about *hounds*?"

"That's about the only word that does mean something to me, and especially in the context of that statement. 'Beware the hounds' I think is a direct reference to the Dominicans and also, as a matter of interest, helps us to date this parchment. The order was formed in the early twelve hundreds in France by the Spanish priest Saint Dominic de Guzman, and was approved by the pope shortly afterward. The order was established to do two things, both dear to the heart of the Catholic Church at that time. The monks were supposed to preach the gospel, which sounds innocent enough, but also to combat heresy, and that was a much darker side of their activities. Over the years they essentially became the pope's personal torturers, working in the darkness of castle dungeons and employing ever more sophisticated methods designed to cause the maximum possible amount of pain to the people—both men and women—who fell into their clutches."

"But how does that help date the parchment?"

"When the order was formed, it was known simply as the Order of Preachers, the *Ordo Praedicatorum*, and it wasn't until the fifteenth century that they became commonly known as the Dominicans, after their founder. But when that name became commonly used, somebody realized that it was a sort of pun, and that the word *Dominican* sounded somewhat similar to *Domini canes*, which would translate as the 'Hounds of the Lord.' And that's why I think that because the author of this text is telling us to 'beware of the hounds,' he has to have been writing no earlier than the fifteenth century."

"That makes sense, and I suppose the most obvious

explanation for the information that the writer has already conveyed in this parchment is that he was drawing on a number of contemporary sources that described what had happened to the Templar order. So at least we know what one of the words in that sentence refers to, assuming you're right, of course. But I don't think we're any further forward in working out what cipher text we should be using to decode the next section."

Mallory nodded and turned his attention back to the translated text.

"The way I read it," he said, "I don't think that first sentence contains the clue that we're looking for. It looks to me as if that's just a general statement, maybe outlining a course of action that we need to follow—that could be the meaning of the expression 'three trials,' for example—but the second sentence seems to me to be far more specific. 'Rely two times on him who came before and carried the burden and the rank.' That's almost a definitive instruction. So all we need to do now is work out exactly what the writer means by "him who came before.'"

"Easy," Robin said.

"Really?"

"No, actually. I was making a small joke. But seriously, if that is the clue, then at least we know that we're looking for a person, for a name, rather than some vague concept or idea that we might never work out. So, who do you think that 'he who came before' might refer to?"

"I suppose logic would suggest that the writer is obliquely referring to somebody well-known in the order, and fairly obvious choices there will include people like Jacques de Molay, the last grand master, and maybe the first, Hugues de Payens, as well as some of the other famous names associated with the Knights Templar. Actually," he added after a pause, "probably not the first grand master, because there would have been nobody 'coming before him': by definition, he was the first. I think maybe we'll start with Jacques de Molay, because so much of the text has been dealing with him and what happened to him at the end in Paris. Perhaps the writer was assuming that we would assume, if you see what I mean, that he was the most important name ever to be associated with the Knights Templar. He's certainly the one person that everyone who reads about the subject knows."

Robin nodded.

"So, who came before Jacques de Molay?" she asked.

"I can't remember," Mallory replied, "but I'm sure that the Internet will supply the answer in a couple of seconds."

He opened his browser, typed in "Knights Templar grand masters," and started the search. Predictably enough, the very first search result was from Wikipedia. Mallory clicked on the link to open the page and then scanned down it until he reached the end of the list of names.

"There you go," he said. "The last grand master of the order before Jacques de Molay was Thibaud Gaudin. We can try that name and see if it gets us anywhere, but let me just check something else."

He quickly did another search.

"I thought so," he said. "If you look at the names of the list of Templar grand masters, you'll see that most of them are single names with an associated place-name. Bernard de Blanchefort, for example, or Bernard of Blanchefort. I think Blanchefort is a town or village somewhere in Southern France. Thibaud Gaudin was also known as Tibauld de Gaudin, so there are at least two different ways of spelling his name, and it can be with or without the *de* as well."

He entered another search term and looked at the results.

"There's nowhere in France just called 'Gaudin,'" he said, "but Tibauld was believed to have come from the Loire region, and there are a couple of towns in that area that include the word in their names. And of course one of them might just have been called 'Gaudin' in those days."

"I suppose we'll just have to try all the possible options," Robin said. "But what about this burden he was supposed to be carrying? Is there anything on the Web about what that could mean?"

Mallory scanned quickly through one of the articles on Tibauld de Gaudin. "I don't know if it would count as a 'burden,' but it looks as if Tibauld was one of the very few members of the Knights Templar order who managed to escape the fall of Acre in 1291. The night before the fortifications were overrun by the Mamluk besieging army, he sailed away with a number of noncombatants—women and children, presumably—as well as the entire treasure of the Knights Templar in the Holy Land. He wasn't stealing it, because he held the position of treasurer of the order, and he had been ordered to leave Acre by the marshal of the Knights Templar, a man called Pierre de Sevry, who was then in command of the fortress.

"I don't know all the details of the siege of Acre, but I do know that almost every Christian who had taken refuge in the Templar fort there was slaughtered by the Mamluks when they finally breached the walls. Reading between the lines, my guess is that de Sevry knew for sure that Acre was doomed, and didn't want the treasure to fall into the hands of the infidels, so he made certain that it was transported to safety before the final battle began."

"I think you could describe that as a 'burden,'" Robin said. "Presumably Tibauld would have been one of the last surviving Knights Templar in the Holy Land, and to be entrusted with the entire wealth of the order would be a massive responsibility. What did he do with it?"

Mallory read on. "The short version is that nobody actually knows. He sailed first to Sidon, and while he was there he was elected grand master following the death of Pierre de Sevry at the end of the siege of Acre. Although the Templars were determined to resist the approaching Mamluk army, they were too few in number to defend the entire city of Sidon, and so they retreated to what was known as the Castle of the Sea. It had been built in the thirteenth century as a fortification just off the coast of Sidon, and was approached by a narrow and easily defended causeway about one hundred yards long.

"But before the Mamluks arrived, Tibauld de Gaudin got back into his ship and sailed off into the Mediterranean, an act that could easily have been interpreted as cowardice, and which was certainly not what most Templars would have expected their new grand master to do. The other way of looking at it is that de Gaudin knew that the number of defenders in the castle was wholly inadequate to resist the vast Mamluk army, and his plan was to sail to Cyprus to raise enough reinforcements to allow him to return to the Holy Land and drive out the infidels. And, probably, to get the order's treasure to a place of safety.

"What followed was by all accounts something of a shambles. The Templars who had remained behind in the Castle of the Sea fought as bravely as members of the order invariably did, but when Mamluk engineers began constructing a new and wide causeway to link the castle with the mainland, they accepted that they had no choice but to retreat. They took to their ships and sailed to the city of Tortosa, in Syria. But even that proved too big and too difficult to defend, and later that year both Tortosa and the castle of Athlit were evacuated, the Templars assembling at the small sea fort of Ruad, about two miles off the coast of Tortosa, as their final redoubt. But when Sidon was abandoned, that realistically marked the end of the presence of the Knights Templar in the Holy Land."

"I take it that Tibauld didn't raise any reinforcements, then?" Robin asked.

"Correct. He apparently did almost nothing on Cyprus. In fairness to him, he did have other problems, including trying to defend the Kingdom of Armenia from Turkish forces, and there were domestic difficulties on Cyprus as well, because of an influx of refugees. He was probably also not a well man, because he died the following year, 1292, and it looks as if all mention of the Templar treasure of Acre died with him. Interestingly, at the same meeting of the hierarchy of the Knights Templar that confirmed Tibauld's appointment in October 1291, a senior knight named Jacques de Molay was named marshal of the order, succeeding Pierre de Sevry. He, of course, then became the grand master of the order after Tibauld's death."

"Well, de Gaudin sounds to me like a pretty good candidate for 'him who came before and carried the burden,' so unless you've got any better ideas, why don't you try using his name as the cipher text?"

"I'm already doing it."

But despite trying numerous different combinations and spellings, none seemed to work, just converted gibberish to different gibberish, and eventually Mallory sat back, frustrated.

"I have no idea where to go now," he admitted. "I think I've tried just about every possible combination."

Robin was again looking at the section of the parchment text that they'd already deciphered. And suddenly she saw three words that hadn't really registered with either of them before.

"Look," she said, pointing at the translation. "It says 'Rely two times.' That has to mean something."

Mallory looked at it for a moment. "I just thought it was an emphasis, you know, meaning you could really rely on him, something like that. Now I wonder . . ."

His voice trailed away; then he looked up at Robin, who was standing beside him.

"Unless that's a kind of oblique instruction about the decryption," he suggested. "A double transposition rather than just a single one? If so, it's probably the earliest example ever."

"But it's worth a try?"

"Definitely," Mallory said, taking a fresh sheet of paper.

Working out exactly what spelling of the man's name to use took a bit of trial and error, and Mallory tried numerous different combinations, together with the other word or words that would have to follow the name to make up the required twenty-six letters.

He prepared another table, as he'd done before, and entered the alphabet and the cipher text underneath it:

A	B	C	D	E	F	G	H	I	J	K	L	M	N	O	P	Q	R	S	T	U	V	W	X	Y	Z
T	H	I	B	A	U	D	G	A	U	D	I	N	M	A	G	I	S	T	E	R	P	C	C	T	S

"Are you sure that'll work?" Robin asked.

"No," Mallory said, "but that seems the best fit for the twenty-six letters. That's the shorter version of Tibauld's name, his abbreviated title—he was the *magister generalis*, the Latin for 'grand master,' and the last five letters are the initials of the full name of the order, *Pauperes commilitones Christi Templique Solomonici*. Anyway, we'll find out when I try it."

Then he noted down the letters that encrypted the same expression and wrote the result under the alphabet:

A	B	C	D	E	F	G	H	I	J	K	L	M	N	O	P	Q	R	S	T	U	V	W	X	Y	Z
E	G	A	H	T	R	B	D	T	R	B	A	M	N	T	D	A	T	E	A	S	G	I	I	E	T

And finally that combination worked, which meant that it was a double transposition cipher, which incidentally meant the history of cryptography would have to be amended.

There were quite a number of duplicate letters in the cipher text, which inevitably caused delays in the decrypting, or more accurately the translating, of the Latin plaintext, but steadily the two of them worked their way through the remainder of the text. Everything yielded apart from the very last section, twenty or so lines of cipher text. Nothing Mallory tried seemed to work on it, and eventually they reluctantly decided to just ignore it.

When they'd finished, Robin read through what she'd written down, made a few small changes to make it sound rather better, more like modern English, and then read out the whole of the translated text to Mallory, who listened with great care to every word she said.

"Well, that's a bit of a bugger," he said when she'd finished.

52

To say Silvio Vitale was annoyed barely hinted at the level of his irritation, and the proximate cause of his anger was the man standing in front of his desk: Marco Toscanelli.

"I had expected far better from you," he snapped. "I would have thought that a team of six experienced operatives, all of you armed and with the clearest and most specific of instructions, would have been able to eliminate a harmless British bookseller and recover the object that we sought. Instead you have returned to Rome outwitted and outmaneuvered by this same man and his secretary, or whatever that woman turns out to be. Four of our operatives are dead, three of them killed by your own hand—"

"I explained that to you," Toscanelli interrupted. "The first police car had just arrived and I knew that—"

"Never interrupt me when I am speaking," Vitale said coldly, and Toscanelli immediately fell silent. "Irrespective of the reasons that you decided justified your action, the fact remains that you yourself killed three of the men under your orders, and I am far from satisfied that you were correct in doing this. And even if there genuinely had been no other possible course of action, your execution—and that realistically is the only way to describe what you did—meant that our masters were asked a number of questions by an official representative of the British embassy here in Rome, questions that we would far rather have never had occurred to anyone. Obviously the answers given were very carefully prepared and worded to avoid the order becoming incriminated in any way, but the fact remains that what we had intended to be an entirely covert operation ended up attracting a huge amount of publicity in Britain—not only the local papers but also the national dailies there are running the story even now, trying to work out exactly what happened in that quiet seaside town—simply because of what you did."

Vitale paused for a moment and glared across the desk, his hostility almost palpable. "And then, to make matters even worse, when you and the remaining two men finally located and captured the two targets, and that in my opinion was more a fluke than an indication of any kind of coherent plan, they not only managed to get away from you, but also probably took the relic with them, though I note that you never even bothered checking that it was actually in their possession. They also took back the computer that you had removed from the flat in Dartmouth, and in the process maimed one operative and killed the other. If Dante talks, make no mistake: I will issue a termination order against him, and another one against you. You might have done better to kill him as well, because while he still breathes, your life is in serious jeopardy."

Vitale stopped talking for a moment, his cold black eyes never leaving Toscanelli's face.

"In fact," he continued, "throughout that entire operation, absolutely the only thing you actually did right was upload the data from that computer to our servers here in Rome, during the extremely brief period while you had it in your possession. That is the only reason why you're standing in front of me now. If you had not got that information to us, I would already have had you killed. In fact, I would probably have done it myself, and I promise you it would not have been a quick death."

Vitale fell silent again, and after a brief pause Toscanelli decided he had to respond. The trouble was that every single statement made by the head of the order was absolutely true. It had been, by any standards, a catastrophe, the team selected by Vitale and led by Toscanelli failing to achieve any of the objectives for which they had flown to Britain. And the death toll was simply unacceptable, given the opposition—if such a word could actually be used to describe the two people they had encountered in Dartmouth. But Toscanelli was certain there was more to it than Vitale seemed prepared to accept, and he was determined to make his views known.

"That man Jessop might just be a bookseller now," he began, "but the way he reacted to the situation he found himself in proves to me that he is far more competent and experienced in close combat than we had any reason to expect. I strongly suspect that he has some kind of military background, and if we had known that before we landed in Britain, we would have approached him in a very different manner. And the other—"

But before he could continue to elaborate the excuses for his team's failure, there was a sudden peremptory knock on the door.

"Come," Vitale called out.

The door opened almost immediately, and a black-clad man stepped into the room and crossed immediately to the desk, where he handed Vitale a folded sheet of paper.

The leader of the order opened it and read the information written on it. Then he glanced at the messenger.

"What's the source for this?" he demanded.

"The local newspaper in Dartmouth. We are monitoring each edition as soon as it is published on the Internet. According to the report we read, that information was released by the British police yesterday."

Vitale dismissed the man with a gesture, and as soon as he had left the room, he switched his attention back to Toscanelli.

"So you think the bookseller might have spent some time in the British army, do you?" he asked.

"That or some other branch of the military, yes," Toscanelli replied.

"Interesting. Because according to this news report, the detectives investigating the triple murder in Dartmouth have now confirmed that the apartment and the antiquarian bookshop that was on the ground floor of the building were owned by the same person, Robin Jessop."

Toscanelli looked puzzled.

"We knew that," he said. "In fact, we knew that before the aircraft took off from Rome."

"Yes," Vitale replied, "but up to now the authorities in Britain had not released the name of the owner of the property. They simply referred to it as a bookshop in Dartmouth with an apartment located above it, without confirming the name of the owner."

"I still don't see the significance."

"The significance is that the British police have now identified Robin Jessop as the owner of the bookshop, and stated that she lived in her apartment on the second floor of the building. 'She' and 'her,' Toscanelli," Vitale emphasized. "So not only have you been comprehensively outwitted by a British bookseller, but it now turns out that she's a twenty-eight-year-old woman, not some hulking former soldier."

For a few moments, Toscanelli didn't reply, processing the new and unexpected information.

"But I thought Robin was an English male name," he finally spluttered.

Vitale permitted himself a brief smile.

"Actually," he said, "so did I, but apparently it isn't exclusively masculine. So who exactly was the man who was with her? Her boyfriend? Or a minder, a bodyguard? And if so, why would she have a bodyguard?"

"I have no idea," Toscanelli replied. "So how does this affect our mission?"

"I don't actually think it does. If you see them again, either of them, your orders are quite clear: you kill them. If possible, try and make it look like an accident, but if you can't, just kill them anyway. And if you do run into them, make absolutely sure that you either recover the relic or totally destroy it."

Vitale pulled open the top drawer on the right-hand side of the desk and reached inside it. Toscanelli tensed, wondering for the briefest of instants if, despite his last remarks, Vitale had changed his mind and was reaching for a pistol to shoot him, there and then. But then he relaxed when the other man simply extracted a buff envelope and held it out for him to take.

"These are your orders. We have had a team working on decrypting the text ever since you uploaded it, and although they haven't quite finished it yet, we believe it is clear that what we seek must lie somewhere in the eastern Mediterranean."

"Based on what?" Toscanelli asked, feeling on firmer ground now that the threat of his immediate execution had diminished somewhat.

"On the name Tibauld de Gaudin, the man who was the second-to-last grand master of the Knights Templar. There's an oblique reference to his name in the text that has already been decrypted. He ended his life in Cyprus, and it therefore seems likely that the object of our quest was in his possession when he arrived there, and as far as we know from checking our own records of the interrogations and all other relevant contemporary sources, we can find no evidence to suggest that it was ever removed from the island. That appears to have been the last place it was ever sighted."

"I'm sure the orders you have given me will explain everything," Toscanelli said, "but can you provide me with a quick summary of what you want me to do?"

Vitale nodded. "There's a diplomatic passport in that envelope. Pending the full decryption of the text, you are to fly to Cyprus and wait there for further instructions. The professor believes that the text will explain in some detail exactly what Tibauld de Gaudin did with the objects that were placed in his care. Otherwise we have no idea why the parchment should have been prepared in the first place. Once we have succeeded in cracking the code for the final section, I will contact you on Cyprus using our encrypted e-mail facility—obviously you will take a laptop with you—and tell you precisely what you are to do and where to look."

"How big a team do I have this time?"

"Team? Team?" Vitale almost laughed aloud. "What team? You left Rome with five other men, and within forty-eight hours or thereabouts four of them were dead and one was in the hospital with a broken arm. Members of our order are used to obeying orders immediately and implicitly, but given your record so far in this matter, how many people do you think would be prepared to accompany you on this mission? To save your brain overheating, I'll tell you, because I did ask some of our operatives. None is the answer. Not one. In fact, I was only asking the question as a matter of interest, because I never intended that anybody else would get involved in this phase of the operation.

"You are the only member of our order who has actually seen Jessop and the man who was with her in Dartmouth. If they also manage to decrypt the text, as I believe they almost certainly will, then they will probably end up in Cyprus as well, and when they do you will find them and kill them. You will also locate the objects that we seek and when you have done so, then and only then will you contact me to arrange the recovery operation. You will also find and either recover or destroy the relic, the parchment."

Vitale's gaze bored into Toscanelli. "This is a solo operation. You can complete this by yourself, or simply do not bother ever returning here, because if you fail you will die. Whether by my hand or the hand of somebody else does not matter, but failure is not an option we are prepared to tolerate, and especially not a second failure."

The head of the order stood up, rested his hands on the desk in front of him, and leaned forward. "You will be traveling to Cyprus alone and operating independently. But I will also be sending another team of operatives to the island—in fact, they have already set out—and their entire responsibility will be to monitor your actions and, if they feel it necessary, eliminate you. This is your last and only chance to redeem yourself. Fail me, and you will die.

"And if you believe that you can simply get lost some-where in the world and never make it to Cyprus, just re-member the reach of this order. Wherever you go, we will find you. And when we do I can promise you that you will wish you had never even been born."

53

France

"So, actually, I was right in the first place," Mallory said, pointing at the sheets of paper lying on the desk. "This really is a treasure map, of a sort, anyway. I mean, it's not actually a map, but it does state that clues were left on the ground to help somebody find these two objects. Are you sure that you're reading the Latin correctly?"

Robin nodded.

"I'm quite sure that I'm right," she replied. "The text claims that Tibauld provided markers—I suppose that's the best translation—that could be followed if they can be interpreted. That's the obvious meaning of this phrase 'read the signs to know the path.'"

"Don't forget that there's that one last part of the text we still haven't managed to unscramble," Mallory said. "Maybe that would tell us exactly where to start looking."

Robin shook her head. "Actually I think it's the other way round. The last sentence says 'search for truth at the end of the path to begin anew.' I know that's not specific, but I think it means we follow the trail Tibauld is supposed to have left and when we find what he concealed we'll also find a clue to allow us to read the last section of the text."

Robin looked down at the translation she'd prepared. "I'm still puzzled about the way the writer refers to two separate things: the 'treasure' and the 'wealth.' Or the 'assets,' I suppose, would be an alternative translation. But even when they're mentioned in the same sentence, he seems to be making it clear that they are two different things, not two different words being used to describe the same object. And that is peculiar. I think most people would assume that the treasure of the Templar order was also its wealth. I really don't understand why the writer is adamant that the two things are separate."

"I suppose he could be talking about two different treasures," Mallory suggested. "In fact, that might be it. Tibauld de Gaudin would have been in charge of the treasure of the Knights Templar in Outremer, the Holy Land. That's the lost treasure of Acre, the hoard that vanished from the historical record in the confusion surrounding the order at the end of the thirteenth century. But they wouldn't have had all their assets in one place. Their main headquarters was in France and it would make sense for the Paris preceptory to hold the bulk of their assets, because that would probably be seen as the most secure and well guarded of all their properties. In 1307, of course, it became very clear that being based in the French capital city offered them no security whatsoever when the king of France turned on them."

"That's a good point," Robin conceded, "and you might even be right. But that still doesn't really explain why the writer of this text consistently uses two different words: *treasure* and *wealth*. If he was referring to a cache of Templar assets secreted away in the Holy Land, and another second group of assets located in France, then I would have expected him to call one 'Outremer assets' and the other one 'French assets' or something similar. But whatever these two things are, what we have to do now is to decide what we're going to do about them, bearing in mind what's happened so far with these murderous Italians. Do we really want to get involved any further in following a kind of medieval treasure trail that has already nearly cost us our lives? Twice," she added.

Robin looked at Mallory.

"There could still be some danger," he admitted. "We have the original parchment, but those Italians had your computer for long enough to copy the information on it, so the leader of the group could have it on a memory stick in his pocket or have even sent it to his bosses. Of course, they'll have to decipher it, just like us, and until they do they'll have no idea where to look."

"So, should we carry on? Continue this quest, I suppose you could call it."

Mallory nodded. "I think so, yes, just keeping our eyes open for these men in black. Apart from anything else, if there's even the slightest chance of finding any part of the Templar treasure, I'd be happy to take a few risks, because the reward could be literally incalculable. My vote, if this discussion is going to be in any way democratic, is that we forge on and see exactly where the trail leads us. What do you think?"

"Oddly enough," Robin replied, "I agree. Selling antiquarian books is not what you might describe as a high-risk occupation. In fact, it is quite startlingly boring almost all the time, and I've tended to get my kicks not exactly on Route 66, but on the track or in the dojo. It actually makes a pleasant change to be doing something so completely different. And, as you said, the potential reward makes taking the odd risk definitely worthwhile."

She stood up and held out her hand.

"We're kind of partners already," she said, "but let's make it semiofficial. I want to see this through to the end, with you. Equal risk, equal reward."

Mallory stood up as well and took her hand in a firm grip.

"Sounds like a plan," he said. "Fifty-fifty. You and me against the world, and especially against any more gun-toting Italians who turn up to try to ruin our day.

"I suppose it's worth saying that I was wrong about one thing," Mallory added, sitting down. "It looks like this trail is going to take us quite a long way away from France. In fact, I think the first place we have to go is Acre."

But half an hour later he changed his mind.

"I'm wrong," he said, leaning back from the desk where he had been alternating between bending over the written translation of the parchment text and staring at information he had culled from the Internet on the screen on his laptop. "I don't think tramping round Acre would help us very much."

"But we know the treasure was there," Robin pointed out, "because contemporary accounts show that Pierre de Sevry specifically ordered Tibauld to escape with it by sea. And we also know that he followed those orders, because the next place he turned up was at Sidon, the nearest Templar stronghold to Acre. So why wouldn't going to Acre be helpful? It's the start of the trail."

"Just because of what happened after the ship left. Within a matter of days or even hours—there's some dispute about the timing—the Mamluk army attacked the Templar fortress, and at the same time the miners who had tunneled under the foundations of the fort set fire to the piles of wood and other flammable materials they'd stacked in those tunnels. At the height of the battle for the fortress, the foundations gave way and most of the walls collapsed, killing both the attackers and the defenders, and when the dust had settled—literally—the Mamluks overran it and destroyed everything that was left."

Robin nodded. "I see what you mean. So if Tibauld had left any kind of clue or message anywhere in the fortress, and the parchment suggests that he *did* leave markers to allow somebody to follow the trail, it would almost certainly have been completely obliterated by the time the Mamluk army moved on to its next target. And I suppose the other side of the coin is that it's difficult to think of any good reason why he would have left anything there anyway. He was about to escape the coming massacre in a ship full of women and children and a few chests full of coins and bullion, and when he left the jetty behind the Templar castle that night, he could have had no idea where he was going to end up or what was going to become of the Knights Templar in the Holy Land. It must have been a really depressing voyage to make in those circumstances."

"So I suppose Sidon would have been the first place Tibauld could have left the treasure of the order or some indication where he was going to hide it," Mallory said. "Or more accurately, at the Sidon Sea Castle, which is where the Templars had taken refuge, and where Tibauld first made landfall with his strange mixed cargo."

Robin nodded again. "And that presumably is a castle at Sidon itself, is it? In the city, I mean."

"Not exactly."

Mallory opened the search box on his browser again

and typed in "Sidon Sea Castle." A lot of results were listed, but he clicked on the first entry from Wikipedia.

"This is as good as anything else," he said, and pointed at the images on the screen. "Sidon is in Lebanon, and it's almost certainly Phoenician in origin, and has probably been occupied since about four thousand BC. When the Templars arrived in the area and decided to use Sidon as one of their bases, they soon realized that the city was far too big to be properly defended by such a relatively small number of knights, so they decided to do a bit of lateral thinking, I suppose you could call it, and they moved their base offshore.

"A very short distance off the coast at Sidon was a small island connected to the mainland by a narrow causeway less than a hundred yards long. When the Templars arrived, all that was on the island were the ruins of a former temple to the Phoenician version of Heracles or Hercules, a mythical figure named Melkart, though it was possible that it had been of much greater importance centuries earlier, perhaps even being the location of a royal palace. The Templars were interested in its strategic value and took it over, building a fortress that covered the entire land area. That gave them a formidable castle that could easily be defended from attack by sea, though that wasn't a common method of assault in those days, while the narrow causeway prevented any large-scale assault from the mainland. It could be defended by quite a small number of determined men, and the Templars were nothing if not determined.

"When Tibauld de Gaudin arrived, he was the most senior Templar knight at Sidon and no doubt the other Templars looked to him to provide leadership and guidance, but as we know that didn't happen. He disembarked the passengers from his ship and very shortly afterward he set sail to Cyprus, with the laudable intention of raising reinforcements, creating a new Templar army that would sweep back from Cyprus and once and for all rid the Holy Land of the infidels that infested it."

"And he failed."

"Exactly. He completely failed to raise reinforcements, probably because just about every fighting man he approached would have realized that the Mamluks were essentially invulnerable, just because of their vast numbers, and to volunteer to fight against them was simply suicidal. Not even mercenary soldiers were interested, no matter what sums of money Tibauld offered them. That, incidentally, is another reason why it's certain the treasure was taken to Cyprus, because if Tibauld de Gaudin hadn't had the funds, he couldn't have even begun approaching any mercenaries. Don't forget, all Knights Templar took a vow of poverty when they joined the order, so Tibauld would have had almost no money of his own. For him to try to recruit mercenary soldiers, he would have had to use Templar assets."

Robin nodded in slow agreement, then shook her head. "Hang on a minute. If it's certain that Tibauld de Gaudin did take the Templar treasure to Cyprus, is there any real point in going to Sidon, to this castle? We already know there'll be nothing to find there."

Mallory gestured at the decrypted and translated Latin text.

"You could be right, but I think it's possible that there might be," he said. "Just look at this sentence in the text that we've just deciphered. 'The burden conveyed from the Tower of the Flies of Ekron to rest at the fortress on the water.' Ekron was an ancient biblical city believed to be ruled by Baal-zebub, the Lord of the Flies, and for a time the Crusaders believed Acre was Ekron, hence the name of the tower. It was an important defensive fort on a tiny island at the entrance to the protected harbor at Acre, and would have been the last point that Tibauld de Gaudin's ship would have passed as he left the harbor that night. And the fortress on the water has to mean the Sidon Sea Castle."

"So that means whatever Tibauld was carrying on board the ship was taken to Sidon," Robin said, "but then he sailed to Cyprus, didn't he? Why would he have left anything at Sidon?"

"We know he went on to Cyprus. That's in the historical record, but this parchment confirms it, talking about the 'island of copper.' Nobody knows where the name 'Cyprus' came from, but in antiquity the island was known to be such a good source of copper that in Classical Latin the metal was referred to as *aes Cyprium*, or 'metal of Cyprus,' which was later shortened to *cuprum*, and hence *copper*. The probability is that Tibauld knew Cyprus quite well, because he'd been in the area, around the eastern Mediterranean, for some time. And I think that's important because of this reference."

Mallory pointed at the next translated sentence.

"'And in that place he marked that place,'" he read out.

"The Latin word is *locus*," Robin said. "It's got several different meanings, but 'place' is as good as any."

"I know, and as it stands that sentence doesn't make too much sense. But pick a couple of alternative meanings and it does. 'And in that location he marked the spot,' for example. I wonder if Tibauld knew before he set out from the Sidon Sea Castle where he was going to land on the island, and also where he'd find a safe hiding place for the treasure he had been entrusted with. So I think that sentence means he left some kind of mark or message at Sidon, a statement of his intentions, if you like. That might just have been a precaution, a way of telling the other members of the Knights Templar where the assets were going to be deposited, so that if some accident befell him after he'd arrived on Cyprus, the treasure wouldn't be lost forever."

"Couldn't he just have told someone what he was going to do with it?" Robin asked.

"He could have, certainly, but he would have known that the Mamluk army was probably already marching toward Sidon. And after seeing what had happened at Acre, I don't think Tibauld would have been happy to entrust his secret to any one Templar, or even to a number of them, because of the very real danger that they would be slaughtered in the battle that was going to take place at Sidon within a few days or weeks. If he was going to provide any information about his intentions, the only safe way to do so would be to create something concrete, something that would endure for centuries, like a carving. It would also have to be meaningless to the Mamluks and only make sense to a fellow Templar, which would be quite a difficult trick to pull off.

"That's just a theory, mind you, and I could be completely wrong, but the way the text talks about a trail suggests that there might be clues left on the ground, as it were, that we can follow."

"So now we have to go to Lebanon?" Robin asked.

"I think we should, yes, and just hope if Tibauld *did* leave any kind of clue in the Sea Castle that it's still there, because the place was pretty badly knocked about after he left Sidon."

Mallory used the touch pad to move the cursor to open a new browser window and entered another term in the search box. "Anyway, I think the first thing we have to do is work out how to get to Lebanon. We want a route that's quick and easy, and that probably means hopping on a plane, so I'll just do a quick search and see what's available."

While Mallory checked flights from various French airports to the eastern Mediterranean, Robin looked again at the text they had finally translated.

"I think you're right about following a trail," she said, "because that *is* the way this passage reads. But I just wonder how easy it will be to spot any clues Tibauld left behind him over seven hundred years ago, far less work out what they mean."

"That will be the real trick," Mallory replied, "and all we can do is hope that we're smart enough to see a hidden meaning in what other people have dismissed as unimportant over the centuries."

54

Sidon, Lebanon

Traveling to Sidon didn't prove to be as difficult as Mallory had been expecting. They drove to Paris Orly and took a flight direct to Beirut, landing at the airport that lay just to the south of the city. Once there, they hired a car and drove the relatively short distance—about twenty miles—down the Mediterranean coast of Lebanon to Sidon.

"I'm actually rather enjoying this," Robin said, leaning back in her seat and looking through the side window of the car at the sparkling blue waters of the Mediterranean as Mallory steered the hired Renault south. "I just wish we had the time to stop and lie on the beach for a week or so, and let all our troubles just waft away. But I can't stop thinking about the problems still waiting for us back in Devon, festering away quietly in the background."

"And they're probably getting worse as well," Mallory said. "I'm quite sure that the pointed hat brigade will be getting more and more irritated with every day that passes when they can't haul you into the nearest police station and give you the third degree about what happened in your apartment. When you do eventually go back and face them—because obviously we can't keep doing this forever, running around looking for lost treasures—I still think your best plan is to simply deny all knowledge of what happened. Tell them you walked out of your apartment to meet your new boyfriend and, quite unexpectedly for you, he turned out to be a kind of white knight who whisked you off for a prolonged dirty weekend that turned into a week spent bouncing around the eastern Mediterranean."

Robin smiled at him.

"I don't really see you as a white knight," she said, "and we haven't had any kind of dirty weekend. But you're probably right. The obvious objection to that scenario is my failure to go and talk to the police once I knew that those three men had been killed in my apartment. I suppose I could say that I thought it was Betty having a joke with me, trying to spoil my fun, but I really don't know if they would believe that."

"I don't think that it really matters whether they believe it or not. What they can't prove is that you were there when the murders took place, because you weren't. The old triumvirate in law enforcement, and especially for murder, is means, motive, and opportunity, and of those the only one that really fits you is opportunity, simply because you own the property. Means is a bit of a gray area because it will be clear to the police that the men—or at least two of them—were armed when they arrived, and so they could argue that you seized one of their pistols and shot the three of them. But that still leaves motive. You didn't know those three men, and you certainly didn't have any valid reason for wanting them dead, so it's difficult to see how they could mount a successful prosecution against you for their murders. Apart from anything else, I don't think any reasonably fair-minded jury would believe that tiny little you would be able to overpower three hefty men armed with pistols and then shoot them, with or without your martial arts skills.

"In fact," Mallory continued, "if my reading of what happened after we made our getaway is correct, I'm the one who needs to be worried. That last Italian could dump the murder weapon in my car so that the police will find it when they recover the vehicle. I suppose with hindsight it probably was a good idea to report the car stolen, because at least that will muddy the waters. If the vehicle wasn't in my possession, then I couldn't have placed the murder weapon in it. But I still think I'm going to need a flock of high-priced lawyers back in Britain if I'm going to be able to talk my way out of this."

"Then let's hope there really is some kind of treasure at the end of this, because then you'll be able to afford the best legal brains money can buy," Robin said.

They drove on in silence for a few more minutes, and then Mallory pointed ahead.

"There it is," he said, gesturing toward an old gray stone fortification, much of it in ruins, located just off the coast on their right-hand side, on the northern edge of Sidon. It was approached by a stone causeway that linked the small island to the mainland.

"It looks as if it's suffered a bit over the years," Robin remarked.

"It has," Mallory confirmed. "After Tibauld left to sail to Cyprus, the remaining Templars here prepared to defend the castle against the Mamluks, but they almost certainly knew from the start that they were doomed. And they were right. The enormous Mamluk army, fresh from their overwhelming victory at the siege of Acre, arrived at Sidon and quickly overwhelmed the defenders of the castle. The few members of the order who managed to survive the battle escaped by sea and made their way to Tortosa, but it quickly became apparent that there were simply too few of them there to make the slightest difference, and that for the garrison to remain would simply be suicidal.

"The Knights Templar weren't scared of dying in battle—in fact, they welcomed it—but they were also very aware of military tactics, and they would have known that if they stayed in Tortosa to face the oncoming Mamluk army, they would all die. If that happened, there would be even fewer Christian knights in the Holy Land able to combat the menace of the infidels, and throwing away their lives to no purpose would only serve to weaken their cause."

"So they left, presumably," Robin said.

"They left. Both Tortosa and the one other remaining mainland Templar castle in the Holy Land, Athlit, were abandoned that same year, before the Mamluks were able to lay siege to either of them. But the Templars did make a kind of last stand on the fortress island of Ruad. That's located a couple of miles off the coast of Tortosa, today's Tartus in Syria, a few miles north of Tripoli. In fact, in 1300 Jacques de Molay, who was by then the Templar grand master, took part in a complicated and ultimately unsuccessful plan involving not only his own order but also the Knights Hospitaller and the Teutonic Knights, supposed to be supported by a large force of Mongol warriors that conspicuously failed to materialize. The idea was to use Ruad as a bridgehead to attack and recover Tortosa, but all they actually managed to achieve was to launch a few raids on the mainland, seize a handful of prisoners, and engage in a bit of plunder. Because the

Mongol army was delayed by bad weather, they didn't have a sufficiently large force to even attempt to engage the Mamluks. And after a certain amount of deliberation, most of the combined forces withdrew and returned to Cyprus, leaving behind a small garrison on Ruad.

"The pope then got in on the act, and with typical papal generosity and arrogance, and ignoring the territorial claims of any other nation, he gave Ruad to the Templars. Jacques de Molay organized the reinforcement of the fortress island, and stationed a large force of knights there, some hundred and twenty, who were supported by five hundred archers and four hundred servants. He was obviously hoping that the island could eventually be used to stage an invasion of Tortosa, but it all came to nothing.

"In either 1302 or 1303 the Mamluks sent an invasion fleet of sixteen ships to Tripoli, and from there they besieged Ruad, setting up their own encampments on the island and finally starving out the defenders. After the final surrender, the Mamluks behaved with their normal duplicity and disregarded the terms they had just agreed to. All the archers were executed and the majority of the Knights Templar were taken in chains to Cairo and imprisoned under appalling conditions, most of them dying through ill treatment and starvation. And the surrender of Ruad," Mallory finished, "marked both the end of the Crusades and of the presence of Christian knights—whether Knights Templar or from one of the other two military orders—in the Holy Land. There were plans and schemes after the event, mainly orchestrated by the pope, but none of them ever came to anything."

Mallory braked the car to a stop conveniently close to the end of the causeway linking the Sea Castle to the mainland, and for a couple of minutes the two of them just sat in silence, staring out at the ruined fortress in front of them.

"So, what happened here?" Robin finally asked.

"When the castle fell to the Mamluks, they did their best to demolish it. That seems to have been almost a kind of policy with them: whenever they took a Templar stronghold, like Acre, the order's main power base in the Holy Land, or the castle of Athlit, they systematically dismantled the fortress, presumably in an attempt to make sure it couldn't be reused, or not without a lot of rebuilding work. Here at the Sea Castle, they apparently changed their minds a bit later on, because they then came back and rebuilt it themselves, and also constructed the stone causeway that you're looking at right now. That wasn't the end of the story, because the castle was later abandoned, but it was rebuilt yet again by a local emir in the seventeenth century. It was extensively damaged in later conflicts, so it's had a long and somewhat traumatic life."

Mallory pointed at the old fortifications. "Pretty much all that's left now are the two towers you can see and a wall that connects them. The rectangular tower is the better preserved of the two, but in some ways the east tower, the other one, is the more interesting. That was built by two different groups of people at different times. The lower levels date back to the days of the Crusaders, the Templars, while the upper part was constructed by the Mamluks. The wall that links them is interesting, too, according to what I've read. That includes Roman columns, built into it as horizontal strengtheners, and that was quite a common technique in areas where Roman remains were found, because the stones they used were strong and regularly shaped and offered an easy way to increase the speed of construction."

Robin looked at him.

"Well," she said, "we certainly aren't going to find any kind of clues or information Tibauld might conveniently have left for us sitting here in this car staring at it. Let's get over there and take a look."

The rectangular western tower was, as Mallory had explained, in quite good condition, given its turbulent history. It was over to the left of the entrance of the site as they left the causeway, and when they walked in they entered a very large room with a vaulted ceiling. There were a number of carved capitals in the room as well as several rusting iron cannonballs, presumably a legacy of the later conflicts that had raged around the building.

A staircase wound its way up the internal walls and gave access to the roof of the building, on which a small mosque had been constructed during the reign of the Ottoman Turks. More impressive was the view of the harbor and the old city from the roof, a wide and unobstructed vista. But they weren't there to sightsee. They spent a few minutes on the roof, then walked back down the staircase into the large room, waited for their eyes to become accustomed to the much lower level of lighting inside the building, and then began their search, working their way around the groups of tourists wandering in and out of the building.

They took their time, first looking around the interior but without seeing anything that immediately struck them as being interesting, and then began a much slower and more careful inspection of the lower levels of masonry, the parts of the building that would most likely have been standing when the Knights Templar were in occupation.

"It would be a help," Robin said, more than a trace of irritation in her voice, "if we had the slightest idea what we were actually looking for."

Mallory grinned at her.

"That's the problem," he said. "What we're doing could be a complete waste of time. We still don't know if Tibauld left any kind of clue here, and if he did there's really no way that we could guess what it might be. Obviously I'm assuming that it wouldn't be anything very obvious—not, for example, an outline map of Cyprus with a large cross in one location and a note in Latin beside it saying 'the treasure is buried here'—but I'm hopeful that he might have left something. He would also have known there was a good chance that the castle would fall to the Mamluks within a matter of weeks or months, and that it would then be badly damaged and possibly even demolished by them, so if he *did* leave any kind of indication, it would almost certainly be carved into a single stone, not inscribed on a number of them, in case the wall or whatever was demolished."

"That's slightly interesting," Robin said, "but not actually helpful. You know more about this sort of stuff than I do, so let's look at it from the other side, as it were. I agree that marking a single stone would make good sense, and he would most probably have picked a stone that forms a part of the foundations or the very lowest levels of the fortress, because those would be the parts of the structure most likely to be left standing after the Mamluks had done their worst. So I suppose we're looking in more or less the right place. But what form could any clue possibly take? And there are a lot of symbols and letters and even whole words carved on these stones, many of them medieval graffiti and in everything from Latin to Arabic, so picking out the right inscription or carving isn't going to be easy."

Mallory considered for a moment.

"Okay," he said. "Let's think it through logically. He

obviously knew that he was going to take the treasure to Cyprus, because the island was not only under the control of the Knights Templar, but for a while they'd actually owned it and had set up their headquarters in Limassol. They bought it from Richard the First, Richard the Lionhearted, back in 1192, and he'd captured the island a year earlier during the Third Crusade. The Knights Templar later sold it to Guy of Lusignan. The island has a long history of conflict that's still the case even today with the Greeks and Turks arguing over it. With their toehold in the Holy Land becoming ever more tenuous, Cyprus was really his only possible destination. So there'd be no point in writing the name of the island or drawing a map of it, because any member of the order would already know that was where he would have to be going. But what he might have done was draw a map of a particular section of the island, or possibly write the name of the place he had chosen to secrete the wealth of the order. And I suppose that he might also have included some kind of Templar symbol, something unmistakable, so that anyone following the trail would be able to recognize the significance of the inscription. Maybe a drawing of the *croix pattée*, something like that."

"That's still really vague," Robin said, "but I'll let you know if I see anything that might fit the bill."

They worked their way diligently around the walls, moving in opposite directions until they finally met up again near the entrance door.

"I didn't see anything that looked helpful," Robin said, "though some of the Latin graffiti was interesting, not to say inventive. How about you?"

Mallory shook his head. "Nothing at all. Maybe we'll have better luck in the other part of the castle."

The other principal section of the castle, the eastern

tower, was in a much more dilapidated state, lacking a roof and with large sections of the walls damaged or missing completely. The only good thing about the tower's poor state of preservation was that the missing roof meant it was much easier to see and interpret the marks on the stones. And there were a lot of those, spanning the ages.

There were fewer visitors in this part of the fortification, probably because there was less to see in the ruined tower, and just as they had done in the western tower, they circled the interior of the building looking for anything that stood out and could possibly be a clue.

"Keep your eyes open for initials as well," Mallory called out to Robin.

"I am," she replied shortly.

But again, their search appeared to be entirely fruitless and, somewhat despondently, they met in a spot near the center of the ruined tower to compare notes and share the lukewarm contents of a bottle of water. It was a hot day, and they both knew the dangers of dehydration, of forgetting to drink when you were busy doing something else.

"I didn't see anything," Mallory said. "I've looked at dozens of crosses scratched into the stones. I've seen Christian, Coptic, and Greek Orthodox symbols, crosses in squares, and crosses in circles, but what I haven't seen anything like a *croix pattée*. No sign of the splayed ends that are so characteristic of that Templar symbol."

"What about initials?" Robin asked. "Nothing useful there, either, I suppose?"

Mallory shook his head. "No. I've had my eyes peeled for *TDG*—Tibauld de Gaudin—all the time we've been here, and I've looked at dozens, maybe hundreds, of letters and initials on those stones, and that's one combination I've yet to see."

Robin took the bottle from him and had another long

swallow. But as she handed him back the plastic water bottle, a sudden thought struck her.

"Hang on a minute," she said. "If Tibauld *did* write his initials, he probably wouldn't use those three letters. The name Tibauld de Gaudin is what we know him as, the way that history records his name, but the 'de Gaudin' bit isn't actually a part of his name, is it? That simply tells us where he came from. He was a man named Tibauld who came from a place called Gaudin, and if he walked up to us right now and introduced himself, he would just call himself Tibauld."

"I hadn't thought of that," Mallory admitted. "So if he was going to write his name in shorthand, as it were, what would he do? What letters would he use?"

"That I don't know for sure, but if you look at the way shorthand forms have developed over the years, one very common characteristic is that you lose the vowels, because it's really the consonants that give the word its shape. So *thanks* becomes *thnx*, though that's probably not a very good example. But if Tibauld was going to use an abbreviated form of his name, it would probably be something like *TBLD* or perhaps just *TBD*."

"Now, that," Mallory said, "does ring a bit of a bell with me. I'm sure I've seen the letters *TBLD* somewhere in this place."

"What, where we are now?"

Mallory shook his head. "No. I think it was in the other tower."

Without saying another word, the two of them abandoned the eastern tower and quickly walked back into the other structure.

"Where did you see it?" Robin asked.

"That's the tricky bit," Mallory replied, "because I can't remember exactly. I think it was over on that wall there"—he pointed to the opposite side of the large room—"but I can't be absolutely certain. We'll just have to search until we find it. What I do remember is that the letters were quite large and whoever had inscribed them had enclosed them in a kind of square box. And don't forget," he added, "that even if I've remembered the initials correctly, there's no guarantee those letters are anything to do with Tibauld de Gaudin."

"I know," Robin said briskly, "but that's absolutely all we have found, so let's take a look at it and try to work that out."

In the event, finding the four initials—and Mallory had been right about them—didn't take very long. Only a couple of minutes after they'd walked over to the opposite wall, Robin lifted her arm and beckoned him over.

"Is this what you saw?" she asked.

On the old gray stone directly in front of her was a rough square, itself divided into two equal parts by a horizontal line. Below the line and centered in the lower half of the square were the letters *TBLD*, clearly and accurately carved, in contrast to some of the other marks they had found, which were little more than surface scratches. These letters, and the line that formed the bisected square, had apparently been incised with a metal chisel, and had been done with considerable care. Above the dividing line and also centered were four other letters— *SOIM*—which made no sense to either of them.

"It doesn't look to me as if whoever carved this was simply some mindless little git who wanted to make his pathetic mark here for posterity," Robin said, tracing the outline of the letters with the tip of her forefinger. "This was obviously done using proper tools and looks to me like a deliberate and thoughtful carving, intended to last for eternity. The only problem is that there's no sign of a

Templar symbol anywhere near it, so I really don't think that we're any further forward. This could have been carved by Tibauld de Gaudin, or probably more likely by someone acting on his orders, or it could equally well have been put here by some unknown bloke called 'Thomas Brian Liam Doyle' or another equally forgettable name. Though if it was, I don't know why he would have taken so much trouble over it."

Mallory nodded, and gave her a brief smile.

"You're absolutely right," he said, "except for one thing. When we started looking here, I suggested you keep your eyes open for any depiction of the *croix pattée*, but I think now that I was wrong. The Templar cross was so well-known as the symbol of the order that it would simply be too obvious a shape to carve. Anybody seeing it, and especially somebody on the track of the Templar treasure and looking here, would immediately be alerted. The fact is that there's a Templar symbol right in front of us, but it's much more subtle than the *croix pattée*. What we're looking at is actually an accurate representation of the *Beauseant*, the battle flag of the Knights Templar."

"It is?" Robin sounded something other than totally convinced.

"It is."

Mallory pointed at the square carefully incised into the gray surface of the old stone and traced the outline.

"The *Beauseant* was one of the simplest flags that has ever been created," he said. "All it consisted of was a roughly square piece of material dyed black at the top and white at the bottom, the dividing line occurring at the halfway point. Some later versions also contained the *croix pattée*, but in these circumstances that would have been too much of a giveaway. But I think what we're looking at here is the simplest possible design of the Templar battle flag, with a shortened form of the name of the newly elected grand master carved into the lower half. I'm certain this is the clue that Tibauld de Gaudin left here before he sailed to Cyprus."

Robin still looked doubtful.

"Don't you see?" Mallory said urgently. "Tibauld would have known the likely fate of the Sea Castle, so he couldn't have left an overt message or other indication, for fear of it being too obvious. But this"—he pointed again at the carving—"this is just a bunch of letters in a square. It only makes sense if you already know that Tibauld de Gaudin was here, and that he was the former treasurer and then the grand master of the Knights Templar, and that he had been entrusted with the treasure of the order and was leaving imminently for the safe haven of Cyprus."

Robin looked at him, and then back at the carved letters and lines on the stone. Then she pointed at the part of the stone directly below the carved inscription. There were a number of other marks inscribed, with equal care but nothing like as deeply carved, in that area.

"Are those a part of it, do you think?" she asked.

Mallory took a small black aluminum flashlight out of his pocket and shone it where Robin was indicating. He could see an unusual shape, somewhat like large and small capital letters *L*, the small one directly above and to the left of the larger one, and joined to it.

"It could be," Mallory agreed. "It looks as if it's been incised with the same care as the main carving, but I haven't the slightest idea what it means."

A couple of inches over to the right was what looked like a letter *V*, but lying on its side with the apex pointing to the left. And to its right were three other, smaller, shapes, each of which also looked like the letter *V* but inverted, the middle one slightly smaller than the other two but more deeply incised and with a short horizontal line directly below it.

"I also have not the slightest idea what these might mean, if anything," he added. "But I'll take a bunch of pictures of them, just in case."

While Robin stared at the shapes, Mallory fished around in his computer bag, which—inevitably—he had brought with him from the car, and took out a small digital camera. He checked that the flash option was set to "Auto" and then took half a dozen pictures of the inscription and the marks underneath it in quick succession, altering the angle of the camera each time to ensure that he was capturing the entire image, and hoping that by doing so any other marks or incisions that they hadn't spotted in the fairly poor light would be recorded by the camera.

"Why did Tibauld inscribe the shorthand version of his name in the lower half of the flag?" Robin asked. "He was the newly appointed grand master of the Templars by this time. Surely his name should go at the top of the flag, as the leader of the order, instead of these other four letters?"

"I don't have an answer for that. The Templars were always modest in their outlook. They took vows of chastity, poverty, and humility, so perhaps Tibauld thought it more appropriate that his name should appear lower down. It does seem odd, though, because it implies that the *SOIM* was more important than he was. The short answer is that I don't know."

"So, if this is the clue," Robin persisted, "what does *SOIM* stand for?"

"That's the rub, I'm afraid," Mallory replied, replacing the camera in his bag, "because I have absolutely no idea. But what I do know is that those four letters have to mean something. They could be the shortened name of a person, but I think it's much more likely that they indicate a place-name or something of that sort on Cyprus, and the only way we're going to be able to work out their meaning is to get ourselves over to the island. I'm sure that's where the answer lies."

55

Rome

Silvio Vitale had carefully considered everything that Toscanelli had told him. Some of what he said Vitale had discounted as little more than excuses for the embarrassing failure of his men, but much of it clearly had a basis in fact: the deaths of four people and the maiming of a fifth allowed for no other interpretation.

Obviously there was much more to the female bookseller Robin Jessop and her unidentified male companion than met the eye. Vitale was not a man known for making assumptions, and he had immediately instructed members of his staff to gather all the data that was available on Robin Jessop. This turned out to be precious little, almost no more information than he already knew about her ownership of the bookshop. The only significant piece of extra data his staff had managed to collect was that she was an occasional amateur racing driver, holding a competition license and generally doing well in the handful of events that she bothered to enter each year.

But even the most diligent of inquiries had failed to

reveal much about the man who was accompanying her. Toscanelli had noted the registration number of the Porsche Cayman that he had been driving, and that information, channeled through the senior police officer who was a tertiary, a kind of unofficial lay member of the Dominican Order, had generated the name David Mallory and an address in Cornwall, but almost nothing else.

However, there were a number of official channels open to Vitale, and he had instituted a number of checks through these. And almost immediately he had begun to gather results.

Within the Schengen area, routine passport checks were almost nonexistent, but travelers were still required to produce their documentation whenever they did certain things, the most obvious of which was flying as a fare-paying passenger in an aircraft, and passenger records were held for some time. They were also confidential, but there were numerous ways in which they could be accessed by law enforcement agencies and other bodies.

Within six hours of Robin Jessop and David Mallory flying to Beirut, Silvio Vitale was looking at a printout of the passenger list for that flight, and that told him precisely where in the world she and Mallory were heading.

Vitale knew that Toscanelli would still be in transit to Cyprus, but he sent him a long encrypted e-mail anyway, telling him what he had discovered. Beirut, he was absolutely certain, was not Jessop's final destination. He knew the history of the Knights Templar better than almost anybody, and from the deciphered parchment text he knew that there was a strong probability Tibauld de Gaudin might have left clues, clues that could conceivably have survived to the present day, and that the first of these was most likely to be found at Sidon, at the Sea Castle.

In fact, he hoped that this was the case, and that Jessop and the man with her would find it and then travel on to Cyprus, which was where both logic and history suggested that the lost treasure of the Knights Templar was to be found, or at least the treasure de Gaudin had taken from Acre, the treasure of Outremer.

But Vitale was still frustrated by one thing: despite a brute-force attack mounted by three of the most powerful computers the order possessed, the final section of the encrypted parchment had still not been deciphered. He had been assured by Fabrini that it would eventually yield, but he had no idea when they might achieve a breakthrough. It could take hours or months, and nobody had any idea which.

But perhaps whatever information remained to be discovered at the Sidon Sea Castle would be enough for Jessop to discover the hiding place. And for that reason, Vitale had had a change of mind with regard to the orders he had given Toscanelli. Instead of acting alone, he was to link up with the advance party that had already reached the island of Cyprus, and they were then to identify Jessop the moment she arrived and follow her and her companion until they discovered where the treasure was hidden.

Once that had been done, the encrypted e-mail concluded, Toscanelli's original orders were to be followed: the woman and her male friend were to die, and Vitale frankly didn't care how, so Toscanelli and the other men could enjoy themselves with her if they wished.

Vitale read through the text of the message one last time, making sure that everything he had said was perfectly clear and unambiguous, and then he sent it. And after that, there was nothing he could do but sit back and wait.

56

Cyprus

Getting from Lebanon to Cyprus hadn't proved to be anything like as difficult as Mallory had expected. There were no ferries, apart from one that plied the route between Mersin in Turkey and Girne on the north coast of the island. But flying was easy, and even the timing had worked. They got back to the airport in Beirut just after five that afternoon, and once Mallory had returned the rental car, almost as a formality he and Robin wandered over to check the departure boards before attempting to find a hotel for the night.

But what they saw changed their minds immediately: Cyprus Airways had a flight leaving for the island at seven fifteen that evening, and they were in good time to catch it. Mallory bought two tickets with cash, choosing a return flight in three days' time. Hopefully by then they would either have located what they were seeking or have to acknowledge that they were wasting their time.

The flight landed precisely on time at Larnaca at seven fifty-five, and they were among the first of the passengers to walk out after passing through customs and immigration. The sun was a glowing yellow ball in a solid blue sky, dipping slowly toward the horizon, and they knew that the heat would hit them like a hot and muggy blanket when they started their search the following day.

"We need two things," Mallory said, looking around the interior of the airport building. "A car—obviously air-conditioned—and somewhere to stay, and that had better have either really thick walls or air-conditioning as well. In that order," he added.

"Well, don't just talk about it," Robin said, pointing at a sign for a hire car agency. "Get over there and sort something out."

"And the other thing we need to do is keep our eyes open. I paid for our air tickets with cash, but we had to show our passports, and that could mean the bad guys know where we're heading. In fact, they might even be here already."

Half an hour later they were sitting in a white right-hand drive Renault Clio, Cyprus being one of only two islands in the Mediterranean—the other being Malta—where traffic drives on the left-hand side of the road, a hangover from the colonization and occupation of the island by the British at the end of the nineteenth and first half of the twentieth centuries. Although the light was already beginning to fade, he had the air-conditioning running at full blast to try to bring the temperature down to a manageable level because the car had been standing in the full sun all day. Inside the vehicle, Robin and Mallory were looking at a road map of Cyprus that had been supplied by the rental agency.

"I don't know why," Mallory said, "but I always thought Cyprus was quite a small island. In fact, it's big. Really big. According to this, it's the third biggest island in the Mediterranean after Sicily and Sardinia. More important for us, it's about a hundred and fifty miles long and over sixty miles wide at its widest point, and that means it's a hell of a big area to search."

Robin nodded. "So we absolutely have to decipher what Tibauld de Gaudin meant by those four letters. Otherwise this is going to be a complete waste of time."

Mallory pointed at the map.

"Right now," he said, "we have no idea where our search is going to take us, so I suppose it doesn't really matter where we decide to stay, at least for tonight. According to this map, the airport is just to the south of Larnaca itself, so why don't we just head north into the town and drive around until we find a small hotel that looks halfway decent? Then we can take a couple of rooms for a night or so while we sort ourselves out."

"Go for it," Robin instructed.

Mallory slipped the car into gear and moved away from the curb where the vehicle had been parked. He drove slowly down the road, alternating his attention between his mirrors and the buildings lining the road as they entered the town from the south. He saw no sign of anyone following them, but the traffic was so heavy that spotting any surveillance was extremely difficult.

Neither he nor Robin had ever been to Cyprus before, so it was all new to both of them. It looked typically Mediterranean, the seafront road dominated by a mixture of newish high-rise hotels and apartment buildings and a handful of much smaller and older individual houses, almost all of them painted white, presumably to reflect the ever-present sunlight, and with red-tiled roofs. There were cars everywhere, and motorcycles and scooters whizzed through the traffic with a cavalier disregard for any rules of the road.

"There've been a lot of problems here in the past, haven't there?" Robin asked. "Between the Turks and the Greeks, I mean."

"There still are problems," Mallory confirmed. "The island's basically divided into two separate parts. Down here in Larnaca, we're more or less in the heart of the Greek sector, which occupies about two-thirds of Cyprus. Then up to the north of us there's a dividing line running roughly east to west, and above that is the smaller Turkish area. I don't think today that there's too much open hostility between the two parts, but it's certainly true that they don't get on with each other very well."

"I saw something on television a while ago about property problems, people buying land in some areas of Cyprus, building houses, and then being told that the ground actually belonged to a Greek citizen, and that the Turkish vendor didn't actually have any legal right to sell it in the first place. I think some houses had actually been demolished as a result."

"I saw the same program," Mallory confirmed. "The start of the troubles was when Cyprus became independent in 1960 after the British occupation."

Robin nodded.

"Remind me not to buy anything except food and drink while I'm on the island," she said. "Definitely no real estate."

Mallory drove the Renault farther through Larnaca and away from the center of the town, where he guessed that hotel prices would be fairly high, and headed north toward the outskirts, looking out for somewhere that appeared both welcoming and inexpensive. He still had a substantial amount of cash in his wallet, the money he had taken from the Italians they'd clashed with back in Devon, but those funds were not inexhaustible. He had avoided using any of his credit cards since they left Britain, so that the British authorities wouldn't be able to trace them through credit card transactions. In their position, cash really was king, and using it essential if they were going to stay below the radar.

About twenty minutes later he braked the car to a stop on the side of the road and pointed through the windshield, again checking the mirrors and again seeing no sign of any vehicle or person who could be following them.

"How does that look at you?" he asked, indicating a white-painted hotel on the opposite side of the road and a short distance ahead.

"Pretty much the same as about a dozen or so that we've already passed," Robin replied. "Why have you picked that one?"

"Two reasons," Mallory said. "The signs beside the entrance."

Robin shifted her glance slightly, and then nodded. "I see what you mean. That should do us nicely."

On one side of the entrance a cheaply painted board announced GOOD ENGLISH SHE IS SPOKE HERE, while on the opposite side another sign proudly proclaimed AC ON ALL ROOME.

Mallory drove the short distance down the road, swung the car over to the right, and stopped it in one of the half dozen or so parking bays that fronted the small hotel. He left the engine running to drive the air conditioner and opened his door.

"You stay here for a minute or so," he said. "I'll see if they've got any vacancies and check just how good the English is they spoke, because my Greek is nonexistent."

He came back out about ten minutes later, two room keys attached to large brass fobs in his left hand.

"They had two rooms left," he announced, opening the driver's door and reaching inside to turn off the engine. "They're next to each other at the back of the building with quite decent views of the sea."

They removed their bags from the trunk of the car. Mallory locked it and then they walked inside the hotel.

A little over eighty yards away, in a narrow side street, a tall and well-built man kept his compact binoculars focused on the two figures as they walked away from the car. He was wearing a pair of cutoff jeans and a T-shirt, and he was sitting astride a middle-sized Honda motorcycle, powerful enough to keep up with almost any car on the twisting roads that characterized some areas of Cyprus, but small enough to be maneuverable in the crowded streets of Larnaca or any other town. In a leather pouch on his belt was a smartphone, and a Bluetooth headset was positioned over his right ear.

"They've just walked into the hotel," he reported in Italian. "They're carrying their bags, so I'm sure they've taken a room there. Just confirm that you've made a note of the address. You already have the registration number of their rental car."

He listened to the reply, his gaze never leaving the entrance to the building.

"I'll give it five minutes," he said, when the man at the other end of the call stopped talking, "just in case they've forgotten anything, and then I'll do it."

The man calling himself Salvatore—a randomly selected work name—had been waiting inside the airport building, sitting at a table in one of the cafés that offered an unobstructed view of the arriving passengers, and had identified the two targets almost immediately. The description that Marco Toscanelli had supplied was both accurate and detailed. They hadn't known which flight the targets would be likely to arrive on, and so Salvatore had been visiting the airport to meet every aircraft that had come from Lebanon. Toscanelli had explained that eventually the order would be told which flight they'd taken from the passenger list, but getting access to the list would take time, and the flight duration was very short, only about forty minutes, so physical surveillance had been the only option.

As soon as Salvatore was certain of his identification, he had called Toscanelli's mobile phone to confirm that the two people had been on that flight, and had kept the line open until Jessop and Mallory walked over to the rental car desk. Then he'd ended the call temporarily, folded up the newspaper he'd been pretending to read, and slipped it into his pocket. He waited until the targets had completed the formalities and were walking toward the exit doors, then followed them out of the building, keeping a few yards back.

Outside, he had walked over to the edge of the parking area where he had left his motorcycle, pulled on his helmet, and again opened the line to Toscanelli to update him on the situation.

As soon as the targets had been positively identified, Toscanelli had suggested sending another member of the group to join the surveillance operation in a car. Salvatore had agreed to this, but recommended holding the second vehicle out of sight and in reserve, because he really didn't believe that any car could elude his motorcycle on the streets of Larnaca. And he'd been right.

When the two targets had put their bags in the trunk of the rental car, Salvatore started the engine on the Honda and waited for the Renault to move away. Then he followed the car, never getting closer to it than about fifty meters and often dropping back to over two hundred meters, and using the heavy traffic on the streets to shield him from the view of the driver as much as he could. Through the Bluetooth headset he kept up a running commentary so that Toscanelli knew exactly which route the two targets were following, just in case something unexpected happened and he lost contact with them.

But it had been almost too easy, the driver of the Renault apparently having not the slightest idea that he was being followed, and Salvatore was completely certain that he had been unobserved. Now he only had one final task to perform, which would take him under a minute.

He continued looking at the hotel, but there was no sign at all of the two people he had been following, and he guessed that they were in their room, maybe unpacking or just freshening up. He didn't want to leave it any longer, in case they decided to return to the vehicle and drive off somewhere for a meal. The window of opportunity was quite small.

Salvatore nodded to himself, checked his watch, and then spoke into his headset.

"I'm going in now," he said.

He restarted the engine of the motorcycle and drove up the road before swinging right into the parking area of the hotel, stopping his machine right beside the white Renault. He glanced round to make sure that he was unobserved, then reached into the pocket of his jeans, took out a small black plastic object about half the size of a box of matches, and flicked a tiny switch on the side. He checked that the small green light at one end was flickering faintly, then bent down and in one fluid and practiced movement he positioned the box against the metal on the inside of the car's rear wheel arch, the powerful magnet the device incorporated almost snatching it out of his hand.

Then he simply turned his bike around and rode un-hurriedly away from the hotel, as if he'd just changed his mind about going into the building.

"The tracker's in position," he said into his headset as he changed up into third gear and accelerated gently down the road that led out of Larnaca. "Confirm that you have a good signal?"

"Confirmed," the voice in his ear stated. "Remain within sight of the hotel, just in case they decide to move later this evening. Ensure that you have a full tank of fuel and a spare battery for your mobile."

Even as Toscanelli issued his instructions, Salvatore was turning left into a street that would virtually com-plete the circle and bring him back to a position from which he would be able to observe the hotel again. Until he was completely certain that the two targets had retired for the night, he had no intention at all of leaving the area.

He didn't even bother to reply to Toscanelli. He was a professional, and knew exactly what was expected of him. Being given pointless orders by the man who had presided over one of the most spectacular failures in the order's recent history was not something that sat well with him.

"I've been in worse places than this," Robin said, placing her bag on the end of the double bed in her room and looking around.

The walls were a kind of faded grayish green, not an unpleasant shade but one that was beginning to look dis-tinctly tired, while the shutters on the windows were newly painted in white. The en suite bathroom was small but possessed all the necessary equipment, and it looked fairly clean. Like the bathroom, the floor of the bedroom was tiled, which probably helped combat the heat, at least to a certain extent, but as far as she was concerned the single most important object in the room was the rounded white oblong shape fitted above the window that bore the name Mitsubishi in red: the air-conditioning unit. Mallory's room next door was virtually identical.

On one of the two small bedside tables were two remote controls, one for the small flat-screen television mounted on a bracket and attached to the wall opposite the bed, and the other for the air conditioner. Mallory seized the latter, aimed it at the window, and pressed the appropriate button. Almost immediately the vents on the front of the unit opened and a faint hum indicated that it was working. A welcome breeze of chilled air wafted across the room toward them.

"It works," Mallory muttered.

"Excellent," Robin replied. "Now I'm starving, and I could also do with an infusion of alcohol of the gin-and-tonic variety, so let's take a walk."

They stepped out of the front door of the hotel and strolled down the street that paralleled the seafront, Mallory again checking for any indication that they were being watched. They picked a bar that overlooked the beach, found a table with a good view of the dark sea, and enjoyed a long cool gin and tonic each. The sun was about to dip behind the mountains to the west of the town, and Mallory knew that quite soon darkness would fall. In the Mediterranean, the transition between day and night is sudden, and the lingering dusks familiar to residents of the British Isles simply don't happen. They finished their drinks and then stepped back out into the street in search of food.

Almost all the local restaurants seemed to be open and they had plenty of choice, eventually settling on a fish restaurant that looked clean and welcoming, reasoning that if you couldn't get decent fresh fish in a restaurant within spitting distance of a fishing harbor in the Mediterranean, where could you?

The food was as good as they'd been hoping, well cooked and presented, and they washed it down with a decent bottle of white. Mallory paid the bill in cash, as usual, and then they strolled slowly back to the hotel. They enjoyed a final cup of coffee out on the terrace, looking at the lights of Larnaca and listening to the nighttime sounds of the town, then went up to their rooms.

Salvatore had eaten a much simpler meal.

He'd consumed two cups of coffee while ostensibly reading a newspaper in a café a short distance down the street from the hotel where the two targets had taken a room, and it was with a certain sense of relief that he finally watched them step out of the building and stroll down the street. Once they'd passed him and had walked about fifty meters down the street, he folded his paper, stood up, and began to follow them on the opposite side.

When they walked into the bar, he sat on a low wall on the opposite side of the street close to a lone streetlight and again appeared to immerse himself in his newspaper, despite the gathering gloom. But within just a few minutes, he could no longer even pretend to be able to see the print, so he folded the paper and stuck it in his pocket and then just sat there, watching the street.

Once the two targets had entered the bar, Salvatore contacted Toscanelli to explain where he was and what was happening, a call he ended when the two people emerged. He stayed behind them, merging with the early-evening crowds and easily keeping them in view, as they continued walking down the street. When they eventually chose a restaurant and disappeared inside, he strolled on farther and picked up a snack from a street vendor. He daren't take the risk of sitting down in a restaurant, because if he did that he wouldn't be able to leave quickly if the targets suddenly emerged, and he had no intention of ending his surveillance until he was certain that the targets had returned to their hotel for the night.

Just over an hour later, they did just that, walking out of the restaurant, apparently entirely unaware that anybody was paying them the slightest attention, and retraced their steps down the street to the hotel.

As soon as the main door of the building had closed behind them, Salvatore continued walking along the street, past the building, to the side street where he'd left the motorcycle. At the corner, he paused for a couple of minutes, staring back down and across the street toward the hotel.

Then he shrugged, pulled on his helmet, started the bike, and rode away.

57

Cyprus

Robin and Mallory walked down to the hotel dining room for a somewhat belated breakfast a little after nine the following morning, sitting in a coffee shop–cum-bar at the back of the hotel on the ground floor. It opened onto a small terrace with three tables each surrounded by four metal and plastic chairs, from which they had quite a decent view across the rooftops of Larnaca to the eastern Mediterranean beyond, a solid band of bright blue flecked with the occasional whitecap.

The terrace was deserted, and they decided to have coffee out there once they'd eaten. Robin sat down at the table on the right-hand side in the shade of the umbrella and placed the road map of Cyprus on the table in front of her, weighing it down with a glass ashtray. Then she removed a pair of large sunglasses from her bag and put them on, shielding her eyes against the glare.

A minute or so later, Mallory walked out onto the terrace, the strap of his computer bag over his shoulder and a cup of coffee in each hand, and sat down beside her.

They lingered over their coffee, trying to decide whether or not to stay in that hotel for a further night, or to move somewhere farther inland on the grounds that it might be a bit closer to the area they were going to have to search. Assuming, of course, that they did actually manage to interpret the clue they believed Tibauld de Gaudin had left at the Sidon Sea Castle over seven hundred years earlier.

"I like it here," Robin said. "Larnaca seems like a pleasant town, and this hotel isn't bad. And to me, it doesn't seem to make very much sense to drive somewhere else on the island until we've got some idea where we should be looking. Why don't we take the easy option, at least just for one more night, and stay here?"

"That's fine with me," Mallory replied. "Now, if we're going to crack this we need to get moving."

Together they scanned the map, looking at the terrain and place-names that were displayed, hoping for inspiration.

"This isn't going to be easy," Robin pointed out, "and I know I'm stating the obvious, but what we have to look for is somewhere that satisfies two separate criteria. First, it has to be somewhere that actually existed at the beginning of the fourteenth century, and I don't know enough about the history of Cyprus to know which of the towns and settlements shown on that map today were around in Tibauld's time. Do you?"

Mallory shook his head.

"No, not really," he admitted. "This hotel has Wi-Fi, so I can do a bit of research on the Internet, but a good first step might be to try and buy a tourist guide to the island, which will hopefully tell us a lot more about the history of the place. You said two criteria," he added. "What was the second one?"

"Oh, just the names," Robin explained. "This place is called Larnaca today, but I have no idea what it might have been called back in the medieval period. Or if it even existed in those days. So we need to find somewhere that had already been built in medieval times and find out what name it had in that period. And, of course, it has to be somewhere that will make sense of the *SOIM* clue."

Mallory sat in thought for a couple of minutes, staring down at the map and digesting what Robin had said. He knew she was right, and at that moment he couldn't think of any easy way of narrowing down the search. He had no doubt that if he went to the Internet and re-searched, say, Larnaca or Limassol or Nicosia, he would quite quickly be able to find out what those places were originally called and when the first settlements had been established, but he couldn't do that for every village and town and city on the island because it would take far too long.

Driving around Cyprus and hoping for inspiration was never going to work, either, because according to the abbreviated table of facts and figures on the road map, the island boasted over eight thousand miles of roads, roughly two-thirds of which had paved surfaces, while the other third were unmade. The island was both much bigger and much more developed than he had ever antici-pated. Finding any object here that had been hidden, and hidden competently by people who knew what they were doing, over seven hundred years earlier was going to make finding a needle in a haystack look like an absolute doddle by comparison.

Random searching was never going to work. They defi-nitely had to work out what Tibauld de Gaudin had been thinking when he landed there and what he could possibly have done with the Templar treasure of Outremer.

"I think," Mallory said slowly, after a few moments, "that we can probably ignore the towns and other built-up areas."

"That's a big jump," Robin replied. "How can you justify it?"

"I'm trying to imagine what might have been going through Tibauld's mind when he arrived here on Cyprus. He had been present in the city of Acre, in the Templar fortress that had been one of the principal fortifications of the order for something like a century. Although he had left a matter of hours before the final attack by the Mamluks, he would obviously have known almost as soon as he got to Sidon that Acre had fallen, and probably guessed that the entire Templar garrison there would have been slaughtered. He would also have looked at the fortifications and defensive strength of the Sea Castle when he reached it and realized that neither the strength of the fort nor the size of the garrison would be anything like enough to withstand a determined attack by the Mamluk army. Don't forget, he'd already seen the Mamluks in action, right up close and personal.

"So by the time he landed in Cyprus, Acre would already have been lost and Tibauld would most probably have been expecting to hear quite soon that Sidon and, very probably, Tortosa and Athlit as well, would be either destroyed or abandoned in the face of the Mamluk hordes. In short, he would have known that the Knights Templar had effectively been expelled from the Holy Land and, unless a miracle happened, they were extremely unlikely to be able to return in the foreseeable future."

Mallory took a sip of his coffee and glanced at Robin, who nodded encouragement.

"I can't fault your logic so far," she said. "Carry on."

"Right, so the Templars have basically been defeated,

and Tibauld is sitting around on the island of Cyprus with a bunch of treasure chests full of bullion and coins and stuff. I'm sure he probably did do his best to try to raise a reinforcing army, but my guess is that he already thought it was a lost cause. So I think that when he chose a hiding place for the Templar assets that had been placed in his care and control, he would almost certainly have assumed that it might be years, possibly even decades, before the Knights Templar presence could be reestablished in the region and the treasure recovered."

"You're obviously presuming," Robin said, "that transporting the treasure back to France or one of the other Templar strongholds in mainland Europe wouldn't be another option for him?"

"I am," Mallory agreed, "but that isn't necessarily the case. Don't forget that the Knights Templar divided their assets between their various headquarters. Traveling in those days was an extremely dangerous operation, and although the ostensible reason for the founding of the Templar order was the protection of pilgrims on the roads to Jerusalem, in later years the order developed an incredibly safe and very secure means of facilitating trade, which works very much like modern banking.

"A trader in Paris who wanted to go to Rome, say, to purchase goods, would take sufficient funds—and these could be coin, bullion, jewelry, or anything else negotiable—to the Templar preceptory in Paris and deposit it there. In return, he would be given a document, issued by the Templars and with the appropriate seals and signatures or whatever to establish its authenticity. He could then travel with that document, which would be of no use to anybody but him, all the way down through Europe as far as Rome. When he got there, he would take the document to the Templar stronghold closest to the city, hand it over, and receive the equivalent value in coin or whatever he wanted, less a commission that would be retained by the Templars. Their banking charge, if you like.

"Now," Mallory went on, "the only way this system could possibly work in medieval times was if every Templar stronghold held substantial assets. A trader had to be absolutely certain that if he deposited money in one Templar preceptory, he could then go to the corresponding stronghold of the order in another country and be able to draw the money he required immediately. So unless Tibauld de Gaudin was convinced the order was finished in Outremer, he would have wanted the assets stored somewhere safe to allow the order's banking system in the eastern Mediterranean to keep functioning."

Robin nodded. "I remember you saying earlier that the Templars actually owned the island of Cyprus for a while, and it was obviously an important strategic refuge for them for some time because of the attempt to take Tortosa from the island of Ruad, so all that makes sense. Of course, once the order was disbanded in 1307, everything would have changed. But that's another story. But I still don't know why he wouldn't have hidden treasure in a town."

"Just because of the time factor," Mallory explained. "If Tibauld guessed that the future of the order in that part of the world was uncertain, and he must have been an intelligent man to have become the order's treasurer and later the grand master, then he would have known that hiding it in a town would simply be too risky. The thing about towns, about a settlement of any size, is that they are in a constant state of flux, of change. A building is demolished to make way for a larger structure; cellars are removed to allow stronger foundations to be built; the paths of streets and roads are altered. Over time, everything changes. The one thing he would definitely not have wanted to happen was for the treasure to be tucked away in a cellar somewhere and then to be found fifty or a hundred years later or whenever by somebody simply enlarging their property. I think he would very deliberately have chosen somewhere where he felt the treasure could lie safely hidden for as long as it took for the Knights Templar to rise again and reclaim the Holy Land once more for Christendom."

"Very messianic," Robin commented.

Mallory smiled somewhat sheepishly. "Sorry about that. I do get a bit carried away sometimes over the Templars."

"So, where did he put it?"

"I still don't know," he admitted. "But I think it would have to be somewhere well away from the centers of population, perhaps in a cave or another kind of natural hiding place, or just possibly in a building that already existed, maybe a castle or a monastery or something like that. The trick, of course, is going to be finding it."

For the next two hours or so they pored over the map, looking for anything, any structure or geographical feature whose name could possibly be rendered in a shorthand form that might read *SOIM*. But nothing they looked at seemed even remotely likely. They saw no names that shared more than one or two of the letters of the abbreviation.

Finally Mallory leaned back in his chair with an expression of frustration on his face.

"I think we're wasting our time," he said. "Unless we've missed it, that abbreviation doesn't refer to any of the geographical features shown on this map, and certainly not to the castles and other buildings that could have been around when Tibauld was here. I was really hoping that he might have picked one of the old castles on the island, because they were definitely here in that period, and they would almost certainly have been occupied by the Templars and would have been fairly safe and obvious places to secrete any valuables. But the names are completely wrong: by no stretch of the imagination can I get *SOIM* out of *Buffavento*, *Kantara*, or *Hilarion*, so obviously Tibauld didn't do what I would more or less have expected him to do.

"Part of the problem is that this is a new road atlas. I'm quite sure it doesn't label all the geographical features, and obviously any names that it does include are going to be the current spellings of names that might originally have been written in Greek or Latin. As I said before, we need a decent guidebook to Cyprus that will include a really comprehensive history of the island and whatever the local equivalent is of a British Ordnance Survey map, a map that will chart and name every significant geographical feature on the island."

He stretched his arms above his head and took a deep breath. The sun was rising steadily higher into the sky, and the day was already hot. It was also, Mallory noted with sudden surprise, almost time for lunch, and despite his recent breakfast he was already feeling hungry.

"There's really nothing else we can do at the moment," Mallory said, "though I suppose I could go on the Web and just do a bit of background research on Cyprus, see if I can find any of the old names of various places, that kind of thing, but I can do that later just as well. Why don't we take a wander down the street and see if we can find a bookshop and then grab an early lunch so we've got the afternoon free?"

"Good idea," Robin replied. "I don't know about proper bookshops that will sell you the kind of map you want, but I can pretty much guarantee that we'll find a souvenir shop down the street where you can pick up a guidebook."

Proper bookshops, as Robin had described, seemed few and far between. One was closed, and had clearly been so for some considerable time. The other they located obviously relied upon the sale of paperback novels in multiple languages for much of its income, but they found a small map section tucked away in a corner of the very back. The proprietor spoke reasonable English, so Mallory was able to explain exactly what he was looking for.

There wasn't really an Ordnance Survey type of map available, but he was able to purchase a modern copy of a seventeenth-century map of the entire island, as well as a current and fairly detailed topographical map. Between the two of them, they hoped that those would reveal the information they were looking for.

Finding a guidebook was a lot easier, and they emerged from one of the souvenir shops along the street with three volumes, two of them illustrated current guides to the island, and both lavishly illustrated with color photographs. The other was a much more serious tome detailing the history of Cyprus from the earliest days, but noticeably lacking any kind of illustration apart from a handful of maps and a few line drawings.

Everything went into Mallory's computer case, and they continued along the street.

"We'll just grab a quick lunch," Mallory said when they'd selected a restaurant. "I want to get back to the hotel and start studying those two new maps. The name we're looking for has to be out there somewhere."

*   *   *

Salvatore, their faithful but invisible shadow, had appeared outside their hotel at just after six that morning, just in case the targets suddenly decided to leave the building. The tracker on the car would allow the vehicle to be followed, but Toscanelli was insistent that he wanted them tailed if they left the hotel on foot as well. Apart from Toscanelli himself, who needed to keep out of sight of the two targets, the only member of the team who had actually seen them, and so could be relied upon to definitely recognize them immediately when they emerged, was Salvatore. He was the only choice in a field of one.

He'd wandered up and down the street, merging as best he could with the few pedestrians who were already out and about, and then took a seat at an outside table as soon as the first café opened its doors for business. Ordering himself coffee and breakfast, he paid as soon as the waiter brought his meal so that he could leave immediately. The café was on the opposite side of the street, which gave him an excellent view of the hotel, and his motorcycle, with a full tank of fuel, was parked a few yards down the street.

The two people he was watching out for finally appeared late in the morning, by which time he'd read the entire contents of his newspaper twice and listened to two somewhat acrimonious telephone calls from Toscanelli, who appeared to be convinced that Salvatore must have missed them. The fact that Toscanelli seemed to doubt his competence was another black mark against the man, in Salvatore's opinion.

When the targets finally stepped out of the building, he heaved a sigh of relief. He had been beginning to wonder if Jessop or the man had somehow detected their surveillance and had slipped away during the night.

They seemed to be in no particular hurry, just ambled down the street like a couple of holiday-makers, intent on nothing more than lunch and sightseeing, although Mallory seemed to be frequently searching their surroundings, probably checking for surveillance.

But Salvatore realized they had some vague plan in mind after he'd made a brief call to Toscanelli to tell him they were on the move. Their visits to the bookshop and the souvenir store confirmed that. In each case he managed to get close enough to glance through the window while they were inside, and although he couldn't see exactly what the man was purchasing, he could at least tell that it was a couple of maps and a few books.

After they'd left the second shop, he called Toscanelli again, briefing him on what he'd seen. The update pleased the disgraced operative.

"They know something," Toscanelli said confidently. "They must have some kind of lead. That's the only reason they'd be buying maps. Make sure they don't see you."

Salvatore watched as the targets walked slowly past the handful of restaurants lining the street, pausing to look at the menus posted outside each one. He took the opportunity to move some distance ahead of them: people who think they're being followed tend to only look behind them, but he could observe them just as well from in front.

Eventually they selected a restaurant and disappeared inside, then reappeared a few seconds later to sit at a table outside. Salvatore mirrored their actions, glancing at a number of menus before sitting down at a table just inside a different establishment that lay between the hotel and where the two targets were sitting. He ordered a small beer and a main course, and paid the bill as soon as his food arrived. From his position, he would easily be able to see Jessop and the man as they returned to their hotel.

They didn't take as long over their meal as Salvatore had expected, and strode past the front of the restaurant after about an hour. And, exactly as he'd done before, the Italian stood up and dogged their footsteps all the way back.

"Do you want to work out there on the terrace again, like we did this morning, or upstairs?" Robin asked, as they walked into the reception hall. They could see the terrace through the rear doorway of the hotel. The brilliant Mediterranean sunshine was bathing it in light, the only shadows the small circles of darkness cast by the umbrellas above the tables.

"I think we'd be better up in your room. The Wi-Fi signal will probably be stronger up there, inside the building, and the computer screen is really difficult to see in sunlight."

Robin nodded, looked through the windows at the bright blue strip of the Mediterranean beyond the town, and suddenly shivered.

"Cold?" Mallory asked.

"No. Somebody just walked over my grave. Which I hope is only an old saying. I've got a lot of life I want to live yet."

Mallory switched on his computer and placed it on the dressing table while Robin sat on the newly made bed and spread out the maps they'd bought that morning.

They started with the current topographical map, sitting side by side on the bed and each looking at roughly one half of the representation of the island on the unfolded sheet. Examining every geographical feature and place-name took a considerable length of time. It was over an hour before Mallory finally shook his head and stood up to stretch his aching back.

"I haven't seen anything, any name at all, that could realistically be abbreviated to *SOIM*," he said. "Have you spotted anything?"

"Not to put too fine a point on it," Robin replied, "sod all. I'm beginning to think we're barking up the wrong tree here."

Mallory picked up the topographical map and folded it.

"We're not done yet," he said. "Don't forget that some of the names will have been changed, perhaps as recently as the nineteen seventies, just because of the conflicts between the Greeks and Turks. Let's take a really good look at that copy of the old map."

The seventeenth-century map was quite different from the current version. In contrast to the sharp modern lettering that had identified geographical features on the topographical chart, the older map's annotations were written in a stylish cursive script, like italics. The labels were also much more difficult to read, the letters tiny and indistinct, and frequently confusing, not least because the labeling was in French.

After another hour, neither of them had seen anything that was even faintly possible as the location to which Tibauld de Gaudin had been referring. Either they were on the wrong track altogether, or the clue that they believed they'd found at Sidon was actually completely irrelevant, just a piece of unusually well constructed graffiti.

Mallory picked up the map and tossed it onto the chair in front of the dressing table; then he and Robin lay down side by side on the bed, staring at the ceiling and alone with their thoughts.

"Maybe we're wrong," Mallory said finally. "Maybe

when we saw that shape at the Sea Castle I was just clutching at straws. I mean, it does look remarkably like the *Beauseant*, but you could also argue that it was just a square with a line across it. And perhaps because I assumed it was a representation of the Templar battle flag, I kind of talked you into believing that *TBLD* was a shorthand form of *Tibauld*."

Robin shook her head. "I don't think you talked me into anything. In fact, I'm not that easy a person to persuade. I still think that you were right, that the mark on the stone had been carved on Tibauld's specific orders. I don't believe that it was just a piece of graffiti. It was too carefully and accurately carved for that to be the case, so I still think we're on the right trail. We just need some final piece of evidence or a different way of interpreting the information."

"I'm glad you think so," Mallory said. "I was beginning to wonder if it was all in my mind, if I was seeing far more in the codes and clues than was really there. I know that you can always interpret—"

"Wait," Robin interrupted urgently, sitting up and looking at Mallory. "I just thought of something, right then when you mentioned codes and clues. I've just realized something that doesn't make sense."

Mallory was caught up in her excitement, and stood up from the bed.

"What?" he demanded.

Robin stood up as well, crossed to the desk, and grabbed a piece of paper and a pencil.

"Look," she instructed.

She wrote the name Tibauld on the sheet, and then the abbreviated form *TBLD* right beside it. On the line below she wrote the other clue they'd found at Sidon: *SOIM*. Then she pointed at the piece of paper.

"What do you see?" she demanded.

Mallory shook his head.

"Only what's there," he said, unsure where she was going. "The full name Tibauld, the abbreviation of it, and the other abbreviation that we still can't make any sense of. What are you seeing that I'm not?"

"Look at the two abbreviations," Robin said. "What's different about them?"

Mallory looked back at the page.

"The letters, obviously," he replied. "All the letters are different, and the only similarity is that each abbreviation has four letters, but I guess that it could just be coincidence."

Robin smiled at him mischievously. "There's something else you're missing. Remember when we were back in Sidon and I told you that one of the commonest ways of abbreviating any word or name is simply to take out the vowels, because it's the consonants that shape a word? That's how you get *TBLD* from *Tibauld*. But *SOIM* is different, because it hasn't been formed by stripping out the vowels. It can't have been, because two of the letters actually *are* vowels. Now do you see?"

"I hear what you're saying, and I see what you mean. What I'm not sure of is how this helps us."

"Right from the start of this adventure, or whatever you like to call it, almost everything we've touched has had something to do with codes and ciphers. I think that Tibauld de Gaudin decided to apply a final further level of secrecy to the location of the Templar treasure of Outremer. For the abbreviation of his name to be recognized, he would have had to leave it simply as *TBLD*, but I think he basically tried to encrypt the abbreviation he'd used for the location. My guess is that he chose his hiding place, abbreviated the name by stripping out the vowels, and then encrypted it, probably by using plain vanilla Atbash. That's how we've ended up with two vowels in an abbreviation where there really shouldn't be any."

Mallory didn't reply, but scrabbled among the papers he'd removed from his computer bag when they returned to the bedroom, and plucked out the one on which he had written the first, simple, and uncomplicated Atbash cipher. It took him less than ten seconds to decode the four letters *SOIM*.

When he'd done so, he picked up the discarded map of Cyprus and looked at one particular area on the north coast of the island. Then he opened one of the guidebooks, checked an entry in the index, and swiftly found the corresponding page and read the first part of the article that was printed on it.

He put down the book, turned back to Robin, and impulsively kissed her full on the lips. She looked somewhat startled but made no move to resist.

"Sorry," he said, the excitement palpable in his voice. "I just felt I needed to do that, because you're absolutely right. That's the only thing that makes sense. The straight Atbash decode of *SOIM* is *HLRN*, and the most obvious interpretation of that is the castle of Saint Hilarion, up on the north coast of the island, a castle that was originally built in the eleventh century and that the Templars definitely occupied. That must be where Tibauld de Gaudin stashed the treasure of the order, and so that's where we're going right now."

Fifteen minutes later they had packed their bags, paid the bill, and checked out of the hotel. Mallory opened the trunk of the little Renault and put everything inside it, then sat down in the driver's seat and started the engine while Robin looked at the map, working out the best route to take to the north coast of the island.

"I think we'll take the long way round," she said. "The problem is that we're down here on the south coast at Limassol, and the castle of Saint Hilarion is on the other side of Cyprus on the north coast, and between the two places are the Troodos Mountains. There are roads that go over the mountains, but it's quite a long way and they'll be twisty and steep, so I think the fastest route will actually be to head east along the coast and then follow the main road north to Nicosia. Then that will carry us pretty much straight on to Girne or Kyrenia, and that's more or less the location of the castle."

"Suits me," Mallory said, reversing the Renault out of the parking space. "I'm just the driver. All you have to do is tell me where to go."

"They're on the move," Salvatore announced when his call was answered, speaking softly into his Bluetooth headset, "and my guess is they've checked out of the hotel because the man has just put all their bags in the car."

He was again sitting at a café on the opposite side of the street—a different one this time—a coffee cup and a newspaper on the table. He watched as the Renault stopped just short of the main street, the driver checking the traffic in both directions before pulling out.

"They're heading east," Salvatore continued. "I'll give them a couple of minutes, then catch up with them on the bike. Confirm you still have a good signal from the tracker?"

"Confirmed," Toscanelli said. "Nico is in his car about half a kilometer from you, and he'll become the primary unit once they leave the built-up area. I'm in the secondary unit, and we've just got mobile from the hotel. Make sure they don't see you. If you think the driver has any suspicions at all, turn off as soon as you can and then hang well back for the rest of the journey. Whatever happens, they mustn't know that they're being followed."

"Copied," Salvatore said, ending the call. He tucked his newspaper into the pocket of his jeans and walked away from the café toward his parked motorcycle.

58

Cyprus

Following Robin's directions, Mallory steered the car through the center of Larnaca, heading northwest toward the interior of the island. The afternoon traffic was heavy, and they made fairly slow progress.

"We're on the B2 at the moment," Robin said, looking up from the road map that she had open on her lap, "but if you see a sign for Nicosia, or for the A2, follow it. It looks to me as if the B2 was the old main road, and the A2 is a newish motorway that follows the same route."

"So we could stay on the B2."

"Yes. But it's already late afternoon and we need to find somewhere to stay tonight, so the sooner we get across to the other side of the island, the better."

The traffic thinned out as they drove farther away from the center of Larnaca, and Mallory joined the A2 Motorway as soon as they reached the junction. Then he increased speed considerably, and they began covering the distance much more quickly.

"Does this take us all the way to the north coast?" he asked.

"No. In ten or twelve miles this motorway merges with the A1 and swings around to the north. Obviously we just keep on going all the way to Nicosia, which is where the motorway ends. Then we have to hack our way through the town and out the other side, but then we'll only be fifteen miles or so from the north coast."

She looked down again at the map, then glanced back at Mallory.

"Stupid me," she said. "I knew that the castle of Saint Hilarion was on the north coast of Cyprus, but I've only just realized that means it's in the Turkish area. Is that going to be a problem, crossing from the Greek sector to the Turkish sector, I mean?"

"I really don't know," Mallory said, "and I hadn't really thought about that. I think for a few years there was a wall separating the two parts of the island, so I suppose then it would have been a bit like the situation in Cold War Berlin. I hope it's a bit easier now, though I suppose there will be regulations governing the movements of Cypriots. But we're tourists, so hopefully we'll just be able to drive from one sector to another, maybe with just a passport check or something in the middle."

The border crossing wasn't that difficult, but it also wasn't as easy as Mallory had hoped. Nicosia was crowded, and the traffic was moving so slowly that they decided to stop at a café for a drink and a snack while they were still on the Greek side, in case they had problems finding anywhere once they crossed the border.

Mallory, inevitably, was carrying his computer case, and while they waited for their meal to be prepared he took out his laptop and surfed the Internet, using the free

Wi-Fi system offered by the café. It didn't take long to find a couple of sites that listed the procedure to be followed for vehicles crossing from the south to the north of the island.

"It's lucky we're not going the other way," he said after a few minutes, closing the lid of the laptop and putting it back in his case. "If you hire a car in the north of the island, you're not allowed to drive across what they call the Green Line into southern Cyprus. The only vehicles allowed to cross the border in that direction are those owned by Turkish Cypriots. But going from south to north, we'll be okay, with a couple of wrinkles, obviously."

"What kind of wrinkles?" Robin asked suspiciously.

"The main one is that the car insurance isn't valid in northern Cyprus, just like insurance bought in the north of the island is invalid in the south, so when we get to the border we've got to buy an additional policy."

"Typical," Robin said. "That's like an English driver having to buy insurance for Scotland once he gets to the border. Anything else?"

Mallory nodded.

"We also need visas," he said, and held up his hand to forestall the objection that he could already see forming on Robin's face. "But the good news is that getting these seems to be just a formality because we have British passports. We just have to fill in a form each."

"And that's it?"

"As far as I can see, yes. But there may be a fee or two to pay as well, in addition to the extra insurance we'll have to buy."

"Oh well. It's only money. And not even our money, come to that."

When they'd eaten they got back in the car and Mallory followed the instructions he'd read on the Internet and had taken the trouble to jot down. The site had told them to look out for road signs to "Keryneia," which were not particularly plentiful or very clear, but they did eventually find their way to the Metehan crossing point.

The Greek border guards seemed surprisingly relaxed, and barely even glanced at the vehicle as they drove past. The Turkish officials were equally casual, but they did halt the Renault to inspect their passports and vehicle paperwork.

The visa form wasn't particularly difficult to complete, requiring little more than their names, nationalities, and passport numbers, and obtaining the additional insurance that was a legal requirement didn't take long. Less than fifteen minutes after Mallory had switched off the engine, he started it again and they drove on, into northern Nicosia.

On the other side of the border, both the language used on the road signs and the flags were different, the familiar blue-and-white symbol of Greece being replaced by the crescent and star on the red flag of Turkey. But otherwise the Turkish part of Cyprus looked remarkably like the Greek sector. Just as in Larnaca, it soon became obvious that the northern part of the island also relied heavily upon tourism for its income, and there seemed to be just as many bars, cafés, restaurants, and hotels as they had seen in the south.

"Under no circumstances let me go inside a place like that," Robin instructed, pointing at the brightly lit window of a shop they were driving past in the late-afternoon traffic.

Mallory glanced in the direction she was pointing and nodded. There was absolutely no doubt about the goods on sale. Arranged in different-colored pyramid shapes in the window were piles and piles of Turkish pastries, dusted with icing and probably handmade somewhere in the local area.

"I reckon you're looking at roughly a million calories in each heap," he said. "God alone knows why all the Turkish girls don't weigh about a quarter of a ton each. They must have the most amazing willpower."

"They probably daren't go near the shops selling the stuff," Robin said, then turned her attention back to the map. "Now we need to head for Girne, so keep your eyes open for a sign. We should be able to find a hotel somewhere there."

The main road ran more or less due north out of Nicosia, across the Mesaoria Plain and straight toward the Kyrenia Mountains, the long and narrow range that stretched east-west for roughly one hundred miles along the north coast of Cyprus, defining that part of the island. They only rose to about half the height of the Troodos Mountains in the center of Cyprus, but had historic importance because they'd provided locations for watchtowers and fortifications since the earliest days, offering unrivaled views across the Mediterranean.

The transition from the level plain to the mountains was somewhat abrupt, but crossing to the other side of the range was easy, the road swinging almost due east to follow the path of a long valley before turning back to the north. As soon as they emerged from the end of the valley, they saw the lights of Girne in front of them, a twinkling carpet in the gathering gloom of early evening.

"Pretty," Mallory commented. "Do you want me to head for the town center, or what?"

"Might as well," Robin replied. "There's a harbor and quite a few tourist attractions, according to this map, so finding a hotel shouldn't be difficult. In fact, it looks as if there's a large interchange on the outskirts of Girne. If you turn right there and head north, that should take us straight toward Kyrenia Castle—Kyrenia is the old name of the town—and that's one of the most popular historic sites in the area."

"There was something about that in the tourist guide, wasn't there?"

"Yes," Robin said, opening the book that she'd occasionally been looking at during their drive and finding the appropriate page. "It was originally probably a Templar stronghold, but the fortification there today is much more recent. It dates from the sixteenth century and it was built by the Venetians, modified later by the Ottoman Turks and later still by the British. It's apparently quite an impressive building."

A few minutes after Mallory made the turn off the main road, he stopped the Renault in the car park of a small hotel located in a back street between the castle and the harbor. The sign outside the building, written in rather better English than they'd seen back in Larnaca, promised not only vacancies but also en suite showers and toilets, plus free Wi-Fi for guests, and for a fairly low quoted price.

Robin looked at the building with a certain amount of suspicion.

"It looks very cheap for what it's offering," she said.

"We're staying here for one night, not buying the place," Mallory pointed out. "If it's no good we'll find a better hotel tomorrow, but it's getting late and I don't want to spend the rest of the evening driving round the town looking for something else."

In fact, it wasn't too bad once they got inside, though the showers and bathrooms were cramped and clearly fairly recent additions to the small adjoining rooms they took. But they were clean, and the receptionist who took Mallory's cash and handed them the keys spoke good, though not fluent, English.

They had a drink in the bar-cum-lounge situated just off the reception hall, sitting at a corner table while they planned what they were going to do the following day, the topographical map of the island unfolded on the table in front of them.

"I don't really have much of a plan," Mallory said, looking at the entry for Hilarion Castle in the guidebook. "It all depends on what we find when we get up there."

Robin nodded. "I think our biggest problem is that the castle is a major tourist attraction and has been for quite a long time. That means people have been walking all over it and—probably—digging all around the area while work was being done on the place for several centuries. I know you're convinced that we're on the trail of this lost treasure, but I really don't see how something that was hidden the best part of one millennium ago could still be lying there, just waiting for us to turn up and find it. Surely somebody would have found it already?"

"I don't know, and it's very difficult to prove a negative. But I've read a lot about the Templars, and so far I haven't found any indication that it was recovered. If somebody had stumbled across the hoard since the thirteenth century, I would have expected to see a reference to it somewhere. The Templar treasure definitely arrived here in the care of Tibauld and he certainly died here, and all references to the treasure seem to have died with him. But I take your point. Logically you would expect that the treasure had been recovered at some point. If it wasn't, if nobody knew where he had hidden it, I can only assume that he concealed it really well, in some part of the castle that was hidden from view or that nobody knew was there."

Robin smiled at him. "And you really think that we're going to be able to just walk in there and find it?"

Mallory shrugged.

"I don't know," he said again. "The only clue we have is that piece of graffiti we found at the Sidon Sea Castle, and all that seems to say—assuming we're reading it correctly, of course—is that Tibauld concealed the hoard at Hilarion. What it obviously doesn't tell us is exactly *where* he hid it. And I don't think there's anything much we can do until we actually get up to the site and see what it looks like."

"I'll go inside and check," Salvatore said into his Bluetooth headset. "I speak enough Turkish to ask for a coffee or a drink."

"If they're not in the bar, don't push your luck," Toscanelli replied. "Don't let them even guess that you're watching them."

Toscanelli was still a couple of miles outside Girne, the car having got stuck in a line of traffic waiting to cross the border into northern Cyprus. Salvatore had had no such problems on his motorcycle, and Nico, in the second car, which was equipped with the receiver to follow the tracker attached to the target car, had driven across the border only three or four minutes behind the Renault. Nico had followed the targets, and Salvatore had followed Nico, and they had had no trouble at all in tracing Jessop and her male companion to the hotel they had chosen.

In fact, Salvatore didn't really need to go into the building at all, and he knew it, but he wanted to make absolutely certain that the two targets were there simply because he had lost sight of them on the journey across the island. And, if possible, he also wanted to get some idea about what they were doing.

He ended the call without any further comment, tucked his headset into his pocket, switched his mobile to silent, secured his crash helmet to the motorcycle, and strode into the hotel. Inside the building, he walked casually into the bar, where about twenty people were sitting, drinks on the tables in front of them, the low buzz of conversation interspersed by occasional laughs, the riffle of cards, and the chink of glasses.

Salvatore hadn't eaten since lunchtime and was still uncertain what the evening would bring, so drinking alcohol was not an option. He ordered and paid for a coffee and a cake and took them over to a small round table on the opposite side of the room to where the two targets were sitting. He'd identified them the moment he stepped into the bar. Sitting down, he took out his now rather tatty newspaper and placed it on the table in front of him, then bent forward, appearing to read it while covertly studying Jessop and her companion.

Five minutes later he finished his snack, picked up his paper, and walked outside. As soon as he was clear of the building, he called Toscanelli to update him on the situation.

"They're in the hotel," he confirmed, "and my guess is that they won't be leaving tonight. It looks to me as if they're making plans for tomorrow. They've got a guidebook open in front of them and they're studying what I think is a topographical chart, but I wasn't close enough to confirm that. So my guess is that they'll make an early start tomorrow."

"They're working out where to start looking," Toscanelli said.

"Exactly. Nico can do the overnight surveillance, because I need to eat something and get some sleep. I'll be back here, covering the hotel, tomorrow morning no later than six."

59

Cyprus

The castle was located on the northern side of the Kyrenia Mountains, and Robin had worked out that probably the fastest way to get there was to retrace their route of the previous evening and head back toward Larnaca and the south coast of the island, then head up into the mountains when they were on the south side of the range.

Once they left the main road, their driving slowed as the narrow road wound its way up the steep side of the mountain and around hairpin bends, gaining height all the time. Mallory could see at least three cars in front of them, and about the same number behind, together with a couple of motorcycles.

"According to this guidebook," Robin said as they drove through some kind of military area, following the signs directing them toward Saint Hilarion, "the best time to visit the castle is early in the morning—as we're doing now—and before most of the coach parties begin arriving. Apparently it's very popular with Russians, for some reason, and they tend to arrive en masse. It's a big place, by all accounts, but it can get very crowded during the tourist season. Which I suppose is more or less right now."

Mallory nodded. "If this level of traffic is anything to go by, this early in the morning, the guidebook is probably right. With any luck, we'll be able to take a quick look round before it gets too crowded. And once we've done that, we'll have a much better idea—I hope—about where we *should* be looking."

"Because wherever the treasure is," Robin finished for him, "it won't be anywhere that's visited by tourists, obviously."

"Exactly. It's certainly a hell of a long way up," Mallory said, swinging the car round yet another tight corner. "I think when I looked at the history of the place it was reckoned to be almost impregnable."

"That's right," Robin said, looking again at the guidebook. "Obviously no castle can ever withstand a siege indefinitely, but Saint Hilarion's Castle did a lot better than most. It was one of the last fortifications on the island to fall to the Knights Templar when they arrived here at the end of the twelfth century, and about forty years later it became the stronghold of the Lusignan king Henry the First in his conflict with the Holy Roman emperor Frederick the Second, and it held out for four years, though it wasn't besieged for that entire time. When there was finally an outbreak of peace in the thirteenth century, a lot of rebuilding work was done on the castle, and it became a summer residence for the rulers of the island.

"But the most destructive enemy the castle faced never actually laid siege to it. When the Venetians took control of Cyprus late in the fifteenth century, they concentrated their defenses down on the coast, at fortifications like

Kyrenia Castle, near where we stayed last night, and ignored the forts located higher up. It's possible that they actually began dismantling Hilarion and the sister castles of Kantara and Buffavento, apparently to save the cost of providing a garrison for each of them."

Mallory nodded. "And that's another reason why it'll be a waste of time looking in the obvious places in the castle, because if the Venetians even partially dismantled it, they would certainly have found the treasure if it had been placed anywhere within the structure. That is if the hoard hadn't already been found when the place was being rebuilt and expanded."

"And I didn't know this," Robin said. "The castle became a stronghold again, but much more recently. In the nineteen sixties it was used as the headquarters of the Turkish Cypriots, and they put a small garrison there that managed to defend the place against attacks by EOKA. That was the Greek paramilitary force that was trying to drive out the British as well as the Turks and basically make Cyprus a part of Greece. And another decade later, it became the center of a fight for control of the pass that runs through these mountains. It's obviously seen more than its fair share of conflict over the centuries, and that must mean that the castle has been thoroughly explored by almost everybody involved."

Robin closed the guidebook and stared through the windshield at the narrow ribbon of road unrolling in front of the car.

"And you still think it's worth carrying on?" she asked. "In view of its history, are you sure that we're not just wasting our time?"

"I can't be certain of that, no, but I still think that if the treasure had been found, there would be some report about it, somewhere. And I also think that Tibauld de

Gaudin wasn't a stupid man. He would have known that the castle of Saint Hilarion, just like any other castle, would very probably be besieged at some point, and might even be taken by enemy forces, and so the last thing he would have done would be to secrete the treasure anywhere that it was likely to be found. I think he probably concealed it near enough to Hilarion so that the castle became a kind of marker, but far enough away that you would have to know exactly where to look to discover it."

"So, how do we find out where to look?"

Mallory shrugged and grinned at her.

"I've said that I don't know so often since we began this that it's almost become my motto," he replied. "I'm hoping that once we've had a look at the castle itself and the surrounding area, we might have an idea where to start. When we've done that, we'll take another look at the pictures I took of that piece of graffiti in Sidon and see if it makes any more sense. I suppose the one advantage we do have is that, assuming what's written on that old piece of parchment is correct, at least we know there *is* something here to find, even if we don't know exactly where to look for it. Without that single piece of information, I suppose it's at least possible that nobody has ever come up here looking for the Templar treasure. That's not much of a plan, I know, but right now it's all I've got."

At the fork in the road, Mallory swung the car right, following the signs for the castle, though he hardly needed them: the battlements and crenelated walls that adorned the top of the mountain were clearly visible. It looked like something out of a fairy tale, a pointed peak surmounted by an ancient Disneyesque castle.

There weren't many parking spaces at the end of the

road below the sprawling outline of the castle, and although they were early Mallory didn't want to get boxed in by other visitors, so he turned the rental car around and stopped it about fifty yards down the road, pulling off onto the stony verge on the left-hand side.

Then he turned off the engine and for a few moments they both sat there staring through the side windows at the ancient ruin that stretched up to the peak above them.

"It's much bigger than I thought it was going to be," Mallory said. "I'd kind of envisaged something a bit like the Sidon Sea Castle, a fairly compact fortification."

"You can probably describe this place in lots of different ways," Robin replied, "but 'compact' certainly isn't one of the words that immediately springs to mind."

Mallory glanced back, toward the end of the road. Drivers of other cars were maneuvering their vehicles into the marked parking places or choosing spots beside the road, as he had just done. There were a couple of buildings there, one of which obviously contained a café, and presumably a section where admission tickets could be purchased, and probably a gift shop as well, the Turks not missing an opportunity to capitalize upon a captive audience.

"According to this book," Robin said, "the climb up to the top of the castle takes about an hour, and it's pretty steep, but apparently the views are really spectacular."

Mallory nodded.

"If we were here on holiday," he said, "I'd suggest we should do just that, climb all over the place taking pictures that we'd probably never look at again, exactly like tourists everywhere. But I think the one thing we can be certain about is that the treasure isn't anywhere that a person buying a ticket is going to be able to visit. So actually visiting the castle is going to be a complete waste of time and effort, not to mention bloody hard work, from the sound of it."

Robin smiled at him. "You're just a cheapskate, too mean to buy a ticket."

"Not really. Just to prove it, I'll buy you a coffee and a cake or something in that café back there, and I'll find the best book about this place that the gift shop has to offer. Wandering about here is going to be pointless until we've got some idea of the layout."

He took his computer bag out of the trunk and locked the car, and then they walked back along the road until they came to the entrance to the gift shop. There were numerous guides to the castle on the shelves, written in about a dozen different languages. Mallory flicked through them and selected a volume containing two different maps, one showing the layout and structure of the castle itself, while the other was a detailed topographical chart of that section of the mountain range. He bought the book and they walked into the café.

The temperature was already starting to climb up outside, and instead of coffee they both decided that a couple of glasses of cold fresh lemonade would hit the spot rather better, accompanied by two generous slices of baklava. Once they'd finished eating, he moved the plates to one side and opened the first of the maps, the one showing details of the castle. The extensive structure seemed to be divided into three main areas. At the very top, nestling between the twin peaks that formed the summit of the mountain, was the upper ward. This contained the remains of the royal apartments and King John's tower, and was the ultimate destination of most visitors because of the spectacular views it offered over the north coast of Cyprus.

Below that was the middle ward, where there were further royal apartments and a number of other structures including Saint Hilarion's Chapel, the gatehouse, and the Belvedere, the name deriving from Italian and simply meaning a structure designed to take advantage of a particularly fine view. The lowest section of all, predictably enough called the lower ward, was delineated by the impressive wall that dominated the landscape close to the approach road, and which also contained one of the entrance gates and the barbican.

"And a barbican is what, exactly?" Mallory asked, pointing at the label on the map.

"It just means a fortified gate or entrance," Robin replied. "They were a common feature of castles and fortified towns in the Middle Ages, and they were usually positioned just outside the main wall to act as a first line of defense for the gateway, the weakest point in the defensive wall. The barbican was normally linked to the main wall by a short corridor protected by thick walls, usually referred to as the 'neck,' so that if the enemy forces seemed to be gaining the upper hand, the defenders could leave the barbican and get back inside the city or castle and continue the fight from there. They fell out of use during the fifteenth century because of changes in siege tactics and the kind of heavy weapons that had started to become available then."

They continued studying the map for several more minutes, but nothing struck them as being particularly significant. The whole structure had clearly been built, rebuilt, demolished, and built up again over roughly half a millennium beginning in the tenth century, and as Mallory had believed all along, if the Templar treasure had been hidden away anywhere within the grounds of the castle, somebody would certainly have found it during that period.

"Interesting, but not helpful," he said, folding the map and tucking it into the sleeve inside the back cover of the book. "Let's take a look at the general area, and see if inspiration strikes us then."

He took out the second map and spread it out on the table where they were sitting. It was much more comprehensive and detailed than the topographical chart of the island that they had bought back in Larnaca, and just showed that section of the Kyrenia range where the castle was located. Again they studied the markings and details, but without seeing anything that seemed important.

"It's like looking for a needle in a haystack, to use a cliché," Robin said, "when you're not actually sure you're looking in the *right* haystack."

Mallory stood up and felt in his pocket for some coins. "Would a coffee help?" he asked.

"It certainly wouldn't hurt. White, no sugar, and not too strong, if that's possible, bearing in mind we're in Turkey."

A few minutes later Mallory carried the drinks over to the table and sat down again.

"Let's have another look at the pictures you took at the Sidon Sea Castle," Robin suggested. "Maybe that will generate some kind of spark."

Mallory quickly had the laptop running and they studied each of the images that he had taken of the symbol scratched on the wall of the old Templar fortification, displaying them on the screen one after the other.

"There are a few other marks on the stone," Mallory commented. "I can see those inverted V shapes underneath it, and the V lying on its side, but I have no idea what their significance is, or even if they're just a few random shapes scratched on it by somebody centuries later."

"I don't know," Robin said thoughtfully, studying the new picture on the screen. "Hang on a minute," she continued as Mallory pressed the key to display the next image. "Go back one."

She stared at the picture again, then nodded.

"You've seen something?" Mallory asked.

"I don't know, but I was just wondering if there might be some significance in the positioning of the letters."

"Which letters? Oh, you mean the *SOIM* and *TBLD*?"

"Yes." Robin pointed at the picture on the screen. "If we're right—and after all this I hope to God we are—I still think it's a bit peculiar that the abbreviated form of Tibauld should be positioned in the lower half of what you think is the *Beauseant*. After all, he had been a senior member of the Knights Templar for several years, and by the time this inscription was carved, he was the grand master, the leader of the order. So if his name was going to be put on the *Beauseant*, I would have expected it to be at the top of the flag."

"Maybe." Mallory didn't sound completely convinced. "Don't forget that the order made a big thing of poverty and humility, and perhaps Tibauld didn't think himself worthy of having his name at the top of anything, grand master or not."

"But this is just a piece of well-carved graffiti, something that was never really intended for public consumption, not like an actual flag to be hoisted above a group of Templar knights or flown from the battlements of a castle. We're assuming that this carving was made for one purpose only: to indicate to members of the order arriving at the Sidon Sea Castle at some future date, long after the original garrison had either left or been slaughtered, that the treasure of the order had been taken to Cyprus and to show its location. Or at least to provide a clue, a starting point, if you like, to allow these later Templars to recover it."

"Okay," Mallory replied, "I can't argue with any of that, but I don't really see where you're going with it."

Robin pointed at the screen again.

"I think it's significant," she went on, "that the *SOIM*, which we're fairly sure is *HLRN*, the abbreviated form of Hilarion encrypted in Atbash, is placed above the *TBLD*. Tibauld was the treasurer of the order. The treasure was placed in his care and after that he became the grand master, so maybe he was using his own name as a synonym for the treasure itself. After all, he couldn't really spell out exactly what he was hiding, because if he did, then anybody—Templar, infidel, or just somebody looking for booty—would be able to follow the trail and recover it. But only a Templar would know that Tibauld was the treasurer, and that he had taken the wealth of the order to Cyprus."

"I think I see what you mean. You reckon that the *TBLD* refers to the treasure. And because the letters *SOIM* are placed above the *TBLD*, that means the hiding place is underneath the castle."

"Exactly," Robin said. "Tibauld was too intelligent a man to hide the treasure within the castle, or even in an existing cellar or dungeon or anything like that, because he would have known that it would almost certainly be discovered in the future. So I think that he may well have ordered an underground cavity to be excavated somewhere in the lower area, the lower ward, of the castle and buried the treasure in it. That would, if you like, be a literal—in the proper sense of the word—interpretation of the carving. The treasure would be under the castle. So that would be *TBLD* under *SOIM*, or rather *HLRN*, just like the carved inscription."

Mallory nodded slowly. What Robin had said certainly made sense, though there was an obvious problem.

"If you are right," he said, "that does present us with a certain amount of difficulty. You can see the size of the castle, and especially the lower ward. If that was where Tibauld hid the treasure of the order, any markers or indicators he might have left to show where it was will almost certainly have been obliterated during the last seven hundred years. And there's also an obvious practical problem. Even if we could somehow manage to find the location of the hoard, digging it up would probably prove to be impossible. I somehow can't see the Turkish authorities letting us chew up the interior of one of their principal tourist attractions with a JCB digger, and we'd probably need to use something like that to have any hope of finding it."

"So that's it, then? We just pack up and go home?"

"Maybe. In fact, yes, if you're right. This really is the end of the trail."

For a few seconds the two of them just sat there, staring blankly at the computer screen. Then Mallory shook his head.

"That really is a bit of a bummer," he muttered. "I really didn't expect that we would manage to get so far, to follow the trail for as long as we have, and then meet something like this. We can't go to the Turkish authorities and tell them what we've discovered, because we haven't really found anything, just an old bit of parchment and some scratches on a stone in the wall of a long-abandoned castle. None of that is what you might call solid evidence, is it?"

"No," Robin agreed, glancing at Mallory.

She looked back at the screen, and then her expression changed.

"Hang on a minute," she said. "There's something about this that doesn't make sense. About the timing, I mean."

"Timing?"

"Yes. Think it through. Tibauld de Gaudin traveled from Acre to Sidon with the treasure, and when he got there he was elected grand master of the order. But he left almost immediately to carry the treasure to Cyprus, and according to the historic record he never went back to Sidon because he died on the island quite soon after his arrival. So that carving at the Sidon Sea Castle must have been done on his orders after he arrived from Acre but before he left for Cyprus."

"Obviously," Mallory interjected.

"Sorry. Just getting my facts in a straight line. So if that timeline is correct, Tibauld must have known before he left Sidon exactly where he was going to store the treasure on Cyprus. That must mean he knew the layout of this castle and local area in enough detail to have selected a suitable spot in advance. If that was the case, then I don't think his solution to the problem was to dig a hole somewhere and bury it. He must have had somewhere more permanent in mind, but somewhere that still fitted the general description of being under the castle of Saint Hilarion. Maybe some building or structure lower down the mountain."

Mallory thought for a few seconds, then reached out and picked up the topographical map. Down one side of it was the usual legend, explaining the meaning of the various symbols used on the map and other relevant information. When he read one particular sentence, his face brightened immediately, and he pointed at it.

"I think you could be right," he said. "Just read that."

Robin looked down at the tiny writing. "I don't understand. 'The Kyrenia range is sedimentary in origin and principally formed of limestone with some marble deposits,'" she read out. "I thought marble was limestone," she added.

"It is, I think. Or a kind of limestone, anyway. The point is that there's something interesting about limestone and the way it reacts to acidic water. When rain falls, it will absorb a certain amount of carbon dioxide from the atmosphere, and it picks up more from decaying plant material once it hits the ground."

He paused and glanced back at the topographical chart before turning again to Robin.

She looked puzzled and faintly irritated.

"So?" she demanded. "I really don't want a lesson on meteorology, if you don't mind."

"It's not meteorology," Mallory pointed out, "just some basic chemistry that I can barely remember now. The point is that the addition of carbon dioxide to water produces a form of carbonic acid. Limestone is actually calcium carbonate, and that reacts chemically with carbonic acid, causing a slow but consistent erosion of the rock. And that produces cavities that grow larger with the passing millennia."

"So?" Robin demanded again.

"So one of the principal characteristics of limestone is the ease with which caves are formed in it by this chemical process. I don't think Tibauld de Gaudin had any intention of just digging a hole and burying the treasure of the Knights Templar or sticking it in a building near here. I think he knew that the mountain underneath the castle of Saint Hilarion was riddled with caves, and he picked one of those to be the final resting place of the wealth of the order. So what we have to do now is find which one he chose."

On the other side of the café, Salvatore was becoming restless, and debating the advisability of buying another cup of coffee, just in case he had to go to the lavatory and the targets chose that moment to leave. To add to his discomfort, the seats were hard, and he was slowly growing numb.

He was also puzzled because he had no idea what the targets were planning on doing next. Like Toscanelli, he had expected that once they arrived at the castle they would head to wherever they believed the treasure was hidden, but unless they thought it was somewhere in the café—which seemed unlikely at best—it didn't look as if they were doing anything other than a bit of research, studying images on a computer and a map taken from a book the man had purchased in the gift shop.

Not for the first time, the Italian wondered if their masters in Rome had got it all very badly wrong. Perhaps Jessop and her male companion were simply taking a holiday. But the more he thought about that, as he pretended to be engrossed in the newspaper open on the table in front of him, the less likely it seemed, simply because of the places they had visited since they slipped away from Britain. Tourists would be unlikely to visit the Sidon Sea Castle, a fortification constructed by the Knights Templar, and then the castle of Saint Hilarion, known to have been used by the order, unless they were looking for something, and obviously something to do with the Templars.

But at that moment something changed. Jessop, who had until then appeared somewhat morose, suddenly smiled, wrapped her arm around her male companion's shoulders, and kissed him on the cheek. Both of them were visibly more animated for a few seconds. Clearly they had made some kind of discovery, because the man moved the computer to one side and began studying the map in much more detail.

Jessop murmured something to him and he nodded. She got up, walked over to the counter, and ordered two more cups of coffee, which at least made Salvatore's immediate decision slightly easier. As soon as she had sat down again, he left his seat to collect another drink for himself. Clearly the two targets wouldn't be leaving the café for at least a few more minutes.

He watched them as closely as he could without making his surveillance obvious. They seemed to be alternating their attention between whatever was displayed on the computer—and because of the angle of the screen Salvatore couldn't see what that was and he wasn't prepared to risk walking close to their table—and the unfolded map.

For almost a quarter of an hour, the targets appeared to be engrossed in their task, and then it looked as if they had found what they were looking for, or at the very least had reached a decision, because the man closed the lid of his laptop and slid the computer into the bag he had with him while Jessop folded the map. Moments later, they both stood up and walked out of the café.

As they passed his table, Salvatore took his mobile from his pocket and pressed the speed-dial key for Toscanelli's phone. His call was answered almost immediately.

"*Sì?*"

"They're on the move," Salvatore said in Italian. "They've been looking at something on the man's computer and studying a map."

"Something on the Internet?" Toscanelli asked.

"I don't know, because I couldn't get close enough to see," Salvatore replied, standing up and following the two targets out of the building. "Wait."

He had expected them to purchase tickets and then enter the grounds of the old castle, but instead they did the opposite, heading away from the buildings and walking down the road toward their hire car.

"It looks like they're leaving the place," Salvatore reported. "They're either going back to their car or heading somewhere else on foot."

"I didn't expect that," Toscanelli said. "Nico's already inside the castle, waiting for them. I'll get him back straightaway and into the car. You follow on foot until we know what they're doing."

"Where are Emilio and Flavio?"

"In the other car, waiting down the road, just in case the targets leave the area. I'll alert them as well."

Salvatore pressed the button on his Bluetooth earpiece to end the call and turned in the same direction as the targets, following them down the road fifty or sixty meters behind. As they approached their vehicle, the man took a set of keys from his pocket and seconds later the hazard warning lights flashed to indicate that he had unlocked the car. The moment he saw that, Salvatore crossed to the other side of the road, took out his mobile phone, and speed-dialed Toscanelli's number while he pretended to use the device to take photographs of the castle wall that towered above the road.

"They're definitely on the move," he reported. "I'll head back and collect the motorcycle. Make sure that Emilio knows they could be heading his way."

Salvatore ended the call, then turned away and walked up the road up to where he had left his motorbike. Behind him, he heard the sound of a car engine starting, and the crunch of tires on gravel or stone as the vehicle began moving.

Just before he pulled on his helmet, a few minutes later, his phone rang.

"They haven't gone that far," Toscanelli told him, now obviously making a conference call. "There's a parking area for coaches just down the road, where it forks right to lead up to the castle. Emilio was parked just beyond that. The two targets have turned in there, and now they're following a rough track that runs around the side of the mountain. They're driving slowly, and I think they're looking for something."

He paused for a few moments, apparently making a decision.

"Salvatore, don't go down the road for the moment. Stay near the castle and find somewhere that will give you a good view of the track. I want to know the moment they stop and what they do then. Nico and I will follow them. Emilio and Flavio, you cover the end of the track, because it doesn't go anywhere and they'll have to come back the same way. This could be the endgame," he finished. "I don't know how they've done it, but somehow they must have discovered where the hoard was hidden. So all we have to do is wait until they recover it and then take it off them.

"Remember," Toscanelli finished, "the orders from Rome are quite clear. The targets are not to leave the island. When they find what we're looking for, they can take its place. It's been undiscovered for over seven hundred years. With any luck, their bodies will remain hidden for centuries. As a bonus, you can all take a turn with the woman before you kill her. Or even afterward, if that's your thing."

60

"Are you sure about this?" Robin asked as the rental car bounced along the rough track, throwing up a cloud of brownish dust behind them.

"Frankly, no. But as far as I can tell from the topographical chart, this track will take us into the area directly below the castle, and that's about as close as we can get to the caves that are marked on the map."

"I don't want to rain on your parade, but surely if the caves are marked on the map, people will have explored them already. The people who did the survey for the topographical chart, for example."

"Not necessarily. Mapmakers make maps: they don't normally also explore the landscape. It's quite possible that they will simply have noted the entrance to a cave and its approximate internal dimensions, and left it at that. I doubt very much if they would also have explored or surveyed the caves, because that really isn't their job."

Mallory grunted as the front wheels of the car dropped down into a deep rut and the whole vehicle bounced and shuddered. "But you're right about other people wandering around the hillside and having a poke about inside any caves they noticed. If we're reading the clues correctly and Tibauld did store the treasure here, that does make sense because he would have needed to choose somewhere with fairly easy access, but at the same time it would have to be a place that offered some kind of security, so that no opportunist just wandering into a cave would be able to find the chests or whatever the treasure was stored in."

Mallory glanced through the windshield at the shape of the castle on the mountaintop above and to their left, then turned his attention back to the track in front of them. "According to the map, there's a turning area at the end of this path. We'll park the car there and then start walking."

"And you still think that's the right place to search?"

"I hope so. But now that we know the shape of the castle, it does make sense of that strange mark, the kind of stylized double capital letter *L*, the small *L* on top of a large *L*, that was scratched underneath the carving of the *Beauseant* we discovered at the Sidon Sea Castle. The layout of the main walls of the castle is exactly that shape, the lower walls forming the larger letter and the upper ward the smaller. And the mark that was carved on the right-hand end of the larger letter *L* could easily be interpreted as an arrow, pointing us in more or less the direction we're going now. In fact, the turning area or whatever it is at the end of this track is more or less directly in line with the lower wall of the castle, so I think that's probably a pretty good place to start looking."

A minute or so later he pulled the car to a stop in a roughly circular area of rough ground. Then he started moving forward again and turned the car around so that it was facing back in the direction from which they had come. He parked it on one side, so that any other vehicle following them would also be able to turn around easily.

Before he did anything else, Mallory stared back along the track they'd just driven along, then looked back up the slope towards the old castle.

"What is it?" Robin asked.

"Just checking that nobody's followed us," he said. "I haven't seen anyone taking any interest in what we're doing, but by now those Italians probably know we're on the island, even if they don't know exactly where we are."

But he saw nobody. No car had followed them down the track, and he couldn't see anyone near the castle looking in their direction.

"I think we're okay," he said.

"I hope so," Robin replied. "I'd hate to have the bad guys turn up now, not when I think we're so close to the end of the trail."

They got out of the car, and while Mallory opened the trunk to remove a rucksack containing a couple of large bottles of water, a heavy flashlight, and a packet of spare batteries, plus a few tools that he had thought might be helpful, Robin looked up toward the peak of the mountain.

"I see what you mean," she said. "This spot is almost directly in line with that lower wall. But where do we go now?"

Mallory looked back the way they'd come, then stared at the steep slope that lay beyond them, in the opposite direction.

"If that symbol was an arrow," he replied, "then what we're looking for must be somewhere over there. And if the inverted V shapes on the carving represented caves, which seems to me to be the obvious explanation, then we're looking for three of them, probably situated fairly close together, and almost certainly the important one is in the middle."

Because they had expected to do a fair amount of walking, both were wearing stout lace-up leather shoes with heavy-duty soles and trousers and had lightweight anoraks, because they knew the temperature would fall the higher they climbed. In fact, it was quite a bit warmer than either of them had expected, and so the anoraks stayed in the trunk of the car, along with Mallory's computer bag.

"Are you sure about that?" Robin asked. "I thought you normally slept with it."

Mallory smiled at her.

"I do, almost," he said. "But I think in the circumstances, bearing in mind that we're going to be scrambling around inside caves—or at least I hope we are—it's probably actually safer left locked up in the car. The last thing I want to do is drop it." He tapped one of the zipped pockets on his trousers. "And I've downloaded everything that's really vital onto this external hard drive, so I do have a backup as a last resort."

Mallory picked up the rucksack and hoisted it onto his shoulder, and after a final check to make sure that the car was locked, they set off, picking their way horizontally across the slope in front of them, trying to maintain a more or less straight path. The air was warm, thick, and muggy, and within just a few paces both of them had started to perspire.

"I know we've only just started," Robin said, "but how far do you think we'll have to go? I mean, are we there yet?"

"Probably not all that far," Mallory replied with a chuckle. "If we get a long way from the peak, then I think we can be fairly certain that we've missed it, because then it wouldn't be 'under the castle,' which I still think is what Tibauld meant. My guess is that the hiding place was probably within visual range of the castle, simply so that the garrison, or perhaps a few trusted and selected members of it, could see if anybody approached it. And practically speaking he wouldn't have wanted the treasure to be too far away in case he needed to access it. So the short answer is that we shouldn't have that far to go."

Within about eighty yards, the slope they were walking across terminated in a rock face that barred any further progress. A short distance over to their left was a cleft in the rock that presumably was one end of what looked like a fairly narrow and constricted ravine. Mallory ignored that, and instead turned to his right and began making his way along the cliff face, looking for any indication of a cave or an opening.

And almost immediately they found one.

The cliff face was rugged and uneven, and had a considerable amount of vegetation growing along its base. Behind two large bushes growing quite close together, Mallory spotted an opening. It was roughly square in shape, perhaps six feet wide and five feet high, but even without entering the space he could tell that it was small.

"It's a cave," he said, "but not a big one, and unless the others are really well hidden, it seems to be the only one along this stretch of cliff."

"But we are going to check it out," Robin insisted.

"Definitely," Mallory agreed, reaching into his rucksack and taking out the flashlight.

They stepped forward, moving through the entrance to the cave and into the gloom that lay beyond. The contrast between the brilliant sunshine outside and the darkness within was startling, and for a few seconds they just stood there side by side as they waited for their eyes to become accustomed to the lower levels of light inside. Then Mallory switched on the flashlight and moved the beam slowly around the interior of the cave.

Like the entrance, the interior of the cave was roughly square, but it was small, perhaps only eight or ten feet in length and about the same in width, while the roof height varied between about five and seven feet. Close to the entrance, one of the walls was somewhat blackened, presumably evidence of fires that had been lit there in the past, a deduction that was supported by a rough circle of stones that had clearly been used as a rudimentary hearth.

"Somebody's obviously been in here," Mallory said. "Maybe a shepherd or a goatherd has used this cave as a temporary shelter in the winter, if they bring their animals this high up. Otherwise I suppose a wandering hiker or two might have used it. But I don't see any evidence of a medieval presence here. Do you?"

"None at all," Robin agreed. "But at least this proves that you were right and that there are caves in this area. It just means we haven't found the right one yet."

They stepped out again into the bright sunlight and made their way slowly along the cliff face, looking out for any other openings in the rock. But the outcropping was not particularly big, and in a few minutes they had reached the end without finding any other caves or openings apart from a couple of narrow cracks barely wide enough to accommodate a human hand.

"The carving back at the Sidon Sea Castle indicated that there should be three caves here—assuming that our interpretation of those inverted V shapes is correct, of course—and so far we've only found one," Robin said. "There was nothing over to the right of it, so maybe the other two are over there, on the far side of the entrance to that ravine."

They walked back the way they'd come, retracing their steps along the base of the cliff. But although they followed the cliff face as it curved around to the west, beyond the entrance to the ravine, and looked carefully behind every single patch of vegetation, they saw no sign of any openings or gaps in the rock that would accommodate anything much bigger than a rabbit.

"I suppose that kind of proves a negative," Mallory said. "We now know that wherever the three caves are, they aren't anywhere along this cliff face."

"I have a feeling that we might have more luck in that ravine," Robin replied. "Just thinking back to that carving at Sidon, the representations of the caves were lined up horizontally on the stone. If the purpose of that stylized letter *L* was for us to walk away from the castle, then the implication is that we would pass the caves as we did so, while we were heading more or less northeast. But if the caves had been located along this rock face, then I think the carver—Tibauld de Gaudin or whoever was acting on his instructions—would have placed the symbols one above the other, in a vertical line, because that would have been a more accurate representation of the geography."

A few moments later, they turned left and stepped into the entrance to the narrow ravine. The shape struck them immediately. It was as if some mythical giant in the days of the ancients had swung a massive ax, smashing the head down and driving a narrow gully through the stone. And that wasn't the only impression that they both immediately had.

"Sidon again," Robin said, and Mallory could hear the excitement in her voice. "That other shape carved into the stone, the letter *V* lying on its side and pointing back toward the carving of the *Beauseant*. That's exactly the shape of this ravine. This could be it. It really could."

"Right. Let's hope so," Mallory agreed, realizing immediately that she was right. The ravine was shaped like an elongated *V*, the apex pointing back toward the old castle, and it was aligned roughly southwest to northeast, more or less along the extended line of the lower wall of the castle of Saint Hilarion. It did all seem to fit with the image they had found carved on the old stone back in the Sidon Sea Castle.

"This ravine is pretty narrow," he said, "so why don't we split up? You cover the left side and I'll take the right."

The left-hand wall of the ravine was almost sheer and largely featureless, just a few small shrubs and bushes hanging on to life and clinging to what soil there was in the few cracks and ledges on the stone. The vegetation growing at the base of the cliff was comparatively sparse, and Robin was quickly able to confirm that there were no obvious caves or openings visible.

Mallory, on the other hand, was faced with thick undergrowth that necessitated him pulling branches aside in order to see what, if anything, lay behind them. Nevertheless, within a couple of minutes he had discovered an opening. Another fairly small cave, which he looked inside briefly before calling Robin over and pointing it out to her.

"If you're right," he said, "this could be the first of the three caves indicated on that stone, so rather than waste time looking inside this one, let's see if we can find the other two."

Because it was clear that there was nothing to find on the left side of the ravine, Robin joined forces with Mallory and the two of them began working their way along the right-hand side, taking it slowly and ensuring that they didn't miss anything. But it wasn't until they were almost at the end of the ravine that they found a second cave. Before they went into it, Mallory and Robin walked out of the northeastern end of the ravine, but there was no sign of any other opening in the rocks as far as they could see.

"Two down and one to go," Mallory said, striding back into the ravine. "In fact," he added, "if this is the second cave, the middle one, then this is what we've been looking for."

"That seems too easy," Robin objected. "This cave is right down here at ground level. Anybody could walk in and stroll away with anything they found. I was expecting Tibauld's cave to be either pretty inaccessible or really well hidden."

"Sometimes the easy option is actually the right one."

"What's that? 'Philosophy for a Really Lazy Man, Chapter One'?"

"Not really," Mallory said with a smile. "Just a random thought, I suppose."

They stepped inside the gloom of the second cave, but apart from a handful of discarded beer and soft drink cans in one corner, there was no evidence that anybody, and especially not a group of medieval knights, had ever been in there.

"I hate to say it," Mallory said, "but this looks like a busted flush. Either that or we haven't found the right cave yet."

They stepped outside again and for a few moments both stood in silence, looking up and down the ravine. Then Mallory shifted his gaze upward, to look at the upper levels of the rock walls on either side of them. The rock on the western side was almost sheer and clearly possessed no openings of any sort, and because of its orientation it would have been in sun for most of the day. The eastern side, in contrast, was comparatively broken up, had at least twice as much vegetation growing on it, and it was possible that some parts of it would normally be in shadow. There was also what looked like a ridge running along most of that side, perhaps twenty feet above the floor of the ravine, and whatever was on it was invisible from where they were standing.

To Mallory, that looked like a much more interesting—and a far more likely—prospect.

"I think we should go and have a look up there," he said, pointing toward the edge of the ridge.

"Suits me. I think we're just wasting our time down here."

There were no paths leading up from the floor of the ravine, but the broken surface on that side meant that it was a comparatively easy climb. A couple of times they each lost their footing, but without mishap, and within about five minutes they were standing on a long and narrow ledge, a mixture of rock and grass underfoot. Presumably because of the fractured nature of the stone on that side, the area possessed thick undergrowth, which would clearly conceal any cave that might be there. There were no signs that the ledge had been visited by anyone at any time, and all Mallory could see on the ground were a few droppings probably from either goats or rabbits: he wasn't a competent enough biologist to know the difference.

They made their way slowly forward, pulling back branches on bushes to check behind each one as they made steady progress along the ledge. But every spot they looked at displayed only the featureless surface of the rock, and both began to feel increasingly despondent.

"I don't think it's here," Robin muttered.

But at that moment, Mallory pulled back a hefty branch from a large and bushy shrub, and behind it both of them immediately found themselves looking into the darkness of a small cavity in the rock.

"Bingo," Mallory said.

The undergrowth largely obstructed the entrance to the cave, and for a fleeting moment Mallory wished he'd brought a machete. But within a couple of minutes they had made their way inside the cave and were able to look around.

"You do realize that this is roughly halfway between those other two caves we found in the ravine?" Robin asked.

"I do now," Mallory replied, and switched on the flashlight to flood the cave with light.

It wasn't a particularly impressive sight. The entrance was probably only about four feet wide at the base and perhaps five feet high, the sides narrowing markedly higher up, while the cave itself was bigger than the entrance suggested, perhaps fifteen feet wide at the maximum, at about the halfway point, and roughly twenty feet deep, the far end tapering almost to a point.

But there was not the slightest sign that it had ever been used for any purpose at all by human beings.

"I'm beginning to get a bad feeling about this," Mallory said. "Apart from the fact that it's a bit bigger, this cave looks exactly like the others."

"You're right, but that doesn't mean we're not in the right place. This cave is inaccessible, and it's also hidden from view, which is what I would have expected if Tibauld had chosen this as the place where he was going to hide the treasure." She paused for a moment and walked back to the entrance, glanced around outside, and then strode back. "Part of the castle wall is visible from here," she added, "and that's another point in its favor."

"It can have as many points in its favor as it likes," Mallory retorted, "but that doesn't alter the fact that there's nothing in here now. This is just an empty shell. If this cave ever was used to store the Templar treasure of Outremer, either Tibauld himself or some other member of the order must have come along at a later date and removed it. Maybe they did decide to take it back to France or just to another location in Cyprus or some-where else in the eastern Mediterranean, and for some reason that fact was never recorded in the Templar ar-chives."

"That's not necessarily true. I wasn't expecting to walk into the cave and find half a dozen ironbound chests just sitting there. Tibauld wasn't stupid, and even with the entrance to the cave being virtually invisible and very probably being watched from the castle above, he would still have wanted the treasure to be concealed. There might well be some kind of hidden partition or some-thing of that sort in here."

Mallory laughed shortly. "You mean that sometime in the fourteenth century, in a moderately inaccessible cave in the middle of Cyprus, some medieval engineer turned up and built a false wall? Like a Bob the Builder of the Middle Ages?"

"Don't knock it. Medieval engineers were a lot clev-erer than most people think. Don't forget the book safe."

Mallory nodded.

"Point taken," he said, bent down, and picked up a fist-sized lump of rock from the floor of the cave. "If there's a false wall in here, I promise you that I'll find it."

He stepped over to the left-hand side of the cave and rapped the stone sharply against the wall. The unmistakable sound of stone on stone rang out. "Solid as a rock. In this case, literally."

He moved on, working his way down the side wall of the cave and using the stone as a hammer, listening out for any indication of a cavity. At the far end, he had to work his way around a pile of fallen rocks to reach the right-hand wall and return toward the entrance, where Robin was waiting.

"I'm sorry," Mallory said, "but unless I'm missing something the walls are absolutely solid." He tossed the stone onto the ground in disgust. "If the Templar treasure ever was here, it's long gone now. I'm afraid we've been wasting our time, chasing shadows and following ghosts. Let's get out of here."

But Robin didn't move, staying right where she was and staring toward the back of the cave.

"What is it?" Mallory asked.

For a few seconds, Robin didn't respond, just continued looking in the same direction.

"What is it?" Mallory repeated.

"It's the rocks," Robin said. "They're wrong."

Mallory switched the flashlight on again and shone it at the pile of tumbled boulders at the far end of the cave.

"What do you mean 'wrong'?" he asked. "It's just a pile of old rocks."

Robin shook her head. "No, it isn't. When I came in here and looked around for the first time, I saw the rocks just as you did, and like you, I guess, I assumed that that was a result of a rock fall centuries ago. But I was wrong, and so are you."

Mallory lifted the flashlight beam so that it illuminated a part of the cave roof, then dropped it down again, back to the rock pile. "You're obviously seeing something that I'm not. What I see is a pile of old rocks. What do you see?"

"I see a pile of old *weathered* rocks," Robin replied.

For the first time, Mallory actually focused his attention on the rocks themselves, rather than on the shape of the pile. And he realized that Robin was right. Unlike the walls of the cave itself, which were largely clean, untouched by wind or rain, the rocks at the far end of the cave had clearly spent many years exposed to the elements. They were, without a doubt, weathered rocks. What he didn't see was why that should be important. "So?"

"So why would anyone bother to climb up to this moderately inaccessible cave in the middle of Cyprus—I think that was how you described it—and then carry about half a ton of rocks into it from the outside? That just doesn't make sense. Or rather it only makes sense in one context. This *was* the cave in which Tibauld de Gaudin concealed the Templar treasure of Outremer, exactly as we thought, and he hid it in a hole at the far end of the cave. Then he covered it over, probably with heavy wooden planking, and piled rocks on top of it to hide it from prying eyes. The only mistake he made was to have his men collect rocks that had been outside for years, but he probably had no option because there weren't enough inside the cave to hide what he'd done."

She pointed at the rock pile. "And unless somebody thought it was a good idea to remove the treasure and then replace the wooden planking and all the rocks again, to hide the hiding place, as it were, it looks to me as if the treasure is still buried over there, in the place where Tibauld de Gaudin's men originally put it."

61

Shifting the rocks was hard work. Obviously there was no moving air in the cave, and although it was much cooler inside than out, within a few minutes of starting work both Robin and Mallory were sweating profusely. But at least the cave was big enough to allow them to just roll the rocks out of the way, to move them to one side. They didn't have to carry them anywhere, which was a bonus.

Just before they started, they'd taken a moment to look at the area covered by the boulders, which was roughly circular, and Mallory was surprised that he hadn't spotted this apparent anomaly himself. A rock fall would not have been anything like as neat.

It took them almost half an hour, but when they'd finished they were standing together at the end of the cave and surrounded by a kind of perimeter of boulders. At their feet, barely visible under a thick layer of dust and dirt, was a flat surface delineated by a number of straight parallel lines, the unmistakable shape of a wooden platform of some sort. But before they attempted to move it,

Robin and Mallory shared the last of the lukewarm water in the first bottle. Despite their eagerness to shift the wood and find out what lay beneath, both of them knew the importance of avoiding dehydration.

"I don't know if these are individual planks or some kind of platform, the lengths of wood nailed together," Mallory said, "but we'll soon find out."

As well as the water and the flashlight in his rucksack, he had assembled a selection of tools that he'd thought might be useful in their quest, despite not knowing exactly how it would be likely to end. Two of the pieces of equipment he had selected were a small crowbar and a collapsible trenching tool, which combined both a shovel and a pick.

He took out the crowbar, used the point to locate the ends of the lengths of wood, slid it underneath what seemed to be the center of the platform, and pushed down hard. There was a faint creaking and cracking noise, but nothing else happened.

Mallory changed position, sliding the point of the tool under the end of the adjacent plank of wood. This time he placed his foot on the other end of the crowbar and pressed down firmly. With another creaking sound, this one much louder, the wood lifted a few inches. He abandoned the crowbar, slid his fingers underneath the end of the wood, and pulled upward. The wood was stiff and difficult to move, lifting only when he applied all his strength to the task, and it came free very slowly and with great reluctance. Giving a final heave, he wrenched the wood upward, and with a loud cracking sound it lifted clear of the ground and he was able to shift it to one side.

It wasn't a platform, he had realized immediately as he lifted the wood, but a number of thick wooden planks lying parallel to each other and covering a hole excavated in the floor. In fact, it was a double layer, because underneath the length of wood he had just moved were half a dozen other planks laid at right angles to the top layer, obviously intended to provide additional support to cope with the substantial weight of the rocks.

With the first plank moved, shifting the others was comparatively easy, and within a few minutes, with Robin's help, Mallory had lifted all the planks from the top layer and placed them to one side. He again used the crowbar to lift the end of one of the planks situated underneath and moved that length of the wood out of the way as well. That provided an opening that allowed him to look down into the cavity below.

"What can you see?" Robin asked.

"A whole lot of nothing at the moment. Pass me the flashlight."

Mallory shone the beam vertically downward into the hole, and they both stood there, staring down.

A visible tremor of excitement ran through Robin. Directly below them, through the gap in the wooden planking that Mallory had created, they could see the unmistakable shapes of two ironbound chests. They weren't very big, perhaps two and a half feet long by eighteen inches wide, and about the same in height, though it was difficult to estimate that with any degree of accuracy from where they were standing. The iron on the top of each chest was chased into an intricate pattern, and large metal handles were fitted at their ends for ease of lifting and carrying.

For a few moments, neither of them spoke; then Mallory handed Robin the flashlight.

"I'll need to shift the rest of these planks before we can get them out," he said, matter-of-factly.

"Yes," Robin replied, equally calmly. "You will."

"I suppose the biggest problem," Mallory said, levering up another heavy length of wood and moving it to one side, "will be deciding what we should do with the stuff once we've got it out. I mean, I have no idea how Turkish law treats buried treasure. Do they have anything similar to the British law of treasure trove, which guarantees the finders either the object they've discovered or its cash value?"

Robin snorted in derision.

"I have no idea," she replied, "but from what I've heard about the Turks I think we'd be more likely to find ourselves thrown into jail and charged with looting important national artifacts while a bunch of local officials split the proceeds between themselves. Did you ever see that film *Midnight Express*? Well, I don't suppose that conditions in most Turkish slammers have improved much over the years. In my opinion, absolutely the last thing we do about this is tell anyone in authority. Our best bet will be to get it out of here and bury it somewhere ourselves, preferably on the Greek side because I think it's easier to get to from the outside world, and then take a number of holidays in Cyprus over the next couple of years, putting the odd gold bar or bunch of coins in our luggage before we leave the island."

"You're obviously assuming that these chests are full of treasure. They might be empty."

Robin shook her head.

"Not a chance," she snapped. "Nobody would go to this much trouble to hide a couple of empty boxes. Okay, I don't know what's inside them, but I'm prepared to lay money that they won't be empty."

"We'll soon find out," Mallory replied. "One thing does strike me, though," he added doubtfully, "because it really doesn't make sense. Those are just two quite small chests. Unless they're both stuffed full of really valuable stuff—gold bars and coins, that kind of thing—they're really too small to hold all the assets of the Knights Templar in Outremer. I was expecting chests about twice that size and perhaps half a dozen of them."

He shifted the last piece of wood planking and then lowered himself into the cavity. Robin passed him the flashlight and he looked around before touching either of the chests, and immediately made a surprising discovery.

"That's odd," he said, shining the beam toward the back of the cavity.

"What?"

"I'd more or less supposed that this was just a hole excavated in the floor of the cave, but it isn't. It looks as if there's some kind of underground passageway here, leading back into the mountainside."

"Interesting, but not helpful," Robin said. "Now stop messing around and lift those chests up here."

"Hang on a minute."

Mallory took out his mobile phone and snapped a number of pictures of both the chests, first showing where they were positioned in the cavity and then several more showing each close up. Then he bent down and seized the handles on the first chest and tried to lift it. He relaxed and glanced up at Robin.

"You win your bet," he said. "I don't know what's in them, but they're definitely not empty."

He bent down again, grasped the handles once more, and with a sudden expulsion of breath lifted the chest to waist height. "Christ, this is heavy."

Grunting with the effort, he lifted it higher still and maneuvered it sideways onto the floor of the cave, to where Robin was standing waiting. Then he bent down and repeated the operation on the second chest, which was at least as heavy as the first. Mallory pulled himself out of the cavity, and together they crouched down to examine what they'd found.

The wood seemed to be in quite good condition, bearing in mind its likely age, which was presumably due to the extremely dry conditions in the cavity under the floor of the cave. The ironwork was covered in a thin patina of rust, but seemed to have retained its strength, again almost certainly because of the lack of moisture in the air.

"They don't look to me as if they're seven hundred years old," Mallory said. "Those handles I was using are still really strong."

"They might not look it, but the evidence we have suggests that they really are as ancient as that."

"But the problem is they're too small. They simply can't hold the treasure of the order. I think these are something else."

"What?"

"I don't know. I just think we need to be really careful with them."

Mallory looked closely at the first chest. The wood on both the lid and the sides was covered in an intricate pattern of ironwork, complex and convoluted, which would probably also have helped give the chest even more structural strength. The sides were straight, while the lid was semicircular in cross section, supported by a hinge at the back that ran the full length of the chest, and secured at the front by a lock and a type of over-center catch.

"I don't suppose there's the slightest chance that it's unlocked," Robin murmured.

"I doubt it," Mallory replied, sticking the point of the crowbar under the catch and levering it open.

Then he tried the lid of the chest, but it remained firmly closed.

"I'll just try the other one," he said, "but I think it'll be the same result."

Again he used the crowbar, but his prediction was correct: although he had no trouble freeing the external catch, there was no movement whatsoever when he tried to lift the lid.

"I don't suppose that the key's down there?" Robin asked hopefully. "Tucked away in a corner somewhere?"

"Fat chance."

But he lowered himself back down into the cavity anyway and shone the flashlight carefully all around, searching for any kind of metallic glint or a box or anything that might contain the key. Unsurprisingly, when he stuck his head up again, he had found nothing.

"Nada," he said, climbing out of the hole. "No sign of it. But it wouldn't have been the brightest of ideas to lock the chests and then hide them with the key in the same place, and we're pretty certain Tibauld de Gaudin wasn't stupid."

Robin stared down at the two ironbound chests. "I don't want to damage these, because they're probably quite valuable in their own right, so how are we going to get them open?"

At that moment a shadow moved across the entrance to the cave and an unwelcome voice called out:

"I think we can help you with that."

62

Cyprus

Robin spun round immediately, but Mallory was looking in that direction already.

Two men stood silhouetted in the entrance to the cave, their faces and bodies in shadow and unrecognizable. But Mallory didn't need to see the face of the man who'd spoken to know who he was. His voice was an extremely unpleasant reminder of the last contact they'd had with him, back in Devon. Even more unpleasant was the realization that both men were carrying pistols while he and Robin were completely unarmed.

The pistol and ammunition that Mallory had acquired were tucked under the seat of the Renault Mégane rental car, and that was sitting in the long-term car park at Paris Orly. He'd known there was no possibility of getting the weapon onto the flight and, in any case, he had hoped he wouldn't need it anymore.

"What did you do with my car?" Mallory asked.

"I dumped it, but that should be the least of your worries right now," Toscanelli responded.

"How did you find us?" Robin sounded almost more curious than afraid. "You can't have followed us all the way from Devon."

Toscanelli shook his head as he and the other man each moved slightly sideways, away from the entrance, still aiming their pistols directly at Robin and Mallory.

"No. The trail went cold as soon as you managed to shake us off in Exeter. I had no idea where you'd gone, but fortunately my masters possess the ability to track almost anybody, almost anywhere, these days. Once you used your passport to take that flight to Beirut, we knew exactly where you were going, and we were able to anticipate your actions. We were too late to follow you on the ground at Sidon, so we didn't know what you might have found there, but as soon as you booked a flight to Larnaca, whatever you had discovered became irrelevant.

"We had expected that the trail would end here on the island, simply because this was where Tibauld de Gaudin died. One of my men picked you up at the airport, and my people have been following you ever since. Right now I have two men guarding the end of the track you drove along to get here, and another watching the cave entrance from the top of the cliff on the opposite side of the ravine. It was all really quite simple."

"Obviously," Robin said bitterly.

"And your men arrived on the island by boat, I suppose, which is why you have weapons?" Mallory asked.

"No, by air. Our diplomatic passports make sure we aren't ever stopped or searched." Toscanelli gestured with his pistol. "You make me nervous, standing there," he said to Mallory. "Get back down into that hole."

"One thing I don't understand," Robin interrupted as Mallory climbed back into the cavity in the floor. "When David and I left my apartment in Dartmouth, your three

men—I'm assuming that you were in charge of them—
were alive. A bit battered, certainly, but they were all still
breathing. Somebody then visited the place and killed all
three men, shooting them through the head, as if they
were executions. Did you order that to be done, or did
you do it yourself? And why?"

Toscanelli inclined his head.

"That was my work," he replied, "because my orders
were absolutely specific. All three of those men knew exactly why we were in England, and my masters had told
me it was imperative that the purpose of our mission
should remain secret. There wasn't enough time to get
them out of the apartment, and I knew that the police
would arrive at any moment. I couldn't take the risk that
they'd talk, so killing them was the only option I had
left."

"You shot three of your own men in cold blood just to
preserve a secret? What kind of monster are you?"

In the gloom of the cave, Toscanelli smiled, a thin and
humorless expression.

"Not a monster," he replied. "Just a man acting in the
best interests of his masters."

"And who are your masters, exactly?" Mallory asked.

Toscanelli inclined his head slightly, almost a bow.
"Like my colleagues, I have the honor to serve as a member of the *Ordo Praedicatorum*."

"I should have guessed," Mallory replied. "The Dominicans, *Domini Canes*, the Hounds of the Lord. The
Black Friars and the pope's personal torturers. The parchment even warned us against you. Your order carried out
the interrogations of the members of the Knights Templar, interrogations that remarkably few people survived,
and most of those who did perished in the execution fires
afterward. I'm frankly surprised that you're still around."

"The eradication of heresy is just as important now as it was in the Middle Ages. The Templars may have suffered pain during their earthly trials, but we know we saved their immortal souls when we put them to the cleansing flame."

"And you believe that crap, do you?"

Toscanelli shook his head.

"My beliefs are no concern of yours," he said. "We are part of a small group, a special section of the Dominican order, if you like, and our function today is unchanged. We act to protect the pontiff and the Holy Mother Church by whatever means are deemed necessary."

"So why are you searching for this buried treasure?" Robin asked. "It's got nothing to do with the Catholic Church."

Toscanelli shook his head. "That's where you're wrong. Members of our order were charged by the pope with recovering the assets of the Knights Templar so that their wealth could be redistributed to other medieval orders that were untainted by heresy. This is simply unfinished business that my masters wish to bring to a close."

"I don't understand," Robin said.

"I think I do," Mallory said, filling the pause that followed her remark. "Philip the Fair of France purged the Templar order because he was bankrupt. The entire purpose of his actions was to seize the Templar treasury, and he coerced the pope into supporting him. Once Philip had taken what he could, because most of the treasure disappeared before the raids in October 1307, the pope ordered the remaining assets held by the Poor Knights of Christ to be handed over to the Knights Hospitaller. The Dominican inquisitors were instructed to find the hidden Templar assets, and that was why the most brutal tortures were applied so enthusiastically. But the Templars never told you, did they? The treasure was never found."

"That is exactly the point. We were given our orders over seven hundred years ago, but the passage of time is irrelevant in our eyes. We have been searching for both the Templar assets and the lost treasure for almost a millennium, and we will continue to do so until both are recovered."

Mallory glanced at Robin.

"What do you mean about the assets and the treasure?" he asked. "Surely they're one and the same thing?"

Toscanelli smiled suddenly.

"You really don't know?" he asked, his tone disbelieving. "The assets were what you'd expect—bullion, coin, and the rest—but the treasure is a single object the Templars revered beyond all price."

"What object?" Robin demanded.

"You'll never know," the Italian replied, "not now."

Robin pointed at the two wooden chests standing on the floor of the cave by her feet.

"And now you think you've found it?" she asked.

Toscanelli shook his head.

"Probably not," he replied. "We believe that those chests contain one part of the Templar treasure of Outremer, but that is simply a tiny fraction of the total wealth that the order was known to possess. Our present search for the hidden assets of the Templars has only just begun, but the real treasure probably lies elsewhere, a long way from this place."

"How did you find out that we were involved?" Robin asked.

"We embrace and employ the latest technology. Our technical staff monitors Web sites, blogs, and the search strings used on the major search engines. The moment you searched the Web for information about the *Ipse Dixit* relic, we knew that you must have found something significant. In fact, we already knew of the existence of the parchment you found, but it had vanished from sight sometime in the fifteenth century, and no copies of the text were known to exist. Once we had established where you were from your IP—Internet Protocol—address, I was sent to England with a team of men to recover it."

"But you didn't do a very good job of it, did you?" Robin asked. "You had the relic, and the two of us, in your possession for only a few minutes before we got away, and the body count on your side was quite impressive. You shot three of your own men, David killed another in self-defense, and the fifth member of your little group ended up slightly broken as well."

Toscanelli shrugged. "Shit happens, as you English sometimes say. But no matter. We have these chests now, thanks to your efforts, and we have no further use for either of you. You can both go back into the hole that the treasure chests came out of. That'll give the archeologists of the future something interesting to investigate."

The sentence of violent and painful death, so casually pronounced, sent a chill through Robin.

"So what now?" Mallory asked.

"This is the end of the trail, and the end of your lives," Toscanelli replied. "We'll kill you both, break open the chests, and recover the treasure. We'll take it back to Rome with us. Our diplomatic status will ensure that we won't have any problems doing that."

He turned to the other man and issued a string of instructions in Italian. His companion nodded, tucked his pistol into the waistband of his trousers, and walked back toward the cave entrance, pulling a mobile out of his pocket as he did so.

"My other three men will be here in a few minutes," he said, "and then we can get started. This is the end-game, and so it's only fair that we wait until they arrive. So you have just a few minutes longer to make your peace with whatever god you worship. I will offer a prayer for your souls before we kill you both."

"I'm an atheist," Robin snapped.

"Then you are truly damned."

The second man returned, and again Toscanelli issued instructions to him in Italian.

"There's no reason why we can't open the chests while we're waiting," Toscanelli said, and gestured toward Robin with his pistol, as he'd done with Mallory. "You're too dangerous to stand there while we do that, Jessop, so climb down into that cavity and stay there while Nico works his magic on these old locks."

Robin had absolutely no option. She knew beyond any doubt that if she didn't do as the Italian had told her, he would probably shoot her down where she stood, and she was determined to make use of every extra minute of life she had left. Maybe there was still something that she and Mallory could do, though right then she had not the slightest idea what that might be.

As soon as Robin was standing beside Mallory in the cavity in the floor of the cave, only their shoulders and heads visible, the man Toscanelli had called Nico walked over to the two chests and bent down in front of them. He took a small leather pouch from his pocket and opened it on the ground beside him. He extracted a couple of precision tools from it, inserted both into the lock on the first chest, and began probing the mechanism, closing his eyes as he concentrated on what his fingers and his ears were telling him.

After only a couple of minutes there was a click from

the lock and Nico seized the catch and lifted the lid a bare fraction of an inch. Then he lowered it again and turned his attention to the second chest, the lock on which offered little more resistance than the first. After he checked that the lid would open, he replaced the tools in the leather pouch, stood up, and walked away. He returned to his place on the opposite side of the cave to Toscanelli, took out his pistol again, and aimed it at Mallory.

"This is a great moment for us," Toscanelli said. "The culmination of a search that has lasted for centuries, or at least the end of the first part of that search. We will wait until all my men are here before we open the chests."

An uncomfortable silence descended on the cave while all four people waited, anticipating very different events.

"If you want to say good-bye to each other," Toscanelli said, after a few minutes, "now would be a good time to do so. You will both be dead in about ten minutes."

Standing beside him in the hole in the floor of the cave, Robin wrapped her arms around Mallory, who bent his head forward until their lips were almost touching.

"Is there anything we can do?" she asked.

"I'm not dead yet," Mallory replied, "and neither are you."

"You've got a plan?"

"Not exactly, but there might just be a way out of here."

He bent closer toward her and lowered his voice to a barely audible whisper.

"Remember the book safe," he finished, and they both turned and looked toward the cave entrance, where three other men had just appeared.

Like Toscanelli and Nico, the three new arrivals were heavily built with black hair and swarthy complexions, all typically Mediterranean in appearance. They stepped inside the cave and looked with interest at the two iron-bound chests, and at Robin and Mallory, still standing together in the cavity.

Toscanelli greeted the three men briefly, then switched his attention back to Mallory and Robin.

"I've decided that killing you both is going to be quite messy and take some time," he said, "so I think it would probably be better if we removed the treasure first. Then my men can take their time with both of you. And I'm sure you'll also be interested in seeing one small part of the wealth of the Templar order, and you can die knowing how close you came to getting it for yourselves."

Toscanelli waved two of the new arrivals forward, and each one knelt down before one of the chests.

As the two men stretched out their hands to the lids, Mallory again bent forward and whispered something to Robin.

On a single word of command from Toscanelli, the two Italians flung back the lids of the chests, a brilliant flash lit up the cave, and for the briefest of instants time seemed to stop.

Then the screaming started.

63

Cyprus

"Now," Mallory said, ducked down, and began half crawling, half running, down the passageway he had spotted when he first jumped down into the cavity, Robin following a couple of feet behind him. The light from the flashlight bounced and shimmered on the walls of the passage as they concentrated on putting as much distance as they could between themselves and the cave. There were other openings off the passage, but Mallory ignored them, keeping to the main tunnel. But then he spotted a narrow cleft that ran upward and made an instant decision.

"We'll go up there," he said, "just in case they start firing down the passageway."

They scrambled up the narrow opening and found themselves in a small closed chamber, barely big enough for them to crouch down on their hands and knees. Behind them, they could still hear an agonized moaning from the cave, overlaid by angry shouts and commands in Italian.

Mallory switched off the flashlight and immediately a

darkness so total that they could literally see nothing at all enveloped them.

"What the hell happened?" Robin demanded. "What was in those chests?"

"It looked to me like rocks," Mallory replied, "and that would certainly explain the weight. They were really heavy."

"I didn't mean that. There was a flash as they opened the lids, and both those men were badly hurt. What caused that?"

"That was two different things," Mallory replied. "The first was the flash from the camera on my phone. I wanted to get a picture of that Italian and I knew that was the best chance I was going to get, while all their attention was focused on those chests. As for what happened when the chests were opened, I can't tell you for sure because I only stood there for a split second before we headed down the passageway. But I was thinking about the book safe, and that brutal antitheft mechanism it contained. That started me thinking.

"If the Templars were prepared to protect a piece of parchment with a device like that, it struck me that they might well have incorporated a similar kind of protection into their treasure chests. I don't know exactly what it was, but it looked to me as if there were two long curved blades built into each chest and hinged on the edges of the lid. When the lid was lifted a couple of powerful springs swung the blades outward in a scything motion that would be almost guaranteed to do serious harm to anybody standing or crouching directly in front of the chest. Exactly as has just happened, in fact.

"Obviously I had no idea what sort of mechanism it was going to be, but I guessed it was going to be quite brutal and certainly attention getting, and that's why we're·

up here now and safe—at least for the moment—and not being beaten to death back there in the cave."

"But they'll come after us, won't they?"

"I don't know. That man's got problems. He's got two men badly, maybe even fatally, injured, but knowing his past record, if they're not dead yet he'll probably just shoot them. The treasure that he came here to recover isn't here at all, unless my eyes deceived me. The last thing he is going to do is take a quarter of a ton of boulders back to Rome with him. The chests are no good to him, and we've just vanished from sight. Obviously he knows where we went, but there are lots of junctions on that passage we came down, and finding us could take him quite a long time. And a man carrying a pistol in a narrow tunnel is actually not much better armed than a man lying in wait with a rock in his hand, and I think those men are certainly bright enough to know that."

Mallory paused for a moment, listening to the sounds that they could still just about hear from the cave. There was a muffled thump, followed a few seconds later by another almost identical sound.

"A silenced pistol?" Robin asked.

"Almost certainly," Mallory agreed. "That will be the Italian, killing the wounded. So if you want my guess, on balance I think he and his two surviving men will probably just walk away from this. Their only reason for coming down here after us will be revenge, but I don't think any of them will be too enthusiastic about trying to explore a tunnel system like this just to find us and kill us, because they must know that there's a good chance they could come off worse, just because of what happened in the past."

For a few moments, they lay there in silence, just listening.

Then Mallory heard another sound that he couldn't immediately identify, a kind of metallic thumping that seemed to be getting closer.

"What's that?" Robin asked.

Suddenly Mallory knew exactly what it was, and realized that there was another course of action the Italians could follow that he had never even considered.

"Cover your ears," he said urgently, doing precisely that himself, "and open your mouth."

And then the echoing thunder of the explosion of the grenade drowned out everything else.

64

Cyprus

Almost an hour later, David Mallory stood up cautiously inside the cavity in which the two chests had been hidden, and peered around the cave.

As he had expected, the three surviving Italians had left. But there were two dead bodies, a lake of dark blood surrounding each of them. Each had a single bullet wound in the head, a coup de grâce that would probably have been welcomed by the victims. Both men also had two deep and savage cuts across their abdomens, cuts so deep that their intestines had spilled out through them. They would both have been in unutterable agony until they'd been put out of their misery.

There was no sign of the instruments that had inflicted the wounds, so clearly the Italians had emptied the chests—the two piles of rocks told that part of the story—and taken both away with them.

"It's all clear," Mallory called out, and moments later Robin appeared beside him.

Both of them were covered in dust, vast clouds of which had been created by the explosion of the grenade.

"I'm amazed we survived that thing going off," Robin said.

"If we'd been down in the main passageway," Mallory replied, "we probably wouldn't still be alive. But grenades are antipersonnel devices, designed to target soft flesh. They're not much good at blowing holes in rocky tunnels that have existed for millennia. We survived because we climbed up into that separate chamber, and the blast got nowhere near us."

"My ears are still ringing," Robin said, "and I'm sure I'm shouting."

Mallory smiled at her, hoisted himself out of the cavity, and then gave her a hand to climb up to the floor of the cave again. Robin walked over to the scene of carnage and looked down. She wrinkled her nose in distaste at the sight of the bodies, then looked at the two small piles of brownish boulders.

"You were right," she said. "They were just full of rocks, and that device built into the lid is obviously still disgustingly effective, even seven hundred years after it was built. I'm really glad that those Italians came along before we had a chance to open them up."

Robin shook her head and walked away toward the entrance to the cave and took several deep breaths of fresh air. Then she stepped back inside and walked over to where Mallory was standing.

"It does raise the question, though, doesn't it?" she said.

Mallory nodded. "Yes. Why fill two expensive booby-trapped wooden chests with rocks and then bury them out of sight in a cave? It wasn't done by accident, obviously, so they must have had a reason, a good reason. I had my suspicions from the start, and I'm wondering about the last section of that manuscript, the text that we never managed to decipher. I think there's some clue here that would allow us to decipher that section. That was one thought I had."

"And did you have another thought as well?"

Mallory nodded. "Yes. The section of the manuscript we decoded that refers to three trials. It's possible that Tibauld de Gaudin realized that the Templar cause in the Holy Land was lost forever, or at least for the foreseeable future. But I think it's more likely that it wasn't Tibauld at all, because by then he was essentially a broken man, but the next, and incidentally the last, grand master of the Knights Templar, Jacques de Molay. It's known that the two senior Templars of the order—the then grand master and his successor—spent some time together on Cyprus, and when he was near death Tibauld would probably have told de Molay where the treasure was hidden and the clue he'd left at the Sidon Sea Castle."

"But why fill the chests with rocks and hide them?"

"I think it's at least possible," Mallory replied, "that by then Jacques de Molay already knew that the writing was on the wall, that Philip of France was planning on purging the order, and de Molay was already making his preparations to ensure that the Templar treasure would not be seized. If Tibauld had told him he'd left that clue at the Sidon Sea Castle, he would have assumed that sooner or later—probably later—somebody would pick up the trail. But because of the nature of Tibauld's carving, interpreting it could only be done by somebody either who was a member of the Knights Templar or who knew a lot about the order. Perhaps he was hoping that after the dust had settled and Philip the Fair had gone to his grave, the order might somehow reemerge. And because the treasure had vanished from the pages of history, eventually somebody would obviously begin backtracking the last days of the order to try to find out what happened to it.

"After France, the biggest Templar presence was in Outremer, and the treasure of the order out here couldn't possibly have fitted into two small chests, unless they were packed full of solid gold. But this underground cavity is big enough to hold half a dozen or more large chests, which could have been big enough. So I think Jacques de Molay had it removed, probably secretly shipping it to France, and left the two small booby-trapped chests in its place. Then, when anyone followed the clues Tibauld had left, there would be something here to find. A Templar would have known that the treasure of Outremer couldn't have fitted inside these chests, and so wouldn't be caught out by the booby traps, which would take care of a normal treasure hunter. A Templar would know that the chests simply provided a clue to follow for the next trial, or trail."

"If you're right," Robin said slowly, "then that means whoever provided that encrypted text on the parchment must have known about the chests, and whatever clue was hidden in them. The two things must have been linked. But that couldn't have been Tibauld de Gaudin, because he died on the island."

"Exactly. We're back to Jacques de Molay again. Tibauld de Gaudin may have started this treasure hunt when he sailed to Cyprus with the order's treasure, but it was de Molay who finished it. He probably didn't actually write the text on the parchment, but he would have provided the information the author needed. Nothing else makes sense."

"So we've come away from this little adventure empty-handed," Robin said.

"Yes." Mallory nodded. "But if I'm right about this being the end of the first trial, then those chests must have held a clue that would allow us to move on to the next level, if you like. And I have an idea where that clue is."

"You have?"

Mallory nodded, pulled out his mobile phone, and scrolled through to the gallery. He selected a close-up picture of the lid of one of the chests and showed her the image.

"Both chests were different, and the patterns in the metalwork are too intricate to just be decoration. I don't know what it is, but there's some symbology hidden in those shapes that we have to crack, because I'm sure that will provide what we need to decipher the last section of the text on the parchment."

"And then we can embark on Jacques de Molay's second trial, you mean?"

"Exactly," Mallory said. "And we can't hang about, either, because those Dominican thugs now have the actual chests, and I'm certain they'll be doing exactly the same, working out the clues. This is a race, and it isn't over yet."

"But first we have to go home," Robin said slowly, "and of course we'll have to face the music. At least it was helpful that the Italian admitted killing the three men in my apartment. I switched on the audio recording function on my mobile as soon as he walked in, so hopefully I'll have a clear record of what he said."

Mallory grinned at her.

"Funnily enough," he said, "I did exactly the same, though I was standing a bit farther away from him so my copy might not be as clear as yours. But I have got a decent picture of him—I've already taken a look at it—so we will have something to show to the Devonshire plods. And then I suppose we'll have to do a bit of fast talking and perhaps a certain amount of editing. As far as I'm aware, there's no evidence to tie either of us to that site in the woodland where the other Italian died, so it might be helpful if we could lose that bit of the recording. I'll tinker around with it before we head back to Britain, just in case the thin blue line is waiting for us on arrival."

"What about the Italians?" Robin asked. "Where have they gone?"

"My guess is that they'll head back to Rome. They followed us to the end of this trail, found nothing, and lost two of their men. The mission wasn't what you might call a raging success for them, but as far as I can see there's nothing to keep them here on Cyprus any longer. And they'll want to get those chests examined by their experts as soon as they can."

He looked around the cave and nodded.

"And there's nothing else for us here, either," he said.

Ten minutes later, Mallory and Robin stepped out of the cave and retraced their steps down the side of the ravine and on across the more open ground to where they'd left the car.

As the sun sank with typical Mediterranean sudden-ness behind the mountains to the west, Mallory started the engine.

"Are you sure you want to go on with this?" Robin asked him. "It's been expensive, dangerous, and ulti-mately fruitless, not to mention the problems we'll have in England trying to convince the woodentops that we're entirely innocent of all charges."

Mallory paused for a moment before he put the car into gear and looked across at her. "Of course I want to go on with it. This is the most exciting thing that's ever happened to me. We could be on the trail of the most valuable lost treasure of all time, which is a pretty good reason by itself. More to the point, it's entirely due to that old piece of parchment that I met you, and for me that's even more important."

"No bullshit. Do you really mean that?"

"Hell yes. Of course I do."

Robin smiled happily and reached out for his hand.

"Good enough for me," she said. "Let's see where the next chapter of Jacques de Molay's quest takes us."

Read on for an excerpt
from James Becker's

THE LOST TESTAMENT

Available from Signet.

Byzantium

AD 325

"Bring him forward."

Two trusted soldiers from the emperor's personal body-guard saluted their master, then turned and strode out of the temporary council chamber, each step they took accompanied by the metallic clattering of their armor and weapons.

Moments later, the two soldiers reappeared, a nervous-looking civilian now walking between them. They continued to the very end of the chamber, where Flavius Valerius Aurelius Constantinus Augustus, accepted only the previous September as the fifty-seventh emperor of the entire Roman Empire, sat flanked by a coterie of advisors.

"So, Flavius, what did you discover?" the emperor asked.

The civilian looked even more nervous at that moment, and Constantine had a sudden realization that he wasn't simply overawed by being in the presence of the most powerful man in the world. Flavius had been in his employ for years, and had spoken with him countless times. There had to be something else that was disturbing him, and if Flavius was worried, then that was a real cause for concern.

Before the man could speak, Constantine raised his hand, demanding silence, then glanced at his advisors.

"This is a private matter," he said. "Kindly leave us."

Without a word, the half a dozen or so officials standing on both sides of the throne filed out of the chamber, followed by the servants and other retainers stationed elsewhere in the room. Constantine then instructed the two soldiers to retire to the opposite end of the chamber, out of earshot, but ordered the guard commander, the officer in charge of his personal bodyguard, to remain close beside him. Constantine was far too cautious a man to allow himself to be left entirely alone with anyone, no matter how apparently trustworthy and loyal, and Marcellus had proved his loyalty beyond doubt on numerous occasions.

"It is not as we had hoped, Our Lord," Flavius began. "I have seen the original document, and the claims made in it are powerful and very damaging."

Constantine gestured, and the guard commander stepped forward, took the document Flavius was offering and handed it to his master. The emperor unrolled the parchment and read the Latin text written on it. Then he read it again.

Constantine was not a scholar, but he had no doubt of the authenticity of what he was holding. The report he had just read was, he was quite certain, both authentic and accurate. And that posed a major problem for him, and for his empire.

"Where did you find this?" he asked.

"It was in Rome," the man replied. "I walked into the

archives and searched through the documentation relating to Cohors I Sagittariorum until I found it. Then I brought it to you."

For perhaps two minutes the emperor remained silent, staring at the parchment in his hand, reading and rereading the words, his acute political mind pondering the direct implications of the document, and how best to use it to his own advantage. From the first, he'd realized that the matter he'd sent Flavius to investigate posed an indirect—but still a potent—threat to him, and would call his leadership and political judgment into serious question if it ever came to light. But it was also clear that without the document he had just been handed there was no direct proof of certain statements made by a notorious troublemaker almost one and a half centuries earlier. He held the key to the matter—held the single surviving item of undeniable proof without which the story was nothing more than an unsupported allegation in his own hands. And the only other person who knew anything about it was Flavius himself.

In fact, Constantine suddenly realized, the document was less of a threat to him than a potent weapon he could use to his own advantage. He was starting to distrust the ambitions of the leader of an emerging religious movement that was beginning to spread its influence across the empire. But he could bring that group to heel anytime he chose, simply by threatening to reveal what this document stated.

And that left only one other matter to be taken care of; and the emperor had made his preparations for this step as well.

Constantine gestured to the guard commander, who took a couple of steps forward and then stood waiting, his right hand resting on the hilt of his *gladius*. Behind Flavius, the two other soldiers of the bodyguard strode swiftly into position, standing a few feet behind the civilian.

"I thank you for your diligent efforts on my behalf, Flavius, in this matter as in many others over the years," Constantine said, "and I apologize for the necessity of what I now have to do."

"I don't understand." Flavius stared at the emperor, the truth dawning and a look of fear spreading across his face.

With another gesture, the two soldiers stepped forward, seized Flavius by the arms and held him firmly in place.

"I dare not risk anything of this matter becoming known. I know you would not willingly divulge what you have learned, but I cannot take any chances. I'm sorry, but this has to end now, my old friend. I bid you farewell."

"No, no, Our Lord, I beg of you. Please, not this."

Constantine ignored Flavius's agonized pleas and turned to the guard commander.

"One blow, so he doesn't suffer."

Marcellus nodded, drew his sword and stepped directly in front of Flavius.

"Keep a firm grip on his arms," he ordered, as the doomed man struggled ineffectually in the steady grasp of the two soldiers.

The guard commander drew back his right arm and with a single and massively powerful blow drove his sword right through Flavius's body, the pommel slamming into the man's ribs as the point of the blade burst out of his back in a spray of blood.

For a second or two, Flavius just stared ahead, his eyes wide, his mouth open in a soundless scream of unbearable agony. Then a gout of blood poured out of his mouth and his head fell forward.

Marcellus let go of his weapon and stepped back.

"Drop him there," he ordered, and the two soldiers lowered the limp body of the dead man to the stone floor of the chamber.

Then Marcellus took a dagger from inside his tunic and handed it to one of the soldiers.

"Cut me," he ordered, "in my left shoulder. Twice. Not too deep."

Obediently, the soldier ran the lethally sharp blade across Marcellus's left upper arm, making two cuts that immediately started to bleed copiously. The man didn't even flinch.

"Now drop the dagger beside him," he went on, and then turned around to face Constantine.

"As you ordered, Our Lord," he said.

"Excellent," the emperor purred. "Now summon help."

When the other soldiers and advisors ran back into the council chamber, the scene spoke for itself. The treacherous Flavius, so long a trusted emissary of the emperor, had suddenly changed his allegiance and drawn a dagger to make a cowardly attack upon the ruler of the empire. An attack barely foiled by the selfless heroism of Marcellus, himself badly injured in the assault.

As the bloody body of the "traitor" was dragged out of the room, and Constantine was congratulated on his lucky escape from death, nobody thought to ask what had become of the parchment Flavius had been carrying when he had entered the chamber.

That was the first time in over three hundred years that blood had been spilled because of that single sheet of parchment, but it was destined not to be the last.

*　　*　　*

Vatican City, Italy

25 November 1965

"Stop! I heard something."

Instantly both figures froze into immobility beside the wall. They could almost have been twins, though they were unrelated, both slimly built men of a little below average height, wearing black close-fitting clothing and dark-colored climbing shoes. Even their hair was black, and they had the typically swarthy complexion of people who live around the Mediterranean.

Neither man had begun his working life as a professional thief. They had both worked as members of an acrobatic troupe in a traveling circus, honing their climbing skills to a high degree of perfection. But after retiring they'd quickly acquired a reputation in certain circles in Italy: these men could be relied upon to get into the most heavily protected of buildings, complete the job they had been hired to do, and keep their mouths shut afterward.

And that was precisely why they were then in the midst of Vatican City, carrying out perhaps the most dangerous commission they had ever been given.

For a minute, the men remained immobile, two dark and silent shadows against the light-colored stone of the wall, listening intently. Then Stefan took a half step closer to his companion and murmured in his ear.

"What did you hear?"

"It sounded like a stone falling, something like that. Are you sure there are only two guards on duty tonight?"

"That's what we've been told: one two-man patrol, nothing more; and they should be a long way from where we are right now. I've checked the patrol route, and the gardens are not a high priority."

"I hope you're right. I suppose we'll find out soon enough. Let's go."

Dragan grinned at him, his teeth a white slash in the darkness. Then he opened the black fabric rucksack at his feet, extracted a metal grappling hook, the points and shaft coated in thick rubber to muffle any noise, and seized the rope about two feet from the end where it was attached to the hook. He whirled the hook in a circle half a dozen times, then released it. Both men watched critically as the hook sailed up into the air and then vanished over the top of the wall. There was a muffled clunk as the hook came to rest somewhere out of sight.

Cautiously, Dragan reeled it in, pulling the rope toward him and down the wall hand over fist. Suddenly the rope went taut, and he took a step backward and peered up toward the top of the wall.

"I think I can see it," he whispered. "Just check it out, will you?"

Stefan reached into his pocket and took out a small but powerful torch, black tape placed in a crisscross pattern over the lens to cut down the amount of light that would be emitted. When he switched it on the narrow beam clearly showed two of the four hooks jutting out over the top of the wall.

"That looks secure to me," he said quietly. "Do you want to go first?"

"Yes."

Dragan picked up his rucksack, closed the flap and slung it over his shoulders. Then he seized the rope with both hands and climbed up it with as little difficulty as if he'd been ascending a flight of stairs. At the top of the wall, he paused for a moment to check the positioning of the grappling hook, then gestured for his companion to join him.

Moments later, both men were in position, sitting

astride the wall as they repositioned the hook so that they could descend into the gardens that stretched out before them. Once they were down at ground level again, this time on the inside, Dragan flicked the rope expertly to dislodge it. The rope represented their escape route, and they dared not leave it in position in case the roving patrol passed by the wall and noticed it dangling there. As soon as the hook fell to the ground, he picked it up, coiled the rope and replaced it in his rucksack.

"That was the easy bit," he said. "Now we have to do a bit of proper climbing."

Neither man had set foot inside the Vatican before, but they moved with unerring certainty. Both of them had spent the previous two weeks studying detailed plans of the Holy See, and they now knew their way around with as much familiarity as if they'd been regular visitors.

Their objective was the Apostolic Library, located off the Belvedere Courtyard underneath the Apostolic Palace, the Pope's official residence. The library had been founded in 1420 by Pope Nicholas V with an initial endowment of some nine thousand books, but was later incorporated into the Vatican Museum and by 1965 it contained more than a quarter of a million volumes.

The two men couldn't enter the building at ground level—that would be impossible to do undetected—so they would be taking a very different route to get inside. The Stradone dei Giardini runs along the side of the Belvedere Courtyard, between the line of linked buildings and the gardens to the west, and that would be where they would make their entrance. A couple of minutes later the two men stopped near the Fountain of the Sacrament to make absolutely sure they were unobserved before they crossed over to the side of the building.

"I don't see or hear anything."

"Neither do I. Let's go."

The two dark shapes, deeper black shadows in the blackness of the night, flitted silently across the roadway, then crouched down beside the wall of the building, again checking in all directions. The next few minutes would be the most crucial of the entire operation, and if they were spotted neither man was in any doubt about what would happen to them.

"Still clear," Stefan said.

Dragan nodded, and then both men took a step back and stared upward at the vertical wall that formed one side of the building. Ten feet away from where they were standing, a water pipe ran all the way down the wall from the gutters at the edge of the roof high above them. The pipe was in excellent condition—the Vatican, as one of the richest organizations in the world, didn't stint on the maintenance costs of its buildings—and within seconds the dark shape of one of the two men, a coil of rope looped around his shoulders, was already a dozen feet off the ground and climbing swiftly up toward the roof.

They didn't need to climb all the way up. Near the top of the building, a balcony beckoned, though it was a few meters from where the water pipe ran down the wall. But just below the balcony was a narrow ledge, barely wide enough for a human foot, and that would provide the means of access they needed.

When he got almost opposite the balcony, about thirty feet above the ground, Dragan stopped to catch his breath—he wasn't as young, or as fit, as he used to be—locking his hands around the back of the water pipe while his climbing shoes rested on one of the junctions. Then he stretched out his right foot, the thin sole allowing him to test his foothold on the ledge before he trusted it with his full weight.

It felt solid, and after a couple of seconds he released his grip on the pipe and flattened himself against the wall as he began edging his way along the ledge. When he neared the balcony, he reached up, stretching as high as he could go, until his hand closed around the carved stone that formed the top of the wall around it. He took a firm grip, then pulled himself up and onto the balcony itself.

Moments later, he lowered the climbing rope he'd been carrying and waited while his companion attached their two rucksacks to the end of it. Then he hauled them up to the balcony and waited a couple of minutes for Stefan to follow in his footsteps and climb up the pipe.

At the back of the balcony was a set of double doors flanked by two windows, all of which were locked, a fact that surprised neither man. They had expected no less, but glass is fragile, and once they were satisfied that the roving patrol they'd been told about was nowhere in sight, the curved end of a crowbar swiftly disposed of one of the panes of glass in the door, and within a minute both men were standing inside the building, the door closed again behind them.

"This way."

They walked cautiously out of the chamber accessed by the balcony and stood for a moment in the passageway outside, where a single dim light was burning. It provided just enough illumination for them both to study the plan they had been given. Then they moved on, heading for one very specific part of the building.

"The Sistine Hall," Dragan murmured a few minutes later, pointing at the sign beside the doorway. "That's it."

None of the interior doors in the building appeared to be locked, the staff presumably believing that the external doors offered sufficient deterrent to thieves, and as soon as both men were inside the room, they split up and began their search.

By any standards, they were surrounded by treasures: glass cases containing ancient manuscripts and other relics, intermittently illuminated by the narrow beams of their torches. In one case lay an enormously valuable fifth-century New Testament written in Greek. In another, documents signed by Martin Luther. In yet others were a collection of love letters sent by King Henry VIII to Anne Boleyn, an essay written by Galileo to the Cardinal who later became Pope Urban VIII, a letter from the painter Raphaello, and another letter, this one sent by Michelangelo to the Superintendent of St. Peter's. But they barely glanced at any of these priceless exhibits. They were looking for two very specific objects, and in a couple of minutes they had found them both.

"Over here."

The two men stood side by side looking down at one particular case.

"That's it?" Stefan said, comparing what was written on the sheet of paper in his hand with what they were looking at inside the glass case.

"Yes," his companion agreed. "In fact, that's both of them."

The glass on the locked display case wasn't armored in any way and offered no more resistance to the crowbar than the pane of glass on the balcony door.

"These other old books and stuff have got to be worth something."

"More than you or I could ever earn in a dozen lifetimes," Dragan said, "but you know the way we work. We do what we're paid to do and nothing else." He opened up the neck of his rucksack while his companion lifted out the two objects they had been told to steal, and laid them carefully inside it.

As they walked down the corridor between the Hall and the Borgia Apartment the younger thief grabbed the other's sleeve and gestured toward a glass case.

"Look at this," he whispered. "It's gold, a crown of gold."

"Yes, but—"

Before he could finish his sentence, Stefan had already lifted his crowbar and cracked the glass that covered the ancient relic.

"What are you doing?"

"Look, I know what you said, and you're right. But this is gold. We can have it melted down, so it'll be untraceable. We're only ever going to get an opportunity like this once."

Without waiting for a reply, Stefan plucked the gold crown out of the shattered display case and placed it in his rucksack. Almost as an afterthought, he also picked up a small and highly decorated copper-and-enamel box and took that as well.

"Put those on now, and don't take them off until I tell you."

The order was unsurprising. They had encountered their employer only twice before, and each time they had been blindfolded and driven some way outside Rome to a large and clearly expensive villa, and the entire time they'd been in the building the man himself had been out of sight behind a screen, so they had no idea who he was, except that he probably wasn't Italian, because his instructions had been relayed through an interpreter.

This time, the journey to the villa took about forty minutes and, after removing their hoods, they were led through to the same room they had been in previously. There, an arrangement of screens had been placed at one end, and a table positioned more or less in the center of the room, the man they believed to be an interpreter standing beside it.

"Do you have them?" the man asked.

By way of answer, Stefan opened his rucksack, lifted out the two objects they had been told to steal and placed them on the table.

The interpreter smiled for the first time since they had seen him.

"Excellent," he purred. "You have done well. Now leave the room while my employer inspects these two relics."

Stefan reached out his hand to pick up the rucksack, but the interpreter shook his head.

"You can leave that here. My employer will not take long."

The two men glanced at each other, then shrugged and left the room as they'd been told. They had no option but to comply: the presence of two tall and heavily built men standing by the door ensured that. They were ushered into a small anteroom by one of these two guards, who then took up a position in the open doorway.

But the interpreter had been right. Less than ten minutes after they'd been told to leave, the two men were called back inside the room. The scene appeared to be exactly as it had been when they'd left, albeit with three small changes: in addition to the two literary manuscripts they'd been told to steal, the golden crown and the enamel box were also placed on the table—their rucksacks had clearly been searched—as well as a single piece of brown parchment.

The interpreter stared at the two men in a disapproving fashion.

"The instructions we gave you, the most specific instructions issued by my employer, were extremely simple. He wished you to steal these two manuscripts"—he pointed at the two leather-bound objects on the table—"the work of the Italian poets Petrarch and Torquato Tasso, and nothing else. Yet you apparently saw fit to take this crown and box of mementos too. Why was that?"

For a moment, neither man replied. Then Dragan took a half step forward and pointed at the crown.

"It was my decision," he said. "It was obvious that the theft would be discovered almost immediately, and I thought it might help to muddy the waters slightly if we picked up another couple of items from the library while we were there, to disguise the real objective of the robbery."

That was nothing like what had actually happened, but as a spur-of-the-moment improvization, he thought it was quite inventive, and almost believable.

The interpreter stared across the table, his eyes moving from one man to the other; then he nodded, turned and disappeared behind the screens at the far end of the room. The sound of muffled voices could be heard. After about half a minute, he returned.

"We applaud your quick thinking, though my employer does not believe you for a moment. You took the other two objects, intending to keep them for yourselves. However, that is not important because you did recover what you were paid to find. Now we have one other question for you." The interpreter pointed at the single sheet of parchment lying by itself on the table. "What is that?" he asked.

The two men stared at the object.

"I've no idea," Dragan replied. "I've never seen it before. We picked up the two sets of manuscripts from the display case and took nothing else from that room."

"That was at the back of the Tasso collection, but it is obviously not a part of it."

Dragan shrugged. "Sorry. I've no idea."

"Very well. You have already received half of the agreed fee, and later today we will pay you the remainder, once you have completed one further task for us."

"That was not a part of our arrangement," Dragan replied. "We were to carry out the theft, deliver the goods to you and then we were to be paid."

"But you've already broken your part of the agreement by stealing these two other items. My employer is a fair man, and he has agreed you may retain the enamel box and the additional sheet of parchment and try to sell them if you wish. Call it a bonus. And the additional task we want you to perform is very, very simple, but we will be watching you to make sure that you complete it exactly as we order. You are to take the crown and the two manuscripts, place them in a secure metal container we will provide and then throw them away at the precise time and place that we tell you."

"What? I don't understand."

"You don't need to. You just need to do what we ask."

Five days later, the man who had organized and paid for the apparently pointless burglary in the Vatican left Italy in his chauffeur-driven car. Hidden in a secret pocket in one of his sets of matching suitcases were the two original manuscripts, handwritten by Petrarch and Tasso, which he would store securely in his extensive collection of ancient relics as soon as he got back home.

In the meantime, from what he'd been able to gather

from the newspaper reports in Italy, Vatican officials appeared quite satisfied that the first-class forgeries he'd commissioned the previous year were actually the real thing, dumped by amateur burglars who got cold feet. All in all, and despite the somewhat unexpected greed of the two burglars he'd employed, it had been one of his most successful collecting expeditions.

About the Author

James Becker spent more than twenty years in the Royal Navy's Fleet Air Arm and served during the Falklands War. Throughout his military career he was involved in covert operations and numerous classified projects. He is an accomplished combat pistol shot and has an abiding interest in ancient and medieval history. His previous novels are *The First Apostle, The Moses Stone, The Messiah Secret, The Nosferatu Scroll, Echo of the Reich* and *The Lost Testament*.

ALSO AVAILABLE FROM
NATIONAL BESTSELLING AUTHOR

James Becker

THE LOST TESTAMENT

A single sheet of parchment holds the power to bring down an emperor and raze an empire. For seventeen centuries the scroll lay hidden away in the vast Vatican archives, guarded by a select, ruthless few who knew of its destructive potential.

When the parchment mysteriously turns up in the stall of a murdered Cairo market trader, authorities contact the British for assistance in identifying the document. Police detective Chris Bronson and historian Angela Lewis arrive in Egypt to take on the case, but quickly find themselves as targets, pursued by assassins. Stalked across North Africa and Europe, Chris and Angela must decipher the parchment's tantalizing message before their time runs out.

DON'T MISS
Echo of The Reich
The Nosferatu Scroll
The Messiah Secret
The Moses Stone
The First Apostle

**Available wherever books are sold or at
penguin.com**